Bad Boys Ahoy!

Bad Boys Ahoy!

SYLVIA DAY

KENSINGTON PUBLISHING CORP.
http://www.kensingtonbooks.com

BRAVA BOOKS are published by

Kensington Publishing Corp.
850 Third Avenue
New York, NY 10022

All Kensington titles, imprints, and distributed lines are available at special quantity discounts for bulk purchases for sales promotion, premiums, fund-raising, educational or institutional use.

Special book excerpts or customized printings can also be created to fit specific needs. For details, write or phone the office of the Kensington Special Sales Manager: Kensington Publishing Corp., 850 Third Avenue, New York, NY 10022. Attn: Special Sales Department. Phone: 1-800-221-2647.

Brava and the B logo Reg. U.S. Pat. & TM Off.

ISBN 0-7582-1251-8

First Kensington Trade Paperback Printing: February 2006
10 9 8 7 6 5 4 3 2 1

Printed in the United States of America

For my children, Jack and Shanna.
I love you.

Acknowledgments

There are many people who deserve recognition for their contributions. The following list is just the beginning.

Many thanks to:

Lori Foster for offering the Novella Contest and choosing my entry as a finalist. I appreciate your generosity and advice. You're a gem.

Morgan Leigh for liking my entry enough to pass it along to Lori and for being an all-around great gal.

Everyone who voted to make *Stolen Pleasures* the Reader's Choice winner. Thank you so much.

My agent, Evan Fogelman, who has to put up with me. Poor guy.

My mother, Tami Day, who introduced me to romance novels and is my greatest cheerleader.

My husband, Kevin, who always believed.

Samara, for being a friend as well as my sister. I love you.

Huge hugs go out to my critique partners Annette McCleave, Jordan Summers, Sasha White, and Celia Stuart, whose invaluable assistance and support helped me shape the stories within this book.

A giant heaping of undying gratitude to my fabulous editor, Kate Duffy. I can't say enough about her. She's been wonderful to me.

And last, but never least, to the hundreds of readers who visited my website, signed up for my mailing list, and clamored for my stories while I was still aspiring. Your faith in me pushed me forward. Thank you from the bottom of my heart.

Contents

Stolen Pleasures

Chapter One

British West Indies, February 1813

He'd stolen a bride.

Sebastian Blake gripped his knife with white-knuckled force and kept his face impassive. If the beauty in front of him were to be believed, he'd stolen *his own* bride.

He watched as her chin lifted with defiance and her dark eyes met his without fear. She was tall and slender, with blonde curls tumbling down from a once-stylish arrangement. Her lovely watered-silk dress was torn at the shoulder, revealing a tempting display of creamy breast. A sooty handprint marred her flesh, and unable to help himself, Sebastian reached out and rubbed the offending mark away with gentle strokes of his thumb. She stiffened, and lifted her bound hands to knock his away. He met her gaze and held it.

"Tell me your name again," he murmured, his hand tingling just from that simple contact with her satin skin.

She licked her bottom lip, and his blood heated further. "My name is Olivia Merrick, Countess of Merrick. My husband is Sebastian Blake, Earl of Merrick and future Marquess of Dunsmore."

He lifted her hands and stared at her ring finger, noting his crest etched in the simple gold band she wore.

He scrubbed a hand over his face and turned away, striding to the nearest open window for a deep breath of salt-tinged air. Staring out at the water, he espied the debris from her ship bobbing in the waves. "Where is your husband, Lady Merrick?" he asked, keeping his back to her.

Hope tinged her voice. "He awaits me in London."

"I see." But he didn't, not at all. "How long have you been married, my lady?"

"I fail to see—"

"How long?" he barked.

"Nearly two weeks."

His chest expanded on a deep breath. "I remind you that we are in the West Indies, Lady Merrick. It is impossible that you were married only a fortnight ago. Your husband would not be able to await you in England if that were true."

She was silent behind him, and finally he turned to face her again. It was a mistake to have done so. Her beauty hit him with the force of a fist in his gut.

"Would you care to explain?" he prodded, relieved he sounded so unaffected.

For the first time, her bravado left her, her cheeks flushing with embarrassment. "We were married by proxy," she confessed. "But I assure you, he will pay whatever ransom you desire despite the unusual circumstances of our marriage."

Sebastian moved toward her. His calloused fingers caressed the elegant curve of her cheekbone and entwined in her hair. Her breath caught, and her lips parted in response to his gentle touch. "I'm certain he would pay a king's ransom for beauty such as yours."

Through the smoky smell that clung to her, he could detect the arousing scent of soft woman, warm and luxurious. He reached for the blade strapped to his thigh and withdrew it.

She flinched away.

"Easy," he soothed. Sebastian held out his hand and waited patiently for her to step forward again. When she did, he sliced through the rope that tied her hands together, and sheathed his knife. He rubbed the marks on her delicate wrists.

"You are a pirate," she murmured.

"Yes."

"You have taken my father's ship and all of its cargo."

"I have."

Her head tilted backward on the slender neck, and she gazed up at him with melting chocolate eyes. "Why, then, are you being so kind to me, if you intend to rape me?"

He caught her fingers and placed them on his signet ring. "Most would say a man cannot rape his own wife."

She glanced down and gasped at the heavy crest that mirrored the one on her own band. Her eyes flew up to his. "Where did you get this? You can't possibly . . ."

He smiled. "According to you, I am."

Olivia stared up into intense blue eyes and felt certain her heart would burst from her chest. Her mind faltered, stumbling over the shocking revelation that the notorious Captain Phoenix was claiming to be her husband.

She backed away from him in a rush, and he reached to steady her when she started to fall. A whimper escaped as his touch burned her skin. The day's events had shaken her, but it was the gorgeous face of the infamous pirate that made her legs feel weak.

He was tall and broad-shouldered, and his presence sucked all of the air from the tight confines of the cabin. His black hair was unfashionably long, and the darkness of his skin betrayed how much time he spent outdoors. He was wild, untamed—a man of the elements.

She'd watched, fascinated, as he'd swept onto her ship and took command of it within moments. Phoenix had executed the attack with brilliant precision—not one man was seriously injured, and no one had been killed. Having spent most of her childhood on her father's ships, Olivia recognized skill when she saw it.

The way he'd used his sword and barked commands, the way loose tendrils of his hair had blown across his face, the way his breeches had delineated every stretch of his muscular thighs—she'd never experienced anything so thrilling. So exciting.

Until he'd touched her.

Then she'd discovered what excitement truly was.

Now she watched, mouth agape, as his long, elegant fingers went to the open collar of his shirt and plucked at the laces. Phoenix tugged the billowing linen from his breeches and drew it over his head.

"Good grief," she gasped, startled by the heat that tore through her veins and flushed her skin as his chest was revealed to her. Her breasts grew heavy, the tips aching.

Phoenix smiled, well aware of the effect he was having on her. His body moved with arrogant grace, powerful muscles rippling beneath tautly stretched skin. Dark hair spread lightly over his chest, tapering to a fine line that traveled down his stomach to disappear beneath his waistband. His arms bulged as he shook out his shirt and stepped closer.

She'd never seen a bare-chested man. Even on her father's plantation, the workers were required to remain clothed, her doting father's way of shielding her maidenly sensibilities. Despite this lack of knowledge, she was certain no other male could claim Phoenix's magnificent form.

Olivia snapped her mouth shut and waited until he was close enough so she could feel the heat radiating from his skin. It took everything she had to resist touching him, to resist burying her face in his chest and breathing him in. He smelled wonderful, a sun-warmed and salted male in his prime. His hands came toward her, his hot gaze dropping to the exposed curve of her breast.

"Hell's teeth!" he growled as the edge of his blade met his aroused cock. Incredulous, Phoenix looked down at her hand, then again at her face. He released a slow, wary breath. "I wouldn't recommend castrating me, sweetheart. One of your duties, after all, is to bear my heirs."

She inhaled a shuddering breath. "I do not believe for even a moment, Captain, that you are Lord Merrick." But the idea was not distasteful. Romantic notions and girlish fantasies—

Phoenix met both of those and so much more. Her father would never have approved of this man, a pirate worlds apart from the carefully selected earl she'd been told to expect. The pirate would not be to any father's taste, but he suited her secret desire perfectly.

Phoenix's brow arched in sardonic amusement. "But you cannot be certain. Have you ever met your husband?" Her hand shook nervously, and he winced. "Steady, love," he cautioned. "You may one day desire the appendage you are so grievously threatening."

"The only appendage of that nature I'll be desiring is my husband's," she retorted.

She watched his grin come back in full force, revealing a dimple on the left side of his lush mouth. *How could a pirate have a dimple?*

"I'm relieved to hear that." His voice was deep and seductive, purring like a predatory cat. "I wouldn't be agreeable to an adulterous wife."

"I am not your wife!" she snapped, flustered by his charm and her response to it.

"If what you say is true, then you are indeed my countess. And despite—," he shot a pointed glance at his blade, "—your charming introduction, you are not displeased with me as a spouse."

"How can you say that?"

"I didn't. Your nipples did. They are hard and aching for my touch, pressing so delightfully against the bodice of your gown."

With a horrified gasp, Olivia covered her breasts, and he easily plucked the wicked knife from her fingers. He handed her his shirt. "Here. Cover yourself until I can locate your trunks. I have no wish to display your bountiful charms to my men. We've been at sea for months, and their control is stretched." He eyed her appraisingly for a long moment and then chuckled. "Bold as you please," he murmured.

She stiffened, wondering if Phoenix found her deportment unappealing, and was disturbed to realize that she cared if he did. All of her life, she had accompanied her father on his frequent trips to London. With a child's awareness, she'd quickly discerned that Polite Society disparaged them because of their common background and her father's work in trade. To protect her feelings, Olivia had learned to disregard the opinions of others. But the pirate's opinion mattered. More than it should.

"I've learned to care for myself," she said defensively.

His dimple flashed again, momentarily stunning her wits. "I'm not complaining," he assured her. "Your father is well-known to me, sweet. I am aware that he is a busy man. I'm pleased you acquired some independent thought and intrepidness." He moved toward the door, apparently unaffected by the attraction that seared her senses.

"Wait!" she cried. Unreasonably, she didn't want to be left alone. His crew was a coarse lot. They'd pinched and groped her, tugged at her hair, and ruined her gown. Intrepid she might be, but a glutton for punishment she was not. "You cannot leave me here alone!"

Phoenix paused on the threshold, his features softening. "No one will come into this cabin without my permission. You'll be safe here."

She shook her head in denial. Her hands began to shake as they clutched his shirt against her chest, the garment still warm from his body and scented of his skin. "Don't leave me."

"I must go," he replied gently. "I have to give orders to my crew, secure your ship, and locate your belongings." He frowned. "Where is the proxy?"

"It was returned to England with the solicitor immediately after the signing."

"Who signed for me?"

Olivia started at his angry tone, and the first seeds of doubt entered her mind. "Lord Dunsmore," she answered softly.

His eyes narrowed. "And you didn't find it odd that your husband didn't come for you himself? You never wondered why he was unable, or unwilling, to at least sign the proxy even if he couldn't be bothered to marry you properly?"

Her bottom lip quivered at his sudden vehemence, and she bit it to hide the betraying movement. But Phoenix was too perceptive. With a muttered oath, he came back to her. His thumb brushed across her mouth, freeing her lip from her teeth. His gaze remained anchored to the spot where he had touched her. Olivia couldn't breathe. Her lip burned.

"You are a beautiful and desirable woman," he murmured. "Why settle for marriage with a man sight unseen?"

"I'd hardly call marrying a marquess 'settling,'" she whispered against his thumb.

He stiffened, and dropped his hand from her. "For the title, then."

Olivia shook her head. The title was important to her father. All she'd ever wanted in a marriage was passion, like her parents were reputed to have had. "It was my father's wish that I marry Lord Merrick. I could not defy him."

She was all that her father had. To disappoint him or sadden him was more than she could bear.

Phoenix searched her face for a long moment. Then he turned and left the cabin without another word, taking with him all of the crackling energy he exuded.

Sebastian assessed the blessedly minor damage to his father-in-law's ship and cursed his father for putting him in this predicament. He leaned against the railing and closed his eyes as the salty breeze ruffled his hair.

The sea had been his demanding and quick-tempered mistress for five years now. Disregarding his past, she had welcomed him with open arms. She had soothed the hurts that had caused him to flee his home and had given him an existence as distant as possible from the one that had pained him. Now a new life had been created for him without his knowledge or consent. Miserable as he was to admit it, Sebastian had no doubt Olivia was telling the truth.

What exactly the marquess had intended by marrying him off he couldn't fathom. He hadn't been in touch with any member of his family in years. What had they planned to tell the poor girl when she arrived and found her husband missing?

He snorted. "Girl" was incorrect. Olivia Merrick was all woman. His woman. His wife.

Hell and damnation.

Sebastian kicked aside an abandoned sword and cursed so foully that all the men on deck looked his way.

For all intents and purposes, he was married. To the most beautiful woman he'd ever seen and the daughter of Jack Lambert, one of the richest merchants in the world. If marriage had been a goal of his, he'd have been pleased. But he didn't want to be married. He had no desire to return to England and assume the role that should rightfully have gone to his brother, Edmund.

"Phoenix."

Sebastian turned to face Will, his first mate, a burly man whose enormous physique contrasted sharply with his harmless-sounding name. "What is it?" he asked curtly.

"We found 'er ladyship's things." Will's bushy mustache twitched. "I've never seen the like. A bed, and bath, and fresh water stored for the use of it. But when we tried to take 'er trunks into yer cabin, she damn near shot Red's 'ead off."

"*Shot* him?"

"Aye, wiv *yer* pistol."

Sebastian pinched the bridge of his nose in a vain attempt to ward off a headache. Damned vixen, he thought, but a reluctant smile curled his mouth nevertheless. Olivia had fire and spirit—qualities he admired in his bed partners.

Good God! Horrified, he shook the thought right out of his head. No. He was not going to even think about bedding her. Bedding her meant keeping her, and he sure as hell wasn't keeping her. She deserved better than a pirate.

"I shall see to her," he grumbled. "Have the men begin repairs to her ship. I want to return Lady Merrick to her father posthaste."

He was briefly surprised at how easily he used his title to refer to her, and then hastily shoved the thought away.

"Aye, Captain." Will's laughter followed him below deck.

Sebastian rapped on his cabin door. "My lady? 'Tis I. I'm coming in." He entered cautiously, peeking his head around the door and searching out her shapely form. He found Olivia sitting at his desk, drowning in his shirt, leveling a pistol at his chest. The mere sight of her made him ache. Golden and determined, she was a tigress.

"Do you know what you're doing with that?" he asked.

"Yes, of course."

He kicked the door shut behind him and headed toward the sideboard for a much-needed libation. Her gaze burned into his back, causing him to smile. "Care for a brandy, sweet wife?"

"Is there any proof you are my husband?" she asked curtly.

"Is there any proof you're my wife?" he retorted, pouring her a glass of the deep red liquid with the hope that it would soothe her ill humor.

"The ring . . ."

Sebastian held his hand over his shoulder and waggled his ringed finger at her.

She snorted.

"Who taught you the use of a pistol?" he queried as he warmed the liquor over a candle.

"The foreman on my father's plantation."

When he turned to face her, he found his gun resting on the desk and Olivia staring pensively out the window. "Your father approved?"

"My father doesn't know. I wanted to learn. There was no cause to distress him."

Withholding a smile, Sebastian moved toward her, admiring her elegant profile, with its pert nose and obstinate chin. Her bottom lip was caught between her teeth, and the thought of claiming that lush mouth with various parts of his body nearly made him hard. He set her brandy atop his nautical charts and propped his hip against the desk.

"What are you thinking, love?" he prodded gently.

She reached for the snifter without looking, and he pushed it into her hand. "That you should put on a shirt."

"I'm quite comfortable, but I'm touched by your wifely concern."

In the midst of a large swallow, Olivia choked. He thumped her back until she waved him off. "I'm fine!" she gasped. Wiping the tears from her lashes, she glared at him. "What are your intentions, Phoenix?"

Sebastian reached over slowly, giving her time to draw away. She didn't. The pulse at the base of her throat fluttered wildly as he rubbed the cuff of his shirt, brushing the edge of his finger deliberately along her bared wrist. He felt her shiver and hid his satisfaction. The attraction, it appeared, was mutual.

"The men have begun the necessary repairs to your ship. It should be seaworthy again within a sennight, at which time we'll head to the nearest port. I will leave my ship and travel with you to England. We shall arrive on British soil, seek out our parents, and unravel this debacle. Then we can obtain an annulment and part ways."

"Oh . . . I see." Olivia looked out the window again.

Sebastian sat tensely at her silence.

"What if I don't wish to have the marriage annulled?" she queried finally.

His eyebrows shot up. "You wish to be married to a wanted criminal?"

Her brief side-glance was intriguing and arousing, showing a surprising lack of fear. By all rights she should be terrified, yet she appeared completely at ease. She swirled the rest of the brandy in the snifter, watching the play of light with undue attention. "Lord Merrick is not a wanted man."

"Do you believe I am Merrick?"

Olivia shrugged. "I'm reserving judgment at the moment."

He downed his brandy and then moved to the hammock that hung across the corner. Hopping in, Sebastian settled his hands behind his head. "You appear quite comfortable for a woman in the bedchamber of a pirate."

She blew a loose lock of hair off her face. When it fell right back into its previous annoying place, she reached up and freed the entire glorious mass. His body hardened instantly. Olivia Merrick was stunning, a siren.

"I don't appear to have much choice in the matter, and so far you have deported yourself much better than the men under your charge."

"I apologize for your mistreatment," he said, watching her plait her waist-length hair. He'd never observed the act before and was startled to realize he enjoyed the intimacy of it. "It will never happen again."

Tossing the finished braid over her shoulder, Olivia downed the rest of her brandy in one gulp. Her eyes watered, and she waved at them with her hands.

Sebastian couldn't contain the obvious question. "Why would you wish to maintain the marriage?"

A moment passed before she found her voice, and when she spoke, it was husky from the fiery abrasion of the potent liquor. The thrill elicited by the throaty sound made his cock strain against his breeches.

He imagined for a moment that she was hoarse from passionate cries of his name, pleasured sounds he'd call forth with deep, drugging thrusts of his cock into her lush body. Sebastian knew already she'd be hot and wet. Olivia was a passionate woman in ordinary matters. In the bedroom, she would most likely burn a man alive.

"For all the reasons I agreed to the marriage in the first place," she murmured. "To please my father, to run my own household, to have children and the security of a man's name." She ran a fingertip over a delicately arched brow before locking gazes with him again. "No one knows your secret, and I certainly won't enlighten anyone. I will have the protection and status of your name, with none of the inconveniences of a husband. In fact," she said, obviously warming up to the topic, "if you are indeed Sebastian Blake, the situation pleases me in a way it didn't before."

He stroked his hand down the center of his chest, noting the way her eyes followed the movement with ravenous attention. "You would maintain my house, bear my name and my children?"

"Of course," she replied, blushing as her gaze returned to his. "I am aware of my responsibilities as your . . . er . . . Lord Merrick's wife."

"You would have to welcome me to your bed." He paused for emphasis. "Often."

Her eyebrow lifted. "If you are who you claim to be, I would welcome you eagerly."

Sebastian stilled at that. In fact, he couldn't move. The image her words brought to mind had him throbbing painfully. "My title would elicit eagerness in you?"

"I am not that shallow," she said, with a lift of her chin.

"Then my form is what you find so attractive?"

Olivia snorted. "Attractive? You are a heathen."

He shot up, setting the hammock swaying perilously. "A *heathen*?"

"Yes, look at you." She waved in his direction. "Your hair is unfashionably long. Damn near as long as mine."

"It is nowhere near that long!" he argued, put out. "And don't swear!"

"And your muscles," she continued, as if he hadn't spoken at all.

"What about my muscles?" he growled.

"They're huge. You look like a savage." She rose from the chair and moved to stand in front of the window.

"A *savage*?" he sputtered, his feet hitting the floor with a thud.

"Most definitely." She coughed, her shoulders shaking.

Sebastian stalked toward her. "I'll have you know, most women find me irresistible."

"Really?" she drawled, sounding unimpressed.

"Yes, really. I was quite the rake when I resided in London," he bragged, unaccountably upset by her dislike of his appearance.

"I'm certain you thought you were," she choked out. "Or perhaps you were more civilized at that time."

His eyes narrowed with suspicion. He spun Olivia around to face him, only to discover she was laughing, her lovely eyes sparkling with wicked amusement.

"You're mocking me." He smiled against his will.

"Just a little," she gasped, clutching her stomach.

She was either mad from the stress of the day's events or . . . enchanting. Sebastian became engrossed in the intimacy of their shared amusement, the rest of their problems fading into obscurity. His hand came up and drew a line down the bridge of her pert nose, which she wrinkled when he tapped the tip.

Olivia stared at him with admiration in her dark eyes, a look that salved the sting his ego had felt mere moments ago. "A savage with a delightful dimple," she murmured under her breath, brushing her fingertip along his cheek.

"Why are you out here?" she asked almost breathlessly. "You, a nobleman of vast wealth and prestige. Why turn to piracy?"

"Ah . . ." He ached to pull her closer. His throat tight, his hand dropped to her shoulder. "You believe me."

She snorted again, a thoroughly unladylike sound that he found charming. "I'm just foxed is all, and willing to indulge you for the moment."

"My lady, you should pay greater attention to your choice of wording. You have no notion of the indulgences I require." At her confused frown, Sebastian clarified, "I am no gentleman."

"You are an earl, my lord."

"It's a title, Lady Merrick, and it has nothing to do with my character."

"You have been trained and bred for your—"

"I have been cursed," he said hotly. "My older brother, Edmund, was to bear the title, but he was killed in a duel five years ago."

"A duel?" she repeated, her eyes widening. "How dreadful! I am sorry."

"Yes, well . . . so am I, I assure you. Especially since he was defending my honor." He gave a harsh laugh. "As if I had any to quibble over."

"He must have loved you very much."

"Edmund loved the title," Sebastian scoffed.

Olivia met his intense gaze without flinching. "What happened?"

He longed to make some flip, roguish, or snide comment to deflect her prying. He wanted to sneer at her and cut her, scare her, and push her away. But his next words would do the deed just as well. "I foolishly compromised a young lady. When her older brother came to me and demanded that I marry the chit, I refused. She was no innocent, as I knew firsthand. And the way we were caught left no doubt in my mind that I'd been snared in a trap."

Her hand flew to her mouth, and his own mouth curved derisively. "Instead of demanding satisfaction from me, her brother approached Edmund, whose damned sense of honor prevented him from refusing. I learned of the duel only after it was over. My father woke me from my bed with the news." He didn't even attempt to hide the bitter edge that crept into his voice. "I was foxed and debauched when he shouted the congratulations at me, as if I'd planned Edmund's demise." He closed his eyes. "Edmund was groomed for his place. I, on the other hand . . ." His voice trailed off.

Why was he telling her these things? The words falling from his mouth had never left his lips before.

"You, on the other hand, are too wild and untamed for such a station," Olivia finished.

Sebastian opened his eyes to find her facing the window, allowing him a modicum of privacy to collect himself. He moved to stand behind her, close enough so that his breath stirred the strands of hair at her crown and her evocative scent fired his blood. His hands clenched into fists.

"I'd wager you were a wild child," she continued, her honeyed voice pouring down his spine, hardening his cock. "You most likely could not bear to sit through your lessons, got dirty regularly, kissed girls you had no business kissing, and defied your father at every turn just to spite him for having such a perfect firstborn—a sibling you could never hope to measure up to."

Stunned at her perceptiveness, Sebastian stared sightlessly out the window.

"Am I close?" she asked.

"Too close," he admitted gruffly. "How did this conversation progress so rapidly to the deeply personal?"

"Your remarkable eyes betray the ruthlessness of your nature and your restlessness. I've been pondering what circumstance could possibly have driven you to this life you live." She turned to face him. "Did your father tell you how sorry he was that it was not you who had died instead of Edmund?"

His breath hissed out through clenched teeth. Olivia looked through him, into him, seeing things she had no right to see. Her eyes filled with a sympathy he didn't want, damn her. Lust, yes. Passion, admiration—he wanted all of those from her. But pity . . .

His teeth ground together until his jaw ached.

"So you are determined," she continued, flaying him with her words, "to prove to him and anyone else paying attention that he was indeed correct and you are a worthless 'spare' for his heir. Being the man you are, you can do nothing half-measure. No, you had to rebel in the worst possible manner. Perhaps you've even hoped to be caught in the midst of your misdeeds. Then your father's humiliation would be complete. Why else would you wear the signet ring that betrays you?"

He longed to smash something, to tear something apart. Furious, torn open by her censure, Sebastian grabbed her shoulders and yanked her to him. His voice came low and full of scorn. "Your words reveal the astonishing depths of your naïveté."

Her lovely face flushed at his disparagement. "I have given you no reason to be cruel."

"Perhaps I am always cruel," he jeered, his fingers digging into the soft flesh of her upper arms. "You know nothing of the man I am."

Her chin lifted, her eyes sparked with anger. "Unhand me, Phoenix. Now."

He pulled her closer. "What would you know of rebellion?" he growled. "You, the dutiful daughter, marrying a man sight unseen to please your father. I'd wager you've never rebelled in your life!"

"I have!" she yelled, shaking with fury. Her lips, red and moist, parted with her rapid breathing.

He arched a disbelieving brow, his entire body hard with anger and fierce desire. "When?"

"Right now." And then she yanked his head down and mashed her lips to his.

Chapter Two

He wasn't kissing her back.

Olivia noted that fact immediately, but her stubbornness would not allow her to desist, even though her pride begged her to cease her foolishness.

"Kiss me, damn you!"

He'd caused this fever in her blood with his half-dressed state and fierce eyes. Phoenix was driving her mad, drawing her to him while pushing her away.

"Don't swear!" he muttered.

And then his arms came around her, and his mouth moved hungrily over her own. His tongue swept across her lips, teasing, urging. He tasted like brandy and wicked things, and her core throbbed in response. Her lips parted in a breathless gasp, and he took the invitation to slip inside. His tongue sought out hers, brushed across it and under it, finding sensitive nerve endings and stroking them with velvety licks.

Oh. Dear. Heaven. The man knew how to kiss. Her toes were curling in her slippers.

Angry and possessive, hungry and bold, Phoenix took over her senses with blatant skill. Unable to resist, she surged into him, wanting more. More of him.

"Steady," he murmured, securing her body against his strength, his large hand moving to her neck and tucking her head into the crook of his shoulder, keeping her still for the ravishment of his mouth.

Olivia moaned when his other hand slipped beneath his shirt and found the curve of her breast, wrapping around the underside, testing its weight. His thumb caressed in gentle strokes, teasing her. Over and over Phoenix circled the straining peak, causing sparks of pleasure to radiate outward and down to the place between her legs.

Oh, why wouldn't he touch her where she ached?

"Touch me." She grabbed his wrist and thrust her hardened nipple into his palm. "Here." She moaned as her body melted. "Oh, God, . . . touch me everywhere."

"*Olivia.*" His kiss lost its faint trace of gentleness. He devoured her, his tongue thrusting rhythmically into her mouth, his fingers plucking and twisting, pulling on her nipple, until she wept from her core. Olivia ached all over. Her skin was too tight, too hot. She wanted to rip her clothes from her body and press her nakedness to his. Instead she caressed his skin, squeezing the bone and sinew beneath, relishing the way his body shuddered against hers.

Lord, he smelled heavenly, like the wind and the sea, passion and pure male. When the knock came at the door, she didn't even register it until Phoenix pulled away.

"What is it?" he called hoarsely, one hand still working at her breast while the other pressed her heated face into his throat.

"Captain, we're 'aving problems wiv the other crew," Will bellowed through the closed portal.

Phoenix growled his frustration. "I'll be on deck in a moment."

Heavy footsteps moved away from the door.

"No . . ." she protested, lost in the scent of his skin, the warmth of his touch, the taste of his mouth. She would give anything for a respite from the madness that claimed her and knew instinctively that he was the cure.

He pressed a quick, hard kiss to her lips. "I must go, sweeting, while I'm still able."

"No." She tugged his neck toward her open mouth, and at first he resisted, then he crushed her against him, tight enough to feel the heat and hardness of his desire through her skirts. Olivia kissed him desperately, wantonly, hoping to make him as mindless with need as she was.

Phoenix thrust her away with a curse. "You're flirting with the devil," he bit out. "Cease, before you get burned."

She winced as the door slammed shut behind him.

Olivia wasn't certain how much time had passed, but the sun had moved steadily across the sky and she knew the day was close to ending. The wind had picked up, pushing a welcome breeze into the cabin, cooling the air and her blood. Mortified by remembrances of her earlier behavior, her face heated and she squirmed in her seat.

What in God's name was the matter with her? She'd never in her life kissed a man, let alone touched him or begged him to touch her. And Captain Phoenix of all people! A man reputed to be as dangerous and deadly as a viper. Why didn't she fear him? Why did she wish to bare herself to his gaze and open her body to whatever he desired?

A knock sounded, and she moved quickly to the desk, collecting the pistol. "Yes?" she shouted, her heart racing. Had Phoenix returned?

The door opened. "'Tis Maggie, milady," her abigail called.

Olivia released a sigh of mixed relief and disappointment. The young servant entered, followed by three sailors. Two of the men hefted yokes with steaming buckets, and the third held her small hip bath. They poured the hot water and then brought in her trunks. Shooting wary glances at the pistol, the pirates departed the room with haste, and Maggie shut the door behind them.

"Are you well?" Olivia asked with concern, wondering how the young girl had fared in the company of Phoenix's men.

"Um?" Maggie hummed distractedly as she stepped over to Olivia's trunks and began to sort through her clothing. "Oh, yes. Quite well. His lordship made certain of it."

The abigail came to her and easily tugged the huge shirt over her head. When the sleeve caught on the gun, Olivia set the weapon on a trunk and laid the shirt next to it. She missed the garment immediately, infused as it was with the scent of Phoenix's skin.

Maggie began to loosen the fastenings to her gown.

Looking over her shoulder, Olivia asked, "What if he should return?"

The maid chuckled. "Little chance of that happening. He's fixing the main mast."

"*What?*" Olivia shot a worried glance out the window. The wind continued to pick up speed. "Why didn't he delegate the task?"

"He said it was too dangerous with the wind blowing like it is."

"Good God!" Olivia headed toward the door. He could be killed. And for some odd reason, she couldn't bear to think of it.

"Milady! You cannot go out there now. Your gown . . ."

Olivia clutched her bodice and ran from the room. When she gained the deck, she looked up at the sky in horror. Still bare-chested, Phoenix clung to the mast, his powerful muscles bunched with exertion, his silky hair blown loose from its queue and whipping around his face. From her vantage, his large form seemed tiny, and yet he appeared at home in the turbulence. His movements were sure and efficient as he struggled against the gales, no fear evident in the expertise of his actions. In fact, no one around her seemed even remotely fearful. Her heart, however, beat a panicked rhythm, ready to burst from her chest.

She sensed the large presence that moved up to her side, and turned to look at the red-haired man she'd nearly shot earlier.

"Ye shouldn't be up 'ere on the deck," he grumbled. "The men can't 'elp but ogle ye, and the captain won't be liking that at all."

"I tried to tell her," Maggie muttered as she came up behind them.

"What the devil is he doing?" Olivia cried, loose hair from her plait blowing around her face until she could barely see. "Can't the repair wait until the wind dies down?"

Red shrugged. "Surely. But 'e was already up there, so 'e might as well finish."

As the wind whipped by again, she returned her gaze to Phoenix. She screamed as he lost his grip and was blown free, his body dangling precariously by the rigging. He was suspended there as the wind flew by, and then his hold began to slip. Unable to watch, Olivia turned to Red and buried her face in his chest, her fists clutching handfuls of his filthy shirt. No one could long survive being battered against the mast like a flag.

"Damned stupid fool!" she cried into the pirate's chest as the men on deck scrambled into action.

It was unreasonable, this horrid fear that clawed at her vitals and tortured her mind. Phoenix was a stranger of only hours' acquaintance. But they'd been intimate. He'd touched her in ways she'd never touched herself. He'd made her feel reckless and wild. She'd felt alive—

Warm hands gripped her shoulders and turned her, pressing her face into salt-flavored bare skin. "Hush, love," Phoenix's deep voice purred in her ear, his warm breath fanning across her neck, his hair blowing around them.

Olivia sank into him with relief. Her fingers clawed at his back, pulling him closer. "You bloody idiot!" she scolded.

He chuckled. "Don't swear, sweetheart. I'm fine."

She pulled back and slapped his chest with a smack that tingled her palm. "You won't be when I've finished with you! Are you *daft*? What were you doing up there in weather such as this?"

It was then that she saw his arm, bleeding and chafed raw from the coarse rope that had saved his life. "Oh . . . look at your arm." Her hands went to the injury, and her eyes flew up to his.

"It's nothing," he said dismissively, absently rubbing the spot where she'd hit him.

Maggie leaned over. "I can make my grandmother's healing tea. It'll take a bit to cook up, but it works miracles."

"Yes, do that." Olivia returned her gaze to Phoenix as the abigail moved away. "I have some salve to put on this. Return to the cabin and allow me to tend it."

The blue of his eyes darkened. "I suppose you'll insist, and threaten me with some weapon or another."

"If I have to."

He offered a mocking half-bow. "After you."

Clutching her bodice, Olivia hurried down to the cabin, willing her heartbeat to slow. Her entire face was marked with his scent. Salty and spicy, it was a richly masculine smell of hardworking male and pure Phoenix. Every breath she took was redolent of the faint traces of his cologne and his unique fragrance.

She threw open the door and rushed to the smallest of her trunks, all the while agonizingly aware of his presence behind her. Delving around, Olivia found the small jar of medicinal salve and straightened, turning to face her pirate captor. He stood just inside the closed doorway, watching her intently, his hands fisted at his sides. The room drew in, shrinking, until there was nothing but Phoenix and her and the powerful attraction between them.

"Come closer," she urged.

His brows drew together as his gaze dropped. Olivia followed it, catching sight of her gaping bodice offering him an unhindered view of her breasts. She hastily covered herself, embarrassment heating her cheeks. His face was hard, his body as still as stone, a statue of a god rendered in flesh and bone.

Turning her back to him, she set the salve jar atop her trunk and retrieved the shirt he had given her earlier. "If you rub that into your—"

She stumbled into silence when he appeared at her side.

How a man as large as Phoenix could move with such stealth she couldn't fathom. He stood behind her, so close she could feel the heat of his skin and the warmth of his breath as it gusted across her shoulder in unsteady measure. He tugged the shirt from her hands and tossed it away. Wordlessly, he reached for the jar and opened it, scooping up a small amount of the salve. Olivia watched unmoving, arrested by his proximity, as he set the jar aside and picked up her hands. He began to rub the salve into her chafed wrists, his touch strong yet gentle and soothing. The moan that rose in her throat escaped without thought.

"You like my touch," he whispered hoarsely, "don't you?"

Helplessly, she lifted her face and stared into his eyes. She swallowed hard. "It burns."

Phoenix nodded, his gaze knowing. "Offer me your mouth." Although his voice was soft, there was no mistaking the command.

Caught in his spell, Olivia's lips parted as his head dropped to hers. At the first contact, her knees went weak. She would have fallen if he hadn't drawn her close. Her senses flooded with his taste, her body softening instinctively for his. His head slanted, finding the perfect fit, and his tortured groan made her dizzy.

Arms around her waist, Phoenix lifted her feet from the floor and carried her to the small corner table. He kicked the chair aside and laid her on the polished surface. Following her down, his mouth never left hers, his tongue sweeping inside with caressing licks.

He gripped the torn edges of her gown, and with a harsh, impatient tug, he ripped the garment and the chemise below it to the waist. His hands went immediately to her aching breasts, plucking the tips, twisting them, the way he must have sensed she desired. Her sex flooded with moisture. He was ravishing her, pillaging and plundering, and it was just what she wanted him to do, what she'd wanted him to do since he'd first come onto her ship.

Olivia moaned into his mouth. "What are you doing to me?"

"What are you doing to *me*?" he retorted harshly. "Only

hours I've known you, and already you drive me to madness." He nuzzled her throat, then blazed a burning trail of open mouthed kisses to her breasts. "I want to devour you, fill you with my cock, ruin you."

"Phoenix . . . " She shied away from the tumultuous sensations that were entirely new to her, but she could not escape him. The pirate held her pinned, his hard body pressed between her spread legs. He sucked a straining nipple into his hungry mouth, the combined effect of his tongue strokes and the rhythmic pulling causing her to grip his hair convulsively. Unable to help herself, Olivia arched upward and rubbed herself against the straining length of his erection. Pleasure speared through her, hot and searing. Stunned, she sank back onto the table.

"No," he ordered around her breast. "Don't stop . . ." He ground his cock into her, moving his attentions to her other breast, and Olivia moaned loudly, her body on fire. Phoenix pulled back far enough to push the volume of her skirts out of the way. His hand brushed the damp curls of her sex, and he stilled.

His gaze moved to hers as he slid a long finger through the slickness of her desire and parted the soft folds. He circled and rubbed the tiny spot where she ached, causing her back to arch on a startled cry and moisture to flood his hand. Groaning, he eased inside her. She murmured a faint protest, but her hips lifted of their own accord, pushing into the wicked invasion.

"You're so hot, so tight." His finger slid in to the base. With his free hand, he lifted her leg until her slippered foot rested on the surface of the table. Then he pushed her knee outward, completely opening her to his gaze. He stared at her sex and withdrew his finger. Olivia watched, fascinated, as he brought his hand to his mouth and sucked his finger inside. "Ummm," he purred, the sound deeply sexual.

He lifted and spread her other leg as he had the first. She flushed, knowing she looked wanton, her gown ruined, her breasts exposed and damp from his mouth, her sex open and glistening with her lust for him.

Phoenix brought both hands between her legs—one spreading the sheltering lips while the other slipped the long, calloused finger back inside her. He began to pump in and out, his gaze arrested by the sight. Her hands gripped the rounded edges of the table, her lower lip caught in her teeth, as she struggled to remain silent. She wanted to cry out, to scream. It felt so wonderful she could hardly bear it. Tension built, coiling in her stomach and shooting outward in hot waves. She didn't understand it, but her body knew, her hips lifting in counterpoint to his movements.

She was so wet, so wild, for him, Olivia could hear the sucking sounds of her body as it tried to hold the plunging finger within her. And then there was more of him inside her—two fingers, drenched in her cream, thrusting in and out. She released her lip and cried out, her body shuddering.

"Please . . ." she begged, but she didn't know for what.

"Feels good, doesn't it?" he growled. "The feel of me inside you. You'd like my cock, wouldn't you, sweet? Stretching you, filling the emptiness that my fingers cannot."

His intense blue eyes remained locked on the place where he claimed her, as he slowly slid down her body, his skilled fingers never ceasing their torment. He licked his lips, and his scandalous intent became apparent. "No," she whispered in protest.

"You will not deny me this," he bit out. "A small taste of heaven before I return you."

Olivia knew propriety dictated she stop him, push him away, but she couldn't, not when Phoenix looked at her the way he was doing now. She rose onto her elbows and watched his mouth descend, his tongue slipping like fire through the petals of her sex.

She ground her hips restlessly into the table. It was horrible and wonderful and wicked. And she loved it, loved how he made her feel, loved to watch him so totally focused on her. His expert tongue lapped her aching sex in a way that soothed and excited at the same time. Olivia spread her legs wider, arching up into his mouth, feeling empty just as he said she would, despite his rapidly stroking fingers. With frightening understanding, he seemed to know exactly what she needed, his tongue held rigid as it flicked against the source of her torment, the source of her pleasure. Phoenix dropped to his knees, concentrating the full extent of his skill on pleasuring her mindless. Higher and higher he pressed her, making erotic sounds of enjoyment against her flesh, until she couldn't bear it any longer. His fingers moved faster, his tongue lapped harder, his growls grew louder—

Her orgasm made her scream, her entire body stretching taut across the table and shaking with sensation as she convulsed in ecstasy against his mouth.

He remained between her legs, sliding his fingers from her and replacing the loss with his tongue until she regained control of her breathing. Only then did he stand and cover her body with his.

"Phoenix . . . "

He pulled her against him, his body rigid and damp with sweat. Olivia knew he had not felt the same pleasure he had given to her.

"Tell me what to do," she begged against his throat. "Tell me how to please you."

"You did," he assured her in a gruff whisper. "To feel you come in my mouth . . . 'twas a singular experience, love."

"I want—"

"I know what you want," he interrupted dryly.

"Please. I want to pleasure you as well."

"No."

Her eyes slid closed, and her head fell to the side, away from his mouth. "You don't want me . . . that way."

"Look at me." Phoenix clasped the sides of her face in his large hands and forced her to face him. His fiery blue gaze burned into hers. "It is not a question of wanting you, but a question of wanting the best *for* you. I am not it."

Her eyes stung, her emotions scattered and confused. "I just want to please you."

He sighed. "You ask for more control than I am capable of."

She searched his face, so austerely handsome and passion-flushed. Something in his eyes—a wary softening—tugged at her heart. She brushed her fingertips across his mouth, and he pressed an urgent kiss against them. Reaching for his hair, Olivia brought it around to frame his face. "You are the most gorgeous creature I've ever seen. I want to touch you all over, put my mouth on you, make you wild for me . . ."

"Olivia." His voice was a pained whisper as his eyes closed on a ragged breath. "Damn you."

Phoenix stood, and opened the placket to his trousers, moving so quickly she had no time to see him. He leaned over her, and she felt him, hot and hard, in the crease of her sex. She shivered, her body slowly coming to renewed life.

"Hold me tight."

"Yes . . ." She held onto him like a woman drowning.

And then he rotated his hips, moving his cock easily through her slick lips. She tensed, expecting stretching and pain, but it never came. He began to move against her, a driving, urgent rhythm of his hips against hers. His cock was hot and hard as he pumped through the folds of her sex, his tight balls slapping against the damp opening to her body. But he kept away from the full consummation she craved.

"Wrap your legs around me," he gasped. "Move with me . . . yes . . ." His skin turned hot under her hands, his breath heaving from his lungs.

The heavy weight of him moving so feverishly between her thighs renewed the ache within her. Wanting to experience the pleasure again, Olivia writhed beneath him, clawing at his back, as her body rushed for the precipice. She sobbed when the rapture hit her, and then Phoenix tensed, rock hard, against her. Burning dampness flooded across her stomach in pulsing jets.

He cried out her name as he shuddered in her arms.

* * *

Sebastian buried his face in the fragrant curve of Olivia's neck and damned himself for being a heartless cad. His control was a source of pride to him, but he'd had none of it today. From the moment he'd seen her on the deck of the *Seawitch* with her chin tilted defiantly and a far too heavy sword in her hand, he'd been captivated. As the day had progressed, he'd become more and more enamored with her. Her beauty alone was impossible to resist, but the fire, the passion . . . He could no more have resisted touching her than he could have chosen to stop breathing.

She'd been trying to assist him, to tend to his wounds, as no one ever had. And he'd repaid her by staring lustily at her exposed breasts and stripping her of his shirt when she'd wished to cover herself. Olivia had been willing, eager, but he should have walked away for her own good. He could never be the husband she deserved. Despite this, he'd spread her out, a feast for a starving man, and debased her with his ravenous touch.

And damned if he didn't want to do it again. Immediately.

Sebastian rose onto his elbows and gazed down at Olivia's beautiful face, flushed with his passion. He almost inquired if she was well, but the dazed look in her eyes answered the unspoken question. His expression most likely mirrored hers.

Placing a swift, hard kiss against her parted lips, he untangled his limbs from hers. Olivia was all heat and desire, a fiercely passionate woman who, even in her innocence, had pleasured him almost beyond bearing. Untried and unschooled, she hadn't the guile to hide her response or to play any games. He'd felt wanted, needed, in a way no one had ever made him feel before.

Staring at her taut belly, shiny with his seed, Sebastian was swept with an overwhelming wave of possessiveness. He wanted to mark her like this everywhere, brand her completely, so that no other man would ever touch her. Her drowsy eyes followed him with such warmth it took his breath away. The way she looked at him, her palpable panic when he'd slipped on the rigging—how long had it been since anyone had cared for his welfare? So long ago he could scarcely remember it. Only his gratefulness for her tender regard had prevented her complete ruination.

Sebastian ached at the thought of returning her to her father, wishing he could spirit her away and keep her safe from the choices of his past, choices that made it impossible for them to ever be together. Never before had he regretted anything he'd done. Now he regretted it all.

"I'd offer you the bath," she murmured, "but the water is certainly cold by now."

Looking at the small hip bath, he smiled. "It's perfect. Thank you."

He retrieved a towel from the washstand and dipped it in the cold water. Then he went to her and cleansed his lust from her body, his cock hardening again as her nipples puckered under his touch. Olivia was so small compared to him, such tiny, sweetly curved perfection. And he'd rutted upon her like an animal.

Cursing silently, Sebastian turned from the arousing sight of her and quickly stripped from his breeches. With a soft hiss, he sank into the chilled water. He glanced at his wife, biting back a grin as she slid from the tabletop and looked modestly at the wall.

"Aren't you curious to see the part of me that you so recently pleasured?" he asked.

She blushed. Keeping her eyes averted, Olivia moved to her trunks, holding the ruined gown against her swollen nipples. She was a ravishing vision, and his body was already eager for a repeat performance. Sebastian scrunched down in the too-small tub and concentrated on the chilly temperature of the water to cool his blood. It was a testament of paternal love that fresh water was set aside for this purpose.

He frowned when she pressed a bar of fine, French-milled soap into his hand. Scented of musk and bergamot, it was definitely a masculine toilet item.

"Why do you have a man's soap?" he asked sharply.

Damnation. *He was jealous!*

Some of the afterglow faded from her eyes. "'Tis my father's favorite. One more or less will not be missed." She turned away, but not before he caught the hurt evident on her delicate features.

Sebastian almost apologized, and then reconsidered. It was best if Olivia did not come to care for him, a circumstance made more likely by the intense passion they'd just shared. Distance had to be created between them—for both their sakes. Apparently, he had a fondness for this woman—*his wife*—that was too threatening to even consider.

Rushing the rest of his bath, Sebastian dressed in silence, eager to flee the intense feelings Olivia engendered. On his way out, he paused in the doorway. "A few of the crewmen will be down shortly to dump the tub water. I'll order more to be heated for you. For God's sake, don't shoot anyone. It will take some time . . ."

"I understand. Thank you." She remained intensely focused on straightening the already orderly contents of her trunk.

He stared at her stiffened spine and couldn't hold back the feelings that twisted and writhed inside him. He clenched his jaw, forcibly withholding the reassurances she obviously wanted, and deserved, to hear. Only minutes ago they'd shared a blinding closeness, and now they were no more than awkward strangers. Instead of bringing ease from his restless agitation, the gulf between them ripped him deeply.

Miserable, he left without a word, the door shutting behind him with an unmistakable click of finality.

Olivia woke to the feel of a steady breeze. From the rolling view outside the windows, she knew they'd raised sail. She looked around the room and found herself alone. Phoenix had not returned the evening before, nor, it appeared, after she'd retired for the night.

There was a knock at the door, and her heart leapt as she rushed to answer it, eager to see Phoenix again. Instead it was Maggie who stood there. The abigail entered with a bright smile, unaware of her mistress's disappointment.

Olivia tried to hold her tongue, but her curiosity won out. "Have you seen Captain Phoenix about today?"

"Aye," Maggie said with a cheerful lilt. "Early this morning, before he went with the *Seawitch*. We're on our way, milady. The crew said we should put into port in Barbados within a few days."

The *Seawitch*. Olivia's heart plummeted into her stomach. Phoenix had moved to her father's ship to get away from her, that was painfully obvious. Her face heated with embarrassment. He most likely thought her the worst sort of wanton. And hadn't she been?

Wretched, she shook her head. She'd been mindless with desire, but the pirate certainly had not felt the same. He'd had the presence of mind to keep her maidenhead intact, a circumstance that said clearly he did not desire to take her as his wife. He would escort her to England, obtain his annulment, and sail off without looking back. She, on the other hand, would spend her days pining for the husband she hadn't wanted, only to discover he was all she wanted.

Olivia spent the three days it took to reach Barbados ensconced in Phoenix's cabin. Bored and crying miserably every time she remembered her abandoned behavior, she resorted to snooping to distract herself. Rifling through his drawers, desk, and cupboards, she found ribbon-bound letters from the Marquess of Dunsmore addressed to Sebastian Blake. She found legal documents that bore his seal and wanted posters displaying his alias. She'd strongly suspected, of course, or she would never have given her favors so freely. But by the end of the three days, she had no doubt.

She was married to a pirate. The thought thrilled her.

Now she needed to discover a way to keep him.

Chapter Three

Sebastian waited for Olivia at the bottom of the gangplank with deplorable impatience. He hadn't seen her in a sennight, and that was a sennight too long in his estimation. Before moving to the *Seawitch*, he'd ordered Will to secure lodgings for her at the local inn when they docked, certain she would relish the opportunity to sleep in a bed after spending three nights in his hammock. She had probably been exhausted. He knew he was. Her cabin on the *Seawitch* had been hell on earth, a decadent room showcasing a massive, velvet-draped four-poster bed.

The nights had been torturous, the silk sheets infused with her scent, a lingering redolence that burned through his blood. He'd dreamed of her naked and spread beneath him, his aching cock thrust deep inside her body, a ripe nipple trapped between his tongue and the roof of his mouth.

The overwhelming need to fuck had forced him into town to find a lusty wench. He'd found several, fondled a few, kissed a couple, and left them all. Not even the most skilled whore could kiss like Olivia, who kissed him as if she would die if she couldn't have him.

He was quite simply mad for her, thoroughly besotted.

Sebastian rolled his shoulders, attempting to ease the tension there. He rubbed the back of his neck and looked toward the inn, immediately grateful for the cane he affected. It supported his buckling knees when his wife came into view.

The entire town seemed to freeze, the bustling noises fading into obscurity until only the cry of seagulls remained. The crowd parted, revealing Olivia's golden beauty as she strolled toward him. Her rich tresses were piled atop her head—careless, artless curls tumbling in studious disarray. Her taupe-colored gown was of the finest silk, shimmering in the island sun like light on rippling water. It showcased her full breasts, tiny waist, and creamy skin to perfection. She wore a broad, feathered hat at a jaunty angle that shielded most of her face from his view, but revealed the full red mouth that had ruined him for any other. He was speechless, breathless, agonizingly aroused at the mere sight of her. Olivia was a diamond of the first water. And for the moment, she was his diamond.

For the first time in his life, Sebastian was grateful to his father.

During the last several sleepless nights, unable to keep her from his thoughts, he'd contemplated their present circumstances. Olivia wanted to maintain their marriage, if he could prove his identity. He collected that the benefits of such a union would be numerous for both of them. She deserved better than him, of course. He'd tried to tell her. If she insisted on having him, what fool would he be to cast her aside? He was not a foolish man. Reckless and selfish perhaps, but certainly not foolish.

The vision that was his wife stopped before him, and to his amazement, she dropped into a curtsy so low her forehead would have touched the dirt if not for the brim of her hat. Sebastian scowled. *What in hell was she doing?*

"My lord," she murmured in deference.

The town immediately resumed its frenzied activity.

Reaching down, he yanked Olivia to her feet. She shielded her eyes from him with her hat, a meek gesture that was not in keeping with her fiery nature. He wanted, with a soul-deep need, to see her lovely eyes and look upon her beautiful face. Annoyed with her behavior, Sebastian spoke harshly. "What is the matter with you?"

It wasn't possible, and yet her head dropped even lower, until all he could see was the top of her blasted hat.

"I apologize if I have displeased you again, my lord. I meant no offense."

Again? What the devil was she talking about?

Sebastian gripped her elbow and dragged her up the gangplank, not stopping until they reached her cabin, where he thrust her in first and slammed the door shut behind them. Frustrated by her hat, he removed the offending article and tossed it aside. Her lovely visage was revealed to him, as well as her tears. Immediately, he felt contrite. He was a cad.

"What ails you?" he queried, drawing her into his embrace. Olivia stood stiffly for a heartbeat before melting into him.

"You're angry with me."

"No," he denied, his hands stroking the curve of her spine. "I'm confused."

She buried her face in his chest and sobbed. "You think I'm a wanton."

His confusion remained, but his mouth curved against her hair. "Perhaps a little."

She sobbed louder.

"But I like it," he amended hastily.

"You don't!" she argued in a muffled voice. "You left me so I wouldn't throw myself at you again. And I won't. Never again, I vow."

Ah! Sebastian grinned like an idiot.

He kept his voice low and soothing. "I'd have ravished you further, Olivia, if the ocean hadn't been between us. You were distraught. Your ship was attacked, you were abused, and your husband was revealed to be a criminal. It would have been dishonorable of me to take your body under those conditions. Bad enough I took the liberties I did."

She struggled away from him, her eyes flashing dangerously.

"You are not an honorable man! You said so yourself. You refused to marry a woman you compromised, and yet the woman to whom you are married is left a virgin." She stomped a slippered foot. "I am not a fool! Admit the truth."

"The truth?" He arched a brow. "As you wish, sweeting. The truth is, I want you desperately. I want to take your lush body, spread it beneath me, and ride you until you can't move. I want to breech your precious maidenhead and ruin you for any other man. I want to hear you moan my name while you come around my cock. I want to fill you with my seed over and over again, until you think of nothing but me and how well I can pleasure you."

Eyes wide, her tongue darted out to wet her bottom lip. "Good heavens."

"Heaven," he purred. "Yes, I suspect it will be."

"It is your right to . . . to do those things . . . if you truly want to. I am your wife."

Sebastian crossed his arms. "Certain of that, are you?" He bit back a smile. He'd hoped she'd be curious.

Her chin lifted. "Yes, I am certain of it."

"You went through my things."

She nodded.

"And what do you think of this development?"

Olivia clasped her hands, dislodging her lush breasts until they threatened to escape her low bodice. His mouth went dry as the desert, lust and appreciation flaring hot and heavy in his loins. Perhaps when his ardor faded, he would regret claiming his bride, but he couldn't think of that now. He couldn't think at all.

"I think 'tis a good thing you like my wantonness, because I am about to become decidedly more wanton." She took a deep breath. "I want you to seduce me now. Make me your wife in truth, so when we return to England you won't cast me aside."

His heart stopped beating. Or rather it dropped between his legs and throbbed violently. "Why?" he asked, wanting her to admit that she wanted him badly enough to compromise herself. "Are you that determined to please your father? By all accounts you are his pride and joy. You can do no wrong in his eyes."

"I have never done wrong!" she snapped. "In his eyes or otherwise."

Sebastian held his tongue, startled at her vehemence.

Her knuckles were white with tension when she spoke. "My mother died giving birth to me. How could I refuse my father anything, when he lost everything that mattered to him for me?"

"I see."

It shouldn't matter why Olivia wanted to remain married to him. He hadn't wanted a wife to begin with and had no life to offer one in any case. But his stomach clenched into knots, and cold sweat dotted his brow. "So you follow his every dictate, including marriage to a stranger, to keep him happy."

Her gaze burned into his. "Yes, I married you because my father asked, but that is no longer the reason I wish to be wed to you. Now I care only for myself and what *I* wish to have."

Sebastian stood frozen, aching, feeling the weight of her silken net entrapping him and yet unable to fight the pleasure it gave him. The decision was made without thought, only feeling.

Olivia offered him everything a man could want—a family, someone to care for him and miss him while he was away, a home to return to, a passionate body to sink into, a beauty to appreciate, and a strength of spirit to admire. For years he'd disparaged such comforts, swearing he needed only his wits and will to survive. He'd never allowed himself to wish for things that were not meant to be his. Then Olivia had come into his life with the promise of happiness he didn't deserve. Selfish and self-centered as he was, Sebastian couldn't refuse.

"And what do you wish to have?" he asked in a hoarse whisper.

"Oh!" She tossed up her hands and stalked to the window, her spine rigid. "Go away, Merrick. I have embarrassed myself enough for a lifetime."

Sebastian shrugged out of his coat and waistcoat, and yanked his shirt over his head.

"Leave, my lord," she said curtly, her back to him.

"No." He sat on the edge of her bed and pulled off his boots. As the first one hit the floor with a thump, she turned to face him.

"W-what are you d-doing?" she sputtered.

"Disrobing," he replied. "Garments are a hindrance to lovemaking." Sebastian dropped the other boot and removed his stockings. He stood up and shucked his breeches, his painfully aroused cock springing free of its confinement.

Olivia gasped at the sight. "Good grief!"

His cock was huge. Dear God in heaven. "That—"she pointed with her finger—"will not fit!"

Along with the butterflies of fear that took flight in her stomach were tendrils of excitement, rich and heady. From her very first sight of the dashing pirate, he'd had that effect on her. Olivia couldn't deny that it was thrilling to know she had a similar effect on him. It seemed her peculiar boldness was not so unappealing to him after all, a realization that filled her with relief.

His brilliant blue gaze lit with amusement, and his mouth curved, revealing his charming dimple. "Thank you, sweetheart. You've just given me the greatest compliment a woman can bestow upon her man."

Olivia stilled. Her man. Her husband. *Hers.*

She wanted more of him, a lifetime of him. Sebastian Blake—outlaw, pirate, peer—could make all of her fantasies a reality. Whatever doubt she felt melted away.

He was gorgeous. Fully naked and bared to her view, he was perfection. Rippled with muscle, taut with desire, heavy with arousal—her mouth watered at the sight of him.

She tore her gaze from his raging erection and looked up into those intense blue eyes. "You will have me then?"

"With pleasure. Since you are so determined to have me." His gaze softened. "Do not concern yourself with the fit," he soothed. "I'll make you wet and hungry for me, sweet. So dripping and ravenous that my cock will slide deep within you like a hot knife in butter, and you will melt just the same."

Dampness flooded her thighs. "Your voice is amazing," she murmured. "My brain simply ceases to function when you speak."

"Olivia—"

"Release your hair," she interrupted. "I like it better loose."

Sebastian walked toward her, tugging out his queue as he came. Truly his hair was not nearly as long as hers, but it did reach the bottom of his shoulder blades, and when he walked the inky black silk flowed over his broad shoulders. He looked like a pagan god, tanned to the waist and built for pleasure.

Her pleasure.

"I am no marital prize," he warned. "I am not any kind of prize."

"You are a treasure." Olivia took a hesitant step toward him. "Just the way you are."

Sebastian held out his hand, and she flew to him, throwing herself into his warm embrace. She gripped the back of his neck and pulled his smiling lips down to hers.

Warm and sweet, his voluptuary's mouth brushed featherlight across hers. She tried to draw him closer to taste him more fully, but he easily held back, his strength so much greater than hers.

"We have weeks to travel, love," he reminded her gently. "All the time in the world to compromise me completely. No need to devour me whole."

Experiencing the novel sensation of feminine power over a stunning man, Olivia experimented with wielding it. "You are mine, my lord. I can do as I please with you."

Sebastian's arms tightened around her, his breath hissing through his teeth as if she'd burned him.

She cupped his cheek with her hand, studying him. "No one has ever claimed you before," she murmured perceptively, wondering what had happened in his life to mold him into the man he was today—a wanted man. She should be terrified to link her fate with his, but all she felt was wonder. "I do so with pride."

Her husband rewarded her with a searing kiss, his hands cupping her buttocks and pressing her into his steely erection. He released her too quickly, circling her, making her ache simply from the heat of his gaze. And then he stilled behind her, silent, the rapid rush of their breathing the only sound in the room.

Olivia waited. Waited for him to move, to touch her—anything at all. Just before she turned in frustration, she felt his hands, sure and knowledgeable, on the fastenings of her gown. Breathless, she shivered under the faint brushes of his fingertips, fingers that had been inside her body, stroking her to rapture. With a soft press of his mouth on her shoulder and a bold sweep of his arms, Sebastian pushed her dress and corset to the floor.

For a moment, only a moment, Olivia was jealous over his obvious expertise at removing women's garments, and then she wasn't jealous, merely comforted. She was in good hands, skilled hands. Hands that knew all the secrets of a woman's body and the places that brought her the most pleasure.

With infinite slowness, those expert hands slid over her breasts, down her waist, and into the apex of her thighs. They bunched up handfuls of her gossamer thin chemise, the fingers rubbing gently across her sex as they pulled the garment up her thighs bit by agonizing bit.

Her husband's hard chest pressed against her back, his shoulders surrounded her, his heat consumed her, his breath gusted harshly against her ear. He was exceedingly powerful and so much larger than she was. He dwarfed her, yet Olivia was unafraid, finding comfort in his strength and reassurance in the tenderness of his touch. A brush, a sweep, his calloused fingertips teased her mound until she melted against him with a plaintive moan. Her breasts swelled and grew heavy, her body trickling moisture down the inside of her thighs.

Just as she was certain her knees would give way, those

skillful hands dragged up her torso, brushing across her erect nipples before tugging the chemise over her head. She sagged into the shelter of his chest, loving the feel of his bare skin against hers. Sebastian had barely touched her, but already she hovered on the edge he'd pushed her over before. His devilish chuckle rumbled in her ear. He knew it.

"I want to look at you," he whispered, his tongue swirling in the shell of her ear before he turned her around.

Olivia forced herself to remain still as his brilliant blue gaze raked her from head to toe. His large hands reached out and brushed along the top of her shoulders before sliding down her arms, leaving tingles in their wake. His fingers linked with hers, and he pulled her closer.

"Beautiful," he breathed before placing a tender kiss on her forehead. "You are the most ravishing creature."

His hands left hers and slid up her sides in a tickling caress before finally . . . *finally!* . . . cupping her aching breasts. She moaned, drowning in his skilled seduction. She'd known her pirate would be like this, focused and intent, wickedly precise in overtaking her senses with his touch, his voice, his proximity.

Sebastian plucked at her erect nipples, tugging and twisting, before he lowered his mouth and licked the hard tips. "Look at me," he ordered.

Olivia forced herself to meet his gaze, warmed by the need that smoldered there. She licked her bottom lip nervously, and he groaned, his mouth swooping down to press against hers. His tongue thrust deep, hinting at what was to follow. One hand kneaded her breast, while the other grabbed her wrist and brought her hand to his cock.

She gasped as the silken weight of him burned her palm. It was not what she'd expected, smoother and softer than the finest silk, yet hot and pulsing with life. She wondered how it would feel inside her. Would it burn her with heat? Stroke her with softness? Olivia shivered with anticipation. Regardless, she knew it would pleasure her. Everything about her husband pleasured her.

Sebastian curled his fingers over hers and moved her hand up and down his length in a hard, fast rhythm that soon had him shaking against her. Once she had the way of it, he left her to pleasuring him and slipped his hand between her legs.

He was everywhere at once—in her mouth, against her breast, in her hand, inside her sex. It was all too much, and yet it wasn't. She wanted . . . "More," she urged.

He smiled against her mouth. "Siren. Found at sea, and luring me to matrimony."

Olivia pulled back, releasing his shaft.

Another of his fingers slid upward into her heat, and she was trapped, impaled in place.

"I'm not complaining," he assured in a silky whisper.

With an arm around her waist, Sebastian lifted her feet from the floor, his fingers still embedded within her as he carried her to the bed. He turned and lay down first, draping her across him, his arm trapped between them, his fingers still pumping into her. Her eyes slid closed on a moan as her body clenched around the welcome invasion. Desperate, she writhed over his hand.

Her blood was thick as syrup and hot, making her sweat. Olivia dropped her head to his chest and felt his nipple brush her cheek. She turned slightly and sucked it into her mouth, as he had done to her. His breath hitched in his throat, his body hardening beneath hers. Reaching for his cock, she began stroking it again, hard and fast like he had shown her. She felt naughty and wanton, a wild woman in his arms. Her hips rocked against his hand, pushing him deeper.

"No more," he growled. Rolling her beneath him, Sebastian spread her stocking-clad legs with his own. He paused, the hairs on his chest scraping across her aching nipples. His fingers slipped out of her, and he spread the cream from them around her swollen opening. He moved higher, rubbing the slickness over her aching bud, making her squirm and beg beneath him.

"Sebastian . . ."

He buried his face in her neck. "Say my name again."

"Sebastian . . . help me . . . I burn . . ."

"Yes, love," he encouraged, his fingers sliding faster. "Burn for me."

Her back arched, her eyes flew open, she hung on the edge . . . *so close . . . so close . . .*

Olivia cursed him when his hand left her sex and moved to her knee.

"Patience," he murmured hoarsely. "I will take you there."

He pulled her legs to his waist, and the heavy heat of his erection prodded her dripping opening. His gaze locked with hers, his forehead beaded with sweat. He lowered his head and mumbled, "Sorry, my love," just before he thrust hard and deep within her.

Olivia bit back a cry, startled at the pain that obliterated her pleasure. She held still beneath him, tears filling her eyes and spilling over.

Sebastian's tongue lapped up the wetness with the long, slow drags of a cat, soothing her even as he pressed inexorably inside. "If I'd gone slowly," he explained, "the pain would have been worse." He cradled her head in his hands, his eyes soft and tender with regret. "There is some good to this discomfort you feel."

"What is it?" she gasped. She could see his concern, felt it in the reverence of his touch.

"I am well and truly compromised. You shall have to marry me, or I will be ruined."

Unable to help it, Olivia laughed, even though it hurt. "Lucky for you, my lord, that we are already wed."

"Ah." He withdrew and then slid forward again, frowning when she winced. "I am a lucky man. My reputation is saved." The pain began to lessen even as he finally buried his cock to the hilt. His ragged groan made her shiver. Dropping his head to her breast, he suckled her.

His big body strained and flexed as he started a rhythm and maintained it, pumping deep within her, his raven hair a curtain around them. His mouth was magic, his tongue swirling around the erect crest of her nipple. The steel of Sebastian's cock began to burn, a wondrous sensation that intensified with the erotic sounds he made.

"Spread your legs," he begged, gasping with obvious pleasure when she opened, giving greater access to his thrusts. "Press your body against me. God, yes . . . Livia . . ."

The fierce Captain Phoenix was clay in her hands.

Olivia arched upward, feeling his skin cling to hers with his sweat. She gripped his contracting buttocks, amazed at their feel, hard as stone. He swirled his hips, grinding into the source of her pleasure, and tingles spread outward, flushing her skin. He pressed into her again, repeating the movement, drenching her body in sensation.

His hips thrust and circled in an endless cycle, over and over, sweeping her higher. His touch was oddly gentle, despite the pistoning haste of his movements. His tenderness swept into her heart, bringing tears to her eyes. Olivia whimpered, lost in his possession. He felt so good, the friction so deep, the stretching exquisite.

"Yes, love . . ." His voice, thick and slurred with pleasure, enflamed her. "You feel . . . so damn good . . ."

He filled her with quick, hard strokes, no longer able to be gentle, and she didn't care. She didn't want gentle. She wanted passion—his passion.

Deep inside, her womb began to clench, then spasm. Arching her back on a scream, she shattered, her inner muscles clutching greedily at his invading shaft. Sebastian pinned her hips, holding her in place for his thrusts, drawing out her pleasure until she thought she would die of it. Only when she sagged into the mattress did he follow her, shuddering against her, gasping her name, filling her with scalding heat.

When it was over, Olivia lay stunned, clinging to her husband as the only anchor in a whirl of decadent pleasure.

It was forever before he spoke, his voice still passion-hoarse. "Hopelessly compromised," he murmured, and promptly fell into a deep sleep.

* * *

Sebastian crossed the moonlit wharf in rapid strides. He was late for his meeting, but his tardiness was of little consequence to him. All that mattered at the moment was his sleeping wife and the panic she would feel if she discovered him missing.

Olivia was uncertain of his attachment to her, as he was himself, but she had given her body to him regardless, trusting him to be a gentleman and claim her as his bride. Nothing could force him to do the honorable thing. He was certain he could return her to her father and successfully fight the proxy. She was intelligent, and he'd been honest about his history, but she had taken him to her bed despite the risks.

She was the first person in his life willing to give him the benefit of the doubt, the first person who truly wanted him, not just for an hour's pleasure or two, but for the rest of her life. He refused to lose her regard. Especially over the distasteful errand he was presently attending to.

Sebastian entered the seaside tavern and paused on the threshold, allowing his eyes to adjust to the interior.

"You're late, Phoenix."

He turned his head toward the voice. "Pierre," he greeted coldly. "Dominique."

The French pirates lounged by the door, and Sebastian felt a twinge of satisfaction. Their position was excellent. After what he planned to say, a hasty egress might well be required. In anticipation of trouble, he had set his own ship to sail that morning, lessening the targets that could be used to wound him.

The two identical brothers remained seated, gazing at him with soul-weary eyes. Sebastian was aware that most of the lightskirts in town found the Robidoux brothers attractive, but not a one would service them. The siblings' sadistic carnal tastes were well known to all.

He looked them over with loathing. Many times over the last year he'd regretted his decision to join with them. One evening, inebriated and wretched, hating his life and the depths to which he'd sunk, he'd shared a bottle with the Frenchmen, and they'd shared an idea—rotating voyages with a split share. At the time, it had sounded like a reasonable plan and one that would lessen his risk.

Now it was his most lamented decision. Where he made every effort to spare lives and had yet to take one that wasn't actively trying to take his, Pierre and Dominique killed and tortured just for their amusement.

"Word has it we're divvying up an amazing booty," Dominique drawled in his unctuous voice. To the ignorant eye, he appeared to be the more civilized of the twins. Sebastian, however, knew him to be the more vicious. "I saw part of the spoils crossing the wharf to you this afternoon—a prime article. The curtsy was a nice touch. You've broken her well, Phoenix, although I personally prefer a bit of spirit in my lovers."

Sebastian's insides coiled with repressed violence, and his hand slid to the blade strapped to his thigh. The thought of these men within viewing distance of his wife made him physically ill. He'd known this confrontation would be difficult, but he'd failed to consider the danger to Olivia, assuming her to be far removed from the devil's bargain he'd made long ago. "There has been a change of plan," he said. "I'll be paying your share in coin."

Pierre leapt to his feet, his chair crashing to the floor. "Bastard!" He shot a furious glance at his brother. "I told you he couldn't be trusted!"

"Calm down," Dominique growled. "I'll see that you receive your fair share."

"Like hell!" Pierre retorted, his voice lowering, but his rage no less evident. "I'll claim my fair share now. I've heard the tales of the cargo in that fat-bellied merchant—fine French laces and brandy, Oriental vases and plates, rich materials, exotic spices, and chests of gold. We've not had a catch of such magnitude in the last year, and it may be just as long before another like her comes along." The Frenchman turned a feral grin toward Sebastian. "If you refuse to share the wealth, my Judas friend, I may be required to come and get it myself."

"I should like to see you try," Sebastian scoffed. "I'll burn the ship and its cargo before that happens."

Dominique placed a restraining hand on his brother's shoulder and eyed Sebastian speculatively. "You're breaking the code, Phoenix. Slitting your own throat, I'd say. Is that what you want?"

Sebastian laughed. "You've always had a flair for the dramatic, Robidoux." He tossed two hefty purses onto the table. "Take your guineas and be happy. You should be grateful. I've saved you the trouble of disposing of the items."

Pierre snatched up his purse and hefted the weight in his hand. The gleam in his eyes betrayed his pleasure at the sum, but it wasn't enough. "I want the woman too."

"No!" Sebastian said, far too quickly. He took a rapid, deep breath, damning himself for revealing an interest he should have kept hidden.

Dominique's eyes narrowed as he collected his purse. "Give him the woman, Phoenix, and we'll call it even."

"She's not available to you, gentlemen." He took a step back, suddenly anxious to be with Olivia.

"She has a maid," Dominique drawled, his brittle gaze brightening with malice. "And her garments are costly. A devilish good piece that one. I'd wager she's worth something to someone. Beauty like that is expensive, wouldn't you say, Pierre?"

"Yes, certainly," Pierre agreed. "A small fortune for that bit of fluff."

Sebastian paused. "Leave the woman out of this. You have your shares. Our transaction is completed."

"But I feel as if I've pulled the short stick," Pierre whined. Then he smiled. "I'll pay you for her, Phoenix." He opened the purse Sebastian had just given him. "How much?"

"She's not for sale," he bit out, his forehead beading with sweat. The situation was rapidly slipping from his control.

The barmaid came by, setting two overflowing mugs on the table.

"Celia," Dominique purred. "Your sister works at the inn, *non*?"

She eyed the pirate warily. "Aye."

"Hmmm. What tidbits did she share about the guests? More specifically, what did she say about the wom—"

Sebastian drew his knife and stabbed it into the table with such fury the wooden surface cracked down the center. "There will be no more discussion of the woman!" he snarled. "Forget you saw her, forget you heard of her, forget she exists." He grabbed the startled Pierre by the back of the neck and slammed his face into the table. The Frenchman stared wide-eyed at the knife, which was only a hair's breadth away from the tip of his nose. Sebastian bent over him. "Have I made myself clearer this time, Robidoux?"

"O-of course!" Pierre gasped.

Sebastian shoved him to the floor with a grunt and yanked his blade from the ruined table. "I've finished here."

He backed out of the tavern, his heart racing. Turning, he ran to the *Seawitch*. The alert was given as he hit the gangplank, and the crew leapt into action. They cast off, catching the faint evening breeze and moving with torturous sluggishness from the quay.

He didn't relax until the island was a mere dark shape in the vast ocean. It wasn't finished, he knew. The Robidoux brothers would make trouble, for when Pierre was upset he would not cease his harping until Dominique took action. And Dominique Robidoux was a man to be reckoned with.

Sebastian made his way to Olivia's cabin and undressed silently. He slipped between the silk sheets and curled around her sleeping back. At the first touch of her skin, he became erect and fully aroused, aching for the comfort of her body. He lifted her leg over his hip and she roused, but made no protest. He dipped his hand between her legs, feeling his thick cream coating her sex and inner thighs. Like the beast he was, he found deep satisfaction in the primitive claim.

"Do you wish—" she whispered.

"No." He buried his face in her hair, inhaling her scent. "Yes. But you're sore. I can wait."

"I don't want you to wait."

"But you will. Soon enough you'll be begging me to cease my constant demands."

"I'll never tire of you, my lord," she assured him in a sleep-heavy murmur that caused him to press against her with a groan. Olivia spooned against him, nuzzling her luscious derriere against his enflamed cock with a trust that left him breathless.

His stomach clenched. She'd entrusted him with her life, and he'd endangered it already.

He had to put as much distance between them as possible and at the soonest opportunity.

"Who is she, Dominique?" Pierre asked, staring after the vanishing ship.

"The Countess of Merrick. What would you wager that Phoenix has gone to ransom her for a fortune we won't get our share of?"

"I don't make bets with you. You always win."

Dominique smiled. "And we'll win this time too."

"How so?" Pierre asked curiously.

"You'll see, brother. You'll see."

Chapter Four

Sebastian stepped onto the deck and turned completely around before spotting Olivia. Sitting on a barrel at the foredeck, she looked pensively over the water. He deliberately made his steps heard so as not to startle her. He smiled as she lifted a bottle to her lips and drank from it. "Care to share, love?"

She passed him the wine. "How was your dinner with the captain?"

"I'm not certain. I was distracted."

"Oh? With what, may I ask?"

"With visions of you, naked in bed, eating supper without me."

"As if I would ever eat naked," she scoffed. "And in bed no less. I, for one, do not relish crumbs on my linens." Her mouth curved in a contented smile. "Do you never think of anything other than sex?"

"Certainly. Just this afternoon I wondered what you were doing in the West Indies."

Her smile faded.

It was the first time either one of them had broached the subject of their pasts. There had been a silent agreement between them to live only in the moment, but they approached England far too quickly. Soon they would present themselves to the world as Lord and Lady Merrick, yet they were hardly more than intimate strangers. He knew her body in minute detail, but her past and visions for their future remained a mystery.

Olivia sighed. "My father maintains a plantation there."

"And you prefer it to London?"

"I enjoy the freedom."

Sebastian frowned. There was something she wasn't telling him. "And what of the Season? You are a diamond, my love. Your popularity is assured."

Even as he said the words, his gut clenched. Men would swarm around his wife like bees to honey, her marital status making her even more desirable. The thought of other men drooling over Olivia while he was at sea made him murderous.

She looked out over the water, avoiding his gaze. "In the past, I've enjoyed the Season. I simply didn't feel up to it this year."

There was more, he knew, but Sebastian hesitated to press her further. Their time on the ship had been idyllic, and he didn't wish to ruin it. Harsh reality would intrude soon enough. "And now that you've wed, do you intend to make England your home?"

That comment brought her gaze back to his. "Of course. Your home is my home now."

"My home is at sea."

Olivia nodded her agreement without hesitation, causing a sharp pain in his chest.

What had he expected? That she would cry and beg for him to remain with her? Hadn't he capitulated merely to sate his lust, with the added bonus of acquiring the wife and heirs his cursed title demanded? Simply because he'd found his desire unquenchable and his need of deeper origin than he'd realized, did not mean his wife was experiencing the same.

He placed his hand on her shoulder and absently stroked the side of her throat with his thumb. "I shall visit you often." He felt, rather than heard, her deeply indrawn breath.

Olivia leaned into him. "How often is 'often' to you?"

"I should pose that question to you, sweet," he replied,

passing the decision to her, while in truth he knew he would crave her and seek her out like a thirsty man would water. "We are in this marriage together."

She hesitated before speaking. "Should you decide to come home at least every six months, you will be able to ascertain if I am breeding or not."

Sebastian stilled. "Breeding." Good God. He could imagine it, picture it clearly—Olivia increasing with his child.

"You're hurting me," she whispered, her hand prying at his fingers on her shoulder.

"I'm sorry." Dazed, he handed her the bottle and began to rub the marks left by his fingertips. "You startled me."

"So I gathered. But it was you who said that one of my duties would be to bear your heirs."

Duty. Not pleasure. Heirs. Not children.

Suddenly there was a distinction between them, one that irritated him and made him restless.

He reached for her hand. "I should like to retire."

Turning, she searched his face. He could feel the air altering around them, shifting even as their relationship did. *What was happening?* Sebastian stood rigid under her scrutiny. *What did she see in him with those dark eyes that bored right through him?*

He was profoundly relieved when Olivia placed her hand in his and followed him to their bed, where heady pleasure and drugging forgetfulness awaited them.

Sebastian stared up at the ruby red velvet canopy and sighed with contentment.

Olivia's heated breath puffed across the head of his cock. "What are you thinking?" she asked.

He glanced down to where his wife lay prone between his legs. She'd spent the last hour in studious examination of his member, tracing every vein, caressing every bit of his hard length with her hands and mouth, purring her delight like a cat with cream. She made him feel supremely masculine; a man appreciated completely by his mate, her admiration a welcome salve after a lifetime of feeling insignificant. At least in this one endeavor, that of being Olivia's husband, he had not been found lacking. "You," he answered. "This bed. Our marriage."

She crossed her hands on his upper thigh and rested her chin upon them. "Do you have regrets?" she asked in a steady voice, even as her expressive eyes showed her worry.

He reached down to caress her tumbled hair. "No. Come closer."

Olivia rose to her hands and knees, her full breasts swaying as she climbed along the length of his body. She'd become quite comfortable with her nakedness over these last weeks, and he appreciated their growing familiarity.

She purred with pleasure as she draped her body over his. He reached up and pulled her hair to the side so he could nuzzle her throat unhindered.

"Sebastian."

"Umm?"

"Tell me about your family."

He sighed. "They are a pack of vultures, sweeting. The entire lot of them."

"Surely there must be some members of your family whose company you enjoy."

"I was quite fond of my brother, Edmund."

She frowned. "What about your mother?"

He stared at the canopy again. "There is nothing I can tell you, other than she was very beautiful, and I know this only because I've seen her portrait. I don't remember her at all."

"How did she die?"

He slid his hands through her hair and cupped the back of her head. "I don't know that she is dead. She ran off when I still an infant."

"Oh, Sebastian." Having caught the bitterness in his voice, hers filled with sympathy.

He choked out a laugh. "Don't pity me, Olivia. I won't have it. I don't want it."

"I won't," she soothed. "I know how it is to grow up without a mother. You and I are so alike, in the most unexpected of ways." Her small hands came up to cradle his face. "Do you know why she ran away?"

"Marriage to my father would do it, I would say. You'll never have the misfortune to meet a colder or more vicious man."

"That is something I cannot imagine." Olivia fell silent, her fingertips drawing circles across his chest. "When was the last time you saw your father?" she asked finally.

He didn't want to think about the marquess. Ever. "Five years ago."

"Are you worried about seeing him again?"

Sebastian considered that for a moment. "I don't believe so. After all, I am returning with the bride of his choosing. He should have no complaints, at least none outside the usual, which entails everything else about me."

Olivia took a deep breath, the movement pressing her breasts more fully against his chest.

"Tell me what you're thinking," he urged when the silence stretched out.

She hesitated, then her natural forthrightness won out. "Would I have been your choice for a bride? Or did you—"

"Yes," he interjected, deducing the nature of her query. "If I'd been of the mind to be leg-shackled, I would most definitely have selected your fetter over any other. And no. What is between you and I has nothing to do with my father. If you think on it further, love, you will see that discarding you would have served my rebellion better."

She sighed and offered a relieved smile. "When will we arrive in London?"

"A week perhaps."

"That's all?" Her smile faltered, then faded completely.

Sebastian frowned. "Why so miserable, sweet?"

With a wriggle of her hips, she positioned his cock at her entrance and engulfed him easily, her passage slick with his seed.

His breath hissed out through his teeth as pleasure, searing and almost painful, coursed through his blood. "*Dear God,*" he groaned. It was like fucking his way into a velvet fist, every time more astonishingly rapturous than the last.

"Do you intend to leave me immediately after we return?" Olivia rose up to a seated position, taking more of him into her body until the dark honey curls of her sex tangled with his black ones and he felt the warmth of her womb cap his erection. The visual and physical combination made him swell even further inside her, stretching her until she moaned.

"W-what?" He couldn't think.

She rose up on her knees and then slid back down along his shaft, killing him softly. "Will you leave me in London immediately?"

He caressed the satin skin of her thighs, his entire body consumed with fever. "No . . . I don't know . . ." He gasped as she rode him again. Lightning bolted into his spine and radiated outward. "What do you want . . . me to do?"

Olivia undulated around him, over him, against him, her fingertips swirling over his flat nipples. Damn, she'd become so familiar with his body, she played it with the skill of the finest courtesan. She knew just where to touch him, where to stroke him, to turn him to putty in her hands.

"I want you to stay with me, just for a short time." She moved again, slowly, caressing his throbbing cock with silken, drenched heat. Sebastian gritted his teeth, his back arching against his will. "There will be balls and luncheons in our honor, callers to our home. I don't want to endure it all alone."

She tightened her inner muscles on him and tweaked his nipples. His sac grew tight, his seed rising, heating. Bloody hell, he was ready to spend himself and she had just begun.

"Of course, love," he groaned, willing to give her anything she asked. "There's no rush . . . for me to depart. I'll stay . . . as long as you . . . think is best. Just do that again . . . oh, yes . . . again . . ."

Olivia's smile was triumphant as she rested her palms flat on his chest and began to ride him in earnest, lifting and falling in a pounding rhythm, moaning in a way that drove him insane. The part of his brain that still functioned realized she'd managed him to her liking with the use of her body, but the part of him presently being milked inside her didn't care. She loved his cock—loved to ride it, kiss it, suck on it—and he loved to give it to her. He was mad for her, mad for her pleasure, mad for her touch.

As her body spasmed around him and she cried out his name, Sebastian found he didn't mind being managed at all. He clutched her hips in his hands, holding her still while he thrust upward into her, prolonging her pleasure. Only when her head fell forward in exhaustion did he allow his own release, spurting his seed in endless bursts against her womb, his body wracked with a pleasure so piercing it robbed him of all thoughts but one: she wanted to keep him with her.

"What in hell are you doing?" Olivia cried as she stepped into the cabin.

The knife in her husband's hand clattered into the bowl of water on the vanity, creating a fine mess. Sebastian stood in front of her cherry-framed mirror, naked from the waist up and impossibly gorgeous. As always, her heart skipped a beat just looking at him.

In the last few weeks, he'd shared daily living with her in every way a man would share his life with his wife. He'd observed her in the bath, watched her eat, and assisted her toilette. In return, she'd become fascinated with watching his masculine ablutions. She relished brushing his hair and mending tears in his clothing. She adored taking care of him and giving him the affection he'd gone so long without. Sebastian absorbed every drop with an awed appreciation that tugged at her heart.

"Damnation," he groused, brushing the splattered water off his torso with a towel. "You are like to scare the wits from me, woman!"

"I'll be scaring more than your wits if I ever find you attempting that again!"

He took a deep, slow breath. Olivia set her arms akimbo and tapped her foot indignantly.

"You said it was unfashionably long," he explained, still holding his hair in his hand.

"So it is."

"Well, we're docking in a few hours."

"I'm aware of that." And she hated it, hated that soon they would lose the wondrous intimacy of their long sea voyage and endless days of pleasure in their bed. Within hours, she would be simpering and smiling at the vultures of Society, the very ones who had picked her flesh to the bone only a year ago. And she would have to share her darling husband with them, a man who bore wounds that still festered. The thought made her stomach turn.

"Therefore I'm cutting it," he said curtly.

"No, you are not."

His blue eyes met hers, capped with a frown. "Make sense, Olivia, and hurry up about it!"

She released her breath and stepped toward him, not stopping until her body was pressed against his. She wrapped her arms around his lean waist. "I like your hair the way it is."

Disbelief etched his handsome features.

"I like running my fingers through it when you are sitting down and I'm standing at your shoulder. I like seeing strands of it left on my pillow. I like it swaying around my shoulders when you are thrusting deep inside of me." With gentle fingers, she pried his hair from his tense grasp and rubbed her face in it.

"I was cutting it for you," he said hoarsely.

"Keep it for me," she whispered, meeting his intense gaze. "When we stand in crowded ballrooms, I will see your queue and know that you are mine. I will be reminded of how wild you are, how you struggle against the bonds that hold you, and I will think to myself, 'He chose the bonds that bound him to me.' And I will be happy."

Her hands stroked up the rippled expanse of his torso and came to rest over his heart. It beat beneath her palm in a panicked rhythm.

"God, Olivia," he breathed in a strangled whisper. "Do you have any idea what you do to me?"

Stepping backward, she grabbed his hand and tugged him toward the bed. "We have a few hours left. Why don't you show me?"

Sebastian looked out over the smelly, sooty mess that was the London wharf and, despite his best efforts, felt his stomach tie up in knots. He'd fled England the day after Edmund died and had never returned, had never wanted to, still didn't.

He sighed, taking comfort in Olivia. He would not be alone in this. His wife was thoroughly consummate in the social arts.

"Good God!" she cried from behind him.

Frowning, he spun on his heel. "What is it, love?"

Olivia stood just outside the stairway, resplendent in a blue silk damask gown with lace-edged bodice and sleeves. A shiver of awareness flowed through him, bright and insistent.

Her hand was pressed to her heart. "You . . . good grief . . ." She shook her head slowly. "Damn, you stopped my heart for a moment."

"Don't swear," he admonished with a roll of his eyes.

His wife had spent far too many days at sea with foul-mouthed sailors, which was understandable considering her father's trade. While he admonished her regularly, in truth he found her colorful speech rather charming. The small foible made her seem less perfect and more real, more his. After all, he was a man of overwhelmingly numerous faults.

He waited patiently for her to explain the cause of her distress. Then Sebastian noted the feminine appreciation that lit her eyes and the smile that curved her lush mouth. In fact, now that he was paying attention, he had to admit she looked completely besotted. *With him*. He grinned. "I take it you approve of my attire."

Olivia glided toward him, all graceful elegance and luscious woman. "You look quite dashing. Magnificent, actually."

She pressed herself against him, heedless of the sailors who swarmed the deck and the pedestrians who moved along the crowded wharf. Her hands slid along the lapels of his fine wool coat, down the intricately embroidered silk of his waistcoat, over the bulge of his cock in his snug breeches, and around to the curve of his ass. Thankfully, her wandering touch was hidden from view by his long coat.

"You, my gorgeous pirate, polish up beautifully." With a firm grip on his hips, she tugged herself toward him, smiling wickedly. "Your cock is hard. Do you never tire of bedsport, Captain Phoenix?"

Cupping the curve of her neck, he pressed an ardent kiss to her forehead. "Impossible with a wife as lusty as mine."

He frowned at her use of his alias, reminded of a task he had set for himself and never accomplished. "Wait for me a moment, sweet. I must speak with the captain."

She looked up at him curiously, but did as he asked without question.

It took only a moment to locate the man he sought. "Captain, did you have the opportunity to speak with your crew about my identity?"

The captain's smile peeked out from his bushy gray beard. "Aye, milord, but as I tried to tell you, the men are loyal to Lady Merrick. We've all been with 'er father, Mr. Lambert, since she was a babe. As far as pirates go, yer crew were the only ones what could catch us. You kept the damage to a minimum, and ye didn't 'urt the lass even before you knew she was yer wife. The men on this ship can respect that."

Sebastian nodded, relieved.

A sharp screech from the quay and his name shouted in Olivia's angry voice had him running toward the gangplank. With a quick eye, he took in the rigid set of her spine, the reticule swinging from her fist, and the finely dressed man who covered his face with his hands, cursing foully. It was easy to deduce that she'd been accosted in some manner she'd found offensive and fought back, as she was wont to do.

Filled with furious possessiveness, Sebastian launched himself at the man, no questions asked. Two quick punches, one to the face and the other to the diaphragm, had the lecher moaning in misery.

Satisfied, Sebastian leapt to his feet, straightening his waistcoat, and went to his wife. "What happened?" he asked gently, visually searching for any evidence of injury or insult to her person. Olivia's face was frighteningly pale.

"That man—" she stabbed a finger at her assailant, "—wants a trip to Bedlam! He *kissed* me, then called me his *wife*!"

Sebastian shot a curious glance at the man on the ground and gasped. Now that his face was no longer hidden, the visage was startlingly familiar. "Bloody hell, Carr! What the devil are you doing assaulting my wife?"

"You know him?" Olivia asked in astonishment as Sebastian helped Carr to his feet.

"Unfortunately, yes," he muttered. "This deranged man is Carr Blake, my cousin."

Carr glanced at Sebastian and then Olivia with watering eyes. "Damnation, Merrick! What are you doing here?"

Sebastian arched a brow. "I am escorting my wife to our home. What are *you* doing here? And kissing my wife, for Christ's sake! Are you mad?"

Carr swallowed hard.

Sebastian lifted his gaze and spied the waiting carriage. The equipage was new, not one he recognized, but the crest emblazoned on the door was his. "You've been using my carriage?"

Olivia placed her hand on his arm. "He called me his wife," she choked out. "He came in your equipage."

Sebastian shot a look at her, saw her blanched features, and felt his mouth fall open as the pieces fell into place. "Oh, hell!" He turned to Carr, his nails digging into his palms as he resisted the urge to throttle his relative. "Tell me, cousin, that you are not here pretending to be me."

Carr winced a split second before Sebastian's fist knocked him into oblivion.

* * *

Olivia said nothing during the ride to Dunsmore House. She couldn't have managed speech even if she'd desired to, what with her mouth being dry as the desert and her throat clenched shut with apprehension. Her discomfort only worsened as the carriage rolled to a halt in front of the imposing manse.

Sebastian vaulted down and stared up at the elegant façade. "Remain here."

"No," she argued. "I'm coming with you. You are not facing your father alone."

He looked over his shoulder. "I don't want you anywhere near him!"

"I don't want you anywhere near him either, but you insisted we come." She lifted her chin. "Go in there without me, and I'll follow you, I vow."

Sebastian's face was grim as he assisted her down. He glanced at the footman. "Wait here," he ordered.

Olivia shivered at her husband's starkly austere features. He led her inside, ignoring the horrified butler. They ascended the stairs, heading directly to the study, where masculine voices could be heard. His hand at the small of her back was firm and steady, despite the inner turmoil she sensed. She'd never seen him in such a mood, something akin to murderous rage, and she realized at that moment what had prompted his fierce reputation.

They entered the room, again without knocking, and Olivia paused, frozen on the threshold, shocked to find her father in a wingback chair in front of the fire. Sitting opposite him was a man who looked remarkably like Sebastian and nothing like the decrepit, miserly man she had pictured in her mind.

Jack Lambert stood, his golden hair glinting in the light of the fire. "Livy, sweet!" He came to her and kissed both of her cheeks. "You're late, by weeks. I was worried sick. Agents at the shipping office have kept watch for the *Seawitch*. Your husband made haste to retrieve you when word came that she'd put into port." He looked past her to Sebastian, eyeing him speculatively. "Where is Lord Merrick? And who is this gentleman?"

Sebastian clasped her father's outstretched hand and dipped his head respectfully.

Olivia shot a scathing glance at the marquess. "Lord Merrick, may I present my father, Jack Lambert. Father, this is Lord Merrick."

Her father scowled. "The devil you say!"

"You've been deceived," Sebastian explained softly.

Her father turned to the marquess, frowning in obvious confusion.

Lord Dunsmore rose from his chair with arrogant indifference. He was as tall as his son, but slender and elegant in his build. He was almost frightening, with his cruel mouth and harshly lined eyes. "Sebastian," he drawled. "I see your penchant for ruining the best-laid plans is still in evidence."

Sebastian's arm stiffened under Olivia's fingertips.

Her father's face turned a mottled red. "Explain yourself, Dunsmore!"

The marquess arched a sardonic brow, the depths of his eyes showing no emotion at seeing the son who had been absent for years. "I think I'll leave the explanations to Merrick."

Sebastian stood for a moment, his face an impassive mirror of his father's as the two men stared each other down, the animosity between them palpable. Olivia tugged on his arm to draw his attention back to her father. He took a deep breath. "Mr. Lambert. It is a pleasure to make your acquaintance. I thank you for the hand of your daughter, whom I treasure."

Her father raked Sebastian with a more penetrating gaze. She knew what he saw—a tall, massively built male with the tan and muscles of a manual laborer. With the long hair and icy expression, Sebastian was intimidating.

"Are you satisfied with this union?" her father asked gruffly. "I was able to ascertain some of the character of the man I thought was the earl, but this man next to you is a stranger to me."

She gave a tremulous smile. "I am most pleased, Father. Merrick has been wonderful."

Her father shot her a skeptical glance. "I researched Sebastian Blake thoroughly before signing the marriage agreements. He was known to be a scapegrace in his youth, an incorrigible. But the man I met was polished and civilized." Unspoken was the notion that Sebastian was none of those things, but she heard it nevertheless.

And so did her husband.

Olivia winced, her heart aching. She hugged Sebastian's arm closer.

"We can procure an annulment, Livy," her father persisted. "I want you to be happy."

"No annulment," she said firmly, feeling Sebastian's body become taut as a bow.

"If I know my son," the marquess drawled, "it is far too late for an annulment. Don't whine, Lambert. You bought your daughter an earl, and she acquired one. No harm done."

Olivia gasped at the insult, instantly reminded of how cruel the peerage could be to those they deemed beneath them. Her feelings meant nothing to this man. *She* meant nothing. To him, she was no more than a breeding mare and a fat purse. Despite her lifelong pursuit of indifference, she couldn't deny that the marquess's callousness stung.

Sebastian glanced at her. Attuned to her feelings by weeks of deep intimacy, he leapt to her defense.

"Damn you!" he snarled. "Were you that desperate for an heir to your precious title? To send Carr to my wife . . ." He took a step toward his father, who hadn't the sense to move away. "I'd have killed you both if he'd touched her in my name. I've a mind to kill you anyway."

"Sebastian, no!" Olivia cried as she saw his hands clench into fists. "He's not worth it."

The marquess dismissed his son's fury with an imperious wave of his hand. "You had no knowledge you were even married. You showed no interest in the Dunsmore lands, the tenants, or your duty to the title. Something had to be done."

Sebastian laughed, a hard, bitter sound. "Those are your responsibilities until you die."

"You must learn your place!" Dunsmore barked. "Accustom yourself to your future duties, create issue."

Sebastian shook his head. "Stay out of my life and my business. Stay away from my wife. I won't tell you again."

Her father reached for her. "Come, Olivia. We're leaving."

"She goes nowhere without me," Sebastian warned without taking his eyes from his father. "You are welcome to stay in my home if you like, Mr. Lambert, but Olivia's place is with her husband. With *me*."

"I don't even know you!" Jack bellowed. "How can I trust my daughter to your care?"

"Father!" she beseeched, alarmed at his vehemence. She had no wish to defy him, but Sebastian was her life now. She prayed she wouldn't be forced to choose between the only two people who mattered. "Please!"

"You shall have plenty of opportunity to become acquainted with me," Sebastian said as he returned to her side and reclaimed her arm in an obvious declaration of possession. "My father is correct. It is far too late for an annulment." His implication was clear—she'd been compromised.

Olivia flushed, mortified.

Her father searched her face, his own tight with concern. "Livy?"

"Come with us, Father." She glanced at Lord Dunsmore. "I do not think I can remain here another moment."

Sebastian nodded. "I agree. We've finished our business." He gestured with his free hand toward the door. "Mr. Lambert. Will you join us?"

"Of course." He shot a furious glare at the marquess. "I am not done with you, my lord. You should have held a care for your reputation. I care only for Olivia."

Dunsmore arched a scornful brow. "Of course. You care so much for your daughter, you would marry her to a stranger without even an introduction. You're a paragon of paternal affection."

Jack flushed. "I considered her welfare. You cared only for your own."

Olivia stared at the marquess and was certain she'd never met a man as devoid of emotion. He appeared to care nothing for the enmity directed toward him from all sides. She shivered merely from being in the same room with him and wondered how a man as warm and vibrant as her husband could have come from such a father.

"Where is your gratitude, Sebastian?" the marquess asked. "I procured you a beautiful bride and a hefty dowry. Of course, she's not but a merchant's daughter, but since you weren't here to see to the matter yourself, you should be appreciative in any case. In fact, you strike me as unfashionably smitten, which suits the rest of your appearance."

The hatred that poured from Sebastian poisoned the air. "You may insult me at your leisure, Father, but keep your talons out of my wife. It is only my . . . *appreciation* for her that prevents me from tearing you apart with my bare hands."

The marquess laughed. "I believe you could do it, too. Look at you! You're like a savage. Dark-skinned, long-haired, and built like an ape."

Olivia whimpered in agony, knowing that Sebastian was bleeding from wounds she had helped to inflict. She had teased him with those same descriptions, but now he would wonder and think himself less of a man, when in fact he was more of one than anyone she had ever met.

"He's beautiful," she snapped. "You're a fool for failing to see how wonderful he is. The loss is yours." She tugged at Sebastian.

With a jerky nod, he gestured for her father to precede them.

Just as quickly as they'd arrived, they departed, her father following in his carriage. As they jolted forward, she moved to sit beside Sebastian, wrapping her arms around his stiff body. She watched Dunsmore House roll by the window, wishing it and the man inside a good riddance.

Chapter Five

Sebastian paced the length of his room in furious strides, damning himself for a fool for thinking he could return to England and survive the experience unscathed. Over and over he played the afternoon's events in his mind. What would have happened had he not intercepted Olivia's ship? Would she have arrived and been duped into thinking Carr was her husband?

The ruse wouldn't have lasted long. His father must have intended for Olivia to go straight to Dunsmore House. A few months to assure a pregnancy, and she would have been too devastated to ever leave. The thought made him sick, it was so heinous. And he'd brought his wife back to this cesspool. Now she knew just how vile was the blood that flowed in his veins.

The adjoining door opened softly behind him. When Sebastian turned to face Olivia, he stilled, devastated to see her attired in a white lace night rail and robe that had to be part of her trousseau.

Her dark eyes skimmed over him, noting that he was still fully dressed. "You're leaving," she said flatly.

He stood there, sweat instantly misting his skin. He wanted to say something, *anything*, to erase the wounded look from her eyes, but his mouth was too dry.

"When?" she asked in a pained whisper. "Now?"

His voice came colder than he'd intended. "You said you wanted an absent husband."

"I know what I said." She stared at him, her heart in her eyes.

Against his will, Sebastian held out his hand to her, and she ran into his arms, her softness and redolence enveloping his senses. *How had he thought this would be easy?*

"I don't want to leave you," he murmured into her hair, and then hated himself for admitting the weakness.

"Can you wait?" she begged. "Allow me to settle Father's concerns. A week or two at most, and then I'll go with you."

Sebastian felt his chest constrict painfully and his cock grow heavy with need. "You would do that?" he asked gruffly. "Live on a ship with me, without a home?"

"My home is with you." Her slender fingers encircled his wrist and moved his hand down between her legs. Then she curled her fingers over his to cup her sex. "You're so tense, restless like a caged panther." She arched her hips into his hand, rubbing herself against his splayed fingers. "Allow me to give you ease and help you relax. We can discuss everything in the morning."

Eyes closed, he pressed his mouth into her hair. "I don't trust myself with you. Not at this moment." He was so furious and disgusted, he could barely breathe, and with her body undulating against his hand, all he wanted was to throw her on her back and fuck her until he couldn't think, couldn't feel.

"I know you're angry and frustrated, but you'd never hurt me."

With a perverse need to argue, he spoke harshly. "You know nothing of me. I attacked your ship just for the amusement of it. Perhaps I'd have even raped you if you weren't willing."

"Oh, Sebastian." Olivia sighed. "If you wish to argue rather than make love, I suppose I can accommodate you. But at least be honest. You took my ship without the loss of one life. And rape?" She shot him an amused glance. "A man of your outrageous beauty would have no need. 'Tis lucky for you I am your wife, or *I* might have raped *you.*"

He scowled, even as his soul ached with longing. "You said I was a long-haired savage."

"Heavens, you didn't believe that?" She stepped away from his flexing fingers and moved to the small circular table in the corner. Pouring a large ration of brandy from the decanter, she brought it to him with a provocative sway to her hips, her golden curls tumbling past her waist.

"You are the most decadent-looking man I've ever seen, Sebastian Blake. Dark as sin, more beautiful and seductive than the devil himself, I would imagine. I would not change a thing about you. It amazes me every morning when I wake up and look at you lying beside me. I pinch myself regularly to be certain I'm not dreaming—that you're actually mine, that I bear your name and title." Her eyes locked on his as her voice lowered seductively. "That I'll bear your children."

Sebastian took the glass from her, his hand trembling, downing the liquor in one swallow. "You sound as if you received the better half of the bargain."

"I did." Moving away, Olivia shrugged out of her robe and left it behind her on the floor. She reached the bed and leaned against the edge. "I am assuming by the bulge in your breeches that you wish me to stay in your room tonight."

His hand dropped to his side, his fist close to crushing the empty glass. "Stay if you like. I'm going out."

"With your cock as hard as a poker?"

His mouth curved mockingly. Best she witness the depths to which he could sink now. Fruit never falls far from the tree. "You needn't concern yourself with my cock."

"Whose concern would it be if not mine?' she asked with a soft snort. "You cannot go about town in that condition."

"I don't intend to."

Her eyes widened as she understood his meaning. "You intend to find a whore to sate your lust on?"

"Perhaps." Sebastian shrugged. "Or maybe I'll sample two. My need is fierce tonight."

Olivia stood, her hands clenching into tiny fists. "Why? When I am always eager for you?"

He laughed. "Yes, you do like my cock, don't you?"

"Yes, and I am not ashamed to say so." Her chin lifted, her dark gaze burning into his. "Take me, Sebastian, and spare yourself the coin."

Deep inside, his conscience writhed in shame, but he squelched it ruthlessly. "But after years of pirating, sweet, I have coin to spare. Or have you forgotten what I am?"

Her eyes narrowed. "I am well aware of what you are. You are my husband, and if you walk out that door and take a whore, you'll be my husband in name only—for the rest of your miserable life. Consider that, my lord, before you depart." Turning, she stalked toward the adjoining door.

It took everything Sebastian had to keep his face impassive, when inside he felt scraped raw. His hand reached out to her retreating back, and in his mind, he was screaming for her to return, his heart begging for her forgiveness. But when he opened his mouth, only bitterness came out. "I thought we discussed this when we first met. I can take your body whenever I choose. The law says a man cannot rape his own wife."

Olivia spun to face him. "I'm *offering* myself to you! You've no cause to find a whore."

"I want one."

"I'll be one."

Her statement hit him like a physical blow. "Beg your pardon?"

"If you want a whore, I'll be one for you." She came toward him, licking her lips and swaying her hips like a harlot. "What'll it be, govna? A rut? Or would you rather I suck your cock?"

The empty tumbler fell from his hand and rolled away, forgotten. "Stop it."

She cupped her breasts in her hands, pinching the nipples. "You can fondle these, govna, for a couple quid."

He gripped her shoulders, shaking her. "Stop it!"

Her gaze met his, full of anger and pain. "Fuck me."

With a curse, he threw her away from him. "You're not a whore, Olivia. You're my lady wife. Act like it."

"I'll act the part of anything you need," she said desperately. "The alternative is your leaving and our marriage ending. Despite the way you're acting, I know that's not what you want. You're hurting. Allow me to help you."

Damn her. He could bear anything but her loss, and she knew it. Yet the monster inside him was determined to push her away. "I don't want to make love, Olivia. I want to fuck. Is that what you want? Do you want to be fucked?"

Her lips parted, and he watched her swallow hard. Desire mingled with the other emotions in her gaze.

"Very well, then." Sebastian ripped open the placket of his trousers to ease the unbearable constriction. His cock, hard and swollen, sprung free. "Lift your gown and lay on your stomach."

Her eyes widened. "Sebastian . . ."

"Now," he growled. He watched with primitive satisfaction as Olivia scrambled to do his bidding. His blood heated further as her shapely legs and luscious ass came into view. He stepped up to her and caressed the silken curve of her thigh, rubbing his erection in the valley between her buttocks. Bending over to bite her earlobe, he whispered, "I'm going to use you, wife. Hard and deep, all night. You won't be able to walk in the morning."

Olivia whimpered, squirming against the edge of the mattress. He brought his hand back and spanked her. Hard. She cried out in astonishment.

"Spread your legs. Wider." Sebastian noted the wetness that dampened the curls of her sex. He ran his fingers through it. "Ummm. Always ready for me." He spanked her again, admiring the imprint left by his hand. He was filled with a violent need to possess her, to claim her, to prove to them both that it was too late to turn back now. As horrid and twisted and unworthy as he was, she was bound to him. Forever.

Sebastian licked the side of her face. "Are you scared, sweet?"

Swallowing hard, she shook her head. "I-I . . ."

"You what? You like it?"

"Do anything . . . ." she breathed. "I like everything you do . . ."

"Good girl."

He slid his cock between her thighs, thrusting back and forth to coat the length of his erection with her cream. She arched her hips into the erotic caress, and he rewarded her with the barest penetration. He teased her opening with a shallow plunge and then withdrew, relishing her protest.

Sebastian slid his hands up her straining back, lifting her night rail as he went, licking along the curve of her spine. "Sweet Olivia. Obeys Daddy without question, but inside, she longs for a wicked man to ravish her." His voice dropped to a husky murmur. "A pirate perhaps?"

She gasped and bucked against the scorching heat of his erection. "Please . . . don't tease . . ."

He stroked the burning skin of his wife's bottom. Pressing a hard kiss to her cheek, Sebastian pulled back when she turned her head to capture his mouth. "I won't be gentle," he warned. "I'm not capable of it now. Tell me to stop if this is not what you want." He slid halfway inside her dripping channel, shuddering as he fought to walk away if she asked.

She writhed beneath him, her long nails leaving scratch trails in the velvet counterpane. "Hurry, damn you!"

"Don't swear," he growled, then rammed his cock balls-deep into her.

Olivia cried out in agonized pleasure as Sebastian buried himself to the hilt within her, the force of his thrust shoving her hips hard into the edge of the mattress. He withdrew immediately and plunged again, stretching her almost beyond bearing. She felt a complete wanton, with her feet resting on the floor, her legs spread wide to better accommodate his frenzied thrusting. She was helpless, a stationary vessel for his lust.

He reached down and wrapped his fist in her hair to hold her still while he fucked her. The hard tugging on her scalp as she moved under his fierce pounding only goaded her excitement. "I love you," she gasped.

"God . . . Olivia . . ." His rhythm faltered, his cock burning hot as it stilled within her.

"I love you," she repeated, shuddering beneath him as he swelled until it was almost painful. Lord above, he was massively built. She was so aroused, cream leaked from her body, causing a sweet sucking sound as he pulled out of her. She thrust her hips back, sliding her body back onto his shaft.

"This is what you wanted, isn't it?" he groaned, his thighs quivering against hers. "You like me at your mercy and desperate for you." Sebastian pulled out and then pumped back into her again, his fingers digging with bruising force into her hips.

"Yes, my love," she moaned. "Be wild for me."

And he was.

Pleasure built impossibly fast, the tight, heavy weight of his balls slapping repeatedly against her, until Olivia thought she would go mad with it. Her eyes slid closed as her entire body began to tremble.

Sebastian growled, and she felt the hard jerking of his cock as he began to come in scorching bursts against her womb. The hand at her hip moved between her legs and began a frantic rubbing against the hard nub that ached for his touch. She groaned at the wracking pleasure, face buried in the counterpane, spurred by the feel of his hot semen flooding her womb and the skilled swirling of his fingers against her. Incredibly his pace increased, and she flowed without pause from one orgasm into another. When he finally collapsed against her back, Olivia was certain she would be unable to move for days, just as he had threatened.

It was several moments before his crushing weight lifted from her. Cold air chilled the skin so recently heated by the press of his body. Somehow she found the strength to reach back and clutch his wrist. "Don't leave me."

Sebastian's calloused hand caressed her hip as he rose. "Allow me to undress, sweet."

She turned to face him, noting his averted gaze and guessing the cause of it. "I'm fine."

"I was rough," he muttered.

"Do you regret what just happened?"

He shrugged out of his coat, then went to work on the buttons of his waistcoat. "No."

Olivia pulled her gown over her head and discarded it. "Then cease acting as if you do." She crawled under the covers and rolled to her side, listening to the sounds of her husband disrobing.

"Do you regret what you said?" he asked in a near-whisper.

She hid her smile in the pillow. "No."

His hard body curled behind hers, his mouth pressing a kiss to her shoulder. Lacing her fingers with the ones he held against her stomach, she fell asleep.

Later, she woke to the feel of Sebastian's hands roaming her curves, his body hot and damp behind hers. His skilled fingers slipped between her legs, dipping into her sex coated with his seed, and stroking until she moaned with desire. His mouth found the lobe of her ear. Helpless with pleasure, she arched into him.

His voice was gruff as he breathed in her ear. "Say it again."

"I love you."

Adjusting her hips, he slid into her from behind, filling her completely. He thrust within her, slow and luxurious, his hands kneading her breasts and rolling her nipples with his calloused fingertips. She begged him to hurry, but he continued to move with lazy strokes, whispering raw, carnal words that goaded her passion to a fever pitch. When he finally allowed her release, it stunned her with its force and she cried out, her fingers clawing at his. Sebastian stiffened behind her and then flooded her with heat, his velvety voice gasping and moaning her name in the darkness.

Sated, he held her tightly to him. "I'm sorry," he breathed against her skin. "I would not have done it."

Olivia didn't misunderstand. "I couldn't bear to share you."

"You never will, I vow."

Dawn intruded around the heavy velvet curtains when

Sebastian reached for her again. She rolled into his embrace by instinct, half-asleep yet sensing how much he needed her.

"I'm so sorry," he whispered brokenly. "I don't deserve you."

"Shhh . . ."

"Tell me again."

"I love you." And her heart ached for him, this beautiful, wonderful man who'd had so little love in his life that he would beg for it from her. "I love you, Sebastian."

With her eyes closed, Olivia relied on her other sleep-hazy senses—smell, taste, touch. Every hard plane and ridge of her husband's body was so familiar to her questing fingertips. He whispered to her, incoherent sounds that made her feel safe and cherished. She tugged him closer, her need as fierce as his, until he rose above her and blocked out the whispers of light.

He anchored her thigh over his hip and thrust skillfully inside her. Over and over he brought her to climax, knowing her pleasures, understanding her wants as only an expert and attentive lover could. She could feel his tenderness spreading through every touch, every lunge. Giving a startled cry, Olivia felt the rapture wash over her, through her, and into Sebastian, who shivered against her and gave a low, pained moan.

Olivia woke hours later and rubbed the sleep from her eyes. Her left hand felt weighted, and she looked at it, coming to immediate wakefulness at the sight of the massive sapphire that graced her ring finger. Her heart tightened. She didn't have to look around to be certain.

Sebastian was gone.

As he threw open the door to his father's bedroom, stealth was not the primary goal in Sebastian's mind. Olivia's scent rose up from his skin as his blood heated with fury. His father had deliberately set out to destroy his wife to attain his own ends. Sebastian would not tolerate it happening again. His father would know that for a certainty in a moment.

He watched with grim satisfaction as his father shot up in

the bed, startled by the sound of the door banging against the wall. The marquess glanced around with wild eyes.

"Hang it all, Sebastian! What is the meaning of this?"

"How fitting. The last morning we met was much like this, only it was I in the bed and you the wrathful figure in the doorway." The memory still made the bile rise in his throat. He smiled with wicked intent as his father paled. "Ah . . . so you see my purpose." He leapt onto the bed and pinned his father down, his hand forming a vice around the marquess's neck.

He would not leave his wife at the mercy of this monster.

"You are fortunate that I have no desire to be a marquess, or I would kill you now and be done with you."

His father's eyes bulged from the face that so resembled his own. What an odd bit of fate that was. Edmund had looked like their mother, sharing her reddish hair and moss green eyes.

"Sebas—For God's—" Dunsmore struggled like a man gone mad, his hands scratching at Sebastian's wrists, drawing blood, his legs kicking convulsively beneath the counterpane.

"Listen." Sebastian dropped his face to within inches of his father's. "You will stay away from my wife. Do not approach her for any reason. If I discover that either you or Carr went within seeing distance of Olivia, I'll kill you." His fingers tightened further, until his entire hand ached with the force he exerted. Then he released his father and moved off the bed.

The marquess rolled to the edge of the mattress and cast up his accounts on the Aubusson rug. "I-I'll . . . cut . . . you off . . ." he choked out, his stomach heaving.

Sebastian laughed derisively. "If only that were possible. But everything is entailed except for your money, and I have no need of it. Spend it, burn it. I don't care."

His father spat on the floor.

Sebastian headed toward the door. "Remember, Father. Stay away from my wife."

After making the appropriate arrangements for Olivia with his solicitor, Sebastian stood on the deck of the *Seawitch*, watching the London skyline shrink as he left England behind. Like a coward, he wanted to flee the mess that was his family, and he fought the temptation to give in to the urge. It would be so easy to leave all the ugliness and never return, to escape the life for which he had no desire and find freedom elsewhere. But he had Olivia now, and he would suffer any ordeal, accomplish any feat, journey anywhere, as long as he could have her and be with her daily.

He must free himself of his past—release his men, make arrangements for his ship, and sever his ties with the Robidoux brothers. He wasn't certain how he would survive the upcoming weeks without his wife, but it was too dangerous to bring her with him.

As England faded from view, Sebastian knew he would return as soon as he was able.

He'd left his heart behind, and he could not live without her.

Olivia barely made it through her morning toilet, consumed as she was by a dull, aching emptiness. She'd been so certain she could convince Sebastian to stay, or to at least take her with him, but part of her was not surprised that he had fled. It was a long-standing habit with him to run from his troubles. In his youth, he'd used drink and women to escape. Later, he'd used the sea and, for a time, her body. But apparently she hadn't been sufficient.

She'd stay in bed if she could, wallowing in the linens scented of his skin and their lovemaking, but her father was here and she had to attend to him. Olivia couldn't conceive how she would manage to survive the day, but the effort had to be made.

In the dining room, she filled her plate from the covered platters on the sideboard. Then she preceded the footman to the parlor, where her father sat reading his paper.

"Good morning, Livy," he greeted jovially.

"Good morning, Father." She pressed kisses to each of his rosy cheeks, then moved to the small table and chairs in the corner. When the footman set her plate and juice on the table, she dismissed him with a smile.

"You look positively lovesick," her father commented. "Are you that pleased with your husband?"

"I . . . yes." She had been, before he broke her heart, but she would never tell her father that. There was no way he could have foreseen what would occur when he endeavored to marry her into a title. And truly, wasn't this mess her own fault? She had known how Sebastian was when she'd determined to keep him. Only her own foolishness had allowed her to hope for more.

"I have to say, I had my doubts when I first saw him," Jack admitted. "I know his type, wild and unruly. Not the sort of spouse a father would choose for his only daughter. But after speaking with him this morning—"

Her pulse leapt. "You spoke with him this morning?"

"Yes. We ate breakfast together. He doesn't appear to be the scapegrace I first thought, though he has the looks for it. His handling of the situation last evening impressed me. He appears to be very protective of you, possessive even. I like that. He's also astonishingly well versed in seamanship, seems not the least put-out with my work in trade, and . . . well, anyway, I found I liked him much better than that cousin of his, the one I thought was Lord Merrick."

Olivia stifled a groan at the reminder. As if she hadn't enough problems of her own to attend to, she was now inextricably bound to the rest of the Blake family, and what she'd seen of the brood so far left a marked distaste in her mouth. "Did Merrick mention his plans to you?"

Her father folded his paper and looked at her curiously. "He said he left you a note. Didn't you read it?"

She was out the door in a moment, shouting for the butler. He came running out, panting with the effort to make haste. But he knew nothing of a note, so she lifted her skirts and ran up the stairs. She found a chambermaid making the freshly changed bed.

"Morning, milady," the young servant greeted with a quick curtsy.

"Did you find a note for me?"

The girl nodded and moved to the end table, returning with a slip of folded parchment.

Olivia murmured her thanks and retired to her room to read the missive in private. It was simple and heartbreaking

Trust me. I will return.
Yours,
S

She sank to the floor and cried.

Chapter Six

London, England, June 1813

Stifling a yawn, Olivia perused the ballroom with a jaundiced eye. The event was a crush, therefore the room was hot and, despite the profusion of flowers, smelly as well. She had no desire to be here, but Dunsmore had insisted she attend.

One would think that the last four months would have wrought some change in their feelings for one another, considering how closely they worked together to ensure her social success. But such was not the case. She detested the horrid man as much today as the day she had first met him. Unfortunately, left to her own devices, she'd had no recourse but to seek out the marquess's assistance. She required his support to establish herself as Lady Merrick. Without him, the social acceptance that was due her would have been denied her.

Personally, Olivia cared nothing for the Beau Monde's regard, and if she'd had any choice, she would have remained at home and licked her wounds in peace. Her child, on the other hand, deserved a proper start in life, and it was for that reason alone she feigned interest in Polite Society.

Her hard work was rewarded with unequivocal success. Even Dunsmore was impressed, and she'd sensed an almost imperceptible softening in his attitude toward her. He would be thrilled to learn that she was *enceinte* and that all of his machinations had the desired outcome, but the knowledge was too precious to share. She suspected he would take a perverse pleasure in obtaining the knowledge before Sebastian, and she refused to give him the satisfaction. It was the final act of kindness she would ever bestow upon her errant husband.

She'd been devastated when he left, weepy and despondent. Then she'd turned furious.

She remained furious.

Olivia set her glass of lemonade on the tray of a nearby footman before she snapped the delicate stem in half. Sebastian had broken his word, left her to fend for herself among the wolves while he ran from his troubles. She would never forgive him for that. Never.

"Trust me," he wrote. Ha! He refused to trust her. Why should she be the only party in their marriage to extend such a simple courtesy?

"My lady, would it be too much to hope that you still have a dance available?"

Olivia turned at the sound of the familiar drawl, eyeing Carr Blake with a sigh. The man wasn't truly evil like his uncle, just misguided and easily led. Regardless, she kept a close eye on him and maintained a rigid distance from his friendly overtures. The man had set out to deceive her in the most heinous manner imaginable, and that was an offense she would never forget. Still, she had appearances to maintain, and one of them was a feigned closeness to the Blake brood, distasteful as they all were. "Certainly. The set after next."

His blue eyes gleamed with excitement. "I am a fortunate man."

Again she was caught by the resemblance between Carr and Sebastian. They were very similar, both boasting shining black hair and startlingly blue eyes. But the resemblance was merely superficial. Carr was more like an exuberant puppy, while Sebastian was more of a panther on the prowl.

Olivia rolled her shoulders back and forced a smile, since most eyes were on her. Her relentless pursuit of the height of fashion had been a large part of her success, an expensive accomplishment achieved through her husband's largesse.

She sighed audibly. She would gladly have given up everything if it would have won her Sebastian's love. But it was too late for that now.

"Lady Merrick, I believe this next set has been reserved for me."

Olivia turned. "I believe you are correct, Monsieur Robidoux."

The dashing Frenchman bowed elegantly over her proffered hand. His golden beauty had won him wide regard with the members of the *ton*. It did nothing for her, but she flashed him her best smile.

He grinned as he escorted her to the gathering line of dancers. "You are even more ravishing tonight than usual, my lady."

She arched a brow. "Thank you, monsieur."

Robidoux had been brazenly forward with her since arriving in London a month ago, suggesting strolls through the gardens or drives in the park, all of which she refused. She braced herself at every meeting, his determination to be alone with her making her decidedly uncomfortable.

"Lady Merrick," he purred in his unctuous voice. "The Dunsmore title is an old and respected one, I've been told. And yet the earl who inherits it is not in attendance. In fact, no one has seen hide nor hair of the man in over five years."

She laughed—part in amusement, part in exasperation. The gossips were rife with speculation about the whereabouts of her husband. After all, it was odd for a missing man to suddenly acquire a wife. It was because of this unusual circumstance that Dunsmore's assistance had been necessary to establish her credibility. "I assure you, Lord Merrick is not a figment of my imagination."

Robidoux's fingers tightened on hers. "A beautiful woman should never be neglected."

She suppressed an unladylike snort. The man's advances

were growing tiresome. "I am not neglected, Monsieur Robidoux."

"Where is your husband then? I would very much like to make his acquaintance."

"And so you shall, in good time." The country dance began, and she released a relieved breath.

The Frenchman's smile held no charm as they traversed the length of the line. "Perhaps you'd care to take a stroll in the gardens with me when the set is over?" he asked before they separated.

"No, thank you."

Olivia was grateful when the music faded to silence. One more dance was left in the set, but at least she was marginally closer to escaping Robidoux's company. Something about the man made her uneasy. His smiles never reached his eyes, and the way he looked at her made her feel . . . dissected.

"*The Right Honourable Earl of Merrick*," the majordomo intoned in his booming voice.

The entire room froze, a weighted silence settling over the mass of occupants like a thick fog.

Olivia turned, eyes wide, mouth agape. As the strains of the next dance began, her eyes were riveted on the tall, dark form descending the staircase.

Sebastian took the steps with his customary arrogant grace. It hardly seemed possible, but his skin was even darker, swarthy in a wholly unfashionable way that made her weak in the knees. The way he moved promised hours of untold delight and overwhelming carnal pleasure. Despite her deeply rooted anger, Olivia's mouth watered, her breasts swelled, and her sex clenched with every step he took.

The guests, released from their surprise, came forward to greet him, but Sebastian was oblivious to everyone else, his intense blue gaze locked on her. The heat that flared between them, even from a distance, brought a mist of sweat to her skin. She knew well the look he was giving her and understood she was in imminent danger of being ravaged senseless, yet she couldn't move, her heart racing. It took him mere moments to reach her, and yet it seemed as if an hour passed.

He held out his hand, and Olivia hesitated only an instant before accepting it, watching in breathless anticipation as he lifted her hand to his lips. Through her glove, she felt the spark that moved from his mouth, up her arm, and down to her core. She shivered.

Satisfaction curled the ends of his lips. "I have missed you, my love."

The rest of the ballroom waited anxiously for her reply, the music overly loud in the otherwise quiet room.

Taking a deep breath, she allowed her fury to show in her gaze, then she lowered in an elegant curtsy. "My lord."

Immediately the guests began speaking in frantic whispers.

Sebastian tugged her up, his expression possessive and bemused. "Time to depart."

She looked for Robidoux, prepared to offer his introduction, and frowned. The Frenchman had left the dance floor and disappeared into the crowd without a word of farewell.

"*Now,* Olivia."

"You have only just arrived," she hedged. Being alone with Sebastian would invite nothing but trouble.

He arched an arrogant brow.

She opened her mouth to protest, then snapped it shut. Her husband was not a man who took well to being denied. Certainly not while he looked as if he would lift her skirts and sink into her body right here in the ballroom.

Giving an almost imperceptible nod, Olivia allowed him to tuck her hand in the crook of his elbow. She held her tongue until they were safely ensconced in the carriage, but the moment he reached for her, she slapped his hand away with her reticule.

"Damnation!" he yelped.

She smiled. "You will not be touching me again, I vow."

Sebastian eyed his spitfire wife in wounded astonishment. He'd noted the changes in her immediately. Olivia looked harder somehow, her eyes furious, her lush mouth pursed tightly together. He had hoped for a warm and eager reunion. Instead, his wife vowed never to allow him to touch her. *What in blazes was going on?*

"What in blazes is going on?" he growled.

She shot him an incredulous glance.

Hang it all, she was supposed to be pleased to see him! "Olivia, love—"

"Oh, please," she muttered. Staring out the window, she heaved a disgusted sigh. "You do not know how to love. You merely desire your allotted conjugal visitation."

"My conjug—" he sputtered. "Bloody everlasting hell! What the devil are you talking about?"

"Oh, I apologize," she replied in mock innocence. "Did I shock you? I meant your breeding rights."

"*My* 'breeding rights'?" He crossed his arms over his chest. "This is ridiculous."

"You would think so."

Sebastian sat in an agony of confusion. He had gone directly to their townhouse from the docks, only to discover her out for the evening. Learning from the butler that she had gone to the Dempsey ball, he'd changed quickly into evening attire and hastened to find her.

He'd been torn about making his belated first appearance as Lord Merrick at such a large gathering, and truly, the silence of the ballroom upon his arrival had momentarily flustered him. Then he'd found Olivia, and everyone else had ceased to matter. He would deal with the rest of the world tomorrow. Right now all he wanted, all he craved, was his wife's lush body pressed against his and her dark eyes warm with pleasure at his return.

"What have I done to anger you so?" he asked softly.

"I cannot believe you even have to ask. You left me here alone," she snapped. "In the midst of the vultures, after you promised me you would stay at least long enough to see me settled in Society. You could not even muster the courage to tell me good-bye. Well, my lord, if you cannot honor your promises to me, I am not bound to honor mine to you."

"Hell's teeth," he muttered. "It was in my keeping of that promise that I was forced to leave."

Her eyes narrowed.

"Aren't you going to inquire as to what I was doing?" he grumbled.

"No. It's far too late for that now. You should have discussed your plans with me *before* leaving."

Sebastian gazed upon his wife's luminous beauty, and he wanted to howl. She could not have stopped loving him. He would die if she had. "You love me."

Olivia snorted. "You flatter yourself."

"You do," he insisted. "And by God, you'll admit it!"

"I will do no such thing!"

"You will!" Oh, he sounded like a child, and he felt like one, chastened and eager to win back the love that made him whole. No one in his life had ever loved him besides Olivia. Well, perhaps his mother had, but what good did it do him when he couldn't remember it?

The carriage came to a halt, and before he could move, Olivia stumbled down from the carriage and ran into the house. Sebastian gave chase, startling the footman, who moved to lower the step. She ran past the gaping butler, who held the door open, and flew up the steps.

"Olivia!" he bellowed. He almost caught her, but he tripped on the runner as he rounded the corner, and the extra steps required to prevent falling on his face cost him. She reached her bedroom and slammed the door, ramming home what sounded to be a very substantial bolt. With an oath, he turned and entered his own suite.

Lock him out, would she? He'd just see about that. He strode toward the adjoining door that had no lock.

And realized the portal no longer existed.

She'd sealed the damn thing up and covered the wall with taupe damask so that no trace of it remained. *Damnation, that was the final straw!*

Sebastian exited to the gallery with angry strides and kicked the door to his wife's room as hard as he could, yelling a curse when it budged not one whit.

"It won't work!" she shouted through the door. "It's barred."

"*Barred?*" he shouted back, incredulous.

"Yes, barred. Now go away!"

His chest heaved with furious indignation. "Olivia . . ." he began warningly.

"*Go away!*"

Olivia sat on the edge of the bed, her heart pounding, her arms wrapped around a pillow, as she stared apprehensively at the door. Long moments of silence passed, and still she fretted that Sebastian would return.

She was stricken to realize she had underestimated the power of his attractiveness. In the four months of his absence, she'd managed to convince herself that their passion would fade eventually. Now she knew it would never fade. Her love for him wouldn't allow it.

Still, she was grimly satisfied that she'd managed to thwart his amorous intent, if only for this evening. She was barely surviving every day, her heart aching with his loss. He certainly deserved whatever discomfort she could throw at him.

After a time, Olivia relaxed, somewhat deflated that he had given up so easily. With a sigh, she stood, tossed the pillow aside, and began to undress herself, no easy task with the row of tiny buttons running down the back of her gown. She was doing a fine imitation of a contortionist when impatient fingers brushed hers away. Startled, she screamed and spun to face her husband, who gazed at her with ravenous hunger and barely tempered frustration.

"How did you—" She glanced around his large form, spying the very top of a ladder resting against her balcony railing. "Dear heaven. The audacity."

Arching a brow, Sebastian tugged at his cravat. "I am a pirate by trade, wife. A barred door is no deterrent to me."

"Wh-what are you doing?" she cried as he deftly removed his waistcoat, tossing it over his discarded jacket.

"I've conquered. Now it is time to claim my booty. In this case, *you*." He yanked off his shirt, revealing his powerful torso and rippling abdomen. He *had* become darker in the weeks they'd been apart, his skin was now a beautiful mahogany. Her mouth flooded.

Good grief, she was going to drool.

"Put your clothes back on!" she snapped, clutching her loosened bodice to her breasts. "I'm furious with you!"

He grunted. "I've gathered that." He tore open the placket of his breeches and shoved them to the floor.

"Oh hell . . ." she muttered as his raging cock sprang free, hard as steel and massively engorged. Her nipples hardened instantly. Olivia forced herself to meet his gaze and saw the masculine satisfaction there. He knew damn well the effect his bare body had on her.

"Ah, see how much I've missed you, sweet," he purred in his luscious voice. "It's been too long since I was last inside you."

She swallowed hard. "I don't want you."

"Liar."

"I'm angry," she complained, her resistance melting as Sebastian took his cock in hand and began to stroke the silken length.

"This is how I've spent my nights, Olivia." His fingers curled around his shaft and pumped hard. "Visions of you had me begging for a release that was denied to me. Sleeping in that bed where we'd spent so many pleasurable hours making love was torture." His eyelids grew heavy as he pleasured himself. "Every night I would bring myself relief with pictures of you in my mind. Didn't you miss me as well?"

Olivia licked her lips, her gaze riveted to the dark hand that stroked his cock. She wanted him so badly she ached. She loved him. Despite everything, she still loved him.

"This changes nothing," she whispered. "It is only sex."

His grin was triumphant, and it pricked her pride. Sebastian might think he'd won this encounter, but she would prove differently.

She crossed the short distance between them and dropped to her knees. Grasping his straining erection, she pulled it down to her mouth and sucked it inside, swirling her tongue around the plum-sized head. His hiss of pleasure followed by the convulsive grip of his fingers in her hair betrayed her power. A few quick thrusts of his hips, and his thighs were straining with the effort to remain standing.

"Poor, sweet," she murmured against the wet head of his cock. "Perhaps you should lie on the bed before you collapse."

Pulling her upright, Sebastian possessed her mouth, thrusting his tongue inside just as he had thrust his cock. His skilled hands caressed her curves with disarming familiarity. Within moments, she was clinging to his powerful body, gasping with pleasure. He ripped her gown open, sending scores of tiny cloth-covered buttons flying in every direction. Excitement coursed through her blood, even as her mind still waged its protest.

"This changes nothing," she repeated.

"Remind yourself of that when I'm done," he growled arrogantly, shoving her dress to the floor. He spun her around and tore at her tapes, quickly divesting her of her petticoats and corset without care for the costly garments.

"Sebastian—"

"Umm . . . say my name again, sweeting. I love the way you say it."

She melted. "Sebastian."

He pulled her chemise over her head and tossed it aside before lifting her and carrying her to the bed, his mouth pressed firmly against her forehead. "I've missed you terribly."

Olivia shook her head, her eyes burning with unshed tears. She tugged the ribbon from his queue, freeing his silky raven locks. "I should be stronger. I should resist you. You've hurt me terribly. Perhaps if I had a blade or a pistol—"

"Neither one could keep me from you."

Then why had he left? More important, she needed to know why he'd returned.

"I love you, Olivia."

Stiffening against him, she leaned back to search his face. Sebastian stared back with tender blue eyes, and Olivia bit back a sob. She'd longed for his love, and she longed to believe it was real. But she couldn't trust him, and because of that lack, instead of joy, his words brought only pain.

"Why do you look so shocked, sweet? Surely you must have suspected how I felt." He laid her on the bed as if she were the most priceless of treasures.

"You came back because you love me?" she queried bitterly. "Only a besotted fool would believe that."

"I didn't come back because I love you."

She frowned, confused.

"I *left* because I love you."

Sebastian settled atop her and lowered his lips, effectively silencing her forthcoming questions with devastating kisses. His hard, expert mouth moved over hers, weakening her defenses, reminding her of the pleasure to be found in his arms. He rolled, taking her with him, freeing his hands to roam with questing tenderness. Hot flicks of his tongue caressed the roof of her mouth and stroked against hers. *Lord, she'd almost forgotten how well the man could kiss!*

His mouth was wicked, divine, and he kissed her as if he were feasting on the taste of her. Her womb clenched on the verge of orgasm. She wiggled her hips until his cock was wedged at the moist entrance to her body.

"Wait!" he gasped, tearing his mouth from hers, but she paid him no heed, sliding onto his throbbing cock with a pleasured moan. *"Olivia!"*

Instantly his torso bucked off the bed, lifting her with him, and he was coming deep within her, crying out hoarsely as his hot seed spurted with wrenching shudders. His arms came around her in a crushing embrace, his body shivering with powerful tremors.

Olivia held him close, wondering at the feel of him, hot and hard and jerking beneath her. When he was drained, she followed him back into the pillows.

"Ah, sweeting," he murmured hoarsely, stroking her spine. "I'm sorry. I couldn't stop it. It's been too long."

"I understand."

"Give me a moment to regain my senses, and I will pleasure you until morning."

His words, meant to entice, filled her with dread. She slipped off him while he was still too sated to stop her. Sitting on the edge of the bed, Olivia ran a hand through her hair, dislodging her hairpins. "You left me, Sebastian."

"I had good cause," he insisted, rolling to face her. "Originally I agreed to stay only for the short time you asked of me. But when you told me you loved me, it changed everything. I realized I loved you and wanted to be with you, but I had my men to take care of, and my ship. I had to sever my ties with them before I could begin anew with you."

Olivia brushed away the tear that escaped and took a deep, shuddering breath. So much resentment, fear, and even a touch of wary hope warred within her that she was overwhelmed with emotion.

She looked over her shoulder at her husband, her heart aching at the sight of his resplendent nakedness and his beloved hair, spread out across her lacy pillows. Somehow the highly feminine trappings of her bed only emphasized his potent masculinity. But it was his gaze that most devastated her, full of longing and love and a hint of fear. She looked away, unable to bear it. "You were gone for four months."

His fingertips moved over her back in a rhythmic caress. "I gave my ship to Will and settled my accounts with the crew. It was my intention to cast off immediately and return to you."

"But you didn't."

"No," he agreed. "For good reason. There are twin brothers—pirates, I'm ashamed to say I associated with. I've angered them, and they are not men to forgive a perceived slight. The night we left Barbados they demanded you in payment of my debt."

"Me?"

"Yes, you. Will informed me that the serving maid at the inn where you stayed was approached by one of the brothers. He asked questions about you, Olivia. He learned your identity. I could not allow the situation to progress any further. You were in danger because of me."

She spun to face him. "What did you do?"

Sebastian reached for her hand and laced his fingers with hers. "I waited for the pirates to return to the island, and when they did, I fought with the more vicious of the two and killed him. The other managed to escape. I hunted him, but he's hidden himself away. I have every reason to believe he'll stay hidden. Pierre was never much of a threat without Dominique."

Olivia traced the swirling pattern in the Aubusson rug with her toe. "You could have told me of your plans."

"You were asleep," he explained defensively. "I'd kept you awake the whole of the night and thought it best to leave quietly. I wrote you a letter."

She stood and paced the length of the bed. "That was no letter, my lord. That was a few lines of hastily scrawled words."

"I was reluctant to write more," he admitted.

She paused. "Why?"

He met her gaze with such earnestness that her barely mending heart broke all over again. "If I'd delayed too long—if I'd attempted to say good-bye—I never would have been able to leave you, especially if you'd begged to come with me, which I suspected you might. Denying you would have been impossible, and it was too dangerous for you to accompany me." Sitting up, he crossed his long legs. "Olivia. My wife. My love. Can you understand?" He held his hands out to her, pleading.

"No, Sebastian." She shook her head. "You left for yourself. Not for me. You—"

"That's not true, damn it!"

"It is! You ran because that is what you do. You've been running your whole life—from your family, your responsibilities, everything. This time you were running from me." She growled with frustration and clenched her fists. "Beautiful, damaged man that you are. I thought I could fix you, heal you, but I cannot."

He leapt from the bed and caught her by the shoulders. "Listen to me."

"No, you listen to me!" She stomped her bare foot. "You broke my heart, Sebastian Blake. Left me to the wolves while you regrouped and gathered your defenses—*against me*! I was getting too close, becoming too important, you—"

"Important?" he scoffed, shaking her. "You are *everything* to me. I've given up all that I had for you!"

She snorted. "Well, you shouldn't have. You threw away what we had."

"No." He paled beneath his tan. "Don't say that. God . . . Olivia . . . don't ever say that!"

"I cannot rely on you."

"You can," he promised. "I shall never leave you again. I swear it. I could no more leave you than I could stop breathing."

"You broke your promise before. How can I believe you now?"

She would not survive it if he hurt her again.

"Damn it . . ." His hands slid down her arms. "Sweetheart." His velvety voice became soothing, seducing. "I love you, Olivia."

"Not enough." She pulled away. "It's too convenient for you to run. There is nothing to hold you to me."

"Our marriage, our love. I *know* you love me still."

"Apparently my love was not enough," she whispered bitterly. "Or yours."

When Sebastian caught her again, she could feel the desperation in his touch. "It has to be enough, Olivia. It's all I have." Lifting her, he carried her to the bed.

"You cannot get your way with seduction."

"Perhaps not," he muttered. "But I can sweeten your temper."

Sebastian stared up at the velvet canopy and listened to the sounds of his wife's rhythmic breathing. He'd loved her into exhaustion, but he was no closer to winning back her heart than he'd been before he started.

Of course, it wouldn't be so easy. When had anything in his life been easy?

Releasing a sigh, he admitted that wasn't entirely true. Winning Olivia's love had been easy, almost as easy as he'd lost it. *God, what a mess he was in. If her love was gone . . .*

No, he wouldn't think about that.

She murmured, stirring restlessly. He reached over and tucked the counterpane more securely around her.

Olivia was his wife. He glanced at her left hand and breathed his satisfaction at the sight of his mother's sapphire. In reality, he had the rest of his life to win her back. But the truth was, he didn't have the rest of his life to wait.

He needed her love. Right now.

Olivia had shown him what it was like to be cared for, what it was like to be happy, not merely on the outside, but deep in his soul.

He couldn't take many more encounters with her disregard. His father's neglect had ceased to be of any consequence when he was still a child, but Olivia . . . His sweet, passionate Olivia. Her anger and remoteness were killing him.

Sebastian ran an agitated hand through his hair. Nothing to hold him to her, she said. He would change that.

He would bind himself to her, to the land, to his cursed family. He would prove to her that he could change, as long as she would be his.

As long as she would love him again.

Chapter Seven

Olivia woke with a start, immediately aware of her husband's large body wrapped possessively around her. She froze for a moment, wondering what to do.

"Morning, my love," he murmured in a deliciously sleep-raspy voice.

"Sebastian," she whispered, acutely conscious of the soreness of her nipples and the ache between her thighs. "I—"

"Shush, no arguing today." He moved, freeing her.

She leapt from his embrace and ducked behind the privacy screen, her heart racing with joy at finding him in her bed again.

Silly, stupid heart. A glutton for punishment.

As she washed with the cold water from the pitcher, she heard him rise. When the knock came to the door, she reached for her robe, then stilled midmovement, surprised to hear Sebastian order hot water for her bath, along with strong coffee. She heard the amused giggle of the chambermaid and shot a glance around the screen. Her eyes widened in horror to find Sebastian standing in the doorway wearing only a sheet. Furious, she stormed toward him, yanking him out of the way of the slamming door.

He bit back a roguish grin and arched a brow. "Yes, my love?" His gaze raked the length of her wet and still naked form. "I am always eager to oblige your carnal desires. No need to accost me."

"Oooh!" She turned from him, clenching her fists. "It is indecent for you to call the servants up here while you are unclothed!"

He laughed. "I would have retrieved a robe from my room, but the door appears to be missing."

Olivia turned to face him again, which was a mistake. Sebastian had discarded the sheet and stalked toward her with obvious sexual intent, his erect cock leading the way. "Damnation! Cover that thing!"

"I intend to," he purred. "With you."

She threw up her hands. "After last night, how can you possibly be so amorous? You hardly allowed me to sleep. I'm exhausted."

"'Tis your fault," he retorted. "I was fine until you started traipsing around the room naked."

"I was not traipsing!" she protested, hurrying toward the relative safety of the screen and her robe. "I was merely curbing your ridiculous flirting. She's a mere slip of a girl—"

"Exactly," he interjected, catching her about the waist and easily subduing her. "And my wife is more than enough woman for me. Jealousy and all."

"I'm not jealous!"

He dropped to his knees with easy grace and laid her down. He rose above her, his long hair hanging around them, and she paused her thrashing, arrested by the magnificent sight of him. He slipped a hand between her legs and grinned. "Ah, no foreplay required." Spreading her thighs wide, he thrust into her. "Umm . . . I missed the feel of you. You are even softer and more curvaceous than I remembered." His mouth latched around a straining nipple.

Olivia gasped as he filled her completely, infusing her with drugging pleasure. "The rug . . ."

"We'll buy another." He withdrew and then thrust again. Hard.

She writhed beneath him. "The servants . . ."

"They'll wait." Pulling her legs around his waist, he settled into a fierce, almost brutal rhythm. "God . . . Olivia . . . I love you . . ."

"Sebastian, you—"

"Hang it, woman! Cease talking."

He took her mouth with desperate kisses, his hard body straining over and inside of her. Her hands cupped his flexing buttocks, and she moaned, relishing the feel of his body working its way into hers. Deep inside, she could feel him, stretching, prodding, stroking her deeply with unfailing skill. Tucking his arms under her knees, he held her wide as he pumped inside her, driving her quickly to the edge and then shoving her over. She was crying out her pleasure when the knock came to the door.

Olivia shoved at his sweat-slick shoulders, mortified.

"*Wait!*" he growled, his pace quickening until he was pistoning into her without mercy.

"Sebastian!" she choked out. "They'll hear us!"

"Yes," he gasped. "Come for me again, and let the whole house hear you."

She moaned, arching beneath him, dissolving in voluptuous bliss. When the orgasm swept over her, she cried out again, unable to contain it. Sebastian cursed when he came, his entire body stiffening before melting into powerful shudders.

Sated, he pressed kisses against her throat. "I love you," he whispered.

And though her lips said nothing, her heart replied in kind.

Sebastian watched his wife over his newspaper at the breakfast table and made a concerted effort not to smile. Olivia refused to look any of the servants in the eye, blushing to the tips of her ears when any of them spoke to her. He found it fascinating. After all, the woman had nearly unmanned him with his own blade and threatened seasoned pirates with a pistol. But apparently those were deeds she was comfortable with. Having two footmen and a slip-of-a-girl chambermaid hear their abandoned fucking was more than she could bear with dignity.

He licked a dab of honey from his lip and felt contented. No woman could respond to a man the way Olivia had and remain unaffected. Not that he discounted her fury. He deserved it, after all. And he would pay whatever penance was required.

She was his better half, adept at all of the things he tripped over, and yet a match for the untamed and uncivilized man within him. She was his counterpart, his soul mate, and he'd hurt her terribly, an offense he considered unforgivable. But he would correct his mistake. He had to.

"What are our plans for the day, love?"

She glanced up sharply. "I . . . I have a meeting this afternoon. And then a fitting at the dressmaker's."

"Excellent. I have an appointment as well. What time is your fitting? I'll escort you."

Her eyebrows rose to meet her hairline. "Beg your pardon?"

"Well, I must meet with our man-of-affairs, sweeting, and make arrangements to visit the Dunsmore estates. It should be a lovely trip. We'll take a few months, and see them all."

"A trip?" she repeated, dumbfounded.

"That's what I said."

Olivia stared at him as if he'd suddenly grown two heads. He bit his cheek to keep from grinning.

Her mouth fell open and then snapped shut. "Two o'clock."

"Lovely, just enough time to attend to my affairs." He pushed back from the table and dropped his paper over his plate. "I shall see you then." He gripped the back of her chair, tipping her on the hind legs until she was looking straight up at him.

"Sebastian! Good heavens, the servants . . ."

He kissed her breathless. "I love you."

Righting her chair, he left the room before she could reply, whistling as he collected his hat and cane from the butler and swept out the door. He vaulted into the waiting coach. It wasn't long before he stood on the landing of his man-of-affairs' small, nondescript office.

"Your lordship!" Benjamin Wilson quickly pulled the door all the way open. "I wasn't aware you had returned."

"I arrived last eventide. How are you, Wilson?"

"Quite well, my lord. And you?"

"Good. Did you hire the investigator I requested?" Sebastian handed his cane and hat to his footman, then moved into the office. He sank into a chair facing the desk.

"Of course!" Wilson assured him, slightly offended. "I am sorry to say, the man I hired was unable to gather as much information as I would have liked. After your departure, Lady Merrick quickly became all the rage, rendering it nearly impossible to make inquiries with any discretion."

Wilson opened a locked drawer in his desk and removed a file with a variety of protruding newspaper clippings. "Most of the information gathered about her came from these."

Sebastian made no move to open the folder. "I'll peruse them in depth later. Give me a condensed version, if you will."

"Certainly." Wilson sat back in his chair. "Lady Merrick's first Season was rather uneventful. Very little mention is made of her in the gossip columns other than casual references to her great beauty and sense of style. Her father's business in trade most likely made her unacceptable to most members of the Quality, and it was widely known that Lady Crenshaw sponsored her only because of the large debt Lord Crenshaw owed to Mr. Lambert."

Sebastian grinned. "I'd wager there is many a peer who regrets his pomposity now, eh?"

"Definitely, my lord," Wilson agreed, nodding. "You made a wise choice."

"I suppose I shall have to thank my father for that one day." Sebastian sighed. "Regardless, please continue."

"Lady Merrick's popularity increased tremendously during her second Season, when she caught the eye of Lord Haversham."

"The devil you say!" Sebastian cried, sitting bolt upright in his seat. Back in their Oxford days, Haversham had been a friend of his. But when Sebastian had turned into a completely worthless, dissolute, immoral scoundrel, Haversham had quickly put distance between them.

Wilson frowned. "Yes, Lord Haversham courted Lady Merrick doggedly for the entire Season. There was heavy speculation that he would be offering for her."

"Hell's teeth." Compared to the angelic Haversham, he was Mephistopheles.

"But in the end, Viscount Haversham did not pay his addresses. He cast her off quite unexpectedly in favor of Lady Chelsea Markham, the Earl of Radcliff's youngest daughter. She, in turn, cast him off in favor of Lord St. Martin." Wilson shook his head sadly. "The scandal that accompanied the very public jilting ruined Lady Merrick. She left London soon after and did not return until she came home as your bride."

He understood now why she had been hiding out in the West Indies and why her father had married her by proxy. Olivia had been running, too.

Sebastian was slightly put out to think that perhaps he hadn't been her first choice in husbands, but he quickly passed over the disgruntlement. She was his now; her past meant nothing.

Rising, he headed toward the front door.

"My lord! The clippings!"

"Burn them. I have what I need. Good work, Wilson. I'll be in touch. Make appointments to meet with the family stewards over the next few weeks."

Sebastian leapt into his waiting carriage and headed for home.

Olivia held a hand to her side and released a deep breath. The baby was beginning to move, tiny flutters of life that awed and amazed her.

"Ready, love?" Sebastian asked from the doorway.

She dropped her hand quickly. "Is it time already?" She swept past him, collecting her hat and gloves from the butler.

"Yes." Clutching her elbow, he studied her with a frown. "Are you unwell? You looked peaked."

"I'm fine. A bit tired is all."

He flushed, and she hid a smile. It wasn't fair he looked so rested when she was exhausted.

His touch was gentle and solicitous as he assisted her into the waiting carriage. Tucked against his side, Olivia wished the ride to Pall Mall were longer. If only she could convince him to stay with her forever. Against better reason, she hoped that he would.

As if he read her thoughts, Sebastian hugged her close and said, "I won't leave you again. I'll tell you that every minute of every day until you believe me."

"You may have to do that very thing," she replied, snuggling closer.

"Then I shall, my love. I shall."

And with Sebastian's heartfelt promise, she felt renewed hope. She rested her head against his chest and smiled. "I'm horribly smitten with you."

"Smitten." He grunted. "You're mad for me." He squeezed her and lowered his voice. "As I am for you."

Once they reached the busy thoroughfare, they left the carriage and began to stroll, stopping to window-shop as they made their way to the modiste.

"Lord and Lady Merrick."

They both turned. Olivia smiled at the approaching couple. The man, tall and superbly fit, boasted eyes of the most startling color. Somewhere between purple and deep blue, they were devastating. The woman on his arm, slender and graceful, offered a luminous smile.

"Remington," Sebastian greeted, offering his hand. "How are you, old chap?

Remington shook it heartily and grinned. "I thought that was you, Merrick, although without the presence of Lady Merrick to confirm it, I would not have said anything. You look positively piratical. You need only an earring to complete the picture." He brought his companion forward. "Julienne, this is the prodigal Lord Merrick. Merrick, allow me to present my wife, Lady Julienne."

Lady Julienne smiled and offered her hand, shooting an amused glance at Olivia. "So there is indeed a Lord Merrick."

Olivia choked back a laugh.

Sebastian didn't bother—he laughed outright. "Olivia, love. Have you made the acquaintance of Lucien Remington and his lovely wife?"

She nodded. "I have."

"I've a favor to ask, my lord," Remington said. "I need some new horseflesh and was hoping I could convince you to join me at Tattersall's tomorrow."

"Certainly. Is there something in particular you are hoping to find?"

With a quick tilt of her head, Lady Julienne motioned her over. Olivia went gladly, leaving the men to their discussion. Julienne Remington was one of the rare, truly genuine people she'd met since returning to London. They shared a small affinity, both having once been ostracized by Society. Julienne, an earl's daughter, had married the notorious Lucien Remington, the bastard son of a duke. It had caused a scandal of drastic proportions, or so Olivia had been told. But from the looks of it, Julienne had made a wise decision. Remington was obviously completely besotted with his beautiful wife.

"I can see why you've kept him hidden," Julienne said with a mischievous smile as they strolled away. "Merrick quite overwhelms a girl, doesn't he?"

Olivia laughed. "Yes, he certainly does."

Julienne stopped before a milliner's and peered inside. "Look at that! Isn't it lovely?"

Looking at the feathered hat, Olivia nodded. "It is quite fetching."

"I must have it." Julienne moved toward the entrance of the shop just as a pastry cart passed. Enticed by the delectable scent of peach tarts, Olivia was suddenly starving. Her stomach growled. Loudly.

Julienne laughed. "Poor dear. Pregnancy will do that to you."

Olivia's eyes widened. "How did you know?"

"I've birthed two sons, Lady Merrick. I recognize the signs." She waved her hand toward the vendor. "Go fetch your pastry, and I'll purchase my hat. We'll meet here when we're done."

"A wonderful idea," Olivia said with a grin. She went to the pastry cart and paid for her tart, her mouth watering in anticipation.

"Lovely day, isn't it, Lady Merrick?"

Recognizing the voice, she sighed inwardly before turning. "Good afternoon, Monsieur Robidoux."

As the vendor moved away, the Frenchman bowed to her and gestured toward a nearby bench. She looked past him to find Sebastian still deep in conversation with Lucien Remington. Reluctantly, she moved toward the seat.

And then she felt the barrel of a pistol pressed to her spine. She stilled, her heart hammering against her ribs. "What in blazes are you doing?"

"Go quietly, *petite*, and you will not be harmed. Scream, and I will shoot you down." The tone of his voice drove the point home. He was serious.

What was happening? She'd done nothing to rile this man, had in fact gone out of her way to be polite. No cause was given for him to accost her, and certainly not with a weapon. She looked wild-eyed toward Sebastian, but he'd altered direction and now faced away.

Her gloves grew damp with the sweat of her palms. The baby fluttered, frightening her further. In any other circumstance, she would scream and fight for her life. But she had her child to consider now, and she would do nothing to endanger the precious life.

"*Go!*" he ordered, bruising her back with a sharp shove of the gun.

She stumbled forward. "There are many people around, monsieur. Someone will see."

"I care not. After today I can leave this dreary country and never return."

"If something happens to me," she warned, "Lord Merrick will hunt you down."

He snorted dismissively. "Phoenix will be dead."

"Lord Merrick!"

Sebastian turned toward the panicked voice, startled to see Lady Julienne running toward him, skirts held in one hand and a hatbox in the other.

"Yes? What is it?" He looked past her. "Where is Lady Merrick?"

"I saw her walking away with that odd Frenchman." She turned to her husband, snapping her gloved fingers. "Oh, what is that man's name? The blond Frenchie with the greasy voice?"

Sebastian tensed, his chest tightening. "Robidoux?"

"Yes, that's it!" she cried. "Dominique Robidoux."

He stilled. "You mean Pierre. Pierre Robidoux."

"No, my lord," Remington corrected with a frown. "Julienne is correct. The man's name is Dominique."

Sebastian's gaze swept across the crowded thoroughfare. If what the Remingtons said was true, he'd eliminated the lesser threat and allowed the greater one to get close to his heart. "Which way did they go?"

Julienne pointed down the street. "That way, and just a moment ago."

Sebastian ran, heedless of the gawking pedestrians and the sight he made. He cared nothing for anyone. He never had. The only person who mattered was Olivia.

Blood roaring in his ears, he almost missed her cry. He stopped abruptly and veered down an alley, melting with relief to find Olivia and Robidoux waiting at the end. The minute he saw the Frenchman's face, he knew he'd made a fatal mistake. He'd killed Pierre, not Dominique. His hand lowered to his thigh, vainly reaching for the blade that wasn't there.

"Release her," he ordered, stepping closer. "I'm the one you want."

Robidoux laughed mirthlessly. "Imagine my surprise to discover the lady Pierre wanted was your wife."

Sebastian's hands clenched into fists, his heart racing in near-mindless panic. Olivia stood stoically, but her dark eyes betrayed her fear. "I'll pay whatever you desire if you allow her to go unharmed."

"I want my brother back. Can you give me that?"

Sebastian gritted his teeth and took another step closer. "You know I cannot."

"Very well then." Robidoux shoved Olivia toward him and raised the gun. "Your wife will die in your arms, as Pierre died in mine."

"No!"

Sebastian's agonized cry echoed through the narrow space as he reached for Olivia's stumbling form. He caught her close, spinning desperately to shield her with his back. The report of the shot was deafening, and he jerked as searing pain tore into his shoulder, barely missing his wife.

Suddenly Remington was there with pistol in hand, thrusting them out of the way. The second shot left a horrendous buzzing in Sebastian's ears, drowning out Olivia's sobbing. A quick glance backward assured him Robidoux was dead. Dropping his gaze to the rapidly spreading bloodstain on his coat, he prodded the wound with his working hand.

"It's nothing," he assured her.

She grabbed his lapels and attempted to shake him, her mouth forming words he couldn't hear but understood nevertheless. "Are you bloody mad?"

"Don't swear," he admonished with a roll of his eyes. Then he kissed her senseless.

Epilogue

Olivia rose from the chair next to the bed and felt momentarily dizzy, something that happened often as her pregnancy progressed. Sebastian was at her side instantly.

"What is it? You look pale." He pressed her back into the seat with his free hand.

"You're supposed to be in bed resting," she scolded.

"It's a blasted nuisance to be in bed all day. I'm wearing a sling, for Christ's sake. I'm not dying. You, on the other hand, look positively ill."

"It's nothing, darling. Truly." She'd been attempting to find the right time to tell him about the baby, but in the three days since he'd come home, so much had occurred that she could barely catch her breath.

His gaze narrowed. "I'll believe you when a doctor tells me the same."

"A doctor isn't necessary."

"You're not well," he insisted. "I've never seen you look less than the picture of health."

"I am completely healthy, Sebastian. If you settle a moment—"

"Like hell you are!" His wicked mouth tightened obstinately.

"I'm with child," she confessed with a sigh.

"*What?* Oh, God!" He dropped to his knees before her, his mouth pressing reverently to her forehead. "Bloody hell, why didn't you tell me before?"

"I never had the time. What with your persistent ravishment and the events of yesterday, when did I have the opportunity?" She leaned forward, burying her face in his shoulder, breathing in the scent of his skin.

"Olivia. Sweetheart." Sebastian pressed his mouth to her throat. "I love you. Please. You have to believe that."

"I do."

"I won't ever leave you again. If I have to journey anywhere, you'll travel with me."

She nodded. "I'm starting to believe you, my love."

"Yes. Believe me." He pulled back to look at her, his intense blue eyes filled with heartrending tenderness. "I'm no longer the man I was when I met you. You've given me reason to change, to hope. Reason to love."

Her small hands stroked his back. "Hush, darling," she soothed, trying to stem the flow of fervent words. "You're overwrought."

"*Overwrought*? Men do not become overwrought. *I* do not become overwrought."

Olivia cupped his face in her hands, smothering a smile. "Beautiful, sweet Sebastian. I've upset your delicate sensibilities."

He scowled. "Delicate sensibilities?"

"Yes, dear. I apologize. I'll have to be more careful the next time I tell you such news. You're high-strung."

"High-strung?" He released a frustrated breath. "Bloody everlasting hell, you've gone mad."

She pressed her smiling lips to his. "Don't swear," she admonished.

And then she kissed him breathless.

Lucien's Gamble

Chapter One

London, 1810

"What the devil are you doing in my club?"

Julienne looked across the massive mahogany desk into blue eyes the color of which she'd never seen before. Somewhere between deep blue and purple, they were fringed with thick black lashes that were shamefully wasted on a man. "I need to find my brother," she said, lifting her chin in defiance.

One black brow arched. "A message left with the doorman would have been simpler, Miss . . ."

"Lady. Julienne. And I attempted to leave messages. I have yet to receive a response." She shifted in her chair as the broadcloth trousers chafed the delicate skin of her derriere. The wig itched, too, but she refused to embarrass herself further by scratching.

"Dressing as a man was an original touch."

She heard the laughter in the velvety voice and scowled. "How else was I to gain admission to a gentleman's club?"

Julienne resisted the urge to flee as Lucien Remington rose from behind the desk and rounded it. She licked suddenly dry lips as she took in his height and the breadth of his shoulders. He was even more devastating up close than he had been across crowded ballrooms. Black hair and tanned skin displayed his extraordinary eyes to perfection. A strong jaw and generous mouth bespoke of his sensual nature, which was lauded far and wide by well-pleasured ladies of his acquaintance.

"Exactly, Lady Julienne. A *gentleman's* club. Those garments do not disguise the fact that you are all woman. Ridgely's foxed, or insane, not to have noticed." His perusal paused briefly on her breasts before rising to meet her gaze.

"No one noticed," she muttered.

"*I* noticed."

And so he had. Almost immediately. She'd been in the club only five minutes at most before he'd grabbed her by the elbow and pulled her into his office. But then, it had taken her only five minutes to make a mess of the whole affair.

His voice softened. "What is so urgent that you would take such drastic measures to speak with your brother?"

As he leaned against his desk directly in front of her, the material of his trousers stretched over firmly muscled thighs. He was so close she could feel the heat emanating from his body. She smelled a hint of tobacco and starched linen, and another delicious scent that could only be the man himself.

Remington cleared his throat, drawing her attention. Julienne flushed at the knowing smile that curved his lips.

She straightened her spine, refusing to be cowed despite how beautiful he was or how flustered he made her. "My reasons are my own."

Remington bent, bringing his mouth inches away from hers. "When your reasons include my club, I reserve the right to know what they are."

Julienne's gaze was riveted to his lips. If she leaned forward just a tiny bit, she could touch them with her own.

Would they feel as soft as they looked?

He pulled away, then lowered to his haunches and placed his large hands on her knees. She jumped at the heat that burned through the broadcloth. "Who is your brother?" he asked.

Julienne's mouth parched the instant he touched her, making speech difficult. Lucien Remington was simply gorgeous.

She'd always thought so, always compared her suitors to him and found them lacking in all respects. No one was as handsome, or as interesting, or as . . . wicked.

Her tongue flicked out to wet her bottom lip, and his eyes followed the movement. An ache came to the place between her legs. Julienne attempted to push his hands away, but when she touched his skin, her palms burned. She pulled away quickly. "A gentleman does not put his hands on a lady," she scolded.

His hands slid higher, squeezing gently, his mouth gifting her with a roguish smile. "I never claimed to be a gentleman."

And he wasn't, she knew. His determination and ruthless business acumen were the stuff of legend. If it wasn't precisely prohibited in writing, Lucien Remington would do it. He showed no leniency when it came to expanding his empire. He was widely disparaged for his "vulgar pursuit of money," but Julienne found it rather thrilling. He cared nothing for the regard of others, a nonchalance she wished she could affect herself.

"Now, about your brother . . . ?"

"Lord Montrose," she blurted.

A devilish smile teased the corners of Remington's mouth. "That explains why he hasn't answered your messages, sweetheart. The earl owes me a great deal of money. I suspect he's avoiding me."

She said nothing, but she clenched her fists. Their situation must be worse than she'd thought. It was common for Hugh to carouse and spend days on end with his scapegrace associates. From experience she knew he most likely wasn't in danger. But that didn't ease her worry. Or their predicament.

"Why don't you tell me what you need?" Remington coaxed, his long fingers rhythmically kneading her lower thighs. "Perhaps I can help."

The sensations he elicited spread up her legs and into her breasts, flushing her skin. Her nipples hardened. "Why would you want to do that?"

His powerful shoulders flexed as he shrugged. "You are a

beautiful woman. I like beautiful women. Especially troubled ones who require my assistance."

"So you can take advantage?" She stood, her thoughts and body in turmoil, and his hands fell away. "I should not have come in here."

"No, you shouldn't have," he agreed, his voice soft. Remington rose at the same time, towering over her. The top of her head barely reached his shoulders, and Julienne was forced to tilt her head back to look at him.

She turned to leave, but his grip on her elbow stayed her. Heat radiated from his fingers and spread through her body.

"Unhand me," she ordered in an unsteady voice. "I wish to leave."

She didn't, not truly, but she must. Remington's proximity was doing terrible things to her. Wonderful, terrible things. Things it most likely did to countless other women.

He shook his head and grinned. "Pity that, since you're not going anywhere. Not until morning. You've created enough of a stir as it is, coughing brandy all over Lord Ridgely. Returning to the floor, however briefly, would stir up the whole mess again. You've wounded his pride, and he's a pompous ass."

"What do you suggest I do then?"

The amusement in his eyes never wavered. "You'll stay the night in one of the rooms upstairs. I'll entertain Ridgely and his cronies until the whole debacle is forgotten."

She gaped. "You're mad! I cannot remain in this establishment overnight!"

Remington laughed. The deep, rich sound gathered around her like an embrace and made her shiver. But she wasn't cold. To her dismay, she was growing hotter by the moment. She couldn't help it with the way he looked at her. Julienne had seen that look before. But no man had ever dared to give it to her.

She found she rather liked it.

"You went to a hell of a lot of trouble to get in here," he purred. "And now you're anxious to leave?"

Julienne sidestepped, but he didn't release her. "My need was especially dire. I apologize for any trouble I—"

"You don't sound very sorry."

"I'll leave immediately," she offered.

"You'll leave in the morning. The hour is late. The streets aren't safe."

"My aunt will worry," she argued.

"I'll send Lady Whitfield a note. She'll know you're well."

She stilled, her eyes narrowing. "How do you know about my aunt?"

"I know everything about every one of the members of my club. Especially those who enjoy lines of credit." Remington's thumb began an absentminded caress of the hollow of her elbow. Julienne felt the warmth of his touch all the way to her bones.

"I know your parents died when you were very young and your Aunt Eugenia's been your guardian for years. You and Montrose are always running roughshod over her. Your brother is brash, hotheaded, and still too young for the responsibilities of his title. You're always bailing him out of one mess or another. And now I know how seriously you take that responsibility."

She looked away, flustered that he knew such intimate details. "Do you also know how sick to death I am of that chore?" she said finally, surprising herself with the admission.

His voice turned soft and sympathetic. "I'm certain you must be. But you've done an admirable job. There's not been even a breath of scandal attached to the La Coeur name."

Julienne looked up at him, overwhelmed by his nearness. She felt slightly tipsy, but she couldn't blame it on the brandy. Lord Ridgely was presently wearing most of it.

Remington led her across the room and pulled the bell. "I'll have one of the courtesans give you a night rail. You'll be comfortable. My hospitality is legendary."

She scowled. "That's not all that's legendary."

Unperturbed, he gave her a wink. A lock of silky hair fell across his forehead, and Julienne fought the unaccountable urge to brush it away with her fingertips.

An attendant came, and Remington drew him aside. When

the servant left, she tried again to reason her way out of trouble.

"Mr. Remington, I must insist you allow me to leave. It is most improper for me to spend the evening here."

"And masquerading your way into my club is proper?" Remington's brilliant gaze hardened with determination. "You've created an inconvenience for me, Lady Julienne. The least you can do is minimize the damage."

Everything they said about the man was true. Single-minded. Stubborn. Relentless. She could always slip away. She was good at—

"Don't even consider sneaking out," he warned. "I've already instructed the attendant. You won't get far."

"Of all the—!" she sputtered.

Abruptly the wall opened, revealing a hidden passageway and a young, scantily dressed woman.

"Escort my"—he shot her an amused glance and chuckled—"lady friend to the Sapphire Room, Janice. Give her a night rail, and order her a supper tray."

The courtesan's eyes widened as she studied Julienne with obvious interest.

With a hand at the small of her back, Remington propelled her toward the opening. He bent low, his lips brushing her ear. "Stay in your room until I send for you in the morning. I would hate for you to be seen without your disguise."

Julienne stared at the open portal. "Don't you have one of these that lead out—"

"No. This goes from here to my room. Nowhere else."

She shivered as his breath danced across her throat, the feeling so intimate as to have been almost a caress. "Mr. Remington, is there any way I could convince you of the impropriety of this arrangement? I'm truly sorry to have disturbed you."

His blue eyes darkened, and he opened his mouth to speak. Then he shut it and shook his head. "Go on now," he urged in a husky whisper. "I have work to do."

Muttering under her breath, Julienne followed Janice into

the secret hallway, feeling Remington's eyes on her until she disappeared from sight. It took only moments to reach the upstairs gallery, where the courtesan ushered her into an opulent bedchamber. As soon as she stepped inside, Julienne paused, entranced.

The Sapphire Room was the loveliest room she'd ever seen. The walls were covered in deep blue-and-cream stripes of silk, the massive bed was layered in lush indigo velvet, and the parquet floors were covered with rich Aubusson rugs. She spun slowly, attempting to picture Remington here.

"My lady?"

Julienne started in surprise at the use of her courtesy title. "How did you know?"

Janice smiled. "'Tis impossible to hide good breeding. I'll go now and fetch you something else to wear and some supper. I won't be long."

"Thank you. I'd be very grateful to get out of these clothes."

After the courtesan left, Julienne tossed the wig into the coal bucket and sank into a chair, once again admiring the luxuriousness of her surroundings. Remington's Gentleman's Club was a pleasure den, a bastion of male comfort and iniquity. Hugh had steeped himself in the environment, surrounding himself with erotic novels and scandalous peep-show boxes, as well as a social circle made up entirely of debauched rakes. She'd been forced to study the enemy simply to know what she faced.

Well, that wasn't entirely true. Julienne had to admit she was curious about carnal relations. She hated to be in the dark about anything, and Aunt Eugenia was no help at all, stuttering and stammering every time she was asked anything of a sexual nature. The books and contents of the boxes had answered many of Julienne's questions, but in the process they had raised many more, and unfortunately they had told her nothing about how to remove Hugh from his path of self-destruction.

Standing, she crossed to the window and stared at the darkened London skyline. Remington's was Hugh's favorite establishment, and after seeing the inside of the famous club, Julienne could understand why. He'd been absent for a week, which was not unusual, but the hounding creditors were driving her mad. Usually Hugh dealt with them, charming them into allowing him a few more days. She, on the other hand, had no notion of what to say, and while the duns strove to be polite to her, they grew angrier by the day.

There would be hell to pay when Hugh showed his sorry hide again. But in the meantime, she was inclined to think her adventure had been worth it just for the few stolen moments she'd enjoyed of Lucien Remington's company. The fact was, the possibility of seeing him up close, of hearing his voice, of watching him at her leisure, was what had prompted this plan. Finding Hugh would have been a bonus.

Under no other circumstances would Julienne have been allowed to make Remington's acquaintance. She knew very little about him, since he was not a fit topic for unmarried ladies. Furtive eavesdropping in retiring rooms had only whetted her appetite to learn more. But there was one thing she knew for a certainty: Lucien Remington was a naughty man.

And she rather liked that about him.

He knew how to enjoy himself without running headlong into the poorhouse. In fact, rumor said he was one of the richest men in England. She hoped Hugh could learn similar self-restraint and financial acuity.

Releasing a deep breath, Julienne turned toward the bed. At times she truly hated being an earl's daughter and all of the social strictures that came with that station. She wished she could be like her abigail, who was seeing the neighbor's footman and was blissfully in love. Instead Julienne would be forced to marry for prestige and money. It really wasn't fair. Playing the martyr didn't suit her nature. Hugh made his own messes, and as far as she was concerned, he should clean them up himself. Unfortunately, that wasn't the way it would be.

But her dreams were her own. And if those dreams were of Lucien Remington and his wicked smiles, no one else would ever have to know.

* * *

Lucien strode to the sideboard, poured two fingers of brandy, and tossed the fiery liquid back in one gulp.

He'd lost his damn mind. There was no other explanation for forcing Lady Julienne La Coeur to stay. His hand went to the front of his trousers and rubbed the length of his aching erection. His arousal was ridiculous. She was dressed in men's clothing, for Christ's sake!

Closing his eyes, he pictured the sway of her hips in those trousers as she'd left the room. His cock throbbed in response.

Hell and damnation! He should have shoved her out the door. Gently, of course, but shoved with haste, nevertheless.

Instead he had sent her upstairs to the room that adjoined his. She was an innocent, that was painfully obvious, but despite her unfamiliarity with sex, she was no stranger to desire. She'd looked at him as if she wanted to eat him alive. And, God, he'd love to allow her to. With very little effort, Lucien could imagine sliding his cock in and out of her delectable mouth. It would feel like warm silk . . .

He groaned as his trousers grew even more uncomfortable.

With a muffled curse, Lucien set his empty glass on the desk and walked to the bookshelf. Glancing quickly through the spines, he located the file for the Earl of Montrose. The earl's entire monetary history could be found in here, from the amount he owed his tailor to the balance in his bank account.

Lucien had been aware that Montrose was playing too deep. Any other patron would have lost his credit privileges long ago. But Lucien had left the young earl's accounts open, for one reason and for one reason only—he wanted Julienne La Coeur. He'd coveted her across many a crowded ballroom. Tiny but temptingly voluptuous, with dark blonde hair and mischievous eyes, Julienne had stolen the breath from him at first sight.

He'd wanted to approach her, to beg a dance with her, so he could hold her in his arms. But his reputation as a notorious rake and debauched libertine, as well as his livelihood in trade, had made him vastly unsuitable for even an introduction, let alone a waltz. So he'd allowed Montrose, his one connection to Julienne, to continue playing, to keep him close until he could think of a way to get to his sister.

Lucien wasn't certain what he'd do with Julienne when he caught her. Perhaps he could seduce her and ease his craving. Maybe a longer association would be required. He honestly didn't know what he wanted. He only knew that he wanted. Badly.

Never in his wildest imaginings (and his imaginings could get pretty wild) had he ever thought she would come to him. And dressed as a man, no less.

But he rather liked that she had. It took a formidable will to risk such a scandal. And she'd stood up to him, before whom even some dukes cowered. Julienne La Coeur was no simpering miss.

Now she was upstairs, preparing to slip into one of his beds. He could imagine her curls spread across his silk-covered pillows, her head thrown back with pleasure, as he rode her hard and deep. She'd be ravishing all flushed with passion . . .

Hang it!

He was driving himself mad.

Before he aroused himself enough to do something he'd regret, Lucien returned the file to the shelf and exited to the gambling area. He wandered among the gentlemen of the Beau Monde, keeping an eye on who was winning and who was losing. He directed the courtesans toward members who looked to be in need of a little amusement, and signaled the servers to water the drinks of those who looked to be falling too far into their cups. He socialized with patrons who sought him out, and paid attention to the quantity and quality of food leaving his kitchens.

Busy with work, he was able to pass some time without a full-blown cockstand. But as the hours passed and more gentlemen made use of the courtesans, his mind wandered back to Julienne.

Beautiful, untouchable Julienne.

He'd watched her draw wallflowers out of their shells and

turn the Beau Monde's social dragons into purring pussycats. And he coveted her gentle regard.

Lucien left the main floor and made his way upstairs. Before he realized it, he stood in the bedroom he reserved for his own use when the lateness of the hour or sheer exhaustion made it impractical to go home. He hesitated in front of the connecting door to the Sapphire Room. His erection was back, hot and throbbing in the tight confines of his trousers. He rested his forehead gently against the portal, knowing Julienne was just inside, so close. Achingly close.

He paused and took a deep breath. He reached for the doorknob and was gratified when it turned. Julienne hadn't had the foresight to turn the lock. Fortuitous, or a disaster? Lucien couldn't be certain. A gentleman would walk away. Of course, a gentleman wouldn't have come up here in the first place.

But then he'd never claimed to be a gentleman.

Before he could think better of it, Lucien pushed the door open and walked right in.

Chapter Two

Julienne woke, alerted to the presence of someone else in the room. She was a light sleeper, always had been, and she lay quietly, attempting to ascertain who'd entered.

"You're awake."

She stiffened. That velvety voice was unmistakable. Sitting up in the massive bed, she held the sheet to her neck and glanced toward the door. Light filtered in around Lucien Remington's tall form, casting half his features in shadow. He looked like the devil incarnate, all raw power and luscious dark masculinity.

"You woke me," she censured in a sleep-husky voice, her body taut as a bow. Her dreams had been fraught with images of him. His hands on her, his lips melded to hers, his hard body pinning her down . . . Nocturnal fantasies she enjoyed with only the tiniest amount of guilt. "This is most improper, Mr. Remington," she said sharply, hiding the heady excitement she felt. "Why are you here?"

He came toward her with his long-legged stride, a sexual predator in motion. Stopping by the bed, he lit the taper on the side table. His mouth fell open when the circle of light revealed her.

"*Jesus!* You're naked!" he accused, stumbling backward with an expression of horror.

"Hence the reason you should not be in here." Julienne pulled the sheet up higher and gestured with a toss of her chin toward the transparent negligee slung over a chair. "Being naked seemed no better or worse than wearing that."

He never took his eyes from her. "I should have allowed you to leave," he mumbled, shaking his head.

She colored. "*You* should leave. You have no right to enter my room."

He'd backed up almost to the door when she stopped him. "Has my brother arrived?" she asked eagerly, pushing her hair away from her face.

Remington stood frozen by the doorway. "No," he croaked. "Montrose is not here." He stared at her for a long moment before blurting, "Are you comfortable?"

"Am I—?" Julienne frowned, confused by the sudden change in topic. "Yes, I was quite comfortable."

"And the food? Did you enjoy it?"

"The food was excellent." She smiled. "Your entire establishment is breathtaking. I'd heard rumors, of course, and Hugh—er, Montrose—raved about the beauty of this place, but nothing equals actually seeing it with my own eyes. It's very impressive. I admire what you've accomplished here."

"You ad—?" He swallowed hard. "Thank you. I'm pleased you like it."

"You must hear that often."

"Actually," he admitted, "that was the first instance where someone other than my parents expressed admiration for me."

"Oh." Julienne didn't know what to say. She knew what others said about him, but she was saddened to realize he knew it as well. "Is that why you came? To check on my welfare?"

An uncomfortable silence descended.

"Perhaps I've come to ravish you," he said finally.

She choked and then laughed aloud, even as her stomach did a little flip. "That's the most ridiculous thing I've ever heard."

Remington's eyes widened. "Why? You don't believe I would want to ravish you?"

Julienne rubbed her forehead and shook her head, wondering if she was dreaming this mad encounter. "Mr. Remington, you are the handsomest man in all of England. Your reputation is well known to me. I am aware a libertine like you would have no interest in a green debutante like myself."

He moved toward her again with painful slowness, as if he pulled against his will. "The handsomest man in England?" he queried softly. "Is that your personal opinion, or one you repeat from the mouths of others?"

She twisted at the waist as he approached, hiding her bare back. "Both," she admitted. She raised a finely arched brow. "I did not take you to be a man of vanity, Mr. Remington, but if you are, and you require confirmation of your attractiveness, I would be more than happy to oblige you . . . *in the morning*. At the present time, I would appreciate—"

"I'm curious, my lady," he interrupted, his mouth curving intimately. "How would you confirm my attractiveness?"

Julienne grew wary at the hot flicker she saw in his eyes, the same look he'd given her in his office. She liked it, but Lord above, she was *naked*! The whole situation was . . . thrilling . . . but far beyond her experience. Clutching the sheet firmly with one hand, she held out the other to halt his advance. He stopped immediately. "What do you want?"

"To ravish you."

He said it so simply, his expression so earnest, that she was momentarily rendered speechless. Oh, he was wicked. And far more interesting than the other men of her acquaintance.

"You can have any woman you want."

"No." His smile was wistful. "I can't have you."

Her breath caught.

"You're very good," she said finally, honestly awestruck. She'd never seen such a talented rogue. "Charming, seemingly sincere. I can see how you've managed so many conquests. But really, I am not worth the effort, I assure you, although I am flattered."

Remington laughed. "Sweetheart, you're amazing. You dress as a man to sneak into my club, tolerate my extorting you into spending the night, and then feel flattered when I barge into your room and tell you I want to ravish you." His voice softened when he said, "I wish I could keep you."

The expression on his face made her heart race. Julienne felt light-headed and dizzy all over again. Then she was struck with a thought that made sense, unlike all the others that swirled in her head. "Have you been drinking?"

He moved casually to the chair and sat. "Tell me why you want to find your brother, and I'll tell you why I came in here."

"If you're interested in conversing with me, can you at least allow me to dress?"

His blue eyes glittered with eagerness. "In the negligee or the trousers?"

Her mouth fell open. This really had to be a dream. An odd, wonderful, bizarre dream. "I don't know how to deal with a man like you, Mr. Remington." She was out of her depth.

"You can start by calling me Lucien," he suggested. "Then you should probably begin screaming. Most debutantes would have run from the room in terror by now. I'm a stranger to you except for my scandalous reputation, which decries me as a hedonistic seducer of women."

She smiled. "I'm not afraid of you. You've no need to force yourself on a woman."

"Who said I would have to force you?" he purred seductively.

"Good grief," she muttered, rolling her eyes. "You deliberately cultivate your image, don't you? I'd wager you're not as bad as they say."

One side of his mouth twitched in amusement. "No," he agreed. "I'm much worse. If you weren't the purest, sweetest, most beautiful thing I've ever seen, I would have already had you on your back, with your heels in the air."

Julienne's mouth parted in surprise, and she looked away, her face flushed. He was a perfect scoundrel to say such things, but she didn't care. Strong, virile, and devastatingly handsome, Lucien Remington was her fantasy come to life. He had been since the first moment she'd seen him at the Milton country rout.

Taller than most of the other men there and heavily muscled like a common laborer, Lucien had permanently imprinted himself on her memory when he'd inclined his head toward her with a rakish wink. She'd not passed one night in the month since without dreaming of him in ways no proper lady would dream about any man, not even their husbands.

Ah, what she wouldn't give to be brazen and desirable, if only for a moment. She would love to be the kind of woman who could retain the interest of a man like Lucien. The thought made her sigh aloud.

"Bloody hell."

She looked up in surprise and was startled by the anguished look on his face.

"What is it?" she demanded. "Why do you look like that?"

Lucien stood and rounded the backside of the chair, putting the piece of furniture between them as if she posed some grave threat to his person. "Because *you* look like *that*! I know what you're thinking, and you must cease. Now."

"My thoughts happen to be none of your business." She waved toward the door. "The hour is late, and I'm tired. I'm undressed, and—"

"I wanted to watch you sleep."

Julienne blinked. "Beg your pardon?"

"You asked me why I was here." He cleared his throat. "I wanted to watch you sleep."

She frowned, confused. "Why would you want to do that?" Lucien Remington, notorious voluptuary, watching her *sleep*? How much more intimate that seemed than ravishment.

She studied him, noting his hands gripping the back of the chair so tightly his knuckles turned white. It couldn't be possible that he was interested in her. It was so against his known nature, she simply couldn't credit it. He preferred mature, and usually married, women. "Are you feeling unwell, Mr. Rem—er, Lucien? Perhaps you are slightly in your cups?"

"I am *not* in my cups!" he growled. "But I *am* decidedly unwell. I'm coming undone. And damn it, the way you look at me tells me you feel the same. I'm not an honorable man, and I do not aspire to be one. I'll take your innocence and walk away without looking back. You'll be ruined, Julienne. I've been panting after you for weeks. *Weeks.*" He shoved away from the chair and began to pace. "I wish to God you had not come into my club."

Julienne gaped. From the moment she'd arrived in London at the start of the Season, her life had seemed to turn completely upside down. Her brother was missing, creditors hounded Montrose Hall, and Lucien Remington wanted to bed her. She couldn't decide which event was most disturbing. Her skin grew hot and tight, her body achingly uncomfortable.

"Aren't you going to say something?" he snapped. "Shout at me. Call me a cad, or worse, if you have the coarse vocabulary to do so. Tell me to leave." When she just stared at him, wide-eyed with incredulity, Lucien approached her and grabbed her by the shoulders. He shook her roughly. "Do *something! Anything,* damn it, to make me go." His fingers kneaded restlessly against her skin, as if he couldn't bear not to touch her.

She stared mutely at the ferocious man who held her. His voice, his words, his countenance—never in her life had she seen such passion. To think she had inspired such a display shocked her to silence.

And thrilled her.

"Tell me to leave," he repeated harshly. "Before I do something we'll both regret."

"Go," she said, her voice so soft it was less than a whisper. But it was enough. Lucien released her and walked away with angry strides.

As the door closed behind him, Julienne felt an odd panic, as if once he left she would never see him again, which was partially true. She would never be allowed to speak to him, to touch him, since simply looking at him was a grave offense. Once he walked out that door, her time with him would be over. Forever.

And she simply couldn't bear it.

"Lucien!" she cried in dismay, willing him to come back to her.

Instantly, the door swung open, and he was in her arms.

Chapter Three

Julienne La Coeur smelled heavenly. Her skin was like the finest silk, her breasts full and generously swelled as they pressed against his chest. Lucien didn't understand why she'd called him back, but he wasn't about to ask for an explanation.

"Sweet Julienne," he murmured feverishly against her throat. "You should have allowed me to go."

Her small, delicate hands slipped inside his velvet coat and slid across the smooth satin back of his waistcoat. "I tried."

He rolled to the side and shrugged out of his coat, tossing the expensive garment carelessly to the floor. He turned back to her and then froze in place.

The sheet had slipped down to her waist, leaving her breasts exposed to his gaze. Firm and gently swaying from his near-frantic movements, they were more lovely than anything Lucien had seen in his life. "You are more beautiful than I imagined," he breathed.

He watched in amazement as her skin flushed right before his eyes, rosy color sweeping across her chest before rising to her cheeks. His gaze studied her face, and he saw that she couldn't, or wouldn't, meet his eyes. With his fingertips, he tilted the bottom of her chin upward, forcing her to look at him. "Don't be shy, sweetheart. Not with me."

As he searched her face, he wondered at his good fortune. Lady Julienne La Coeur. Julienne, so lovely, laying in one of his beds, bare from the waist up, her rich blonde hair spilling around her creamy shoulders, her dark eyes staring at him with such desire. He was so damn desperate to fuck her, he thought he would burst with it, but the small portion of his mind not presently between his legs wondered why the beautiful, socially esteemed diamond would be so eager to spread her legs for a bastard like him. With a muffled curse, Lucien leapt from the bed.

He looked around wildly. "Is this a trap?" he bit out. "Is your brother hiding somewhere, waiting to jump out and catch me compromising you?"

"Beg your pardon?" She looked genuinely confused.

"What are you doing? Lying in bed naked? Giving yourself to me so easily?"

A frown marred the smooth area between her brows. "I was sleeping," she answered crossly. "I didn't ask you to come in here. I didn't even want to spend the night here. *You* insisted." Julienne rubbed her forehead, pulling the sheet up once again to cover herself. "Get out," she said coldly.

His hands clenched into fists.

"Leave, Mr. Remington. Before I take up your suggestion to scream."

He watched in amazement as she threw herself into the pillows and turned her back to him. It would damage her more than him to be caught, but why else would she offer herself?

"This is fantastic," he muttered, more to himself than to her.

She gave a disdainful little grunt and punched the pillow.

Lucien wandered around the room, looking behind the thick sapphire velvet drapes and dropping to his knees to look under the bed. Finding no one lurking in the room, Lucien strode to both doors and locked them. He shrugged out of his waistcoat.

Julienne sat up again. "You're mad if you believe I would allow you to touch me now!"

Lucien yanked his shirt out of his trousers and drew it over his head. He smiled grimly when she gasped at the sight of his chest. He knew he was considered too muscled, the result of many hours spent engaged in fencing and pugilism. But the glimmer in her eyes wasn't fear or revulsion. It was desire.

"Why me?" he asked.

She rolled back onto her side. "Go away."

"Why me?" he repeated.

"Why do you find it so hard to believe?" she mumbled into the pillow. "Women throw themselves at you all the time. Why should I be any different?"

He moved toward the bed. "Am I something to boast to your friends about?"

Julienne tucked tighter into the pillows, pulling the sheet with her. "As if I would ever tell anyone that I'd succumbed to your charms. Which I won't!" she added hastily. "Succumb, that is. Now, please leave!"

"What if I spread the tale?" he asked. "What if I tell every member of my club that I rode between your thighs? That I ruined you, and you screamed with pleasure while I did it?" His mouth curved in a predatory smile. "And you *will* scream with pleasure."

She snorted. "I'll do no such thing."

"What if I tell everyone, Julienne?"

"You wouldn't."

"You don't know me well enough to say that."

"You don't know me well either. For if you did, you wouldn't be so fearful of my intentions."

Turning away, Lucien stared into the dying fire. "You are distraught over your brother."

"I am," she admitted, her clear voice telling him as she faced him again. "I will have to bail him out of this mess, just as I've always done."

He sighed. "If I touch you, you'll be ruined, and the marriage you require to save your brother will be jeopardized."

"I'm aware of that. My actions tonight were foolish at best, but I knew the possible consequences and I weighed them carefully. I'd planned to sit in a quiet corner and observe. I wanted to watch you in your element, a place where the rules are completely yours and you are not bound by the strictures that suppress you in Society. It is unfortunate that Ridgely chose my table to share, but not unexpected."

"Lady Julienne. If you'd been found out—"

"The scandal would have destroyed all chances of an advantageous marriage, I know. But perhaps that would be best for Montrose. I don't care much for the thought of being a sacrifice on the matrimonial altar. Facing the consequences of our actions is the best way to learn responsibility, but I am to blame for shielding him too well. As for this moment, is it so wrong to want the pleasure other women experience? Is it so terrible to steal a little passion in a life that will be bereft of it? There are ways . . . ways to . . . ways that would leave me a virgin—"

Lucien turned in stunned amazement. "How would you know of such 'ways'?"

She flushed from the top of her breasts to her hairline. "I read . . . things."

"You read 'things'?" His eyes widened. *"Erotica?"*

Julienne's hair was a golden curtain around her. With her bared shoulders and flushed face, she looked every bit the wanton seductress and nothing like the genteel virgin he knew her to be.

And yet it was the unabashed tilt to her chin and the defiance so evident in her silence that most affected him. An innocent who wasn't quite so innocent. His cock had been aching before. Now the throbbing was downright painful.

Her beauty was what had first caught his eye, her voluptuous figure had kept his attention, but her smile, warm and open, was what obsessed him. Women did not look at him with such sweet interest. They either shot daggers at him for being what he was, or invited him to their beds with seductive glances. When Julienne had first seen him across the Milton's crowded ballroom, she'd smiled so beautifully that he'd found it difficult to breathe. He'd wanted her instantly, wanted to discover what it was she saw that lit up her eyes with such warm regard.

But now that he had her in his grasp, he found there was more to his interest than mere carnal gratification. He was startled to realize he *liked* her, liked that she was unconventional and bold, as well as beautiful and kind.

Abruptly—regretfully—he realized he couldn't take her. Doing so would destroy her, and he could never do that.

"No." He gave a wry smile. "It's not wrong to want passion. And I'm deeply flattered that you want to discover it with me."

Her smile was so brilliant, it made his chest tight.

Lucien ran a hand through his hair. "I enjoy a good debauch as much as any man, Julienne. But sometimes I wish for the finer things in life, the softer things, pure and innocent like you are."

"I'm not so innocent as all that. If you knew the thoughts I have about you—"

"Hush. Don't say any more. I'm having a hard enough time being honorable as it is."

"I rather like you dishonorable, if you don't mind."

He arched a brow and grinned. She was a minx. He never would have guessed. "Haven't you been warned about men like me?"

"Yes." Her lips curved. "But therein lies the problem."

He shook his head.

"You see," she continued, her voice lowering. "Being around you makes me ache. The way you look at me makes me ache, much more so than when I read Hugh's books. I'm a grown woman. Allow me to worry about the consequences."

Lucien groaned low in his chest, a sound filled with defeat and the death of good intentions. He was only a man, an extremely lustful man, with the woman he wanted most offering liberties he shouldn't accept. But would. He couldn't turn away the chance to touch her, to hold her, just once.

"I'll take care of that, sweetheart," he said softly as he approached her. "I'll make the ache go away."

He placed one knee on the bed and then stretched out beside her, clenching his teeth as she rolled and pressed her breasts into his chest. She tilted back her head, offering up her lips, and he claimed them, his tongue sweeping into the sweet recesses of her mouth. Her response stunned him, her eagerness obvious, and he could hardly bear it. He shook with the effort to slow down, to be gentle, when the fire in his blood urged him to hurry.

His hand caressed her shoulder and then moved down to her breast, finding her nipple as he ravished her mouth. He tugged gently with his fingers, loving how she melted against him, completely responsive and unreserved. Pulling her body to drape over his, Lucien caressed the curve of her derriere, kneading the firm flesh until she squirmed.

"Please," she gasped, pulling her lips from his. Her legs spread in silent invitation.

Lucien buried his face in her throat to hide his smile. Julienne was so innocent and yet so wanton. So perfect.

He slid his hands between her thighs, one finger finding the slick opening that betrayed her desire. He slid through the cream, testing her, before sliding just a tiny bit inside. She moaned and instinctively pressed her hips downward, away from the pressure and onto his erection. Lucien groaned along with her.

This wouldn't do. If she did that again, he wouldn't have the presence of mind to keep from plunging his aching cock straight through her maidenhead.

Julienne whimpered when he gripped her waist, pulling her higher over his body so that her breasts hung in his face and the crisp curls of her sex rested safely against his stomach. He held her slight weight easily above him, admiring the sight of her. Her eyes closed, she arched her back, presenting her breasts, while her golden hair drifted around her shoulders.

Lucien was captivated.

Lifting his head, he pressed a reverent kiss to a puckered nipple. Julienne's soft cry encouraged him to go further. He teased her with licks of his tongue before suckling the taut peak into his mouth, intoxicated by the scent and taste of her skin. She arched into him, rubbing her sex along the muscled ridges of his stomach. She repeated the movement again. Then again. Julienne was riding herself against him, her nipple held firmly in his mouth, and he was on fire, every nerve ending vibrantly attuned to the woman he pleasured.

"Please," she begged. "I need . . . more . . ."

He knew what she craved. To be filled with him, stretched by him, and ridden to orgasm with his cock stroking deeply inside her. But he would not do that. Could not. There was nothing about him that was honorable, but he'd make the effort. For her.

"Patience, love," he murmured, releasing her breast. "I will attend to you."

He rolled her over, capturing her other nipple with his mouth while his hand caressed the length of her body and dipped between her thighs. To his delight, she opened her legs eagerly, and he caressed her lips with soft, gentle swirls, pinching them together, then moving his fingers across the hard, swollen nub in matching cadence to his suction on her breast. Her lithe body began to undulate next to his, and he threw a leg across her hips, grinding his erection into her thigh, his body seeking a relief that would be denied to him.

It was a hell of a time to find his conscience.

Impatient, Julienne arched into his hand. Lucien obliged by venturing a finger inside her again, softly stroking. He pulled out with exquisite slowness, then pressed forward again. With a patience that surprised him, he took his time, loving her gently until her body welcomed his touch with a rush of moisture. She breathed his name, and he was nearly lost.

Lucien released her breast, afraid of hurting her as his jaw clenched with the effort to retain his control. His finger, slick with her cream, slipped out, and then he entered her with two fingers. He fucked her faster now, pulling back to watch her face as she struggled against her approaching orgasm, her skin flushed, her nipples tight and hard. Despite her virginal state, she was so aroused that he had no trouble pleasing her, his fingers twisting and rubbing, constantly changing tempo and direction, to keep her on the edge. Julienne writhed, her fingernails digging into his arm, marking him on the outside as she'd marked him on the inside. Her knees fell outward, opening her cunt completely, and then her hips began to move with him, rising and falling to meet his thrusts.

"Don't fight it, sweet," he coaxed softly as her head began to thrash, her skin so hot it burned his. "Just allow it to happen."

The room was quiet except for the harsh sounds of their breathing and the slick sucking noises that accompanied the pumping of his fingers. Julienne turned blindly toward him, her lips parted with panting breaths, and he thrust his tongue between them, loving the taste of her. When she stiffened beneath him, he pulled away, pinning her down with his leg as she arched and cried out his name, shivering beneath him. She held his fingers so tightly in her orgasm, he could barely move them, but he managed it anyway, drawing out her pleasure. He was stunned watching her, never having seen anything so beautiful in his life.

And he would never be allowed to see it again.

Lucien was torn between masculine satisfaction and utter, wrenching despair.

Julienne opened her eyes and wondered if she'd fainted. She felt boneless, languid with warmth. As she realized the heat came from Lucien, her mouth curved with pleasure. She snuggled closer, and then stilled at the sound of his harshly indrawn breath and the feel of his erection against her thigh. She looked at him in dismay. He was suffering, and she'd been too sated to notice.

He rose to his elbow and looked down at her, his face drawn tight. "I have to go."

She lowered her eyes to the hard ridge of his cock. Reaching down, she brushed the outline with a shy, tentative stroke of her fingers. It jerked beneath her touch.

He pushed her hand away with a curse, then caught it back and kissed her fingertips to soften his rejection. "You mustn't touch me, Julienne."

"But I'd like to," she insisted. Her heart swelled, filled with tenderness for him. "That was so wonderful . . . what you did . . ."

His gaze was achingly tender. "I'm glad you thought so."

Julienne pressed her lips to his.

His hand slid to her nape, prolonging the kiss. Then he sighed and rolled onto his back. In a fluidly graceful motion, he left the bed. Lucien grabbed up his shirt and dropped it over her head.

"Stay with me." She shoved her arms through the sleeves and gripped his wrist quickly when he turned to leave.

"I don't think I can."

"But you wanted to watch me sleep." When he hesitated, she pulled the counterpane back in invitation. He was so obviously torn that it touched her heart.

Suddenly he blew out the candle and slid in beside her. He curled against her back, his knees behind hers, his lips at her shoulder. She clung to his arms as if she would never allow him to go, which was entirely the way she felt. With his warmth and scent surrounding her, she quickly fell asleep.

Chapter Four

"Oh, dear, this is dreadful. Absolutely dreadful. We're ruined. *You are ruined!* What will we do? We shall be run from our home and—"

"Aunt Eugenia, *please*!" Julienne threw up her hands. "Keep your voice down! The servants will hear you."

Eugenia Whitfield snapped her mouth closed and bit her lower lip.

Julienne sank into her brother's chair in the study of Montrose Hall and crushed his letter in her fist. The soul-deep satisfaction she'd enjoyed since leaving Lucien that morning was gone, replaced by weary resignation. "I am not ruined."

"You spent the night with Lucien Remington!"

"Aunt Eugenia!"

Eugenia squirmed in misery on the chaise.

"I did not spend the night with Lucien Remington. I merely spent the evening in his establishment, which no one aside from you is aware of. I'd prefer to keep it that way, so lower your voice. Please!"

"What will we do about Hugh?"

Julienne looked at the missive in her hand and wondered the same thing. Hugh had retired to the country for an extended party with some of his friends, leaving her to deal with the aftermath of his debts. As usual, he'd failed to consider notifying her until days after he'd left. Her brother didn't mean to be hurtful. He was simply irresponsible and always leaped before looking, consistently landing in puddles of trouble. It was partly her fault, for always cleaning up after him. Hugh had never learned that every action has a consequence.

She rose from behind the desk and threw the letter into the fire. "Nothing has changed. I had to marry in any case."

"Oh, Julienne . . ." Eugenia sighed. "You've been through so much. I cannot collect how you manage it."

"The same way you've managed Hugh and me. We do what we must."

Julienne turned back to her aunt and smiled. At fifty, Eugenia Whitfield was still a lovely woman. Widowed at a young age, she could easily have remarried. Instead she had taken over the care of her brother's children when the Earl of Montrose and his wife were killed in a carriage accident. While she often wrung her hands and lamented the unruliness of her charges, Eugenia never said a word of regret about the things she'd given up. Because of this, Julienne loved her aunt more than anything.

"I just assumed Hugh was drinking and gambling himself silly in that club," Eugenia said. "I could never have imagined he would leave town at a time like this! It's your first Season, for heaven's sake." She pursed her lips. "That boy needs a switch to his behind."

Julienne choked back a laugh at the picture. Aunt Eugenia had never raised a hand to either of them, although the hugs had been plentiful.

Sinking into her chair, Julienne let her mind drift to Lucien Remington, a man who was free and unrestrained by the rules that smothered her. Just the thought of the scandalous rogue made her body ache with remembered passion. If she closed her eyes, she could recall his richly masculine scent and the gentleness of his touch deep inside her. The memory alone aroused her, making her nipples hard and her skin hot.

If she listened to Society, she would feel some terrible regret or dismay at what she had allowed to happen, but she didn't.

Lucien had made her feel cherished, and while he'd only mentioned his physical attraction, his every touch, every kiss, had been underlain with an aching tenderness. Her entire life she'd been an object of fragile esteem, not considered a woman of passions, but just a female extension of the men in her life—first her father, then her brother, next her husband. Only Lucien had seen beyond the exterior to the woman within.

She was grateful to have had one night of passion with him, for she would have no more for the rest of her life.

Julienne had left him without saying good-bye. And three days later, Lucien still couldn't stop thinking about it.

Usually he preferred to avoid the morning-after farewell, an often messy affair. But Julienne's silent departure had left him bereft. For the first time in his life, he'd wanted to wake up with the woman he'd touched so intimately only hours before. He'd wanted to share breakfast with her, talk with her, and discover what had her so troubled. He'd quite simply wanted to enjoy her company for a few hours more before losing it forever.

Julienne La Coeur intrigued him more now that he knew her than she had as a stranger. He'd watched her closely for weeks, admiring her graceful poise and social adeptness. But that night in the Sapphire Room, she'd been surprised by his interest, not because she underestimated her own attractiveness, but because she so esteemed his. She admired and was drawn to the very things for which he was usually condemned, and yet he didn't feel like he was just a scandalous bit of excitement to her. Instead he felt like a man appreciated simply for being himself.

Her parting had left behind a void that none of the women he'd bedded since had been able to fill. Lucien wondered if she regretted her curiosity that night or resented him for taking advantage of the offer he should have rejected. He supposed he should feel guilty, but he didn't. How could he, when he ached to love her again?

"I believe Lord Montrose has retired to the country."

Scowling, Lucien looked across his desk at Harold Marchant, his man-of-affairs. Most men cowered when Lucien was irritated. Harold, however, took it in stride, which is why the man had worked for him for almost a decade. Lucien had made Marchant a wealthy man and in the process had earned his loyalty. Marchant was, in fact, the closest thing he had to a best friend. "Is the earl destitute?"

Marchant nodded gravely. "Very nearly. In addition to the staggering amount he owes Remington's, merchants have begun repossessing goods and duns have become regular visitors to the Montrose residence here in town. Soon they will set up a veritable encampment on his doorstep."

Lucien whistled softly. In these days of industrial progression, many aristocrats were losing centuries of inheritance due to their own reluctance to engage in trade or invest in the future. As a man of his own means, Lucien had little respect for anyone who allowed his pride to get in the way of survival. "How does his situation affect Lady Julienne?"

"Lady Julienne?" Marchant repeated, his gaze clearly perplexed through his gold-rimmed spectacles. "She's just begun her first Season, which is remarkable only for the timing of it—she's twenty. Why she waited until now to come out is anyone's guess. She has a respectable portion, but the amount is rumored to be unremarkable. Any serious suitor for her hand will accept responsibility for her brother's future debts. Quite frankly, she'll need to marry for money, but that shouldn't be a problem. She's very popular, has excellent lineage, and boasts great beauty."

Lucien leaned back in his chair. "Who is sponsoring her Season?"

"Her godmother, the Marchioness of Canlow." Marchant frowned. "Why this interest in Lady Julienne?"

Preferring to keep his thoughts to himself, Lucien said nothing.

"No," Marchant said suddenly. "Leave the girl alone."

"Beg your pardon?"

"I've seen that look on your face before. Stick with your

demimondaines and bored aristocrats' wives. Lady Julienne has had a rough time of it. Her brother became Montrose at the tender age of nine and has proven to be ill-equipped for the responsibility. She must marry well. Don't ruin it for her."

On any other occasion, Lucien might have found the warning amusing. But this was no laughing matter.

His blasted conscience was to blame for his predicament. He should have fucked Julienne when he had the opportunity and sated his craving. Not even the past three nights of outright debauchery had relieved his desire. Instead he felt soiled. The emotionless encounters had been sad, sordid imitations of the sweet pleasure he'd shared with Julienne.

"Stay out of my affairs," he growled.

"It's my job to manage your affairs," Marchant retorted.

"I don't pay you to censure my behavior."

"You overpay me, Lucien. Allow me to earn my wages."

Lucien shot him a dark glance. "Why the concern for a woman you've never met?"

"I have met her." Marchant smiled at his surprise. "A few months ago, you sent me to the earl's home regarding his growing balance at the club. Montrose was away, but Lady Julienne invited me in for tea, despite my purpose for being there. She was charming and genuine, a true lady. I liked her immensely."

In spite of himself, Lucien smiled. Julienne saw the individual goodness in everyone she met. One couldn't help but bask in the glow of her regard.

"I have no intention of ruining her, Harold."

"I'm relieved to hear that."

"In fact, I'd like to help her. Hire someone to find Montrose. I want to know where he is."

"As you wish." Marchant rose to his feet. "Anything else you require?"

Lucien was silent for a moment. "Yes. I want you to compile a list of suitable marriage prospects for Lady Julienne. Rich, titled gentlemen, neither too old nor too young. Attractive, if possible. And research their backgrounds. No one with any odd fetishes or disagreeable personalities. No one who smells or has uncontrollable vices."

Marchant stood dumbfounded, with mouth agape, the first time in Lucien's memory the man-of-affairs was rendered speechless.

And Lucien was so bloody miserable, he couldn't even enjoy it.

Chapter Five

Julienne drank in the sight of Lucien Remington like a woman dying of thirst. He was stunning in black evening attire, his raven hair and remarkable eyes shining under the chandeliers, his golden skin in sharp contrast to the snowy white of his waistcoat and cravat. She'd thought of him constantly over the last week, wondered what he was doing, whom he was seeing. She suspected she was besotted, which would be the worst sort of foolishness.

"Julienne." Aunt Eugenia tugged on her arm. "Lord Fontaine is heading this way."

She turned her head and watched the marquess approach her with his slow, sultry stride. Greek god handsome, Fontaine was every bit the experienced rake. At the prime age of three and twenty, the young marquess had determined he was in need of a wife, and Julienne appeared to be on his list of suitable prospects. She pasted a sunny smile on her face and queried under her breath, "Are you certain he's kind enough to help Hugh?"

Eugenia maintained her pleasant expression as she whispered back, "Kindness would be a bonus. I can tell you he's wealthy enough. Just remember, a woman can usually get what she desires from a man with the right amount of charm and compromise."

Julienne wrinkled her nose. She didn't want to charm a man into being kind; she wanted him to be that way naturally. She hoped to find someone knowledgeable enough to set Hugh on the path to maturity and financial independence. She felt certain that with the proper guidance, her brother could be turned around. But the hand that guided him had to be compassionate as well as firm.

Lord Fontaine bowed before her. He claimed her outstretched hand and brushed a kiss across the back of her glove. "Lady Julienne, your beauty steals the breath from me."

"And you, Lord Fontaine, are especially dashing this evening."

Allowing her mind to drift, Julienne bantered the standard social pleasantries without thought. She was relieved when he asked her to stroll around the dance floor. As they began to walk, she saw Lucien take the hand of a beautiful brunette known for her scandalous liaisons. Her heart clenched. Their dark beauty as a couple was striking.

She stared, but Lucien never once turned to catch her eye. In fact, he hadn't spared her a glance all evening.

Fontaine followed her gaze and snorted. "That Remington mongrel is a blight on Society. I have no notion why he continues to receive invitations."

"Lord Fontaine!" Julienne was astonished by his rudeness. He offered a dashing smile, but she suddenly found him less than charming.

"His kind has no business mingling with First Society. It taints us all."

She stiffened, and Fontaine easily adjusted his steps to compensate. Knowing it would be proper to hold her tongue, she still couldn't manage it. "Mr. Remington has made a fortune for himself with hard work and determination. I would think that would be cause for admiration."

"I admire his ability to make money, Lady Julienne," he conceded, "but the manners in which he does so are vulgar. He's nothing more than a domesticated pirate, and his . . . *per-*

sonal deportment leaves much to be desired. Lucien Remington is no gentleman."

Julienne stopped abruptly, causing Fontaine to stumble. Lean and sinewy, he recovered quickly.

"I find your comments offensive, my lord."

Fontaine frowned. With a firm hand, he urged her forward again. "I apologize if I have offended. I merely stated the truth."

"Are you that well acquainted with him?" she challenged.

"Now . . . I wouldn't say that."

"Then perhaps there are hidden depths to his character of which you are unaware."

Her gaze drifted to Lucien as they passed him. He engaged his companion with singular attention. He'd found his latest conquest. And here she was defending his character like a lovesick ninny.

"You appear flushed, Lady Julienne," Fontaine murmured.

She was furious with herself, but certainly couldn't say so. "I'm a little warm."

With a mischievous smile, he led her neatly out a nearby set of French doors and came to a stop on the balcony. "Better?"

A reluctant smile tugged at her lips. Fontaine *was* remarkably handsome and charming, if a little on the wrong side of arrogant. She wondered if, given the chance, he could incite her to the heights of passion Lucien had. She felt nothing for him at the moment besides a slight irritation, but perhaps an attraction could grow. In any case, she could not continue to pine for a man who was never meant to be hers. "Will you escort me through the garden, my lord?"

He arched a brow. "Should we find your chaperone before proceeding?"

"Would you prefer that we did?" she asked, knowing she should insist they find Aunt Eugenia, but more concerned about fleeing the sight of Lucien and his lover.

He tucked her hand in the crook of his elbow. "I promise to be on my best behavior."

As they strolled along the nearby gravel paths, she forced herself to relax and to enjoy the slight evening breeze. They found a small bench in viewing distance of the manse and sat down. Fontaine turned to her, taking both of her hands in his. "I would be delighted, Lady Julienne, if you would allow me to escort you to the Derby at Epsom next week."

Julienne knew that to be seen with the handsome marquess at such a public gathering would solidify his courtship in the eyes of Society. "Lord Fontaine—"

"Justin, please."

She was stunned. His offer was an intimate gesture. He could probably count on one hand the number of people who called him by his given name rather than his title.

"Very well . . . Justin." She took a deep breath. She could also offer intimate gestures. Lucien could not be allowed to ruin her for every other man. Certainly she had not ruined him for other women. "I would greatly appreciate it if you would kiss me."

Fontaine looked understandably surprised, then wary, before grinning with delight. If they were caught, it could be a disaster for her. He would either offer marriage to save her reputation, or he would walk away. As a powerful marquess, Fontaine could not be forced into anything, certainly nothing as drastic as marriage, but at the moment she felt reckless, her stung pride and aching heart goading her to further foolishness.

"With pleasure," he murmured, drawing her closer.

Julienne closed her eyes and prayed for passion. His mouth brushed across hers, featherlight and fleeting. The exchange was not the least distasteful—it was actually quite pleasant—but it was sadly lacking in any combustible qualities. Her heart didn't race, her breath didn't catch. But then she hadn't really expected otherwise.

She opened her eyes and hid her disappointment with a smile. "I would very much appreciate your escort to the Derby, my lord."

"Was that a test, Lady Julienne? And if so, might I safely assume I passed?"

Julienne couldn't tell him the truth, so she simply kept smiling. Thankfully, Fontaine didn't press her further. He stood and held out his arm, but she demurred. "Go ahead, please. I want a moment to catch my breath before I return to the ballroom."

"I cannot leave you out here alone," he said.

But she insisted.

Fontaine stood indecisively for a moment, but in the end his desire to earn her regard won out. He gave a courtly bow and kissed the back of her hand. "I will inform Lady Whitfield of your whereabouts."

When she was alone, Julienne acknowledged that it was time to abandon her dream of a grand passion. She couldn't go about kissing men while thinking of Lucien. She needed to marry, and she couldn't afford to be picky. No one in the *ton* married for love or any other elevated emotion, and it was futile to long for her marriage to be different.

"You kissed him!"

Standing, she turned her head toward the low, accusatory voice.

Lucien.

Lucien kept his fisted hands behind his back. It was bad enough he'd barely restrained himself from beating a marquess to a bloody pulp, but to allow Julienne to see how much he cared would be the worst sort of folly. She'd obviously moved past their one night together, while he had not. He couldn't allow her to discover how completely smitten he was.

He'd been watching her all evening. She bore his mark, although only he knew it. There was a new knowledge in her dark eyes, a subtle swing to her hips, a deeper color to her lips, that said she'd experienced passion. Julienne had always been alluring, but now . . . now he could hardly restrain himself from sweeping her into his arms, carrying her away, and fucking her until neither one of them could move.

He'd heard her defend his honor to Fontaine when they passed by him, and her obvious irritation with the marquess had touched him as few things in his life ever had. Lucien knew he was too bold and aggressive to be accepted in the upper tier of Society, but he was too rich to mingle anywhere else. Men envied his business acumen and enjoyed the comforts of membership in his club. Women liked him for his pretty face and sexual appetite. Somehow between the two genders he was invited everywhere, but fit in nowhere.

Except for those all-too-brief hours he'd spent with Julienne. He'd fit then. Perfectly.

Lucien had followed her out to the garden, wanting desperately to claim her, and instead had watched her kiss Fontaine. And now she sat dreamy-eyed on the bench, while acidic jealousy ate at him.

"Yes," she admitted. "I kissed him."

"Why?" He had no right to ask, but he was unable to stop himself.

She smiled—the same sweet, open smile that said she saw things in him worth seeing. "I wanted to know if it would feel the same as when you kissed me."

He wasn't certain what he had expected her to say, but it definitely wasn't that. Satisfaction filled him. She'd been thinking of him, even while kissing another man. His fists unclenched. "And did it?"

She shrugged. "Well, I don't know. It's been a sennight since you kissed me. My memory may be faulty."

He reached for her hand and pulled her into the shadows. Staring down at her upturned face, his heart ached at her beauty and the trust she gave him so readily. His voice was husky when he whispered, "Allow me to remind you." Lowering his head, Lucien kissed her deeply, making no attempt to hide his desire, determined to erase from her memory any thought of another man's lips on hers.

Only a week since he'd held her, yet it seemed like an eternity.

Julienne returned his kiss with similar passion, her hands slipping inside his jacket and caressing his back. Her tongue brushed across his, and he tasted her sweetness. Nothing in the world quenched his thirst like the taste of her mouth.

"Did it feel like this when he kissed you?" he asked.

She moaned. "Dear God, no."

He thrust his thigh between her legs and lifted her against it. Her eyes were closed, her head thrown back, her lips wet and swollen from his kiss. Only a kiss, and she was melting in his arms.

He must have done something in a past life to earn Julienne's passion, because he certainly had done nothing worthy of her in this life.

"Julienne," he murmured, hugging her close. "I need to speak with you. I don't think I'll be able to talk with you here. You're too tempting, sweetheart. I can't resist taking advantage."

Her smile curved against his cheek. "You are incorrigible."

"Is there any way I can meet with you? To talk."

She pulled away, her dark eyes shining with amusement. "Anywhere we meet would have us alone."

Lucien sighed, hating the class distinctions that would forever keep them apart. "That's true, but perhaps in the light of day, I'll be better able to restrain myself."

Julienne giggled, a wonderful sound that warmed him from the inside. "If you want to speak with me, you will have to call on me. I've no intention of dressing up as a man ever again."

"I quite enjoyed the sight of you in those trousers."

She laughed. "You are a scoundrel, Lucien Remington."

"I've been trying to tell you that," he said dryly. "You should run in terror when you see me coming."

"I'm not afraid of you. I know you would never hurt me."

Her utter confidence in the goodness of his character rattled him to the core. God help him if she ever came to care for him. He would never be able to resist her.

"How can you know that?" he challenged. "My intentions toward you are not honorable."

"Is that so? Then why do you wish to speak with me in a place where you can't take advantage?"

"Why don't you ask me instead what I'd do if you went further into the garden with me?"

Julienne crossed her arms and gave him a chastising look. "Why is it so important to maintain your dissolute image?"

Mocking her, he crossed his arms and raised a sardonic brow. "Why is it so difficult for you to collect that it's not merely an image?"

She pursed her lips.

He growled low in his throat. "Damn you, Julienne! Your girlish fantasies about me are just that—fantasies. I've ruined dukes and then tumbled their wives. I've—" His voice choked into silence, his throat refusing to form the sounds that would drive her away.

Be frightened, Lucien thought desperately. *Run from me before it's too late for both of us.*

Her gaze narrowed. "Because if you were really as wicked as you say, you would have divested me of my virginity that night in your club. But you didn't. I'd wager I could lift up my skirts for you now and beg you to take me, and you wouldn't. You *couldn't*!"

"You innocent fool," he bit out, suddenly furious that she would torture him so. "Never challenge a man's virility. You force him to defend himself in the only way possible."

Fuming and frustrated, wishing she would disdain him instead of entice him, Lucien wrapped his fingers around her elbow and dragged her away from the manse, descending the wide grassy steps into the darkened lower gardens. Julienne followed him easily, making no protest, and her acquiesce only inflamed him further. Finding a yew-enclosed alcove occupied by a marble statue, he pressed her against the cold stone with his aroused body and reclaimed her mouth.

His hands moved urgently over her curves, desperate for the feel of her satin skin. He tugged down the bodice of her gown, exposing her lush breasts. Pushing them up with his hands, Lucien licked a tender nipple, watching it pucker as the cool air drifted across the wet peak. "God, your taste . . ." he groaned. "It intoxicates me . . ."

She whimpered, her hands drifting into his hair, holding him close. "Lucien." Her voice, so husky and full of longing, urged him to greater heights of lust, but he held himself ruthlessly in check, gentling his touch even as he suckled voraciously at her breasts. His body shook with the force of his passion, but her pleasure was paramount, more important at this moment than his next breath.

Julienne pushed him away, presenting a tempting picture of wantonness with her breasts pressed upward by her gown, her nipples wet from his mouth. With challenge in her eyes, she lifted her skirts with a courtesan's grace, slowly exposing her long, graceful legs. Then her thighs. And then the honeyed curls of her sex. She widened her stance in open invitation.

"Lucien," she whispered, a blush suffusing the delicate skin of her chest before moving up her throat to her cheeks. "You will drive me to madness before you are finished with me."

He wanted to reassure her and promise her things he never thought he could promise anyone. But he knew it would be wrong to say such things, to offer hope for a future that could never be. Desperate with need, and angry with her for being the cause of that need, he tore open the placket of his breeches and allowed his engorged cock to spring free.

He would show her what kind of man he was and ruin her for any other. She would hate him when he was through, but that was for the best. "I'm going to fuck you," he promised with savage intent, knowing the act with her could never be so base. "I'm going to keep you pinned against that statue, filled with my cock, until you scream from the pleasure."

With one hand under her thigh, Lucien lifted her leg, opening her wider. The head of his shaft found her, and bending his knees, he pressed for entry. She was so tight, but so hot and wet. She felt wonderful, and her helpless moan as he slid deeper into her made him mindless. His entire body was wracked with shudders as he forced himself to press slowly, carefully. He was generously sized, and Julienne was so small. He couldn't bear to hurt her.

He watched her face as he took her, her features pale in the moonlight, like the statue behind her. Her eyes gazed luminously into his, their depths burning with desire and undeserved affection. She should be frightened, but instead she trusted him implicitly. The way she looked at him made it impossible to breathe. He stilled, held rigid by the moment.

Julienne was correct. He couldn't take her like this, like a whore in someone's garden. And he couldn't make her hate him. It ripped at him to even think of it. With a tortured curse, Lucien pulled away, the heavy weight of his erection slipping from her body. She sobbed in protest, and the sound broke the heart he'd forgotten he had.

With his eyes squeezed shut, blocking out the sight of her, Lucien turned blindly away. His chest heaved with his breathing, his body hard, his blood hot. His cock ached with the pressure of unspent desire, every muscle burning with tension.

Damn her! He cursed the day he'd set eyes on Julienne La Coeur. His hands clenched into fists as he struggled to control the shaking of his body and the torment in his mind.

And then suddenly his cock was drenched in moist heat. Instinctively he tried to back away, but Julienne's hands gripped the cheeks of his ass and kept him still. He looked down, his eyes wide with stunned amazement, as she took more of his shaft into her delectable mouth.

In all of his life, with all of the women he'd been with, in all of the positions and places he'd been, Lucien had never seen anything as erotic as Julienne sucking his cock on her knees in the grass, her breasts spilling over the top of her gown, her lush form turned to silver in the moonlight.

Her attentions were unschooled, innocent, and all the more effective because of it. Her tongue swirled around the head, her mouth pulsing with a gentle suction, her fingertips kneading the clenching cheeks of his buttocks. She pulled her head back and then pushed forward again, her mouth stretched wide to accommodate his size.

Julienne rode his erection with heartening enthusiasm, making soft little humming noises as she sucked on him, and her enjoyment increased his a hundredfold. Unfamiliar with the act, she took him with shallow strokes, but the pleasure was still intense, brought on as much by her selfless giving as the burning that spread from his groin and coursed through his veins.

Lucien threw his head back and growled deep in his throat, his hands drifting into the golden curls at her nape, directing her rhythm, taking care not to completely disrupt the stylish arrangement of her hair. His hips pumped in an unconscious tempo, gently fucking her mouth, as his body sought the relief it could find only with Julienne. Her tongue dipped into the tiny hole at the tip of his cock, and his sac tightened, his shaft swelled. "Pull away, sweet," he gasped. "I'm close . . . I can't . . ."

Julienne ignored his direction and sucked him harder, driving him mad, until he came in an orgasm so intense he swayed on his feet, his seed flooding her mouth, pouring out the depth of his lust and longing. Lucien cried out her name, grateful she held his hips so he didn't fall to his knees and crush her. Blood roared in a raging torrent through his veins, making his ears ring and his eyesight fade to blackness.

He had never come so hard in his life, his cock jerking until he was emptied.

When Julienne rose to her feet, wiping her mouth with the palm of her glove, her lovely face was alight with satisfaction. Trembling, Lucien leaned against her in a weary embrace, sated to his very soul.

Chapter Six

Julienne held Lucien tightly to her, bearing his weight as best she could, her heart light and filled with joy that she had given him such pleasure. She licked her lips, tasting him, and felt a surge of female triumph at her accomplishment. The sensation was heady. Unable to contain it, Julienne laughed with delight.

"You find this to be funny?" he asked, his husky voice tinged with wry amusement. "You will be the death of me."

She grinned. "I made you happy."

Lucien pulled back. His handsome face was flushed, misty with sweat, his beautiful eyes glazed with bliss. And *she* had made him look like that. She laughed again.

"Julienne." His voice was gruff but tender. "You're happy to have made me happy?"

She gave him a quick, fierce hug. "Of course." Pulling away, Julienne began to rearrange her dress, restoring her appearance. She watched as Lucien righted his own clothing. When he tried to reach for her, she sidestepped with a giggle. "Oh, no."

His mouth curved with a heart-stopping smile. "It's your turn, sweet."

She ran up the wide, grassy steps toward the manse, but he caught her easily and dipped his head for a kiss. Julienne savored the heady taste of him for a moment before pulling away.

"No, Lucien," she scolded, even as her heart raced at the seductive promise in his eyes. "You mustn't touch me again tonight. With your reputation, it would not be amiss for you to return to the ballroom looking as you do now, but if I were to return looking that way, it would be a disaster."

He ran his hand down her arm, grinning as he saw her shiver. "I shall feel like a selfish cad, sweetheart, if you don't allow me to pleasure you in return." Lucien bent his head to nuzzle her neck, but she backed away with a chastising wag of her finger.

"Now you see how I felt the other evening when you refused my touch." Julienne turned away and neatly avoided his grasping arms. "Remain in the garden for a few moments. I'm certain my aunt must be frantic by now. You may call on me tomorrow at two. Aunt Eugenia has an appointment, and she'll be gone for hours."

"Where shall I meet you?"

"Come through the mews. I'll find you."

The light in his eyes dimmed. "You're putting yourself at great risk to see me."

"I know."

Lucien was right, of course. But her reputation, so vital to the well-being of her family, stood no chance against her desire to steal whatever time she could with him. "But you're quite impossible to resist."

He grasped her elbow when she tried to move away. "You shouldn't like me, Julienne. I'm not good for you."

"Oh, Lucien." She sighed. She brushed his damp hair back from his face and watched his eyes close with pleasure at her touch. How she adored him, this beautiful, wicked man, with his carefully hidden honor. "You act as if I have more control over this than you."

She lifted onto her toes and pressed her lips to his with a soft moan. "Come tomorrow. Or not. The choice is yours." Turning quickly, Julienne left him in the garden.

* * *

"You look . . . respectable," Marchant said, with wide eyes. "What's the occasion?"

Lucien ignored him. "Did you compile the list I requested?"

"Prospective suitors for Lady Julienne? Of course." Marchant slid the file across the desk.

Scanning through it, Lucien grumbled, "Why is Fontaine at the top?"

Marchant arched a brow. "Besides being an extremely handsome marquess with seventeen estates, hundreds of servants, unlimited funds, and considered the catch of the Season by the entirety of the Beau Monde?"

Lucien snorted. "What about his personal life?"

"He's a known womanizer, but he doesn't gamble or drink to excess. I was unable to find any evidence of his siring any bastards."

"And socially?"

"He maintains his seat in the Lords, and he's held in high esteem by the peerage."

Lucien dropped the folder. Leaning his head back, he closed his eyes, remembering the sight of Julienne kissing Fontaine.

From that recollection came unbidden images—Fontaine holding Julienne and caressing her luscious breasts. Fontaine riding between her thighs, plunging into the silken heat of her, as Lucien could not. Sick with jealousy, he clenched his teeth until his jaw ached.

Julienne was a lady to the core. Lucien knew he could do nothing but ruin her, nothing but cause her to be ostracized by her peers, shaming her, until her spirit was crushed and the affection in her eyes faded to bitter resentment.

"Mr. Remington? Are you feeling unwell? You look feverish."

Lucien opened his eyes. "I'm fine."

"Perhaps you should rest a bit. You've been working too hard lately."

Lucien stood and collected the folder. "No, I have an appointment."

"With whom? I see nothing on your schedule."

"It's none of your damn business," Lucien growled.

"Your attire . . ." Marchant glanced at the file in Lucien's hand. "Tell me you don't intend to call on Lady Julienne!"

For the first time, Lucien damned the high intelligence of his man-of-affairs.

But instead of censure, Marchant laughed. "Are you branching out into matchmaking, Lucien? Or do you hope to collect on Montrose's debt through his brother-in-law?"

"Go to hell, Harold," he growled.

Sobering, Marchant asked, "Are you quite certain you know what you're doing?"

"Of course."

"And what is it you're doing?"

Lucien paused on the threshold of his office. "The honorable thing. For once."

"*Marriage prospects?*" Julienne gaped at him, her dark eyes wide with disbelief.

Lucien clutched his hat in his hands. His throat was so tight, it was hard to swallow. Seeing Julienne's golden beauty in daylight made him think of all the things they'd never be allowed to do together. They would never go for rides in the park or strolls down the street. They could never enjoy a picnic or even the simple act of tea. Hell, he'd had to use subterfuge merely to exchange a few words with her. The harsh reminder strengthened his resolve. He had to remove her from his reach before he destroyed her.

Lowering himself to the chaise, Lucien nodded. "I know your brother has deserted you, sweet. You must marry quickly, and I thought perhaps I could assist you with that endeavor."

She set the folder on the seat between them, her eyes downcast, hiding her thoughts.

"Aren't you even going to look at it?"

"Certainly." She cast him a sidelong glance. "But you know far more about my circumstances than I do about yours. So, before I choose my future husband, I want to discover all there is to know about you."

He scowled. The less she knew about him, the better. "I dislike discussing myself."

"Why? I find you fascinating. Your deportment is faultless, your manners impeccable, your taste excellent. You've obviously had some schooling—"

"Didn't you listen to Fontaine last night? I'm a mongrel, a blight on Society."

"No, you are not," she argued. "I'm sorry you overheard that."

"It was nothing I haven't heard before." He smiled and reached for her hand. "Although I thank you for defending my honor."

The feel of her skin against his was heaven. And hell. He glanced down at their joined hands, hers so pale, so tiny and delicate. Lucien remembered the feel of those hands on his body, their gentle exploration belying her ravenous hunger for him. Knowing he would soon lose her touch forever made his heart ache.

Julienne bit her lower lip. "Why say such horrid things about you merely because you are in trade?"

"'Tis more than that, Julienne." He was silent for a moment, wanting to hide the things she didn't know. But the moment was intimate, her gaze tender, and he found himself sharing the things he discussed with no one. "I'm a bastard by birth."

She didn't even blink. "You have no control over such things!"

"It gets worse," he said dryly, squeezing her hand in silent appreciation. "I am the product of a long-term affair between a courtesan and a nobleman."

"Good heavens!"

Lucien waited for her to put the pieces together. It took only a moment.

"Remington. Your mother is *Amanda Remington*? The famous demimondaine?"

He nodded, and wondered if Julienne would think less of him now that she knew he was the bastard son of a prostitute. A very wealthy, extremely discriminating, and, for the last thirty years, monogamous prostitute, but a one-time whore nevertheless. It was common knowledge. The fact that Julienne knew nothing of it proved once again how far removed their existences were from one another.

"How romantic," she sighed, and Lucien almost fell off the chaise. "You're a love child! How lucky you are."

He stared at her, agape.

With gentle fingertips, Julienne urged his mouth closed. "Your blood is almost as blue as mine, Lucien. No wonder you carry yourself with such pride."

"Are you quite mad?"

"Beg your pardon?"

He shook his head. It was almost as if she didn't see his tarnish. Or perhaps she didn't care . . . The possibility made his heart race, a tiny flame of hope sparking to life within him.

"Julienne, every moment I spend with you brings you closer to ruin. Why don't you see that? I'm a hedonistic, self-centered bastard who has taken liberties with you that deserve to get me drawn and quartered. Beheaded. Hanged. Shot. Run through—"

"Fine," she said sharply, pulling her hand from his and straightening her spine.

"*Fine?*"

"Yes. Fine. You are a horrible, wretched excuse for a man. Is that what you want me to say? Do you feel better?" She lifted the folder and opened it. "I will choose a husband posthaste so you will have no further need to seek me out."

Julienne looked briefly at the column of names, then snapped the folder shut. "The Marquess of Fontaine, it is."

Lucien's hands clenched right along with his jaw. He was ashamed by how badly her words cut him when it was his own ill humor that had goaded her into saying them. Stung, he spoke rudely.

"Fontaine will never be faithful to you. He's just like me. He'll bed anything in a skirt."

"I know." Her voice held no censure, no sadness.

Her ready acceptance of another man, one who didn't deserve her any more than he did, infuriated Lucien.

"That doesn't disturb you?" he bit out.

"Certainly I wish things could be different," she admitted, her fingers fidgeting with the file. "But it's a common arrangement, Lucien. You are lucky to have two parents who care deeply for each other. They've been together for many years, have they not? Your mother and the duke?"

So, she knew who his father was. "Yes, almost two-score years now."

"A lifetime of happiness. Some of us will have only fleeting moments of it. Your birth is nothing to be ashamed of. You have choices, many paths you can take. Some of us have only one."

"And what of your happiness?" he asked harshly.

Julienne's smile was brittle. "I am one of those born with only one choice."

Lucien swallowed hard, his gaze dropping to the folder. He recalled every name it contained, men who were considered his superior because their parents had married while his had not. He had more money than every one of them, more property, more affection for Julienne.

If she would give up her station for him, he would give her the world.

Words tumbled out of his mouth before he thought them through. "If you are so open to having a philandering husband, why not wed me?"

The file slipped from her hands, papers spilling out and spreading all over the floor. She dropped to her knees, scrambling to gather the sheets together.

Lucien joined her, noting the shaking of her hands and her rapid breathing. He said nothing, startled by what he'd asked and afraid to say something that would affect her decision.

Long, torturous moments passed in silence.

"Aren't you going to answer?" he asked finally, unable to bear the suspense any longer.

"Beg your pardon?" She turned her head to look at him, her expression bemused.

"Bloody hell! I just asked you to marry me."

Her lashes lowered, shuttering her gaze. Julienne hesitated before choosing her words carefully. "While I admit to the need for haste, I'm not desperate. I have several excellent prospects. There is no need for you to make such a sacrifice."

Lucien stared blindly ahead. He'd never imagined proposing to anyone, but he also never imagined being refused. He felt ill. Maybe Marchant was right. Perhaps he *had* caught the fever.

He set his hand atop hers, stilling its movement. "I realize I cannot compete socially with your other suitors, Julienne, but financially I can hold my own with any of them." He steeled himself inwardly and then bared his thoughts. "I want you in my bed. I need to be inside you so badly, I'm about to lose my mind, and I'm beginning to think one time won't be enough. It might take weeks, *months,* to rid myself of this craving. It doesn't matter how many women I take, and hell, I've had at least a dozen since—"

"Stop!" she cried, leaping to her feet. "I don't want to know."

Lucien straightened, staring at the top of her downcast head. "Julienne." His voice dropped seductively. "I'm extremely wealthy. I can help your brother, and I can give you everything Fontaine can, except for a title. Is a title so important to you?"

She lifted her chin, her gaze soft and liquid with tears. "No. A title does not matter to me, Lucien."

He reached out and captured her hand. "Then take me," he urged, sweat misting his skin. "I'll take care of everything. I'll take care of you."

"Oh, Lucien," Julienne breathed. "I cannot."

"Why?"

Her chin quivered. "Because I couldn't bear to share you if you were mine."

Lucien was stunned. "But you will tolerate a peer's indiscretions? I don't understand."

"I know." She sighed miserably. "We must forget this conversation. Your friendship is important to me, Lucien. I—"

"Friendship?" His hands tightened brutally on hers. She winced, but he couldn't make himself release her. "We are more than friends, Julienne. My fingers have been inside you. I've held your naked body against mine. You have taken my cock in your mouth—"

She covered his mouth with her hand. "Please, don't be angry. I would never take advantage of your desire by forcing you into marriage. You would be miserable tied down in such a way, which would, in turn, make me miserable. I can meet with you. We can arrange to—"

"You will fuck me," he snapped, "but not wed me?" He broke into a sweat, even though his heart was cold.

A tear rolled down her cheek, breaking him, and he fought back in self-defense.

"You act as if my background and social standing were of no consequence to you, but that's a lie, Julienne. You consider me beneath you. Not worthy of marriage. I'm good enough to fuck, but nothing more." Lucien dropped her hand and turned away. He didn't trust himself to touch her. He might do something completely idiotic—like drop to his knees and beg.

"That's not true!" she cried. "You know that's not true."

He shot her a furious glance, and the sight of her tore at him. Her lush mouth, which had loved his body so ardently the night before, was quivering, and she was struggling to hold back tears.

The damned thing was, so was he.

Without a word, Lucien strode through the open French doors and out to the garden beyond. He heard Julienne calling his name, her voice choked and pleading, but he couldn't go back.

God, how he wanted her! His hands were shaking and his breath shuddering as he mounted his horse in the mews. He was completely undone, knowing, as he pulled away from Julienne's home, that it would be the last time he ever spoke to her.

Chapter Seven

Julienne watched Lucien boldly, uncaring who saw her. After weeks of self-imposed exile, he'd reappeared in Society looking leaner and paler, the skin around his eyes shadowed. He didn't look well, but to Julienne he looked wonderful. Beautifully dressed in evening attire, he stood out from the crowd, his presence so compelling and so uncivilized despite his refined exterior.

Lucien must have felt her regard. He turned his head and met her gaze, his expression altering not at all upon seeing her. He turned back to his companion, a voluptuous and obviously smitten woman of the world. An experienced femme fatale, with flame-red hair and lips, who held his arm and rubbed her full breasts against it, while Lucien sliced Julienne through the heart with the cut direct.

She reminded herself that she'd never had a claim to him. Even when he'd rashly offered marriage, Lucien had never agreed to be hers. But that didn't stop her from feeling as if she would cast up her accounts all over the ballroom floor.

"What are you contemplating, Lady Julienne?" Fontaine asked as he leaned over her.

"I'm thinking you should ask me to dance."

Her handsome suitor's mouth curved in a smile that caused

other women to swoon, yet affected Julienne not at all. "Another dance?" he murmured. "How deliciously scandalous."

With consummate skill, he moved her from the edge of the dance floor and into the line of waiting couples. As the music began and they moved with the other dancers, she watched Lucien lead the redhead to a deserted corner, his hand cupping the curve of her derriere. Dismayed, Julienne missed a step. Fontaine's arm tightened, supporting her, his quick response preventing any embarrassment for them.

"Thank you," she said, with a grateful smile, swallowing back her misery.

Justin tilted his head in acknowledgment. "We rub along well together."

"Yes," she agreed. "We do."

His gaze filled with satisfaction. Their nuptials were quickly becoming a foregone conclusion. Soon, very soon, Julienne would have to explain her brother's plight. Raised an aristocrat, the same as she was, the present Marquess of Fontaine knew the workings of upper-tier marriages, and her situation, while pitiable, was fairly common. In fact, she was almost certain he already knew of her brother's troubles.

When the reel ended, Justin escorted her back to Aunt Eugenia before departing for another event. Try as she might, and she did try, Julienne couldn't stop herself from looking for Lucien. When she found him, she clasped a gloved hand over her mouth, containing a sob. Lucien was leaning over his red-haired lover, whispering in her ear and nuzzling her throat, the picture of rapturous attentiveness.

"Excuse me, Aunt Eugenia." She turned away, her chest tight. "I have to sneeze." She moved with haste toward the nearest hallway.

Afraid to go into the ladies' retiring room and hazard running into other guests, Julienne made her way farther down the hall, where unlit tapers offered privacy. She slipped into the third closed door and shut it behind her. For a moment, she was blind in the darkness, but she stumbled her way to an open-sided chaise, where she threw herself down and began to cry in earnest. Arrested by grief, she didn't hear the bolt slide home. When a large, ungloved hand covered her mouth, her eyes flew open in shock.

And clashed with Lucien's furious gaze.

His intent was obvious as he covered her body with his own. Removing his hand, he replaced it with his lips, his wonderful scent overpowered by brandy, which filled her nostrils and flavored his kisses. Her heart raced and her chest ached as she struggled for air, her body coming to immediate arousal, needing him like it needed food and water.

Julienne tasted blood as her teeth cut the soft insides of her lips. He tasted it, too, and it seemed to inflame him, his ardor mounting until he took her mouth with savage intensity. A delicious shudder heated her body. Against her will, she arched upward into his cock, wanting him . . . needing him to fill the emptiness he'd left behind.

Lucien groaned at her response, his hands wandering possessively over her curves, the heat of his erection burning through her satin gown. His feet slipped between her own and then slid outward, forcing her legs as far apart as her dress would allow.

Where once there had been tender exploration and affection, there now was only pain and fury. Lucien's hand gripped her breast convulsively, hurtfully, making her wince. Julienne's hands moved off the chaise, sliding under his coat and waistcoat, tearing at his buttons in her desperation to get to his skin. Lucien yanked her skirts upward, ripping her stockings. The delicate threads of her gown popped, protesting his rough treatment. He lifted his mouth, and she gasped for air.

"You've ruined me." His hands shook as they reached under her skirts. "I've been unable to bed another woman . . . since the last time I touched you."

She smothered a sob, hating the thought that he'd even tried, and deeply, endlessly relieved that he'd failed.

"Julienne . . ."

"Go to your whore," she cried, even as she held him tightly to her. Even as she prayed he wouldn't.

"Damn you to hell!" he cursed, gripping her thigh with bruising strength. "You're so willing to discard me."

His fingers reached her sex, and he gave a tortured groan. "So wet, almost dripping. Can anyone else make you feel like this, Julienne? Or is this only for me?"

"Lucien—"

"Do you want me to stop?" he asked hoarsely as he slid his fingers inside her.

She tried to pull away, but her traitorous body welcomed him with a rush of moisture. "I don't want . . . y-your anger . . ."

"You want *me*," he whispered savagely. "But you'll send me to another's bed." His damp cheek pressed against hers, his hot breath burning across her ear. "That woman out there—she's desperate for me, Julienne, as mad for me as you are, but she won't turn me away. In an hour, I'll be deep inside of her, and she'll be screaming my name . . . while you rot in your virginal bed."

"Bastard," she sobbed, her hands fisting against his back. "Why are you doing this?"

"Tell me to stop, and I will." His mouth moved feverishly, pressing openmouthed kisses against her neck.

"Go to hell!"

"Ah, sweet," he murmured, his velvety voice filling with sadness, his thrusting fingers never ceasing their torment. "You can't say it, can you? You crave me too much."

Julienne moaned as the pleasure built, Lucien's fingers slipping easily through the cream that flowed from her, pumping faster and faster, making her writhe with the need for more than just this.

"Does it feel good, my love?" He pressed his damp forehead to hers. "Your cunt is so drenched, so hot and tight. I could fuck you properly, Julienne. Ram my cock in you until you scream with pleasure. Would you like that?"

She pressed herself against him, her hips lifting to give him greater access. "Lucien . . ."

He ground his erection into her leg. "You'll miss me when you're married to your philandering marquess." He nuzzled the side of her face. "But I'll accommodate you when you want to be held like this . . . pleasured like this. Wear those trousers and come to my club."

"I hate you for this," she sobbed. And she hated herself for loving him anyway.

"Show me how much you hate me, Julienne. I want to feel it when you come around my fingers."

Lucien reached farther into her, stroking skillfully. And she climaxed on his command, a white hot, exploding orgasm that had her moaning his name. He swallowed her pleasured cries in his mouth, groaning along with her, holding her shuddering body tightly against him.

When it was over, Julienne gasped for air and strengthened her resolve. Before Lucien could pull away, she bucked upward, forcing his fingers from her and throwing him to the floor. She was atop him in an instant, straddling his thighs and shoving his palms under her knees, using the weight of her body to pin his hands to the floor. She drew off her long gloves and tore open the placket of his breeches.

He growled. "What are you doing?"

Staring down at his handsome features, Julienne watched the play of emotions that burned in his gaze. Her hands pulled his cock free and gripped him firmly. Her smile was feral.

"You won't have anything left for that woman by the time I'm done with you, Lucien Remington." She bent forward and licked his bottom lip, savoring his taste. Her hands slid along the hot length of his shaft, loving the feel of him. "I'm going to wring you dry."

"I could throw you off easily," he threatened.

"Ah, but you won't." Her thumbs drifted over the engorged head, feeling the slickness of his seed everywhere. "You crave me too much."

He squeezed his eyes closed with a curse, unable to deny it.

"Did you come when I did, Lucien?" She lubricated her palms and then curled her hands around him. "How terribly naughty of you. But you're still so hard, ready to do it again."

His hips began to pump upward as she used both hands to

stroke him off. "Jesus . . . Julienne . . ." Sweat dripped from his brow, dampening the inky hair on his forehead.

"What a shame for your trollop," she murmured. "I have no experience with male anatomy, but I know you're well-endowed. So hot and huge. My hands can barely close around your cock." She pressed her mouth against his ear. "Like a wild stallion. But that woman out there won't have the pleasure of riding you tonight." Biting the lobe of his ear, she whispered hotly, "You will never be mine, but for tonight, at least, you won't be hers either."

Lucien growled.

His fingers flexed against her kneecaps, and his shaft pulsed in her hands. Julienne memorized the beauty of his face flushed with passion, his gorgeous eyes narrowed and watching her, his mouth swollen and parted on heaving gasps. She stroked him faster, running her thumbs over the slickness on the tip, wanting to give him pleasure. Pumping her fists with greater and greater urgency, Julienne relished the guttural cries that tore from his throat.

She loved the feel of him, soft satin over steel, and the way he liked to be pleasured, hard and primitive. His entire body tensed beneath her, his cock swelled in her hands, telling her how close he was.

"Come for me, darling," she urged. "Come until there's nothing left for any other woman."

He cursed, and then twisted his hips, releasing his seed in powerful spurts across the rug. Julienne continued to attend to him, drawing out everything he had, until her hands were covered in his semen, until Lucien slumped in exhaustion, his body twitching, his breathing labored.

Only then did she release him. She brushed featherlight kisses across his closed lids and parted lips, all the while carefully unwinding his cravat. Then she wiped her hands off with it. She stood and tossed the ruined linen on his chest.

"Good-bye, Lucien."

Glorious with anger, she left him spent on the floor.

Chapter Eight

Julienne collected Aunt Eugenia and left the ball immediately.

She was relieved to return to Montrose Hall. With her emotions in turmoil, she longed for a glass of sherry and a warm bath. As the butler closed the door behind them, their housekeeper approached with a letter in hand. "Lord Montrose returned this evening, my lady. I was told to present this to you upon your return."

"Dear heaven," Eugenia muttered. "What now?"

Julienne opened the missive and read quickly. Furious, she stomped her slippered foot on the marble floor. "The idiot returned to London only to leave straight away for a party."

"*A party?* With what we've been through these last weeks?"

"I will need my cloak back," Julienne informed the startled butler. "And have the carriage brought around again."

"No, Julienne."

She turned wide-eyed to her aunt.

Eugenia shook her head. "Our position is too precarious. Risking your reputation at a time like this could lead to our ruin. I'm ashamed of myself for allowing Hugh to run wild like this, and I'm ashamed that you've been the one to go haring after him every time." She sighed. "I haven't done a very good job of being the disciplinarian, I'm afraid. It's time I corrected that. I shall be the one to go after him."

Julienne leaned over and kissed her aunt's cheek. "You've done a remarkable job. But you'll have to trust me. The places Hugh frequents would make you swoon, and we can't have that."

"Oh, I don't know about that. I was married, and you're just a—"

"Do you know what a dildo is?"

Eugenia's eyes widened. "Good grief!"

"Or the Kama Sutra?"

Eugenia waved her hands in front of her face. "Of course, I've heard of such things, but for you to have been exposed . . . Good heavens."

"See? You're already on the verge of a fit of vapors." Julienne grabbed her aunt's elbow and led her toward the stairs. "I shall see to Hugh."

"You cannot go back to Remington's! If Fontaine were to hear of it—"

"I don't believe Hugh went to Remington's," she said dryly. "He owes too much money there."

"Too much . . . Oh, dear God, we're ruined!" Eugenia shook her head, resigned.

"Now, now. Order some hot tea and settle in. Don't worry yourself. I will locate Hugh, and we'll sort this entire mess out." She prodded her aunt up the stairs.

"I don't feel right about you going out alone at this hour, Julienne."

"I know," she soothed. "I won't be gone long."

"The last time you said that, you spent the night with Lucien Remington!"

"Aunt Eugenia!" Julienne glanced around the foyer in dismay. "Keep your voice down!"

Her aunt grumbled her way up the stairs, glancing down at the foyer indecisively every few steps.

Julienne moved into the study to wait for the carriage, and poured herself two fingers of Hugh's expensive brandy. She lifted the tumbler and downed the contents, coughing and wincing as the potent liquor burned its way down her throat.

Her body still hummed vibrantly from her earlier orgasm, but deep inside, her heart was cold. The things Lucien had said . . . that woman he was with . . .

No. She couldn't think of that now, or she would go mad.

She had to think about Hugh, who was in for a surprise. She was weary of his irresponsibility, and at the present moment, she was furious with every male on the planet.

Her brother was about to discover that firsthand.

It was nearly dawn, and Julienne was close to exhaustion by the time the carriage pulled up to the fourth house. She was relying on her coachman to find her brother based on his knowledge of Hugh's favorite haunts. This was her final stop. If this was not the correct party, she would return to Montrose Hall and wait for Hugh there.

Her footman climbed the steps and made the necessary inquiries. Moments later, he opened the carriage door. "Lord Montrose arrived an hour past, my lady."

"Good." She alighted from the carriage and wrapped her cloak tighter around her.

As she walked up the short staircase, Julienne admired the grand Georgian design. It was large for a townhouse, and the beautifully maintained façade proudly boasted the wealth of its owner. The door was held open, and she swept right in, using the hood of her cloak to hide her face.

She found her brother in a richly appointed billiards room, surrounded by a large and boisterous group of gentlemen and demimondaines. Julienne waited for him to notice her in the doorway, unwilling to risk stepping inside. Hugh laughed at a pretty brunette's witticism and then glanced her way. Despite her hood and cloak, he recognized her. His humor fled, turning into wide-eyed, mouth-agape horror. He left his companions without a word and hastened toward her with his long-legged stride. Gripping her elbow, he pulled her into the shadows.

Hugh La Coeur was renowned for a great many things in addition to his propensity for hedonism. He was a beautiful male specimen, with golden hair and dark, heavy-lidded eyes.

He'd emerged victorious from two duels, and was considered to be an expert marksman and swordsman. If only he'd focus that level of intensity on making money, they could climb out of the financial mire they were in now.

"Jules, what the devil are you doing here?" he cried.

"What do you think, Hugh?" Her voice rose with anger. "You irresponsible, self-centered—"

He clamped a tobacco-scented hand over her mouth and tugged her down the hall. Opening a closed door, he pushed her into a dimly lit parlor. "If Fontaine heard word of your presence in this house, it would be a disaster!"

Julienne pulled her arm from his grip. "And then he might not be inclined to offer for me, and you would be ruined in debt. I can well collect your concern."

Hugh had the decency to flush. "You would be ruined as well," he pointed out gruffly.

"At this point, Hugh, I would find the loss of my reputation to be worth it if you would learn your lesson." She slashed her hand through the air. "Your rakehell days are over. I've come to like Lord Fontaine. It troubles me to think of his money being used to pay for your selfish indulgences. I will not allow him to support you forever. You must do your duty to the title. You need to maintain the estates, make the tenants happy, and find someone you can trust to make some investments for you."

Hugh gaped. "Hell's teeth! I will not engage in trade!"

"Swallow your pride," she snapped. "You have squandered centuries of Le Coeur heritage in less than a decade. Now you must find a way to rebuild it." She crossed her arms and lifted her chin. "And you will start doing so immediately. You no longer have the luxury of parties such as these. You should be home, sleeping, in preparation for the day's hard work on the morrow."

"Damnation." His hands went to his hips. "I will not be dictated to!"

"And you will not whore me out to pay for your lifestyle!"

Hugh was shocked into silence. He was still young enough

that his hard living had not yet etched its passing on his handsome face, but that wouldn't last long. If he continued on his present course of endless indulgences, he would age before his time. But Julienne would fight tooth and nail before she allowed that to happen.

He lowered his head. "Ah hell, Jules. You are correct, as usual. I'm dreadfully sorry for having gotten us into this morass." He ran a hand through his hair and looked at her with suddenly weary eyes. "I'm not suited to being Montrose. I never have been. You have no idea how often I wish Father and Mother were still alive. I miss them, and I had so much yet to learn . . ."

"I understand, Hugh, truly. But you are the only one who can do this," she said with a sigh. "We all have responsibilities in life. This is your burden to bear. I will assist you as best I can and help you find your footing, but you will have to do what is necessary to keep yourself there."

He began to pace. "Have you discussed our situation with Fontaine?"

"Not yet."

"But Jules," Hugh cried, "you have to tell him."

Julienne narrowed her eyes. "Exactly how much trouble are we in?"

He flushed, and her gut clenched.

"Cut to the heart of it," she ordered. "I don't have the stomach to listen to an accounting of every shilling."

Hugh quit pacing and faced her squarely. "It's mostly gambling debts."

"I'm aware of that. How much, Hugh?" She rubbed the space between her brows, fighting off a headache.

"Well, I owe White's twenty thousand pounds and—"

"*Twenty thousand?*" she screeched.

"Hush, Jules!" He winced and shot a glance at the door. "Perhaps you should sit."

"Good heavens," she muttered, her eyes widening. Julienne began to tap her foot in a rapid staccato on the Aubusson rug. "Tell me that is your largest creditor."

"Now, Julienne, I realize—"

"Out with it. We don't have all night."

"We should discuss this at home."

"Oh, no. Right here will be sufficient." She arched a brow. "Who is your largest creditor, and how much do you owe them?"

Hugh's shoulders slumped. "Remington's. I owe one hundred thousand pounds."

Julienne swayed on her feet. "*One hundred thousand?*" she breathed as the blood drained from her face. "To Lucien Remington?"

He reached out to steady her. "Don't faint, Jules," he pleaded. "I'm sorry about all of this, but that bastard Remington kept my accounts open. White's cut me off at twenty thousand, but—"

"No more!" she snapped, pushing him away. "Don't blame Lucien Remington for your weakness. I will not have you disparaging him in any way. Do you understand? *In any way.* He has made something of himself, built an empire. *You* have done this to us. You alone are responsible."

Hugh recoiled from her sharp tone, one she'd never used with him before. "He could ruin us!"

"And who gave him that power?" she countered.

He opened his mouth to speak, but she cut him off with an upraised hand. "I'm exhausted, and I don't wish to discuss your problems anymore this evening. Fetch your cloak. We're leaving."

As the door to the parlor closed, the two intertwined figures on the settee separated, and one sat up.

"Fascinating," Amanda murmured, as she straightened her bodice.

Magnus, Duke of Glasser, brushed aside her dark hair to nuzzle her neck. "Not as fascinating as what I have right here," he murmured wickedly.

"Glass, for heaven's sake. Don't you realize we've just met our future daughter-in-law?" She brushed his roving hands away.

The duke heaved a long-suffering sigh and sat up beside her. "We didn't *meet* anyone. We eavesdropped. And it sounded like the chit has her claws in Fontaine. Why would she want Charles?"

"*Charles?*" She rolled her eyes. "For heaven's sake, Glass, pay attention. I'm talking about Lucien."

"Lucien?" he queried, obviously confused. "She's an earl's daughter. And from the sound of it, she's well on her way to being a marchioness. What would she want with Lucien?"

"What woman wouldn't want Lucien? He's the spitting image of you, handsome devil that you are." She smiled seductively. "And didn't you hear Lady Julienne defend him? There's something afoot there. She *likes* him."

"Lots of women like Lucien," Magnus pointed out with a good dollop of fatherly pride. "Doesn't mean he wants to marry them. Who knows if he's even met the gel before?"

Amanda attempted to restore some order to her hair. "Trust me, darling. A woman knows these things. Lady Julienne took a personal offense to Montrose's comments. I can assure you, they've met. You'll see I'm right."

She squealed as she was tackled back onto the settee.

"I've got something to show you," the duke growled. "Right here."

"You look awful."

Lucien scowled as he paced the empty hazard room of Remington's. "To hell with you, too, Marchant."

His man-of-affairs laughed. "It's unusually early for you to be here."

"*You're* here," Lucien retorted.

"I'm always here at this time." Marchant sighed at Lucien's skeptical glance. "You truly have no idea what you pay me for, do you?"

Lucien paused in his pacing and glared. "I'm certain I don't pay you to harass and insult me, so be on your way."

"I have something to discuss with you, Lucien."

"Not now. I'm not in the mood."

"It is precisely your present mood that necessitates my speaking with you."

"Bloody hell and damnation!" Lucien leaned against a hazard table and crossed his arms, his head throbbing viciously. "Out with it then. And make haste."

"I gave you some bad advice the other day."

Lucien arched a brow. "Not something you want to tell me, Harold. One of the things I pay you for is your advice. If it's not worth hearing, I may sack you."

"The employee in me is quaking in his boots," Marchant said wryly. "But as your friend, I must continue regardless."

Lucien closed his eyes and pinched the bridge of his nose. God help him.

"I don't think you should allow Lady Julienne to marry any of the men on that list I compiled."

Lucien's eyes flew open. "Why? What's wrong with them?"

"'Tis not what's wrong with them, but what's wrong with *you*." Marchant's eyes were kind behind his spectacles. "You're lovesick."

"I am not!"

"You are. You're barely tolerable. The employees are avoiding you, the customers are steering clear of your company, you've been drinking yourself into a stupor every night, and instead of going home, you've been staying in your rooms upstairs."

"I own the damn place!" Lucien growled. "I can spend the night here if I wish."

"You are staying in the Sapphire Room because of her," Marchant argued.

Lucien lowered his head. There was no point in denying it. His man-of-affairs was too bright. "You told me to stay away from her, Harold."

"I thought she was merely a temporary amusement. Now it's obvious to me, and to everyone else, that she means far more to you than that."

"My feelings don't signify. I'm not worthy of her."

Marchant sighed. "Will you be able to live with yourself

knowing she is married to someone else? A man you see regularly here within the walls of your own establishment? Will you be able to hold your tongue, and your fists, when he makes use of the courtesans while the woman you covet waits at home for him? How will you feel when Lord Fontaine comes in to celebrate the birth of their children?"

"That's enough!" Lucien shouted, his chest tight with fury and misery. To think of Julienne belonging to another man was too much to bear. If he couldn't have her, he didn't want anyone else to have her either. But that wasn't the way it would be. And somehow, he would have to find the strength to live with that.

"There are some mistakes we can live with, and others we can't. Only you can determine which kind of mistake this is." Marchant turned to walk away.

"Harold."

The man-of-affairs paused.

"Thank you."

"Lucien, darling. Punctual, as always."

Lucien smiled affectionately at his mother as he was shown into her parlor. Shades of pink and mauve embellished with gilt and satin made the room an entirely feminine retreat. Leaning over her, he kissed both of her cheeks. "You look stunning, Mother."

She waited until he took the seat opposite her before beginning tea. "You look like hell," she said bluntly. "Have you lost weight?" She handed Lucien a cup and saucer. "Pining for Lady Julienne La Coeur?"

Startled, Lucien fumbled with his cup, cursing as he spilt the hot liquid. "Beg your pardon?" Setting the saucer down, he stuck his burnt fingers in his mouth.

"I said you look like hell."

"I heard that part," he muttered, wiping his hand on a linen napkin. "It was the rest of it I missed."

"No, you didn't. I met your love last night."

Lucien blinked, his head spinning. "What did you say?"

Amanda dropped two lumps of sugar into her tea. "She's lovely and feisty."

"Julienne was *here*?" He shot to his feet. *"Last night?"*

"Sit down, Lucien. I shall get a neck cramp looking up at you."

Frowning, he sat.

His Julienne? *Here?* In the midst of London's demimonde? He flushed.

"It bothers you that she was here?" his mother asked.

"Why was she here?"

Amanda smiled. "She was dragging her scapegrace brother home."

Lucien stood again. "Montrose is back?" He swallowed hard. This was dreadful. Now Fontaine could pay his addresses.

"Lucien, please! Sit down."

Again he dropped dutifully into the seat. "What happened?" he asked hoarsely, fighting off a mild panic.

"She was quite firm with him, scolding him and ordering him to start accepting his responsibilities."

Lucien couldn't hold back a smile. Fierce, passionate, no-nonsense Julienne.

Amanda smiled over the rim of her cup. "And when Montrose made a nasty comment about you, she defended you. I wish you could have heard her. She was magnificent."

The nausea he'd been fighting all morning suddenly worsened.

Last night. After the things he'd done and said to her, Julienne had defended him anyway.

His head dropped into his hands. Damnation. He would have felt better if she'd maligned him right along with her brother.

This morning he'd been certain there was no more wretched person on earth than himself. He'd believed it wasn't possible to feel any worse.

But he did. Much worse.

How would he ever make amends to her? Fueled by brandy,

jealousy had eaten him alive. Julienne had spoken with Fontaine at length. The sight of them together had crushed him further. They presented a dashing couple—two perfect, blond, beautiful aristocrats. The handsome marquess had staked an obvious claim to Julienne, and Lucien had wanted nothing more than to rip them apart.

He'd determined to make her as jealous as he was, to force her to share in his misery. But when he'd succeeded, when she'd fled the room in obvious distress, he'd followed, unable to do otherwise. The smell of her, the feel of her skin, the taste of her mouth—he'd been consumed by a singular madness. To give her up, to lose her, was nigh unbearable, and he'd wanted her to say she felt the same. He'd wanted her to fight for him, and when she had, when she'd turned the tables, he'd wanted her even more.

"Lucien?" His mother's voice was filled with concern.

He slid his hands through his hair and laced them at the back of his neck. He looked at his mother with a pained smile. "I've made a mess of things again."

The parlor door opened.

"Good morning!" the duke greeted as he entered.

Lucien rose from his chair and extended his hand to the man with whom he bore a remarkable resemblance. "Good morning, Your Grace."

"You look terrible, son."

"So I've been told. Repeatedly."

"Your father thinks Lady Julienne would be perfect for Haverston," Amanda murmured.

"*What?*" Lucien's eyes widened in horror. There was one way for his life to become more hellish than it presently was, and that was for his younger brother, Charles, the present Marquess of Haverston and future Duke of Glasser, to court or (heaven forbid!) marry his Julienne.

His Grace shot a glance at his longtime paramour. "Seems you were correct, love," he conceded dryly.

Amanda smiled with triumph. "Am I not always?"

The duke grunted and bent to kiss her upraised cheek. "I

must depart. Carolyn is having some sort of soiree this weekend, and I'm expected to attend."

"Of course," she replied, showing no sign of hurt or dismay at the mention of the Duchess of Glasser. After all their years together, she was confident in the extent of the duke's love for her and was aware that after the birth of Charles, the heir, he had never touched his wife again. "Return to me at your soonest."

"Never doubt it." Magnus kissed her again.

Lucien watched the exchange as he had often done over the years, but today the scene held new poignancy. It was a harsh reminder that people did not marry below their class. If he were honest with himself, he would admit that the most he could hope for would be to become Julienne's lover after her marriage. The arrangement could almost be perfect. He would not have to marry, and Julienne could have the title she deserved. But Lucien knew he could never share her with another man, and Julienne would never consent to such an arrangement in any case. She took her responsibilities seriously and would never betray her husband, even if that husband were unfaithful to her.

After the duke left, his mother returned her attention to him. "Do you intend to allow Lady Julienne to marry Fontaine?"

"I have no choice."

"Why not?"

"I offered to marry her, and she refused."

"*Lucien!*" Amanda's brow creased with a frown, something she never allowed herself to do because she feared it would cause wrinkles. "You love her." It was a statement, not a question.

Lucien lifted his cup. "I lust for her."

She sighed. "For heaven's sake, darling, I am your mother. You cannot lie to me."

"That's not a lie."

"Surely there's more to it than that."

"Such as?" he muttered. First Marchant, now his mother. Was everyone determined to meddle in his life?

Amanda set her clasped hands on the edge of the table. "Such as why she was so quick to rush to your defense? Against her brother, no less. And one hundred thousand quid, Lucien? You would never have allowed Montrose to become so far in your debt without a motive." Her eyes lit with discovery. "Are you planning to use the earl's misfortune to obtain his sister? Something so underhanded sounds just like you."

"Thank you for the glowing estimation of my character, Mother." But what an interesting idea. He was surprised he hadn't come up with it himself.

Amanda pounced on his telltale smile. "What is your plan?" she queried eagerly.

"I don't have a plan. I was biding my time until one presented itself."

"Come now. You always have a plan. 'Tis how you acquired greater wealth than your brother."

"Mother," Lucien began with quiet emphasis, "I'm not certain what impression you received from Julienne last evening, but I can assure you, she is not in charity with me at the moment."

His mother frowned again. "Do you want her?"

"Of course," he admitted. "I just don't know in what way I want her. Or for how long, which is why she refused my suit." Of course, he'd botched the entire affair by accusing her of things she wasn't capable of and then storming out . . .

"Tell me what was said, and I'll tell you where you erred."

He laughed. "Why is the mistake assumed to be mine?"

She leaned forward, and Lucien was caught by the earnest intensity of her voice. "You deserve to be happy. If Lady Julienne makes you happy, you should fight to the death for her. You *are* worthy of a highborn bride. Never doubt that."

"I'm not worthy of Julienne." There was no bitterness in his voice, just quiet resignation.

Raw hurt glittered in his mother's eyes. "I am the only difference between you and Fontaine. You are wealthier, you are more handsome, and your blood is almost as blue. Are you ashamed of *me,* Lucien? Is it because your mother is a courtesan that you feel unworthy of Julienne La Coeur?"

"No." He reached across the table for her delicate hand and gave it a reassuring squeeze. "It has nothing to do with you. I've never been a good man, never aspired to be one, and I've been perfectly content. I have no desire to change. Julienne is an angel, the purest thing I've ever known. Agreeing to my suit would alienate her from the only life she's ever known. Eventually she would grow to hate me for that."

"I think you underestimate her strength, Lucien. You may find that you won't make her a lesser woman. Instead she may make you a better man." Amanda shot him a quizzical glance. "Does your bastardy offend her?"

"No." Lucien smiled. "She thinks your affair is 'romantic.'"

"And so it is," she said, with a smug smile. "I liked the girl last night. I like her even more now. She seems a very practical sort."

Lucien arched a brow. "I recognize that look. Stay out of my private affairs, Mother. I do an excellent job of botching them up on my own. I don't require any assistance." He stood. "I have to go now. I have work to do."

"And a lot to think about as well."

He grinned affectionately and ignored her comment. "I shall see you next week."

As her son left, Amanda Remington sat back in her chair and contemplated her next course of action. She knew what her son needed, even if he didn't.

And she would see that he got it.

Chapter Nine

Hugh La Coeur, the sixth Earl of Montrose, paused on the step of his carriage and grimaced at the imposing three-story, columned entrance to Remington's. The morning sun shone brightly on the white façade as various members of the peerage exited and entered the popular gentlemen's club. Behind him, traffic was heavy on St. James. The steady clatter of rolling carriage wheels, horses' hooves, and harnesses reminded him that life was still bustling forward for the rest of London, while he prepared to face his largest and most ruthless creditor.

With a deep, fortifying breath, Hugh climbed the steps to the watered-glass, double-door entrance. A footman in black-and-silver livery welcomed him inside, and Hugh handed his hat, gloves, and cane to one of two waiting attendants. He stepped into the round entrance foyer, with its black-and-white marbled floors, and again admired the massive chandelier that hung three stories up, with a large round table centered below it. A gigantic floral arrangement dominated the center of the table, its heady fragrance permeating every corner of the foyer.

Straight ahead was the gaming area. From there, one could find either the staircases that led to the upper floors—where the fencing studio, courtesans, and private rooms were located—

or to the lower floors, where the pugilist rings were kept. To the left was the kitchen. To the right were the offices of Lucien Remington.

Hugh took one last, wistful look at the gaming rooms and then turned to his right. He walked through the huge wooden door, with its oval glass center, and handed his card to the secretary, expecting to wait. He was surprised when he was announced without delay.

Nervous trepidation plagued him as he entered the sanctum of Lucien Remington. He'd never been in the offices before, and he took in his surroundings with a curious eye. The first thing he noticed was the carved mahogany desk, which directly faced the door. The massive piece of furniture was flanked on either side by floor-to-ceiling windows, and the desktop was littered with paperwork, silent confirmation of the strength and breadth of Remington's empire.

The room was done in masculine shades of deep green, cream, and gold. An immense fireplace to the left was the focal point of a conversation area holding a settee and two leather wingback chairs. Floor-to-ceiling bookcases took up all the available wall space. To the right, sunlit windows afforded views of the street below.

"Good afternoon, Lord Montrose. I trust your trip to the country was pleasant."

Hugh turned toward the deep voice and saw Remington standing behind his desk, his famous blue eyes lit with amusement as he waved a hand toward one of the chairs that faced him.

"How did you know where I was?" Hugh asked crossly as he took a seat.

"You owe me one hundred thousand quid, my lord. I'm not likely to misplace you."

Hugh scowled. "A drop in the bucket for you, Remington."

"True. Now, I assume you've come to repay me?"

Shifting uncomfortably, Hugh said, "I was hoping to make payment arrangements with you."

A black brow lifted. "I see. What do you propose?"

"At the end of the Season, I can repay half of what I owe, and then—"

Remington raised a hand. "I won't accept Fontaine's money. *You* owe me. *You* will pay me."

"Damnation!" Hugh flushed with anger and embarrassment. "Money is money, damn it. Why do you care where it comes from?"

"The point is, I do care."

"If you expect me to pay you out of my own pockets, it will take years."

"I'm not inclined to wait any longer. Either pay me the money, or listen to my alternate proposal."

Hugh stiffened warily. "What alternate proposal?"

Remington leaned back in his chair and crossed his arms over his chest. "I wish to see your sister socially. You will smooth the way for me. For every outing, every dance, every private moment with her, I will reduce your debt by ten thousand pounds."

Hugh's mouth fell open. "Bloody hell. This is extortion!"

Remington said nothing.

"Lady Julienne is close to announcing her betrothal to the Marquess of Fontaine," Hugh pointed out. "Your request could seriously jeopardize his interest in her."

Remington remained silent.

"She's a debutante, Remington, not one of your trollops. I won't whore her out for my debts."

Remington's brows rose, and Hugh colored with embarrassment at the silent challenge that said he was doing exactly that.

"Fontaine offers marriage," he argued.

"So do I."

Hugh choked. "The devil, you say! This grows more outrageous by the moment. Julienne can't marry *you*! She's an earl's daughter, for Christ's sake."

"And I am a duke's son."

"Well, yes, but you're . . . well . . . you're . . . Damnation, you know what the hell you are! It's not the same thing at all."

Remington shrugged, not the least bit perturbed. "Marriage is out, so we return to my offer. You may begin this evening. I want one dance with Lady Julienne. Afterward you can deduct ten thousand pounds from your debt to me."

Hugh ran both hands through his hair before massaging his temples. "She's marrying someone else, Remington. Why not find some other chit?"

"My motives are my own." Remington rested his elbows on his desk. "I'm a very busy man, Montrose. Tell me your decision now—the money or ten moments with your sister. What shall it be?"

"This is appalling."

"Indeed?"

"You've gone mad."

"Quite possibly."

Hugh was dumbstruck, and damned himself for landing Julienne in this predicament. She was correct. It was time to get his affairs in order. "What if she refuses?"

"Then I will allow her to do so. But she must refuse me each time."

"Hell's teeth, this is abominable. You, sir, are no gentleman."

Remington smiled. "I have never claimed to be one."

"I have stipulations."

Remington nodded. "I expected you would."

"Outings must be chaperoned."

"Of course."

"If I acquire any portion of the money on my own, I can buy you out."

"Agreed."

"And"—Hugh flushed— "she's untouched. Don't think to ruin her to force my hand, or I will call you out. In case you hadn't heard, I'm an excellent shot. You would not survive the encounter."

"I accept your terms." Remington's confident expression never wavered. "I will claim the last set of the evening with Lady Julienne at the Dempsey Ball tonight. Don't say anything to her. I will approach her myself and afford her the opportunity to refuse."

"Fine." Hugh rose and took another look around the elegantly appointed office. "I shall never wager another shilling in my life."

"Good idea," returned Remington as he picked up his quill. "I don't like to wager myself."

Hugh gaped in astonishment and then started toward the door, muttering to himself. "Doesn't like to wager. Ridiculous. Man owns the largest gambling establishment in town."

Lucien grinned triumphantly as the door closed behind Montrose. "And I just made the biggest gamble of my life."

Julienne surveyed the glittering ballroom with bleary eyes. Hugh's trips to his various creditors that afternoon had been successful. He assured her of the ready cooperation of all, including Lucien Remington, and seemed truly determined to take his responsibilities more seriously.

Having accomplished that, Julienne could have spent the evening at home and considered the day well spent. But Hugh had insisted she attend the Dempsey Ball. Now it was the early hours of the following morning, she was exhausted, her mind tortured by thoughts of Lucien, and her brother insisted they remain until the end. Julienne tried desperately to stifle a yawn.

"Hugh," she muttered, "I'm retiring to the ladies' room for a nap. You send for me when you're ready to depart."

He scowled. "You promised the last set to me."

"Well, then, send for me just before. If I stand here another moment, I shall embarrass myself by falling asleep on my feet."

"Fine," he grumbled. "Go."

Julienne moved away before he could change his mind. Reaching the hallway, she hid a yawn behind her gloved hand.

She screeched as she was yanked without warning into an alcove. Lucien slid the curtain closed behind her.

"What are you doing?" she cried, even as her heart leapt at his proximity. Stunningly handsome, he was impeccably attired in evening black. She hadn't seen him all evening, and she hated to contemplate where he might have been. "Adding to my collection of bruises?" she snapped.

He had the grace to wince. "Julienne." His voice was low and tinged with regret. "Please forgive me for last night. I was foxed. I should never have touched you the way I did."

She lifted her chin and reached for the curtain. "You are correct about that. Now if you will excuse me."

He gripped her elbow. "Julienne, please. Don't go yet."

"Why not? I think we've said all that needs to be said."

Lucien pulled off his gloves and shoved them into his pockets. The longing on his face arrested her. As his palm cupped her cheek, Julienne closed her eyes and breathed in the familiar scent of his skin.

"I've missed you," he whispered. "Every moment I'm not with you, I miss you."

"Lucien, don't . . ."

"Yes, Julienne. Look at me."

Reluctantly she lifted her lids and met his gaze, the austereness of his features stealing her breath.

"I'm so very sorry, sweet. I never wanted to hurt you."

Julienne fought the tears that threatened. "Allow me to explain something to you, Lucien. Something men of your sort don't seem to comprehend. Women are feeling creatures, at least they are until they've been hurt enough to no longer care. We reserve parts of our soul for the men who are important in our lives, places where trust and respect reside. Once those feelings are lost, you cannot reclaim them. Once they are dead, they cannot be revived." She shoved his hand away from her face. "I've heard your apology, and yet it means nothing to me. You want me to make you feel better, to tell you I understand and forgive you, but I don't understand." She turned to leave.

"I didn't touch her," he said quickly in a voice so hoarse she barely recognized it. "Since that day I came to your home, I haven't been with another woman. I've been faithful to you."

Julienne turned, searching his face, and found him in deadly earnest. "Why?" she asked simply.

"You are the only woman I want." Lucien cupped her face with both hands. "When you rejected my proposal, I lost my head. I'm not accustomed to being denied something I want so desperately. I am so very sorry, Julienne. You don't have to forgive me. All I ask is that you believe my sincerity."

His mouth lowered slowly, giving her the opportunity to pull away. With heartrending tenderness, he kissed away the tears she hadn't known were falling. Julienne turned her head to capture his lips, and she was lost. Lost in his scent, his touch. Lost in *him*.

"I believe you," she whispered.

Lucien's mouth brushed along her jaw and down her throat. "Why are you wearing this high-necked dress?" he murmured.

"To hide the bruises."

He froze, his body turning hard as stone. His hands left her face and reached for the buttons on the back of her gown, his impatient fingers working with obvious familiarity of a woman's clothing.

"Lucien, no," she protested, agonizingly aware of the thinness of the curtain that separated them from the prying eyes of the *ton*. "Not here. Not now."

He dipped his head, hushing her with a kiss. Soon her gown gaped in the back, and he pushed it to the floor. He growled, his fingers brushing over their own prints left in the tender skin of her breasts. "Jesus," he breathed.

Pulling her to him, he kissed her throat. His mouth wandered downward, kissing every mark he'd left on her. The touch of his lips was gentle, reverent. He whispered anguished apologies against her skin, and as he dropped to his knees in front of her, she could feel the wetness of his tears soak through her chemise.

The depth of his remorse, his openness of feeling, his willingness to show her his vulnerability, stunned her. This was a side of Lucien she had never seen. Julienne wondered if anyone had ever seen it.

As he pushed up her chemise, his hot breath ruffled the curls of her sex. She shivered, her blood heating, her heart racing. Lucien groaned and buried his mouth between her legs. Slipping a hand behind her knee, he lifted her leg free of her gown and pulled it over his shoulder, opening her to his ravishment.

Gentle fingers parted her, and Julienne sagged against the wall as his tongue delved deeper inside, licking her as if he savored the taste of her. She stared down, watching him, and her heart clenched in her chest. She could never have imagined the sight of the powerful Lucien Remington on his knees before her, his gorgeous eyes bright with grief and other more frightening emotions. With long, slow, sinuous laps he cherished her. He loved her leisurely, as if they had all the time in the world, as if they were alone and not mere steps away from ruination.

Melancholy welled up inside her. "Lucien," she whispered as his tongue thrust into her. "My darling."

Her fingers slipped through his hair and wrapped around his scalp. His tongue probed deep, and she bit her lip to hold back her cries. The coiling tension wound tighter, and her hips thrust forward, seeking to deepen the contact. She rode his mouth, undulating against him, her lips parted as she fought to breathe. He latched onto her and suckled with expert, gentle force, knowing just what she needed.

Her back arched, her breath seized, her fingers tugged at his hair as she came against his mouth. Her orgasm rolled through her, over her, releasing the relentless tension that had gripped her for over a week. A week in which she'd fallen in love and then had her heart broken.

He soothed her tremors with soft laps, gentling her before rising to his feet.

Boneless, Julienne stood unmoving as Lucien dressed her. He drew her against his chest as he buttoned the back of her gown. When he was done, he rocked her gently in his arms. Never in her life had Julienne felt more cherished.

"It's the last set," he whispered.

"I must go," she sighed. "Montrose will be looking for me."

Lucien nuzzled her throat. "This set is reserved for me."

"Be serious," she murmured, kissing the sharp line of his jaw. "You cannot continue to ravish me in public venues. We'll—"

"I am serious. Montrose is aware of my intentions and has promised to offer no objection. Say yes, Julienne." He kissed the tip of her nose. "I'm an excellent dancer."

"You're also a conceited rogue."

"Ah." His smile stunned her wits. "But you wouldn't wish me to be any other way. Now, go out to the ballroom and wait for me."

Tossing a skeptical glance over her shoulder, Julienne exited the alcove and moved down the hallway to the ballroom. Within moments, Lucien was bowing over her hand. She glanced at Hugh, who scowled.

"Do you wish to dance with him?" he asked, giving her the choice.

"Yes," she breathed, waiting for his refusal and astonished when he offered a curt nod to Lucien.

"How did you do it?" she asked as Lucien led her to the line of dancers with a sure hand and a confident step. His powerful body moved gracefully, and she found herself eagerly anticipating the upcoming cotillion.

"Never mind," he said, grinning. "I believe I'm in heaven. Your taste flavors my mouth, and your scent clings to my nostrils." He closed his eyes, breathed deeply, and sighed.

Julienne blushed. "You say the most wicked things, Lucien."

He raised a mocking brow. "You *do* the most wicked things, my love. Underneath that prim-and-proper exterior is a wanton dying to be satisfied. And I am just the repentant rake to do it."

"Repentant?" She arched a brow.

"Definitely."

She glanced around furtively before whispering, "Do you really think so?"

"Think what?" he asked. "That I'm the man to satisfy you?" His mouth curved with devilish amusement. "Do you doubt it? I think I've proven myself rather well, considering I haven't been able to use all of my endowments." His grin widened. "You do remember what I told you about challenging a man's virility?"

"No, not that." Her blush deepened. "I meant the part about my being a wanton."

He laughed. "You liked that, did you?"

She blushed. "It's a relief to know you find me . . ."

"Passionate? Desirable? Interesting? Beautiful?"

Julienne laughed, heedless of the scandalized eyes that watched them cross the dance floor. "You make me feel like I am all of those things. I thank you for that."

"And you make me happy. So it is I who must thank you."

Her eyes dropped shyly.

"Julienne."

She glanced at him.

"I would like to take you on a picnic tomorrow."

"Montrose would never—"

"Leave him to me."

Julienne narrowed her eyes. "Even if that were true, I've already agreed to accompany Lord Fontaine to a literary luncheon tomorrow."

Lucien's lips tightened grimly. "The day after, then."

She nodded. "If you can arrange to garner my brother's approval, I would love to go on a picnic with you, Lucien."

She knew what he wanted. He wished to say good-bye, and she was touched he wanted to make it a memorable event. He cared for her, perhaps more than he knew, but he would never change, and she would never ask him to. Eventually he would resent her for the marital restrictions imposed on his lifestyle. No matter how much he desired her, desire alone would never be enough to bridge the gulf between them.

However, she refused to think about that now.

Instead she threw herself into the dance and allowed Lucien Remington, notorious libertine, to sweep her away. For this moment at least, she could pretend all of her dreams had come true.

Chapter Ten

He was very handsome.

Julienne acknowledged that fact for the hundredth time as she studied Lord Fontaine furtively beneath her lashes. And quite charming. She glanced around the long table where they sat in Lady Busby's London residence. Most of the other women in the room were eyeing him covetously. But Julienne could dredge up no pleasure in the day. All she desired was to be enjoying a picnic with Lucien.

"Is the food not to your taste, Lady Julienne?" Fontaine asked solicitously.

She smiled. "Everything is wonderful. I'm just not very hungry." She glanced at his plate.

"Liar," he teased. "You want a bite of my scone." He broke off a piece with his long, elegant fingers, swiped some softened butter on it with a knife, and brought it to her mouth. She parted her lips automatically, and he popped the morsel inside.

She blushed, knowing everyone at the table had duly noted the intimate gesture. "I sense a scandalous side to you, my lord."

He grinned. "Does that disturb you?"

"You know it doesn't, or you wouldn't indulge me with it."

"'Tis one of the reasons why I like you so well, Julienne." He took a deep breath. "There is something I wish to discuss with you, but now is not the appropriate time. Perhaps tomorrow I could take you for a drive in the park?"

Julienne knew exactly what he wished to discuss with her, and she knew what her answer would be. But first she had one more opportunity to spend time with Lucien. "I'm afraid I must decline. I have plans tomorrow." She saw the troubled frown and sought to allay his concern. "But the following day would be lovely."

He nodded. "Of course. I look forward to it."

Hours later, Julienne returned to Montrose Hall, determined to spend the evening at home so she would be fresh and alert for her picnic with Lucien. She had so much to say to him, so many things she wanted him to know, before they said good-bye.

She ordered tea brought to her in the family parlor and made her way upstairs with the afternoon's post. Julienne sorted through the pile halfheartedly, until she came to a missive that caught her eye.

Delicate pink parchment, scented of roses and bearing a rose seal, stood out from the others. Julienne opened it curiously.

"Good grief," she breathed when she realized who the sender was. And then she tucked into the letter with gusto.

She'd jilted him!

Lucien stomped back down the steps of Montrose Hall in a fine temper. He still couldn't believe it. He'd never been jilted in his life. "Something came up," Julienne had written in her far-too-brief apology. If that "something" turned out to be Fontaine, there would be the devil to pay.

Returning to his phaeton, Lucien cursed at the sight of the massive picnic basket strapped to the back. He'd never in his life been on a picnic. His staff had been forced to run out and buy the things necessary to put one together, including the basket itself. Even with his foul mood, he wasn't about to allow the fine feast Remington's chef had put together go to waste.

He'd visit his mother and take her out for the afternoon. She would enjoy the surprise.

It wasn't long before Lucien was climbing the steps of his mother's townhouse. Heading toward the pink parlor, he scowled when he heard his mother's laughter inside. *Damnation, she had guests.* Perhaps she wouldn't be available for a picnic either. The thought made his mood even more disagreeable. He opened the door and then stood frozen on the threshold.

"What the devil are you doing in my mother's house?" he barked.

Three heads—his mother's, the duke's, and Julienne's—swung toward him in surprise.

He was somewhat pacified by Julienne's radiant smile. "I was invited, of course," she replied.

His Grace stood. "Afternoon, son. Wasn't expecting to see you until this evening at your club, but I'm pleased all the same."

"I'm not," grumbled Amanda. "Run along now, Lucien, and allow me to speak to Lady Julienne."

Lucien crossed his arms and glowered. "If I leave, Julienne is coming with me. Today was my day with her, promised to me for a picnic."

"You whine like a petulant child," his mother scolded as she attempted to shoo him out of the room.

"You have no notion of the trouble that went into preparing that damn picnic," he argued. "And now it's sitting outside, on the back of my phaeton, getting cold." He held out his hand. "Come along, Julienne."

Amanda glared at her son. "She's not going anywhere. She came to see me, and she's been here only a few minutes."

"She has no business being here. We had plans."

Julienne rose from the settee with her customary grace, and Lucien's eyes became riveted to her. The epitome of the *ton*'s esteemed social perfection, she was nevertheless completely at home in his mother's parlor, and he adored her for that. Dressed in a scarlet riding habit, she was stunning, with her glorious hair piled atop her head and her lush lips curved in a placating smile. As she stepped closer, her scent enveloped him, and his entire body hardened, as it always did around her.

She reached out a hand and stroked his tense upper arm. "I'm sorry I ruined your plans for the day. Perhaps we can still go and take your parents with us."

At the slight touch of her hand, he lost his control and gripped her elbows, pulling her closer. He bent over her, lowering his voice so he wouldn't be overheard. "I wanted you all to myself. I looked forward to it."

She laughed. "My maid is here. She would have come on the picnic, too."

"I might have been able to tolerate her," he muttered. "But my mother will hang on every word."

"What could you possibly have to say that would shock your parents?"

His mouth dropped to her ear. "How about how ravishing you look in that riding habit? I want to ravish you right out of it. I'm sporting an impressive cockstand, Julienne, just from looking at you. I want to take you somewhere, lift up your skirts, and lick you until you scream. I want to put my fingers inside you and—"

"G-good h-heavens," she sputtered, fanning her face with her hands. "Incorrigible rogue."

Julienne stared at Lucien Remington and saw the wicked glint in his eyes. She narrowed her own.

Two could play his game.

Her mouth curved in a seductive smile, and she ran her tongue along her bottom lip. "And while your hands are under my skirts, my wicked Lucien, I would have my hands down your trousers stroking that magnificent cock. You would be so enamored with the feel of my hands, you would lie back and allow me to have my way with you. I could take you into my mouth and suck you. Hard, the way you love it. My—"

"Damnation!" Lucien backed away from her as if she had burned him, the crest of his cheekbones flushed with desire.

Julienne grinned and turned to face his parents. "Would you care to join us for a picnic, Madam Remington? Your Grace?"

Amanda smiled. "My goodness, the heat that comes off you two could start a blaze."

She flushed. Lucien was right. She was becoming a wanton.

"Don't be embarrassed, dear," Amanda said with a grin. "I'm aware Lucien proposed to you. He wouldn't have done so if you were indifferent to one another."

"*Marriage?*" barked the duke. "Does no one tell me anything?"

"She refused him," Amanda explained.

"I should think so," Magnus grumbled. "Fontaine is an excellent catch."

Julienne blinked. "Lucien is a wonderful catch as well. Any woman would be lucky to have him."

"Then why won't *you*?" the duke challenged.

"Yes, Julienne," purred Lucien behind her. She spun to face him and found him leaning against the door jamb, with his arms crossed. "Why won't you?"

"You know very well why!"

"I don't," Amanda said. "Tell me."

Julienne lifted her chin. "He wants me for all the wrong reasons, and when he tires of me, he intends to dally as he pleases."

"Hell and damnation, son." His Grace roared with laughter. "Never tell a woman that before the vows are spoken."

"Glass!" Amanda cried, placing her hands on her hips. "I'm ashamed of both of you."

"She'd allow Fontaine to chase skirts," Lucien said defensively, "but not me. It's not fair."

"That's different," returned Amanda and Julienne in unison.

"Indeed?" Lucien said with a quirk of his brow.

"Indeed?" joined the duke as he walked over to his son. "Explain yourselves." The two almost identical men faced their women with identical arched brows.

Amanda rolled her eyes. "Men are so dense." She pierced

Magnus with a steely stare. "Would I allow you to dally, Glass?"

His face colored. "Hell, Amanda. You'd probably unman me."

"And why is that?" she asked.

Julienne saw where the conversation was headed and rounded the settee. "This is entirely unnecessary. We were discussing a picnic and—"

"Hush, Julienne," Lucien ordered. "I intend to hear this."

"Because you love me, of course," the Duke of Glasser said, with a proud tilt to his chin. "And you're damned possessive."

"There you have it!" Amanda gave a triumphant nod. "And you wouldn't take another woman regardless, because you love me in return."

Lucien stood immobile by the parlor doors. "Are you saying, Mother, that Julienne won't marry me because she *loves* me?"

Amanda shook her head. "What I'm saying is, Lady Julienne won't marry you because *you* don't love *her*. Or if you do, you won't admit it."

"And you believe Fontaine loves her?" he choked out.

"Lucien, it's not Fontaine's feelings that matter." His mother rolled her eyes. "You may be a genius with money, but when it comes to women, you're positively dense."

Julienne had quite enough of this conversation. "Thank you very much for your hospitality, Madam Remington, but I'm afraid I must depart now."

"Like hell." Lucien blocked the doorway. "You promised me a picnic, and we're damn well having one."

"I'm not dressed to go out," Amanda complained.

"Then we'll have it here." He craned his neck into the hallway and yelled for the butler. When the servant appeared, Lucien sent the man to retrieve the basket. Then he looked at Julienne again.

"I'm not feeling well," she said hoarsely.

Lucien approached her with a soft smile. "Lovesick?"

Her stricken gaze met his. "To hell with you, you conceited man."

"I'm already there, sweet. I've been there since I met you."

"If I'm such a source of misery for you, why do you seek me out?"

"You are not the source, my love. My own foolishness is."

Her throat tight, Julienne whispered, "Cease calling me that. We both know it's not true."

With gentle fingers, he tucked a stray curl behind her ear, then cupped her cheek. He brushed away an errant tear with his thumb. Lowering his head, he pressed his lips gently to hers, paying no heed to his parents behind him.

"Lucien, your parents . . ." she whispered, her face flaming with embarrassment.

"Don't mind us," Amanda called out. "Just pretend we're not here."

Julienne's mouth twitched. She rather liked Lucien's parents. "What do you want from me, Lucien?"

"A chance," he said softly. "Keep Fontaine at bay until the end of the Season."

She frowned. "Why?"

"Do you love me, Julienne?"

"Lucien . . ." she breathed, dismayed that he'd asked her so bluntly. "You ask for too much."

"I ask for time to win you." His velvety voice curled around her, low and seductive in its promise. "If marriage to me is something you'd never consider, then say so, and I won't pursue you any further. But if the possibility exists that you would consent to be mine, I want you to give me that chance."

She pulled back and searched his face. "You're serious."

"I am," he agreed, with a tender smile. "Would you marry me if I could change?"

"I don't know. I'm not certain we could be happy together. Not for the duration of our lives."

"And you believe Fontaine can make you happy? How could he, when you are in love with me?"

Julienne shrugged as tears gathered in her eyes. "I didn't

choose to feel this way about you, Lucien. This situation would be so much easier if I didn't care."

"Don't cry," he said gruffly, tugging her closer. "I realize I'm asking for too much. You would have to relinquish the life you know and begin anew with me, a social pariah. But I'm obscenely wealthy and the handsomest man in all of England—"

"Good grief! You remember that?" She blushed.

"How could I forget?" Lucien rubbed her bottom lip with his thumb. "How about a lifetime in my bed? I can promise to love your body to distraction at every possible opportunity. I can give you the kind of happiness you never knew existed. I can buy you things you never thought to have. I can make your life so pleasant that perhaps the condemning opinion of others will hurt you less."

And Julienne knew if Lucien Remington set his mind to making her happy, he would do everything possible to ensure that she was. "It certainly sounds appealing," she agreed breathlessly, her heart warming at the picture he presented. A lifetime with him. It wouldn't be easy, but perhaps it could be worth it. *If he loved her.*

"The picnic is ready," Amanda said cheerfully.

They turned to find the furniture moved aside to create a large space in the center of the room. In the middle lay the picnic blanket and all of the food.

The next couple of hours were some of the most enjoyable Lucien could ever remember spending. His father and mother told bawdy stories from some of their infamous parties, and Julienne was obviously both scandalized and fascinated by the tales. The food was wonderful, as he'd known it would be, and the company delightful, surrounded as he was by the people who meant the most to him.

He was extremely disappointed when it came time for Julienne to bid farewell. Lucien escorted her to her mount and watched her until she rode out of sight, accompanied by her maid and two of his mother's groomsmen.

When he reentered the parlor, he saw his parents, arms

around each other, looking out the window. Amanda turned her head to look at him. "We really like her, Lucien."

He smiled. "Everyone does."

She walked over to her escritoire and returned with a letter. "Look at her acceptance of my invitation to tea. So gracious and sweet. The king could not have received a more respectful response."

Lucien glanced down at the missive and nodded. "She has a way of making people feel worthy."

"She adores you. She's too innocent to hide it."

His grin widened. "She's looked at me in that fashion since the moment I laid eyes on her." He ran a hand through his hair. "And I've been a complete idiot where she's concerned from the very beginning. I've said and done things I deeply regret."

"You're in love, son," commiserated Magnus. "It makes fools of all men."

You're in love.

"I'm not—" Lucien began, and then he fell silent, frowning.

His father arched a brow. His mother smiled.

Damn it, was he in love? A man would know if such a thing happened to him, wouldn't he?

But . . . perhaps . . . Perhaps what he felt wasn't lust at all. Though that had to be part of it, or maybe it was because of it. Who could tell? He certainly couldn't—he'd never been in love before.

Still, love would explain his odd behavior—his strange and unaccountable anger, his jealousy, and his inability to be aroused by any other woman. Love could be the reason why he thought of her all the time, why he missed her unbearably, why he dreamed of her every night.

He *loved* Lady Julienne La Coeur.

Lucien's hand gripped the back of a nearby chair for support.

"Goodness, Glass," his mother scolded as she took in his

condition. "You have no tact. You don't just thrust a revelation like that on someone. Can't you see Lucien's in shock?"

"How in hell can a man not know when he's in love?" Magnus complained.

Amanda shook her head.

Lucien laughed, an odd, slightly wondering chuckle. "I *do* love her," he breathed. "All these weeks of torture, and we could have been together."

"Why don't you simply tell her how you feel?" Amanda asked.

"I will." He firmed his resolve. "And I'll prove it to her."

"You don't have a lot of time," Magnus pointed out. "Fontaine is champing at the bit."

Lucien grit his teeth. "I know. But Julienne promised me she would keep him waiting until the end of the Season."

"That's only a few weeks away," his mother reminded. "You mustn't lose her, Lucien. You'll regret it forever."

"Don't worry, Mother." He hadn't achieved his success through good fortune. He'd worked hard for it, and he would work hard for Julienne. "I won't."

Chapter Eleven

"You must be bored stiff."

Julienne looked up from her book and hid a smile. Curled up in a settee in Lucien's office, she watched him surreptitiously while he worked. "What gave you that impression?" she asked.

He was in the middle of purchasing a mill, which would be the cornerstone of several new ventures, and the acquisition was taking up all of his time. She hadn't seen him in two days and finally decided to simply show up unannounced at Remington's. By bringing her abigail with her, she'd deflected any suspicion on Aunt Eugenia and Hugh's parts, and she'd snuck in through the kitchens to avoid being seen. Lucien came for her immediately, dispatching her maid for a tour of the establishment before taking Julienne to his office. She had insisted he work, apologizing profusely for disturbing him, despite his assurances that her interruption was welcome.

"You're too quiet," he said. "And I'm certain you didn't come here to watch me work."

Lucien had removed his jacket and rolled up his shirtsleeves. Something about his casualness and absorption in his task made her hot. The sight of his bare forearms and strong hands made her ache. The way he muttered over contracts filled her with contentment. After years of watching Hugh struggle with money, she admired Lucien's easy handling of it.

A "domesticated pirate" is what Fontaine had called him. Julienne agreed and found it thrilling.

"I quite enjoy watching you work," she murmured.

"Is that so?" Lucien grinned and set aside his quill. "I quite enjoy having you here. I wasn't certain I could accomplish much with you so close at hand, but actually I find your presence quite stimulating."

"That's because you're a scoundrel."

Leaning back in his chair, he asked, "How are things progressing with Fontaine?"

Julienne shrugged. "Yesterday he took me to the Royal Academy of Art. He wishes to ask Montrose permission to pay his addresses and asked if I was open to his interest."

Lucien stiffened. *Not yet.* "What did you say, my love?"

She picked restlessly at her skirt. "I asked him if he loved me."

Lucien swallowed hard. "And how did he reply?"

"He believes he can grow to love me, given the time."

"Did you tell him you would accept his suit?"

Julienne met his gaze with a reproving frown. "You know I would not be here with you if I had. I asked him to wait until the end of the Season, as you and I discussed."

"He must have been curious as to your reasons."

"Of course. I told him there was the possibility that someone I cared for could grow to love me as well, and I wanted to allow the other man sufficient opportunity to do so."

"Bloody hell," Lucien muttered, with a rueful laugh. "I've always loved your honesty, but for Christ's sake, did you have to be so blunt with him? No man wants to hear he's running in second place." He grinned suddenly. "But finding out he's first is very pleasant."

"I told him he shouldn't settle for anything less than love either. He admired my honesty and agreed to respect my wishes." She bit her bottom lip. "He did say he would put up a fight."

Lucien was tempted to reveal his feelings, but feared Julienne would think he was only trying to outmaneuver Fontaine. So instead he rose from his desk and locked the door. He moved to sit beside her and took her hands in his. "Sweetheart, any man would fight for you. *I* intend to fight for you."

She gave him an arch look. "It's extremely disheartening to know that the two men who wish to marry me find falling in love with me such a chore."

"Sometimes it takes a man a while to realize he's found what he didn't even know he was looking for."

"Ha," she scoffed. "Pretty it up all you like. It will not change the cold, hard facts."

Lucien pulled her hand to his throbbing erection. "It's definitely hard, love." He grinned. "But it's not cold."

Julienne's eyes widened just before she laughed with delight. "Lucien Remington, you are without a doubt the most lascivious man I have ever met."

He pressed his lips to her throat. "That's partly your fault. You tempt me constantly, and it's been a while since I last found any relief."

"Shall I relieve you, darling?" she asked in a breathless whisper. "I would love to." She gave his cock a firm squeeze.

"Jesus." Lucien buried his face in her neck with a tortured groan. "You are perfect for me. Surely you see that."

"I'm not the one you have to convince." She placed her hands against his chest and pressed him backward, crawling over him with a playful glint in her dark eyes. "But allow me to give you some added things to consider."

"Such as?"

"Such as how the sight of you at your desk makes my heart race."

He arched a brow.

"And the way you look with your shirtsleeves rolled up." She licked her bottom lip. "Why, it inspires positively carnal feelings in me."

"Carnal feelings?" His eyes widened, even as his cock swelled further. Lord above, how he loved this woman.

"Yes." Cool fingertips brushed his hair back from his face. "And your hair. I just love it. It's thick and soft like spun silk."

Just as she stretched her body along his, someone tried the knob and then knocked on the door. "Mr. Remington?"

"Go away!" he growled, "if you'd like to remain employed." Lucien raised his head to capture Julienne's lips, slipping his tongue between them to taste her sweetness.

There was a weighted pause. "Yes, sir, but Lord Fontaine respectfully requests a moment of your time."

Julienne slid off of him in an instant. Lucien glanced at the door and saw the dark outline of his secretary through the oval-shaped watered glass.

"Good heavens! What does he want?" She glanced down at him. "And what horrid timing."

"Fontaine is a damned nuisance," he complained.

"Hush, or he'll hear you." She bent over and picked up her book. Before she could turn away, he grabbed her wrist and drew her to him, kissing her with deep possessiveness.

"Umm . . . Mr. Remington . . . sir?" inquired the secretary hesitantly.

"Give me one damned bloody minute!" he yelled.

"Of course, sir," came the obviously shaken voice.

"What a horrid temper you have, Lucien Remington," Julienne teased as she opened the hidden panel in the wall. She stopped before she made her way upstairs. "You know, one of these days I would like to see your home. Your taste is excellent, I would wager it's one of the finest in London."

Lucien ran a hand through his hair to restore some order to the disheveled locks. "Marry me, and my home will be yours." He gestured around him. "Everything I have can be yours."

"It's your heart I want." She blew him a kiss before she shut the panel behind her.

Taking a deep breath, Lucien unlocked the door and returned to his desk. The flushed secretary came in bearing Fontaine's card, and a moment later returned with Lord Fontaine.

As the marquess entered, Lucien reluctantly admitted that

the peer was a formidable opponent for Julienne's hand. Fontaine radiated aristocratic privilege from every pore. Tall, with the light-footed grace of a predatory cat, he had an austere, golden beauty. Dressed in light taupe trousers, with matching striped silk waistcoat and brown jacket, he was an impressive sight.

Fontaine settled into a chair and glanced around Lucien's office. "Impressive, Mr. Remington."

"What can I do for you, my lord? I was"—he paused a moment in delicious remembrance—"wrapped up in something important."

"So I gathered," the marquess drawled, with caustic amusement. "I shall get to the point straight away."

"I wish you would."

Fontaine crossed his ankle over his knee, settling into the chair with casual arrogance. "I'm here to pay Lord Montrose's debt to your club."

Lucien kept his face impassive as he rose and went to the sideboard. "Care for a brandy?"

"Thank you," Fontaine said. "I would."

Lucien poured two rations. "Did Montrose send you?"

Fontaine took the offered snifter before answering. "No, but I will have to settle the debt eventually. I would rather see to it now."

Lucien resumed his seat and spun his snifter slowly between his hands. "It is not your responsibility."

"You've never quibbled before, Remington. I have it on good authority that you will take a payment on a debt from anyone." Fontaine's voice turned derisive. "Just so long as you get paid."

Lucien tilted his head slightly in acknowledgment. He wasn't a fool. Money was money, and he never turned it down, especially when it was his own being returned to him. "This situation is different. I've already made arrangements with Montrose. Your assistance is not required, nor is it welcome."

Fontaine's eyes narrowed. "Why are you so eager to hold his debt?"

"Why are you so eager to pay it?"

"I'm marrying his sister, Lady Julienne. I want Montrose's finances to be in order so Julienne feels free to marry without worrying about her brother's affairs."

"Ah," Lucien murmured, with a tight smile. "Shall we be honest? You *hope* to marry Lady Julienne, and you wish to pay off Montrose's debt so she feels *obligated* to marry you."

Fontaine stiffened the instant before he downed his brandy in one swallow. He set his empty glass on the edge of Lucien's desk. "You are the other gentleman she referred to, are you not?"

"I am."

"Are you attempting to buy a highborn bride with a gentleman's debt?"

"I'm not buying anything. I have no hold on Julienne other than her affection for me."

The marquess snorted. "If you had any care for her at all, you would want her to marry someone of her station. Her feelings for you will ruin her life, and you know it."

"Spare me your aristocratic entitlement," Lucien bit out. "I can give her everything you can except for your blasted title. I can assure you, my love for her will more than make up for that."

Fontaine's crossed ankle began to flex rhythmically in agitation. "Well, well. I have always acknowledged your excellent taste, Remington. I see it extends to all areas of your life. But you fail to see that with my title come privileges like social acceptance and respect. Doors will slam shut in her face if she weds you. Will your love be enough to soothe her pride when that happens?"

"Will your title soothe her loneliness when you're warming another woman's bed?" he retorted.

Fontaine flushed.

The two men eyed each other carefully before Fontaine spoke. "I'll make taking her away from me as difficult as possible, Remington."

"I would expect nothing less. But don't forget, Lady Julienne is a very intelligent woman. She will decide what is best for her without any help from either of us." Lucien gestured toward the door. "I think we're done here."

Fontaine stood. "She deserves to be a marchioness, with all the power that comes with that station."

"She deserves to be loved. Good day, my lord."

"Good day, Remington."

Lucien released a deep breath as soon as the door closed behind his nemesis. His entire body was taut with the primitive instinct to protect what was his. Julienne was his. She loved *him*. And at this very moment, she waited for him upstairs. He wanted to go to her and claim her in the most basic way possible. To brand her as his so that no other man could ever have her.

With a sudden ferocious movement, Lucien pushed away from his desk and strode to the door. "I'll be unavailable for the rest of the day," he informed his secretary, then he closed the portal and took the hidden hallway to his suite of rooms upstairs.

As he entered the Sapphire Room, most of his tension fled. Julienne was there, in his element. A small fire lit the chamber. Although it wasn't cold, it added a cheery atmosphere and bathed her in a soft glow. He wanted this welcoming scene greeting him every day for the rest of his life. He wanted to take her to his home, to make love to her in his bed, to wake up with the scent of her on his skin and her hair spread across his chest. His very soul ached for her.

"The colors of this room suit you," she said softly, her gaze soft and adoring, just as it always was when she looked at him. "Your beautiful eyes glow."

His mouth curved in a warm smile. "That's because I'm looking at you."

Her answering smile was fleeting. "What did Lord Fontaine want?"

"He wanted to pay off your brother's debt. When I refused his money, he guessed my involvement with you."

Julienne took a deep breath. "I see."

"Don't worry. He still wants you."

"I'm not worried," she denied, and then she dropped her head. "Well, perhaps that's not entirely true. He's been kind. I think, had I not met you first, I would have been content to spend my life at his side. It's not his fault my affections are engaged elsewhere."

Lucien leaned against the door jamb and crossed his arms. "I want to pay off all of your brother's markers. No strings attached."

"Beg your pardon?"

"I want you to decide between Fontaine and me with your heart, not with your brother's welfare in mind. I'll have my solicitor draw up documents stating all the debts are paid, regardless of which one of us you wed." His voice lowered and throbbed with emotion. "I would give up everything I have, Julienne, to give you a choice."

"No." Julienne rose from her chair. "I don't want you to do that. It isn't money that will decide my mind."

Lucien remained by the door with the greatest of effort. "If I told you I loved you, would you believe me?"

"Lucien . . ."

"Haven't you wondered why your brother has allowed me to see you?"

"Well, yes . . ."

"Extortion."

Julienne blinked.

"He owes me a great deal of money. I leveraged it against him to get what I want—time with you."

She sank back into the chair.

"I warned you I wasn't honorable, my love. I told you I wasn't a gentleman. I'll do whatever it takes to win you. Anything at all. I have no scruples or morals to hold me back." Lucien watched her closely. "Now, if I told you I love you, would you believe me?"

"I don't know," she breathed. "But I want to." She held out a hand to him, and that was all the encouragement he needed.

He reached her in two strides and pulled her into his arms. Heat swirled around them, as did endless hunger. He would never have enough of her, would always crave her. "I need you, Julienne."

Her fingers entwined in his hair. "I'm here, my love."

"Not just now. Forever." His mouth traveled down her neck. "You are mine. You belong to me. I won't allow Fontaine to have you." He tugged at her bodice, releasing her breasts, then laved her nipples until she clawed at his back.

"Marry me," he urged against her breast.

"Love me," she countered breathlessly.

"Sweetheart," Lucien said, smiling, "I already do."

Chapter Twelve

Lucien watched Hugh La Coeur pace behind his desk in Montrose Hall. Unlike his own spacious and airy office, Montrose's study was paneled in dark walnut, with parquet floors covered in Aubusson rugs. With red drapes so dark in color as to be almost black, the room was oppressive and forbidding, nothing like the jovial, irresponsible man who owned it.

Leaning back a little farther in his chair, Lucien released his breath in a quiet rush. Unfortunately, this meeting was going exactly as he had anticipated.

"You're daft!" Hugh cried. "You cannot marry Julienne. It's just not done, I tell you!"

"I realize that," Lucien replied calmly.

"Then why are you here?"

With endless patience, he repeated his request. "To ask for her hand and discuss the settlements with you. I am prepared to be generous."

Hugh shook his head. "Damnation! You can't purchase a bride."

"For God's sake," Lucien muttered in exasperation. "I am not attempting to buy Julienne."

Montrose leaned over the desk, his palms flat on the surface. "Why my sister? Why not one of the other debutantes out this Season?"

"My lord, you are under the false impression that I merely wish to acquire a wife. One of the benefits of being untitled is that I have no need to wed. I am not required to sire heirs to carry on a family name."

"Then why are you here, damn it?"

Lucien didn't have time for this. "We've already established why I'm here. Now here is the proposed settlement." He tossed the thick legal contract onto the desk. Hugh picked it up and flipped through it, his eyes widening. "You keep Julienne's dowry, but I manage it for you. I will make investments as I deem appropriate for the next six months, after which I will turn the balance over to you. I've opened an account in your sister's name, and I've deposited funds equal to her dowry for her own personal use. She will also receive an allowance, the amount of which is detailed in the agreement."

Hugh found the number and paled. "Good God, this is extraordinary. You must be rich as Croesus."

"You will meet with me in my office every Tuesday and Thursday morning for the next six months. I'm going to teach you about money, Montrose. How to make it, and how to keep it."

"Preposterous," Hugh cried in outrage. "I cannot—"

"Hold your tongue," Lucien ordered, in a tone that brooked no refusal. "Your blasted pride got you into this mess. I'll bail you out this one time, Montrose. I've already paid all of your creditors. But I shall have a wife now and, God willing, children. I won't waste their inheritance on you. You *will* learn the skills I can teach you." Lucien watched the young earl flush with embarrassment and relented, slightly. "You were only ten when you came into your title. I don't blame you for feeling overwhelmed. But I won't allow your irresponsibility to continue. It's time to grow up."

Hugh dropped into his chair, the hand holding the agreement falling carelessly into his lap. "Why are you doing this?" he asked, his expression dazed.

"I thought that would be obvious. I'm madly in love with Julienne. You must take care of yourself so she can cease worrying about you and concentrate on me."

Montrose sighed. "Have you already paid your addresses to her?"

"I have."

"Does she return your affections?"

Lucien nodded, his heart still light with wonder. "By some undeserved blessing, she does." His voice softened. "I promise to care for her. She'll never want for anything. I'll adore her and cherish her until the end of my days."

"You'll have to. She'll have nothing else. I will love her regardless, but Society . . ." Hugh took a fortifying breath. "Congratulations are in order then, Remington."

Lucien tilted his head in acknowledgment. Inside he sighed with relief as the Earl of Montrose reached for his quill.

Julienne waited in the master bedroom of Lucien's sumptuous mansion in Mayfair. They had stayed only an hour at the small wedding celebration, both of them eager to return to their own home and spend long-awaited time alone. The carriage ride had been spent sharing loving kisses and plans for their future.

She smiled in remembrance. Who would have guessed the heart inside the rake could be so tender?

And their home . . . Lord, it was every bit as elegant and opulent as she had expected it to be. She was now mistress of this beautiful residence, and she took great delight in anticipating receiving callers here.

Despite Lucien's misgivings, Julienne was hopeful that they would not be the social outcasts he expected they would be. Some very prominent guests had attended their wedding, including the Marquess of Fontaine, the Duke of Glasser, and Lucien's brother, Charles, the Marquess of Haverston.

Fontaine had promised to call on them and to urge his sister and her friends to do the same. Julienne's godmother, Lady Canlow, intended to gather together Polite Society's most powerful matrons to put their efforts toward making them acceptable. It wouldn't be easy, and a positive outcome could never be guaranteed, but they would try. And if their efforts didn't meet their aspirations, Julienne truly didn't care that much. Lucien loved her. That was all that mattered. She'd never wanted a boring existence anyway, and life with her domesticated pirate would be anything but.

The bedroom door opened. She watched as her husband walked in and turned the key, locking out the world at large.

He leaned against the door with a smile. "You're naked."

She pointed toward the end of the bed. "It seemed pointless to wear that."

Lucien looked at the filmy night rail slung over the back of a chair. He grinned and looked back at her. "Are you nervous?"

"No," she denied, a little too quickly.

"Well, I am."

Her eyes widened. "You are?"

"Of course I am. You're the last woman I'll ever make love to, and you're a virgin. What if I bungle the first time, and you never want me to touch you again?" He shuddered in horror at the thought.

Julienne's mouth hung open for a moment, and then she fell over laughing. "Oh, heavens, Lucien. That's ridiculous."

She saw the heartbreaking tenderness in his gaze, which was all the more poignant blended with the devilish curve of his smile.

"Feel better now?" he asked gently.

And then she understood. "You were teasing me," she accused without heat, her heart racing madly that this resplendently wicked man was now hers. Forever.

"Relaxing you a bit," he corrected. "You looked tense when I came in." Lucien strolled toward the bed, untying his cravat. The rest of his clothing was hastily discarded. Then he was pressing her into the bed, his body hard and beautifully built.

"We must set some ground rules here, my lady." His kissed

the tip of her nose. "First of all, I do all of the touching." He covered her protest with his hand. "I've needed you too long; I won't last if you touch me. For the rest of our lives, you can touch me all you want, whenever you want, but not this first time."

He waited until she nodded her acquiesce and then removed his hand, sliding it downward between her breasts, before letting it come to rest on her hip. "Second, it may be painful. You're very small, and I'm fairly large." He bit back a smile at her choked laugh. "But I'll pleasure you, my love. I promise you that."

"I know you will," she said, loving him even more for his reverent approach to her first time.

"And last but not least, I love you, my wife." He rested his forehead against hers. "With every fiber of my being, I adore you. I intend to cherish you and worship you forever." He brushed kisses against her mouth. Slow, sweet kisses that skillfully stoked her ardor. "I thank you for becoming my wife."

"Oh, Lucien," she sighed, and tugged his mouth back down to hers.

With a chastising murmur Lucien disengaged her hands from behind his neck and laced their fingers together. He concentrated long moments on exploring her mouth, his kisses lazy and drugging, until she writhed against him, begging for his touch.

"Please . . ."

He smiled, and her heart stopped.

His mouth moved to the slim column of her throat, licking and nipping the sensitive skin. He began to undulate his body against hers, slow, sinuous movements of his powerful frame, awakening every nerve, making her moan with the torment. Lucien made love to her with his mouth, with his hands, with the gentle friction of his body, murmuring praise and encouragement so sweet she wanted to cry.

"These, my love, are perfection." He lavished long licks of his tongue across her nipples and then blew on them, grinning as they puckered. "There is no greater pleasure than having these in my mouth." Bending his head, he suckled her, the rhythmic tugging pulling at places deep inside, driving her to madness. She began to writhe, yanking at his hands, needing to touch him. Burning, aching, her skin was too hot . . . too tight . . .

"Darling," she pleaded. But he wouldn't cease, wouldn't release her.

Julienne could feel the pull of his mouth everywhere, the sensation making her squirm as her arousal pooled between her legs. She begged him to hurry, desperate to hold him, kiss him, but Lucien paid her no heed as his mouth teased across her stomach with wet, openmouthed kisses. Moving lower, he spread her thighs wide with the broad expanse of his shoulders. She moaned in relief as his tongue finally delved between her legs.

"Yes," she cried hoarsely, her hips lifting, pressing into his mouth, as her nails dug into the backs of his hands.

"You taste so sweet," he murmured passionately, before he thrust his tongue into her, groaning his pleasure. Julienne moved with him, arching and twisting. He worked urgently, building her desire quickly, brutally, until *finally* she felt the first clenches of her orgasm. Her back arched, her body tensed . . .

Lucien pulled away quickly.

"Damn you!" she cried, her eyes squeezed shut as her body trembled with the force of her need.

He laughed softly. "Now is that any way to speak to your husband?"

She opened her eyes as he covered her with his body. "I need you badly," she whispered. "I'll die if you don't take me." Her entire body shuddered, poised on the brink of release and denied.

"I love you," he breathed. And then he was there, the hot tip of him just inside her, stretching her, warning her of what was to come.

Julienne opened her legs wide, her hips arching impatiently, and without further ado he thrust inside, deep and deeper still, until there was no farther he could go. Then he clenched his buttocks and went farther still, filling her, until there was no doubt she belonged to him.

Her breath held in wonder, she felt little of the pain she expected. She merely felt full and hot, her skin covered in a fine sheen of perspiration, her body throbbing around the hard cock that filled her.

Sweat dripped from his brow onto her breasts. Lucien clenched his teeth as he pulled out, despite her protests, and pressed forward again. He rocked his hips against her thighs, slowly working in and out, loosening her.

"Jesus, Julienne," he gasped. "You feel so good . . ."

She shifted slightly, trying to get more comfortable, and he cursed. Startled, she stilled, and he positioned her as he wanted, lifting her leg, opening her, and then he withdrew, only to return with a powerful lunge that made her cry out.

There was no more gentleness after that; Lucien simply wasn't capable of it. As he pounded into her, pinning her hips when she struggled beneath him, Julienne realized why he'd taken such care to arouse her. He'd known, as only an expert lover could, that he would not be able to coddle her through this. He needed her too desperately, had reined in his appetites for too long. Moaning, sobbing, she could only follow his lead, holding still for his pleasure as he stroked his cock deeply within her, almost animalistic in his frenzy.

And it felt so good, she thought she would die of it.

"You're mine," Lucien growled, and he gloried in the knowledge. From the moment he'd first seen her, he'd wanted her just like this. Beneath him, filled with him, completely his in every way.

He plunged into her, gritting his teeth at the overwhelming pleasure of it. She was so hot, so tight, writhing beneath him, mewling, and sobbing his name in a way that made it impossible to slow down or show her a moment's consideration. But she wasn't frightened or timid. Not his sweet Julienne. Her hips met him thrust for thrust, her cream so plentiful his cock was bathed in it, scalded by it.

"That's it," he encouraged, in a voice he barely recognized as his own. He thrust faster, harder, until he was pistoning into her, shoving her up the bed.

And then she tensed, her back bowing beneath him, her cunt gripping him so tightly it slowed his fevered pace. Her eyes flew open and locked with his. "I love you!" she gasped, and then she came, her orgasm milking his cock, luring his seed, until he spilled into her, flooding her, branding her in a way far more primitive than the ring she wore. He threw back his head and growled her name, certain he had never felt such joy in his life.

When he could move again, Lucien rolled, taking his wife with him, draping her limp, sated form over his body. His hands stroked her back, stilling her trembling. He murmured his love, his longing, told her all the things he'd never thought he'd have the opportunity to say. How he loved the smell of her hair and the beauty of her smiles. How he'd dreamed of her and wanted her with a soul-deep desire. How he'd give her the world, because she gave up the one she knew to be with him . . .

"Darling?" Her voice was a breathless whisper that made his cock swell, the sound of a woman well-pleasured.

Lucien smiled at her endearment, pure contentment pumping through his veins. Had he almost given this up? He thought of the infernal list of marriage prospects and acknowledged what a fool he was. Thank God, Julienne had never given up on him. "Yes, my love?"

He was hard again, the sensual heat of her body over his making him lustful. But Julienne was likely sore and tired. He could wait. She belonged to him now. He had a lifetime ahead with her. A lifetime to love her.

She raised her head from his chest, and her mouth curved seductively. "You're so sweet, my love, with your beautiful words. I would never have guessed you could be so romantic."

Her hand brushed his sweat-dampened hair away from his forehead. “But if you don’t mind, could you tell me how much you love me later, and just show me instead?”

With a delighted laugh, Lucien did not hesitate to oblige her.

Her Mad Grace

Chapter One

Derbyshire, December 1814

Rotting.

To Hugh La Coeur's mind, that was the most apt description for the moldering mansion on the hill. Usually the bright white of newly fallen snow brought a peaceful serenity to the landscape. Not so with this property. Even the pristine beauty of winter could not hide the neglect apparent in everything about the place.

He hesitated for a moment, taking in the view with a disgusted snort. Ominous clouds roiled above him, but the sky was darkening for another reason—the day was ending. Thoughts of returning the way he'd come, through the snow and without light, forced Hugh to proceed. If his need were less dire, he'd ride on in search of a more hospitable-looking home. But he was desperate, and the curling smoke rising from the manor's chimneys told him the place was inhabited. Help was at hand, and he couldn't ignore it, no matter how much he desired to.

He tied his mount, one of his prized carriage bays, to the metal ring protruding from a nearby stone pillar. At one time the pillar had held up the park gate, but not any longer. One side of the gate remained upright, while the other leaned precariously atop the frozen ground.

"Atrocious," Hugh muttered to his horse, as he edged his way through the opening and started the long walk up the drive to the main house.

He glanced around with morbid fascination. It was easy to imagine how beautiful the property must have been once, a source of pride for its noble occupants. But fate had dealt a cruel blow to the peer and family who owned the place. It had obviously gone without maintenance for many years. Vines, long dead, crawled over the brick exterior. Places where paint had once brightened the façade now peeled and warped from lack of care.

The wind picked up, and soft, powdery snow began to swirl around Hugh's polished Hessians. His hair blew across his forehead, his hat long lost in a ditch. The storm would be upon them soon. His legs lengthened their strides. He would have to hurry.

Reaching the door, Hugh banged the tarnished lion-head knocker. The sound echoed eerily, and he shook off the shivers. He was an earl, for Christ's sake! The esteemed, if slightly scandalous, Earl of Montrose, an ancient title that carried a wealth of prestige. His station should place him above such childish fears. But frankly, the place looked haunted, and the forgotten air that surrounded the hall filled him with foreboding.

He almost fled, blizzard be damned, when the door creaked open with torturous slowness. A stooped butler, as decrepit as the manse in which he worked, stood in the doorway.

"Aye?" the old man queried in a gravelly voice.

Hugh handed over his card. "Is the lord of the manor at home?"

The butler squinted at the lettering. He lifted the card to an oddly protruding eye and then dropped his hand with a grunt. The servant gestured wildly behind him. "You'll find 'im in the cemetery out back."

Before Hugh could blink, the door was swinging with lightning speed toward his face. Moving with a pugilist's quick ease, he slipped into the hall before the door slammed shut. The butler turned, bumped into his chest, and shrieked in terror.

Rolling his eyes, Hugh steadied the frail man. "Listen, old chap. My desire to be here is far less than your desire to have me here. I require some assistance. If you provide it, I can be on my way."

The butler studied him closely with his oversized blue eye. "Wot ye be needin', gov'na?"

"You may address me as 'my lord,'" Hugh corrected, with a pointed look at his calling card, presently being crushed in the butler's hand. "What is your name?"

The servant sniffled. "Artemis."

"Very well, Artemis. Are there any other men about the place?" Hugh glanced around. "Men preferably capable of physical exertion."

Artemis studied him with blatant suspicion. "'Enry. 'E's a strapping lad wot runs the stables. And Tom, 'e 'elps Cook wiv the vittles."

"Excellent." Hugh released a sigh of relief. "Would it be possible to find decent horseflesh around here?" Even as he asked, he knew it was asking too much, given the sight of the place.

"O' course!" the old man cried, affronted. "'er Grace 'as the finest 'orses you'll ever see!"

Hugh stilled, his mind rapidly disseminating the information he'd gathered so far. His Grace lay in the cemetery, which left Her Grace widowed. There weren't many duchesses, hardly any that were widowed, and only one of whom he was aware who would claim ownership to a sorry place such as this—

"'Her Mad Grace'?" Of all the damnable luck!

"'ere now!" Artemis complained. "We don't take kindly to that nonsense 'round 'ere!"

Hugh cleared his throat. He was leaving. *Now.* "Well, I'm certain Her Grace wouldn't mind at all if I borrowed her—"

"You can't just barge in 'ere and run off wiv 'er Grace's 'orses." The old man straightened as best he could. "You'll 'ave to ask 'er first!"

"*Ask her?* Good God, she's in residence *here?*" The place wasn't fit for man or beast, let alone for a duchess.

"O' course. Where else would she be?" Artemis snorted.

Hugh arched a brow. "Where else indeed?"

"Come along, then, gov'na." The servant shuffled away, stopping only to grasp the candelabra off the console. "You can wait in the parlor while I tell 'er Grace yer 'ere." Shoving open a set of double doors on the right, Artemis gestured impatiently for him to go inside, shoving the candelabra at him as he passed.

Hugh moved into the room and then spun about as the door slammed shut behind him. "Abominable service," he muttered, glancing around.

No other candles were lit, and the grate was cold. Every bit of furniture was draped and covered with thick dust. Even the portrait over the fireplace was hidden from view. Depositing his meager source of light on a cloth-covered table, he set to work building a fire.

Grumbling under his breath, Hugh inspected the coal bucket, surprised to discover it did indeed have coal inside it. Within moments he'd started a fire. He stood and used a nearby dusty sheet to wipe his hands.

Of all the confounded places for his wheel to break, why did it have to be here?

Hugh rubbed the space between his brows, trying to remember everything he'd heard about the dowager Lady Glenmoore. The elderly duke had shocked the *ton* a few years past with a rushed elopement with his second wife. Then His Grace had gone on to compound the astonishment by passing away within scant weeks of his marriage.

It was widely speculated that the new duchess had helped her husband to his final reward. The succeeding Duke of Glenmoore had distanced himself from his stepmother in short order, banishing her to a remote holding, where it was rumored she passed the time scaring the wits out of hapless passersby such as Hugh. The duchess's weird behavior had earned her the moniker 'Her Mad Grace.'

A bizarre noise caught his ear, pulling him from his thoughts, and Hugh held his breath as it drew closer and increased in volume.

The door opened, the squeaking of the unoiled hinges accompanied by the cacophony of rattling china. His eyes widened as he found himself dumbfounded by the vision that greeted him.

A young woman entered, her slim arms weighted with an ancient tea service. The entire arrangement wobbled horrendously, and he gaped at the bouncing, clattering items on the tray. He'd never seen anything like it in his life, and he waited breathlessly for the moment when everything would crash to the floor.

She whimpered suddenly, and the sound galvanized him into action. Hugh closed the space between them, plucked the service from her hands, and set it down. Turning to face the maid, he saw that her entire body shook as if she stood in the back of a cart traveling a very bumpy lane. Pretty, in a plain sort of way, with flyaway brown hair and pale blue eyes, she offered a smile as shaky as the rest of her.

Hiding his reaction with practiced ease, Hugh realized the young woman suffered from a pitiable nervous affliction of some sort, not surprising considering the residence in which she lived and made her livelihood.

She stammered something unintelligible, dipped an odd, crooked curtsy, and fled the room, as if he posed some grave threat to her person.

Hugh shook his head in wonder. Were all the servants plagued with some ailment or another?

Glancing at the service, he was relieved to see the tea had already been prepared. He poured and drank, appreciating the warmth, which chased away his chill. So much time passed while he waited, he nearly finished the pot before the door creaked open again.

Hugh turned to face the newest arrival. He was so amazed at the graceful glide with which the figure entered, he forgot to set his cup and saucer down and merely stared.

Black-clad from head to toe, her face veiled with lace, the duchess swept in with haste and halted just as quickly. She stood a few feet away, her figure short and petite. Because the darkness of her gown blended with the shadows, he could see very little of her, but something about her gave him pause. His body tensed, turning hard all over, and his fingers held the delicate china saucer far too tightly. Sweat misted his brow despite the cold. It wasn't nerves or apprehension that held his attention so completely. No, it was far worse than that . . .

Good God, he was becoming aroused!

Shooting a horrified glance at the tea in his hand, he quickly deduced that the infamous madness must spread through the water. Hugh dropped the cup and saucer on the table with such haste, the remaining liquid splashed over the rim and stained the dusty cloth below.

"Is there something wrong with the tea?" the duchess queried, her voice muffled by the thick veil.

He shook his head. "No. I apologize for the—"

"What do you want?" she snapped suddenly.

"Beg your pardon?" He, of the dry wit and ready retort, could think of nothing more clever to say, his brain feverishly trying to comprehend why his body was ready to mate with an elderly duchess suffering a mental malady.

"Why are you here?" she repeated slowly as if it were he that suffered the brain affliction. "What have you come for?"

Hugh gathered his wits. "My carriage wheel was damaged in a rut. I require the use of—"

"I'm truly sorry, but I haven't the means to help you." She fled the room with as much haste as the maid.

Mouth agape, he decided something truly heinous polluted the water hereabouts. There was no other explanation for this craziness. Flushed, slightly disoriented, and quickly becoming mad as hell, Hugh strode out the open doorway, bearing down on the dark figure who scurried away.

"Oh, Your Grace," he called out with deceptive courtesy. "Another moment, if you please."

Her pace quickened. So did his.

His legs were longer.

She hit the steps, hiking up her skirts, and he lunged forward, catching her elbow. She gasped. He almost did, too, but restrained himself. Her arm was firm and well-formed under his fingers, not at all as he imagined.

"Perhaps I misled," he said dryly. Her lace-covered face turned to his. "I wasn't *asking*."

She stiffened.

"You're ill; I collect that." His gaze narrowed as he attempted to discern the facial features hidden behind the veil. "It appears you are unaware that a blizzard is fast approaching, and this is one of the coldest winters on record. My servant's arm was broken in the fall, and one of my horses is lame—"

"Lame?" she repeated, her voice tight.

Ah! He suddenly remembered Her Grace's love of horses, as professed by the ancient Artemis. Cad that he was, Hugh had no hesitation in playing on her sympathies. "Yes, lame. I'm certain the beast will recover, given the proper care and rest. So, too, will my footman, if also provided with proper care and rest." He released her arm and stepped back, prepared to give chase if she fled again. "I haven't the time to seek out another domicile, Your Grace. I am the Earl of Montrose, not some thief set to rob you. I will return your horses and conveyance to you at my soonest, I can assure you of that."

She stood silently for a long moment, her damaged brain seeking something to say, he was certain. Finally she gave a jerky nod of agreement and turned, taking the steps with remarkable agility for a woman of her vast years.

Relieved, Hugh turned and bellowed for Artemis. He had no notion if the madness was permanent or not, but he had no desire to catch it in any case.

"Go with him."

Charlotte looked out the upper-floor window and watched

the dashing earl hitch the horses to a cart. He was a tall man, broad of shoulder, with the most glorious shade of dark-honey hair. He stood silhouetted by the snow, his elegantly dressed body moving with latent power, his shoulders bunching and flexing beneath the velvet of his coat. She couldn't see his face from here, but she guessed he would be handsome. Or at least she hoped he would be. A man blessed with so fine a form should have a face to match. "It wouldn't be proper."

"Who cares about proper?" came the laughing rejoinder. "We've never done anything properly. And the earl appears quite . . . interesting."

Interesting? Yes, he would be. It had been so long since she'd spoken to someone even remotely her age. She told herself every day that she was content with her life here, but sometimes, at night, she wished for things to be different.

Turning, Charlotte allowed the heavy velvet drapes to fall back into place. Her gaze moved around the spotless, well-appointed room, with its damask-covered walls and Chippendale furniture, before settling on the trim figure who waited with an arched brow. "I don't know. I'd like to help him, but the more assistance we extend, the more he may discover about us."

"Keep him busy then. We can't leave them out in the cold. The horse is injured and must be tended. The footman could use your healing touch. They'll catch their death, and neither one of us could live with that. You've done well enough protecting our secret these last years. I've every faith that you will continue to do so."

Charlotte moved toward the armoire. Opening the mahogany doors, she withdrew a dinner gown and spread it out carefully on the end of the bed. "I still think it's ill-conceived. The duke's orders were clear. The others can help him and send them on their way."

"Neither Henry nor Tom can set a broken bone, and well you know it. Go on now. You are better with those horses than anyone. The earl could use your help."

"But it's late!" she protested.

"Excuses, excuses. It's not late at all, and since Montrose

mustn't see me, I won't be eating dinner with him, so you can put that away. You will have to entertain him alone, but you knew that already. Now hurry up and change, before you're forced to chase after them."

Charlotte sighed. "If you insist."

"I do."

Damning the fates for sending him out in this godforsaken weather, Hugh adjusted the harnesses and chanced another glance at the sky. It was growing dark quickly, the storm clouds rolling in with portentous haste. He worried about his injured footman and his horse. Risking the journey had been foolhardy at best, but his sister, Julienne, had invited him for the holidays. He'd declined at first, but in a fit of boredom had changed his mind and decided to go anyway.

And this was the result, of course. Julienne would point out all the ways he'd handled the journey irresponsibly: He should have written to accept her invitation so she could expect him. He should never have waited so long to leave. He should have stopped at an inn when the weather took a turn for the worse. He should have commissioned a sturdier equipage, instead of one built to impress. And she would be correct on all counts, as usual. One of these days, he'd like to prove her wrong. He'd like to prove to them both that he was capable of managing his own affairs. That he was a man one could trust to lean upon.

Hugh lifted his head and watched the two young men approach him, carrying blankets and flagons of spirits to warm his servants. They were strapping lads, as he'd requested, although one of them stuttered terribly and the other had a lazy eye. Regardless, they would serve his purpose, and they seemed eager enough. Not that he blamed them. If he were in their place, he'd wish for any fortuitous circumstance to leave this forgotten estate.

The soft nicker of a horse behind him urged him to turn around. His gaze moved upward from the snow-covered ground, following the lines of a massive horse. His mouth fell open as he perused long, shapely legs encased in breeches, a slim torso framed by a spread cloak, stunning green eyes, and rich crimson hair. He gaped, at a loss for words, deciding he would've been better off avoiding the blasted tea, because it certainly couldn't be a woman who sat astride the hulking beast. And wearing *breeches* no less!

"My lord," the fantastic vision murmured from her high perch. And it was a *her*. No man could bear that beautiful face or stunning, feminine bedroom voice. A voice that curled around him in the deepening dusk and heated his blood.

He snapped his mouth shut.

"You are . . . ?" he growled rudely. Hugh knew he was suffering from a deplorable lack of social grace, but truly, there were only so many bizarre things a person should be expected to tolerate in one day, and since this afternoon, he'd had more than his share.

"Charlotte," she replied as if that were explanation enough.

"Right."

He frowned, his gaze narrowing as it raked her lithe form for the second time. Her manly attire delineated every soft curve of her legs. The cropped, form-fitting riding jacket, though somewhat out of date, showcased firm, high breasts and a trim waist. Impossibly he felt overheated again, although just moments before he'd been shivering. He studied her intently, noting her perfect posture and uplifted chin. "What are you attempting to do out here in this miserable weather?"

"I'm here to assist you, my lord."

"Right." He should argue further, and would, as soon as his brain was working again. At the moment it was completely occupied with the stunning redhead in breeches, leaving not one thought process free to refuse her.

Charlotte was not young, nor was she old. Five and twenty would be his guess. She was a classic beauty, with skin as clear as the finest porcelain. Her mouth was wide—too wide, some would say—and her lips full and carnal in their plumpness. She had lovely clear green eyes, and they met his with an easy forthrightness he admired.

"Who are you?" he asked.

The infinitely kissable mouth curled in a smile, and his gut tightened. A few moments ago he would have been alarmed. Now he was merely resigned. Apparently, he was getting aroused by all of the female inhabitants of the area.

"I thought we resolved that already," she murmured, her throaty voice threatening to shove him over the precipice of aroused into thoroughly erected.

"A servant?"

"Hmm . . . More of a companion. I've been asked to accompany you."

"For what purpose?" he scoffed. "I must make haste if I've any hope of reaching the next posting inn."

"It's already too late for that, my lord. You'll have to remain here for tonight at least, perhaps even until the storm blows over, if it's as wicked as the skies herald." She chuckled, and his cock twitched.

"Hell and damnation!" It had been years since he'd been troubled by an unwanted cockstand, yet this unusual female had him throbbing in his trousers with a simple bout of amusement.

Her eyes widened at his curse.

"My apologies," he corrected quickly. "My manners seem to have flown." Along with the common sense of every individual he'd had the misfortune of meeting today. "I cannot possibly remain here overnight."

"Why not?"

"Why not?" he repeated.

"That is what I inquired," she said dryly. "Why can you not stay?"

"There's no room, for one," he pointed out.

"There's plenty of room. The manse is quite vast."

He scowled. "How much of it is inhabitable?"

Charlotte laughed. And Hugh was captivated. He decided in that moment he would have her, and suddenly the storm he had cursed mere moments before became a blessing. It would trap them together, giving him the opportunity to seduce her into his bed. His mood brightened. Unlike the rest of his life, he made no stumbles in the bedroom.

"Oh, my lord. Don't be fooled by the apparent neglect. There are several available rooms, all clean and ready for guests."

He arched a brow.

"Truly." She flicked the reins with casual ease, and the huge brute of an animal moved toward the lopsided gate. "We should make haste."

"What exactly can you offer in the way of assistance?" he asked, vaulting onto the driver's seat of the cart, while the two young men jumped into the back.

She patted the bulging saddlebag he'd been too distracted to notice before. "I heard your footman has a broken arm. I can set it and tend to him, while you attend to your carriage."

Hugh nodded, resigned. It would save time, and if she couldn't help John, at least she'd be pleasing to the eye in the meantime. Damned if the sight of her in those breeches didn't make every thought leave a man's head.

He urged the horses forward, and she moved aside to allow him to lead.

Charlotte's hands were quite literally shaking on the reins.

She'd never been studied in such a manner in her life, in a way that made her skin hot and her palms itch. She was no ingenue—her attractiveness had been the backbone of her existence for many years. But it had been a novel experience to be raked by Montrose's warm brown eyes. She felt looked at, truly *seen*, for the first time in years.

At first glance he appeared nonchalant, but she wasn't fooled. He'd perused her in detail, and liked what he saw. It had been thrilling. Arousing. And she wanted the handsome earl, who was an obvious libertine, to strip her with his eyes again.

Charlotte had hoped he would be fine of face, but the reality was far more devastating than she had imagined. He exhibited none of the signs of ennui and dissolution common to men with a marked predilection to excess. Montrose was, in fact, youthful and quite fit. More than fit. Vigorous, actually, and virile. Potently virile.

His mode of dress was understated, almost reserved, which suited him because his physical beauty alone was attractive enough. Any further adornment would simply be too much.

There were varying forms of male arrogance: the arrogance of wealth and privilege, the arrogance of intelligence, and the arrogance of attractiveness. The Earl of Montrose bore all of those traits, and a little bit more. The intensity of his stare, the way his hands had tightened the harnesses, the leisurely, seductive grace with which he moved—it all betrayed him. A man that comfortable in his own skin would know all about sexual pleasure and wouldn't doubt his ability to bestow it. He was a man who fucked often and well. A man few women could resist.

Charlotte watched him closely as they left the grounds and moved onto the snow-covered lane, noting the easy expertise with which he held the ribbons. She was a woman who appreciated men who had a way with horses, because she liked them so well herself. Quite frankly, she respected men who took the time to become experts in the things that interested them. And Montrose was just such a man.

Glancing up, she noted the rapidly darkening sky. Yes, he would definitely be spending the evening with them, and if the turbulent wind was any indication, he might be staying much longer than that. Blizzards could sometimes last for days, with the roads being impassable for weeks after they passed.

She would have to be careful or he could learn more about them than she wanted him to. She would have to keep him occupied so he wouldn't sneak around in his boredom.

And she liked that idea far more than she should.

Chapter Two

"Will he recover?"

Hugh glanced over his shoulder and found the lovely Charlotte lounging against the stall door. "I expect so. A minor sprain, I think."

Returning his attention to the task at hand, he continued to apply salve to the scraped and swollen front legs of one of his carriage bays. Unlike the main house, the stable was warm, well tended, and in excellent shape, a fact that didn't surprise him at all.

"Allow me to have a look," she murmured, coming toward him.

In the tight confines of the stable stall, there was no room to avoid her. She squeezed in between where he knelt and the front of his horse, her breeches stretching deliciously over a lush derriere. Hugh's mouth dried at the sight, his entire body hardening as her scent, a soft mix of flowers, enveloped his senses.

"I agree." Her tiny hands soothed over the raw scrapes, and the animal breathed a soft whinny. Watching the caressing strokes of Charlotte's hands, Hugh swallowed hard. It was a common enough task she was performing, and yet his interest in her was so unusually strong, it made the everyday action startlingly erotic.

Earlier, while struggling to remove his trunks from the disabled carriage, Hugh's gaze had continuously strayed to the beautiful redhead as she set his footman's broken arm and tended to his abrasions. There was a quiet confidence to her deportment and an unflappable air of control that he admired. He'd struggled most of his life to find that sort of confidence in himself, but to Charlotte it seemed innate.

Most women of his acquaintance would have been no assistance at all, but Charlotte had been invaluable. With her help they'd finished quickly and returned to the Kent estate with barely a moment to spare. Outside the wind howled and blew around with such force it was hard to see. Even now, her gorgeous red locks were dampening, the snow in them melting in the warmth of the stable.

"You shouldn't have ventured out here," he said.

"I wanted to be certain you found the salve." Still crouched, she turned to face him, bringing her ripe mouth within inches of his own. Across her nose was a light dusting of freckles, the bane of most women's existence, but a trait he'd always found charming.

Hugh studied her with a frown, trying to reason out why he found her so desirable. Charlotte was beautiful, yes, but no more so than he was accustomed to. The revealing breeches could have much to do with his constant state of arousal, although he'd never before considered men's clothing particularly enticing. Of course his brother-in-law would beg to differ.

"What are you doing out here?" he asked.

She arched a brow. "I told you—"

"No. Not here in the stables, here in Derbyshire."

Charlotte sat and crossed her legs. Hugh did the same.

"I grew up here. I left for a while and then returned."

"Your family is here?"

Hugh reached for a nearby towel and rubbed the salve from his palms. Then he picked up her hands and cleaned them as well, taking note of the calluses and ink stains that marred her fingers. The nails were trimmed to the quick, neat and without vanity, similar to the way she comported herself.

"No," she murmured, a bit breathless. "I have no family."

Finished with the cloth, he set it aside, but kept her hands within his. She didn't protest, for which he was grateful. He enjoyed touching her, relishing the way it made his entire body prickle with a singular sensual awareness.

"Tell me about the duchess."

If he hadn't been holding her hand, he wouldn't have known she tensed at his query. Her adeptness at hiding her feelings intrigued him. She was too young to be so expert at evasiveness.

"What would you like to know?" she asked, looking away.

He snorted. "What *wouldn't* I like to know? Is she mad, like they say? Does she mistreat you? Why does she live like this? The horses live better than you. Why—"

Charlotte covered his mouth with her hand. "No, no, and she doesn't have any other choice." She stood and tugged at their joined hands. He rose to his feet.

"Allow me to show you to your rooms, my lord. You'll see things are not so dreary as they appear at first glance."

"You're avoiding my questions."

She smiled, a potent mixture of sweetness and allure, and his stomach clenched in response. "Not so," she assured him, releasing his hand. "I simply want to answer some of your questions without words."

There was a bit of promise in the sparkle of her eyes, a hint that told Hugh she found him attractive. He was glad of that, for it made his goal much easier to attain. It was bloody freezing outside, and he'd be trapped here for days. The time would best be spent in bed with a lovely companion, and he wanted Charlotte with a sharpness he'd not experienced in a very long time, if ever.

Hugh stepped closer, gauging her reaction, and smiled when she stood her ground, her emerald gaze neither frightened nor wary. "I thank you for your help today," he murmured, reaching for her hand.

She lifted hers to meet his, startling him. "It was nothing."

"It was wonderful. The way you handled James's injuries

and set his broken bone . . . I don't know that I could have done it." He brushed his thumb over the back of her hand and felt her shiver.

"You might be surprised at the things you can accomplish when the need is dire enough."

"You sound as if you speak from experience."

"Perhaps." Charlotte tilted her head and frowned, studying him with a far-too-perceptive gaze. "And you?"

He shrugged. "I never seem to reach the dire point," he confessed, attempting to make the words light but failing miserably. "I'm always rescued before it progresses that far."

Her grasp tightened, giving him a comforting squeeze. "I think you did well enough today, barging into the house and cornering Her Grace. There was no one to rescue you or your servants, yet you managed quite nicely on your own."

Hugh's eyebrows rose.

Charlotte touched his mouth where he was attempting to curb a smile and said softly, "I am a very good judge of character, my lord, but I misjudged you."

"Oh? In what way?"

Her smile matched his. "I was very impressed with you today. Earlier, I wouldn't have thought you'd need to hear that. But apparently you do."

And with just that simple statement, the sharp edge of Hugh's desire honed to a burning point. Suddenly the cozy warmth of the stables was too hot, the air around them crackling with sensual energy. He'd never experienced anything like it, this itching, burning feeling coursing over his skin. That it was brought on by simple verbal praise astonished him. But, then, everything that had happened today astonished him.

Charlotte recognized the change in the atmosphere. Her pupils widened, her mouth parted. Hugh stepped back a fraction, forcibly preventing himself from moving too fast and frightening her. She took a step forward, closing the distance he'd just created.

Against his better judgment, Hugh tugged her nearer. When she came forward willingly, he reassessed her. Charlotte was comfortable with his touch and his bold approach. In fact, he would say her approach was just as bold, belying her innocent exterior.

"Charlotte." His free hand came up to brush across her cheek, finding her creamy skin as soft as he'd imagined it would be. "I believe you are the loveliest thing I've ever seen."

"My lord—"

"Hugh," he corrected. He'd never been comfortable with his title, and at this moment it created a distinction between their classes of which he didn't wish to be reminded.

She leaned into his touch, her mouth curving in a wry smile. "I'm usually immune to charming rogues."

Hugh didn't deny the obvious. Instead he ran his thumb across her lips. "Your mouth is beyond lovely. It's simply perfect."

His free hand moved to her shoulder, then down along the curve of her spine. Charlotte arched into him, pressing her breasts to his chest. Unhampered by stays and petticoats, he could *feel* her, all of her, yet not enough of her.

Lowering his head slowly, he moved his fingertips away, intent on kissing her. She had such a lovely mouth, so full and ripe. And it said such wonderful things.

It was the not-so-gentle bite from his horse upon his shoulder that brought back the reality of the small stable stall and the storm that raged outside. For a moment, Hugh considered ignoring the rude intrusion and continuing anyway, but the warning snort from the beast behind him changed his mind.

"We should go back to the house," he said with true regret. "I believe my horse is jealous."

Charlotte blinked and took a moment to reply, visibly withdrawing from his blatant seduction. "Yes, I suppose that would be wise." The matching note of regret in her voice soothed Hugh's nigh-unbearable frustration.

Hands linked together, they left the comfortable stable and struggled across the courtyard, entering the manse through the kitchen. They were wet and frozen by the time they completed the journey, and the cook stared at them agape as they stumbled inside followed by a billowing cloud of snow. Hugh gaped right back.

The cook was the largest woman he'd ever seen. Impossibly tall and built like a laborman, she quite frankly scared him. Gray hair stuck out in every direction, and grayer eyes raked him from head to toe. With a gleaming knife in her hand and a helpless chicken on the counter, she was a terrifying sight to behold. He might have stood there for hours, arrested by shock, had Charlotte not grabbed his arm and tugged him from the room.

"Good God," he muttered as he followed Charlotte up the servants' stairs to the upper floors.

Minx that she was, she laughed. "Wait until dinner," she promised. "You'll be impressed."

"I'm impressed already." He'd never met an Amazon before in his life.

Traversing well-appointed hallways, Hugh barely had time to register the dichotomy of the house before he found himself in an immense bedchamber warmed by a fire. It was beautifully furnished and immaculately cleaned. He found it hard to believe he was in the same residence he'd entered just a few hours ago.

"Why isn't the rest of the manse maintained?" he asked, glancing back at her.

Charlotte shivered by the door, her hair and garments wet with melting snow.

He held out his hand. "Come warm yourself by the fire."

"Not yet."

The "yet" gave him pause, a tiny intimation that she intended at some point to tarry in his rooms. Their eyes met and held, his with silent query, hers open and clear.

"Go change, then," he said. "Before you catch your death. You can explain to me after you're warmed."

She nodded. "I'll return directly to escort you to supper."

Hugh sketched a quick bow. "I await your pleasure."

* * *

"How long did it take before he started asking questions?"

Charlotte sighed. "Longer than I would have expected."

"How did you answer?"

"I didn't."

"But you'll have to."

Nodding, Charlotte began to strip from her damp clothes. Goose bumps covered her skin, and she stepped closer to the warmth of the fire. "Montrose is very interesting, just as you suspected."

"And handsome."

"Yes, he's quite gorgeous, and a brazen rake, too." Smiling, she thought of the way he'd cleaned her hands for her and the concern he'd shown for his injured footman. "But much nicer than I would have thought. A touch vulnerable, too, which I never would have suspected. I took him for the arrogant sort, but beneath that exterior, I think he doubts himself a little."

"Oh . . . he *is* interesting! Perhaps it's good he's come along, then. You're young and lovely; it's truly a shame you've chosen to dedicate yourself to me. Not that I'd ever send you away. You keep me from going completely mad with boredom."

Charlotte laughed. "It's no sacrifice, as you well know."

"'Tis far different from the life you knew."

"That is not a bad thing." Charlotte sank gratefully into the steaming bath. "My former life had its pleasures, to be sure, but I was ready for a change and a bit of equanimity."

A few moments of silence passed. "I studied the map while you were gone."

Resting her head against the lip of the tub, Charlotte closed her eyes. "I'm sick to death of poring over that blasted thing. When the spring thaw comes, we'll charter a ship and go ourselves. Perhaps then we'll discover something useful."

"His Grace was very ill when he gave you that map," came the soft reminder. "Perhaps he wasn't altogether sane at the time."

Charlotte sank lower into the water. She'd considered that

possibility many times. The books Glenmoore had left behind were cryptic at best, and the map, while comparable to others depicting the same body of water, had distinguishing features she could find nowhere else. Still, what choice did they have? The new Duke of Glenmoore was miserly with the trust and—

"Have you considered any other possibilities?" interjected the lilting voice Charlotte had come to love.

"No," she admitted. "But I suppose I shall have to, in short order."

"Well, in the meantime, enjoy the earl." The soft rustle of muslin betrayed movement. "You should wear your red silk to dinner. You're breathtaking in it. He'll never be able to resist you."

"He's not trying to resist me," she said dryly. She'd never cared for libidinous pleasure-seekers like Montrose, though she'd tolerated them when necessary. Hugh, however, wasn't at all like his appearance led one to believe. In fact, he seemed almost lonely. Much like she was.

"Ah, well, even better."

Charlotte laughed. "I'm certain it's not proper to discuss this sort of thing with you."

"Who cares about proper? We've never done anything properly."

Hugh glanced again at the mirror, adjusting his cravat for the hundredth time, before resuming his pacing. *What the devil was taking Charlotte so blasted long?*

He'd give her a few moments more, then he'd track her down. Who knew what had happened to her in this museum of oddities? Why, he shuddered just thinking about it! It was abominable for such a gorgeous creature to be rusticating out here, in the wilds of Derbyshire. It was a travesty he intended to rectify as soon as the cursed weather cooperated.

When the long-awaited knock finally came, he threw open the portal with such haste that Charlotte stumbled backward in surprise. He was equally astonished.

Dressed in a crimson silk gown of stunning simplicity, she

stole his breath and his wits. With off-the-shoulder sleeves, low-cut bodice, and high waist, the dress featured no adornments of any kind. Charlotte herself wore no jewelry or gloves, and her coppery hair was piled atop her head in riotous curls. Her skin was pale as moonlight, and the scent of her, fresh and flowery, was an arousing counterpoint to the seductive look of her.

It took all of the self-control Hugh possessed to keep from grabbing her and ravishing her upon his bed. Charlotte appealed to him on so many levels, he found it hard to collect them all.

He watched, mesmerized, as her mouth curved in a knowing smile. She was thoroughly aware of the effect the sight of her would have on any man.

"Shall we go to supper?" she asked.

"Must we?"

Her green eyes glowed with warm amusement. "I'm rather starved myself."

So was Hugh, but not for food. However, the thought of her company while eating his meal was somewhat pacifying. He stepped out of his room and offered his arm. The light touch of her bare fingers burned through his coat and shirt to his skin below, making him ache for her. Charlotte was tiny, the top of her head barely reached his shoulder, and from his high vantage, Hugh had an excellent view of the ripe swell of her breasts.

He looked away, staring resolutely down the gallery. Unlike the demimondaines with whom he usually associated, it felt wrong to ogle Charlotte as if she were worth nothing more than a good tumble. She was intelligent and kind, as evidenced by her steadfastness in the face of today's events. Fact was, he rather liked her, what little he knew of her, and since he had a few days to fill, he determined to discover as much about her as he could in that time.

As they moved from one hallway to another and prepared to descend the main staircase, Hugh felt as if he were moving through time. The brightly lit and beautifully furnished part of the house faded into the dust-covered and rotting section as easily as they turned the corner.

"It's less of a burden on the servants to maintain only the areas we use regularly," Charlotte explained before he could ask.

Thinking of the motley crew he'd met so far, he had to agree.

Hugh was relieved to see that the dining room was clean and kept in usable condition, but he was slightly disappointed to see only two place settings on the long mahogany table.

"Is Her Grace not joining us for dinner?" Even as he asked, he wondered why a paid companion would be allowed to dress so beautifully and eat dinner with him instead of with her employer. But he refused to ask. No sane man would question such good fortune.

"She's become accustomed to eating her meals alone."

"Odd, that," he murmured as he held a chair for her. He'd made a habit of surrounding himself with large, boisterous groups of people, rarely spending a moment without company of some sort. Eating alone sounded . . . lonely.

Taking his seat, Hugh settled in to enjoy his meal when a familiar noise drew his attention to the swinging door that led to the kitchen. He shook his head and sighed.

Sure enough, the portal swung open and the young, jittery maid entered. The soup tureen in her hands wobbled alarmingly, and the ladle protruding from it rattled so loudly, nothing else could be heard. Directly on her heels and bearing a pitcher came Tom, the lazy-eyed boy who'd assisted Hugh earlier.

The two servants almost collided, compliments of the madly swinging door. Together they performed an odd sort of spinning dance, stumbling forward and back and around, as they attempted to keep their liquids from spilling out everywhere.

For a moment, Hugh watched the antics in dumbfounded

fascination, and then, muttering an oath, he pushed to his feet and rescued the maid from the soup (or the soup from the maid, depending on how one looked at it).

"'Tis a wonder you don't starve," he muttered, and Charlotte laughed.

"They would have been fine, if you'd have given them a moment."

Hugh shot her a disbelieving glance.

"Truly," she insisted.

"Are you the only normal individual on the premises?" he rejoined as he took his seat.

The lovely full mouth he found endlessly erotic curved in a wide grin. "That depends on what you consider normal. Some would say that a young, unmarried woman who chooses to live with a mad duchess is far from normal." She glanced at the shaking woman at the end of the table. "You may serve now, Katie."

The pretty brunette flashed a tentative smile and moved to fill their bowls with soup. Hugh watched as, despite her affliction, she managed the task without spilling a drop onto the pristine tablecloth.

The meal consisted of a variety of delectable dishes, including curried fowl and braised ham, and Charlotte was refreshing and engaging. She made him laugh with her dry wit and was attentive enough to keep his glass filled with wine. Hugh attempted to broach the subject of the duchess, but like a consummate politician, she directed the conversation to lighter topics, such as the spring dance in the village and Mr. Edgewood's skinny, unappetizing pig. Lost in the pleasure of her company, Hugh was content to allow her evasiveness. For the moment.

After dinner they retired to the upstairs library, and Hugh took the opportunity to study her in greater depth. It was easy to discern that she was not merely a paid companion. There was a practiced grace to her movements and a studious understanding of the customs enjoyed by men of privilege. She brought him a cigar, which she lit with expertise. Moving to the sideboard, Charlotte poured a large ration of brandy, which she warmed over a candle flame before bringing it to him. Her hips swayed softly as she approached, her shoulders held back to better display her lovely breasts. The invitation in her eyes was apparent.

"You're attempting to seduce me," he murmured with a smile, extremely pleased. It was not unusual for women to pursue him, but he was especially enjoying it this evening. Setting his cigar aside, Hugh caught her wrist when she held out the glass and tugged her into his lap. "Would you like me to take you away from this place?"

As soon as the words left his mouth, he acknowledged what an excellent idea it was. Charlotte was far too lovely to be hidden away, and he could easily see himself keeping her for a while.

She didn't reply. Instead, she turned her face and pressed those lush lips to his. Plump and flavored of wine, her kiss was intoxicating. He was held motionless, achingly touched and aroused by the simple gesture. He, a man consummate in the carnal arts, was arrested by a mere kiss. It was Charlotte who took control of the moment, Charlotte whose tongue licked along his lips and teased for entry. Hugh could only groan and pull her closer.

"Montrose," she whispered, her forehead pressed to his.

"Hugh."

"Hugh . . ." She said his name on a sigh, a warm breath that mingled with his before he breathed in and made it his own. "I am a woman of the world. I don't need to be rescued."

Holding her was both pleasure and torment. His cock was hard and swollen against her luscious derriere, aching to fill her. "What do you want, then, Charlotte?" he asked hoarsely. "I'll give you anything you desire."

Her hand came up and entwined in his hair, kneading his scalp, until his eyes closed helplessly, awash in pleasure. The air around them heated, becoming heavy with a desire so intense, it almost frightened him.

The sudden crash in the hall startled them both.

"Damnation," he cursed, setting her from his lap before rising to his feet and striding to the door. Throwing it open, he stuck his head out and found Katie down the hall with a broken pitcher at her feet. Noting the blood that pooled in her palm, he hurried to her side, pulling out his handkerchief as he went.

"Poor thing," he murmured, dabbing at the cut. "It must hurt terribly."

"'Tis nothing. Please . . ."

It was the first time Hugh had heard her speak, and her soft, lyrical voice drew his gaze upward. He found her crying.

Flustered by her tears, he sought to soothe her. "Charlotte will have you good as new in a moment."

"It's not that," she sobbed. "I broke the pitcher."

"That old thing?" he dismissed gruffly. "I shall purchase a dozen more for you when this storm has abated. Then you can break as many as you like."

Katie lifted her face and gave him a grateful, wavering smile. Hugh coughed in embarrassment and looked away, relieved when Charlotte knelt beside them and took the girl's hand. Straightening, he backed up a step.

Charlotte examined the wound. "We must go to the kitchen to tend this." She offered him a silent apology with her eyes. "You can retire. I'll manage."

"I'd like to help."

"Truly, there's nothing you can do but watch. And it's been a long day. I shall see you tomorrow."

Hugh hesitated a moment before nodding his acquiesce. Charlotte was obviously accustomed to handling her affairs alone, and the dismissal was obvious. He would not be seeing her again tonight.

He didn't understand why he wished to help her carry this burden, and any others she might have. He avoided responsibility whenever possible, and Charlotte was made of stern stuff, he knew. Yet there it was, the unmistakable desire to take care of her.

After the two women disappeared around the corner, Hugh entered his suite and locked the door. No longer distracted by his attraction to Charlotte, his thoughts returned to where he was and the situation he was in.

Somewhere on this floor, the mad duchess waited.

He'd never been a nervous sort. In fact, he was known for his steely concentration, which had stood him in good stead through two duels and had given him a reputation as a man with whom to be reckoned. Because of his even temperament, Hugh found the whole mystery of the decrepit mansion and the legend of the duchess rather thrilling. His life had become a tedious cycle of business meetings, women whose names he couldn't remember, and fair-weather friends. He was bored of it all, which was the main reason he'd decided at the last moment to visit Julienne.

As he undressed, he racked his memory trying to recall what he could about the old duke and his hasty marriage. Glenmoore had been an Eccentric, an Original, always haring off on worldly adventures at which everyone else had shaken their heads. Hugh knew Glenmoore's son had always considered his father to be something of an embarrassment.

Now Hugh wished he'd paid greater attention to the talk. When his sister had married Lucien Remington, he'd become adept at avoiding gossip of any nature. For future reference, he'd have to rethink his reticence. Perhaps there was something useful to be gleaned from the chatter after all.

Charlotte was an enigma he *would* unravel. A lady's companion was expected to have a sterling reputation, and yet it was fairly obvious by the way she dressed and her skilled seduction that Charlotte was a bit tarnished.

Every one of the servants had some affliction or another. It was highly possible that the tempting redhead's reputation was hers.

Damnation, he was thirsty!

He'd had nothing but wine since the pot of tea earlier. Shooting a wary glance at the fresh pitcher left by Katie, Hugh sighed in resignation and poured a small ration. There was no help for it. He couldn't drink liquor the entire duration of the storm. With everything that was happening around him, he was better off sober.

He lifted the glass and drained its contents. Then he crawled into the massive bed and promptly fell asleep.

Hugh stiffened but made no other movement. All of his senses alert, he listened carefully for the sound that woke him.

There it was again—the soft sound of material brushing against itself.

Someone else was in the room with him.

Throwing back the covers, he leapt from the bed, startling the dark form that stood at the foot of it. He lunged forward, arms out to capture his Peeping Tom.

And ended up facedown on the rug.

Startled, knowing he should have caught the intruder, Hugh jumped to his feet and spun about, expecting to catch *something* and finding only air. Running to the nightstand, he lit the taper, then looked around, finding no one and nothing amiss.

He cursed as he pulled on his discarded trousers. A man could take only so much.

As he reached for the candle, he noted the pitcher next to it and muttered an oath that would have blistered the ears of a seasoned sailor. If the blasted water was to blame for this, he'd be foxed the duration of his visit and be glad of it.

In the meantime, though, Hugh didn't believe he'd imagined the specter at the end of the bed, and he also didn't believe the individual simply dissipated into thin air. Having Remington as a brother-in-law had taught him a thing or two about appearances, and he'd use what he'd learned to search the walls on either side of the fireplace.

It took less than an hour to find the tiny lever. Hugh engaged it, and the wall slid open without a sound, betraying how well maintained the mechanism inside was.

With a small smile of satisfaction and the thrill of discovery, he picked up the taper and stepped inside.

Chapter Three

Bending over the desk in the study, Charlotte released a deep breath and seriously considered ripping the blasted map she was studying into pieces. She'd spent three years attempting to puzzle out the cryptic thing and had very little to show for her efforts.

If she had only herself to look after, she would frame the map as a colorful memento and carry on. But she had an entire house of people to worry about, and her efforts alone could never support them all. Moving them away, finding a place to live, trying to make ends meet . . . impossible. But of course, that's exactly what Carding intended.

Charlotte tightened the belt of her lined silk robe. Her negligees had been purchased for her past life and were ill-suited to her present circumstances, but she wore them regardless. They reminded her that she was a woman, that she was still young and attractive. Left out here in the country, it was far too easy to forget those things.

Bleary-eyed, Charlotte knew she should retire, but thoughts of the handsome earl just a few doors down made sleep difficult. She hungered for him, hungered for the hard body and impressive cockstand she'd felt while sitting on his lap.

All night he'd looked at her as if nothing else in the world existed. Despite his readily apparent desire and her obvious willingness, he'd restrained himself. He'd kept his hands from pawing her despite the hard, throbbing erection she'd felt at her hip. His slow, leisurely seduction showed he respected her, perhaps even admired her. Bold as she was, she'd considered knocking on his door, knowing the charming rogue would welcome her eagerly. She was considering it now . . .

"Hello."

Startled, Charlotte glanced up, and her heart lodged in her throat. Not but a few feet away stood the Earl of Montrose, wearing only trousers and an endearingly tousled head of dark blond curls. He was such a beautiful man, powerfully built, with shoulders that were a tailor's dream tapering to a washboard stomach and trim hips. His dark eyes were heavy-lidded, seductive, gazing at her with their customary breathless intensity.

"I didn't hear you come—" Her voice trailed off as she looked past him and saw the opening in the wall of the study. "Have you been sneaking around?" she snapped.

Barefooted, he stepped toward her with the top button of his trousers undone, the muscles of his stomach rippling with strength as he moved. "*I* was sleeping," he drawled softly. "Someone else was sneaking around. In my bedchamber."

Charlotte winced inwardly, but kept her face impassive. *Bloody hell.*

"Sounds as if you had a bad dream," she murmured, rolling up the map. "After what happened today—"

"It wasn't a dream, Charlotte."

She froze as Montrose rounded the desk and came up behind her. He smelled wonderful, an enticing scent of softly warmed cologne and aroused male. And there was no doubt he was aroused—the hard length of an impressive erection strained against the front of his trousers. She stood tense, expectant, waiting for him to make the first move.

The earl blew out his taper and set it aside. His chest pressing into her back, he reached around for her hands and stilled their movements. "I've allowed you to be evasive, sweet, but now it's time we discussed the answers to the obvious questions."

"I don't know what you mean," she breathed, her heart racing at his proximity. The heat of his skin burned through her robe. Unable to stop herself, she squirmed against him and felt the hard swell of his cock slide across her buttocks.

He spread the map open, his breath hot and harsh in her ear. "Now where is the sharp wit I so admire?"

Charlotte swallowed hard. He did admire her, and for more than her appearance.

One of his large hands rested safely over hers on the map. The other, however, ventured away, cupping her shoulder before sliding down her back. She arched into his caress helplessly. "This is beautiful," he murmured, stroking the heavy silk of her robe. "The green brings out the color of your eyes and sets off your hair."

"Montrose . . ." Her eyes slid closed. It had been so long since another person had touched her. Too long.

"Hugh," he corrected softly, his teeth grazing the side of her neck. Shivering, she caught her breath in an audible rush. Much taller than she was, he had no trouble looking over her shoulder. "What are you studying so intently?"

"I-it's nothing."

"Hmmm . . ." Hugh's hand moved to her hip and kneaded the flesh gently. "It looks like a map of the West Indies to me."

Charlotte leaned heavily against the desk. "I look at it when I wish to bore myself to sleep."

His hand over hers lifted and came to rest on her stomach, pressing her back into his hard chest. His tongue, hot and moist, licked along the shell of her ear. "Are you having trouble sleeping, then?"

Lord, she felt drugged, her mind working sluggishly to respond to his questions. The earl was a master seducer, she'd recognized that immediately. But to be the object of such skill was completely overwhelming.

"Sometimes," she admitted.

His mouth nuzzled the sensitive skin of her neck, his erection burned into her lower back. "Explain the map to me."

She tried to remember why she didn't want to answer his questions and failed. "I-it's believed t-to lead to a treasure."

The earl's hand at her waist slipped inside the opening and cupped her breast through her night rail. Expert fingers circled with teasing, brushing caresses, while his other hand slowly raised the hem of her gown and robe. "What kind of treasure?"

"Pirate's treasure."

Hugh rolled her nipple between his fingertips. "An interesting way to pass the time."

A moan escaped her, and she arched into his cock. "Ah . . . yes."

His palm cupped her bare thigh, then slid upward. He was taking over her senses, waging a silent battle to force her to lower her guard. And he was succeeding. She'd already revealed far more than she should.

"Are you attempting to seduce me, my lord?" She gasped as his hand cupped her sex.

"Seduction is long past, sweet. Now I'm making love to you. But don't change the subject. Tell me why you have such interest in that map." With a long swipe of his tongue, he licked her neck, then whispered, "And spread your legs."

A breathless laugh escaped her at his arrogance, but she complied with his request, because she could do nothing else. She was rewarded with his stroking fingertips, gentle and reverent, gliding through the slick evidence of how very much she wanted him.

"I promised to find the treasure," she moaned, melting into him.

"For what purpose?" His finger slipped inside her and began to pump in a leisurely rhythm, driving her mad.

"Why does anyone seek treasure?" Her head fell back against his shoulder. "Heavens . . . that feels wonderful." She shivered, and his hand at her breast gripped tighter.

"For money, for fame, for adventure," he suggested, his voice so gruff, it betrayed his arousal. "Which is it for you?"

Charlotte arched her hips into his hand, her body on fire. His teeth bit into her neck, his fingertips tugged at her nipple, his fingers thrust between her legs until her orgasm was almost upon her. She cried out and tensed in expectation.

He stopped, and his hands left her.

"No . . ." she protested. "Don't stop."

With a hand between her shoulder blades, Hugh pressed her gently forward until she lay sprawled across the map. He lifted one of her legs and set it sideways atop the desk, opening her completely.

"Why do you want to seek treasure, Charlotte?" His palms stroked the curve of her bare derriere.

"For the money."

"For the duchess?" He kissed the small of her back. "For yourself?"

"Both." She shuddered, her arousal so painfully acute, she considered relieving it herself. Her hand moved off the desk to do just that.

"Don't even think about it," he warned. And then she heard him remove his trousers. "Tell me you're not a virgin."

Her throat was so tight, she could only shake her head.

"Do you want this?" he growled, thrusting his hard cock through the lips of her sex.

"God, yes," she breathed. "I want it."

He bent over and pressed his damp cheek to hers, his erection resting in the valley of her buttocks. "I want you more than any woman I can recall, Charlotte. Your scent intoxicates me, the feel of your skin drives me to madness, and your mouth . . . I want to do obscene things to your mouth." He kissed her cheek so gently, her heart clenched. "But I need answers, and I expect you to give them to me. Will you do that when I've finished?"

At the moment, she felt like doing anything he asked.

Hugh's hands stroked down her back, soothing, caressing.

"Are you in danger, sweet? Perhaps you hide here to escape something unpleasant?"

Charlotte's hands closed into fists. Seduction was one thing, as long as it was honest and without guile. "Don't pretend to care, Montrose, when I hold no illusions that you do or will. You want sex. Fuck me, and be done with it."

He straightened abruptly, his voice tightening. "I'm not lacking in sex. It's *you* I want."

She took a breath, then released it, sensing she'd pricked him and wondering why that mattered to her. "I swore not to tell anyone, Montrose. Can you collect that? I don't know you. In a day or two you'll leave and—"

She gasped as he thrust his cock into her with no further preliminaries.

Her fingers clawed at the desk and her back arched as pleasure seared her senses. He was large, so unbelievably built, and hard as steel, throbbing within her, until she felt nothing else.

Hugh leaned over her, lacing his fingers with hers. "I'm inside you, Charlotte." He nudged deeper, reminding her of that fact. As if she could forget. "I intend to remain inside you for the next few days. There are things I can do, ways I can take you, that will prompt you to tell me what I want to know just so I'll allow you to come. Or you can be a good girl and just tell me now. Then we can spend the next few days enjoyably discussing ways to alleviate your problems."

Arrogant men were one of her deep irritations. "I am not without skills of my own," she bit out, clenching deliberately around him, pushing herself into orgasm.

He growled, his hands tightening brutally on hers, as she came around his cock. She threw her hips back to take him completely inside her, biting her lip to hold back her cries. It was a breathless, burning release, searing her senses, but it was only a tease, a brief respite, and as he swelled in response, she writhed in torment, needing more.

Hugh withdrew from her, then slid forward again, making

her feel every thick, silken inch, stretching her deliciously, until she thought she would die of it.

"Naughty Charlotte," he murmured. He stroked her again with expert awareness. "We can stay here for hours." Again he withdrew, again he thrust. "Or we can retire to my bed, and you can lay on your back. I could suck your nipples then, sweet. Lick them, bite them, while I fuck you. Wouldn't you like that?"

She ground her teeth together and shuddered all over as he pumped into her again. "Bastard."

"No, I'm quite legitimate. And wealthy. I could help you, sweet." *Out. In.* "Why seek treasure when you have me?" His fingertips stroked the straining length of her spine.

"I don't have you."

He stilled his movements. "You could."

She lay prone upon the massive mahogany desk, spread and helpless, filled with Montrose's wondrous cock, her heart racing so fast she could hear nothing over the rushing of blood in her ears.

What was he saying? What was he offering? And why, when she'd given him what he desired without a fight?

Hugh didn't move, he simply waited, and she knew without him saying so that he wouldn't continue until she replied one way or the other. She didn't understand what he was offering, but whatever it was, she wanted it, she wanted him. Desperately.

She'd spent her entire life caring for herself because there was no one else to do it. She found it difficult to trust others, and she was a pragmatist at heart who believed in keeping her emotions far removed from her sexual liaisons. And yet she found herself wanting to believe a silver-tongued rogue. Knowing she shouldn't, Charlotte nodded her head.

"Thank God," he muttered, his mouth pressing feverish kisses against her skin, belying the control he'd exhibited only a moment ago.

Hands on her hips, Hugh pinned her down. Releasing his desire, he began to fuck her with greedy abandon. Hard and deep, his driving rhythm unfaltering, he brought her to orgasm and then continued to take her, plunging through the grasping depths of her body. He came, she was certain of it. She heard his deep groan, felt his seed pulse and then spill out, but he didn't cease, didn't grow softer.

He slid her knee forward, opening her further, so that nothing impeded his cock from her depths. His sac, tight and hard, slapped against her clit, making her beg. Hugh swore and cursed, and came again. Charlotte could only grasp the edge of the desk and allow the pleasure to take her, to fill her, to sweep away her reservations, until all she felt was Hugh La Coeur and a tentative dream that would never come to fruition.

Chapter Four

Hugh stared at the map and wished he'd paid more attention to the Earl of Merrick's discussions of trade routes in the West Indies.

He snorted. In the last twenty four hours, he'd wished he paid better attention to a lot of things. He'd always been a bit self-absorbed and rarely bothered with matters not directly pertaining to him or Julienne. Now suddenly he found himself concerned for a stranger. It was disconcerting, to say the least, and confusing.

Behind him, in his bed, Charlotte slept on. He'd give her a few more minutes, and then he'd take her again. The need he felt astonished him. He'd been at her most of the morning, and still his cock was hard and throbbing to be inside her once more. Only when they were fucking did he feel even remotely like his normal dissolute self, albeit minus his usual control.

Hugh couldn't grasp why his brain refused to concentrate on the finer points of the sexual act with Charlotte. It was simply base, no finesse, all need and sweat and fierce desire. He'd been unable to pull out before spilling his seed—not once, but every damn time. It was intolerable, but he was unable to resist, assuring himself that one more encounter would sate his lust, one more spine-melting orgasm would appease his craving.

"Hugh?"

The soft sigh behind him made his heart race. It had taken a bit of . . . *persuasion* to convince her to use his given name. Hugh was inclined to think she'd initially been stubborn just to enjoy more of his fucking, a thought that filled him with masculine satisfaction.

He turned and offered a smile. "Yes, sweet?"

Charlotte's eyes dropped to his erection, widened, and then lifted again to his. She licked her lips. Flushed and disheveled, sprawled out across the mess that was his bed, she was breathtakingly beautiful. "What are you doing?"

"Studying your map." He rested his hip against the escritoire and crossed his arms. "It's unusual and cryptic."

She nodded. "There are some books and a journal that I've been using to decipher it."

"Where did you purchase these things?"

"The elder Glenmoore gave them to me."

Hugh frowned. "Why?"

She slid upward on the bed, propping herself against the pillows, caring nothing for modesty. And he was glad of that, for the sight of her creamy skin, firm breasts, and rosy nipples filled him with delight. He could gaze at her for hours, had in fact done that very thing this morning, counting her freckles and admiring her sleeping innocence. Then he'd cursed himself and the madness that had been plaguing him since he arrived. He'd donned his trousers and retrieved the map, determined to think of something other than Charlotte.

"Glenmoore knew his son would give us nothing," she said, with obvious bitterness. "His Grace grants us the use of this home only because it suits him to keep us under his thumb."

"Why not simply institutionalize the duchess?"

Charlotte stiffened visibly. "She's not mad."

She paused, and he said, "It would be best if you divulge everything without prodding."

"I was his mistress," she blurted, lifting her chin.

Hugh gaped. "*The old man's?* Good God."

"No." She rolled her eyes. "Not the elder Glenmoore. The newest Glenmoore."

"Oh." He scowled.

"You knew I wasn't innocent," she reminded softly.

Waving off her statement with a toss of his hand, Hugh bristled at the jealousy he felt for a man she was no longer with. "Yes, Yes," he muttered. "And that doesn't bother me in the least. I'm grateful actually. No other way I could molest you all morning."

She laughed. "I was most willing to be molested."

Hugh arched a brow.

Her wide mouth spread in a delighted smile. "It isn't often that well-endowed, gorgeous men with hearty sexual appetites come to call."

He snorted and ran a hand through his hair.

She sighed. "Your mood is odd for a man who should be sated."

"I don't like that you would have taken any man," he admitted gruffly.

Sliding from the bed and dragging the sheet with her, she retorted, "And I don't like that you think I would have."

He watched her stalk toward the door, her spine straight and proud. She was magnificent, a red-haired goddess who brooked disrespect from no one.

Going after her, Hugh stepped between her and egress. "I'm sorry. Please don't go."

Charlotte tilted her head back and considered him carefully. "You're surly this morning."

"I apologize. You are not to blame."

Evidently satisfied, she nodded and moved back to the bed. "It was beautiful here once," she said over her shoulder. "The first time I visited, the manse and grounds took my breath away." She crawled back into the bed.

"Glenmoore brought you here?" He followed her to the bed and sat on the edge.

"He was Marquess of Carding then and impatient for his father to die." She looked at him with narrowed green eyes. "Do you know him?"

An image of the brawny, overbearing duke came immediately to mind. "I've met him on occasion."

"He's an ass," she said curtly. "He didn't care at all that his father might be offended to meet his mistress. Carding never cared about anyone but himself." She brushed her hair back over her shoulder. "Glenmoore was ill, and Carding left him here, far from his ancestral seat, to die alone and uncared for. The servants were understaffed, no doctor was sent for. It was terrible. I was ashamed to know him."

Hugh reached out and claimed her hand, knowing that, as nurturing as Charlotte was, she would have been deeply distressed by the elder Glenmoore's suffering. She squeezed back, and he felt an odd tugging at his heart that she would take comfort from him. He was certain he'd never been a comfort to anyone.

"One evening I went to Glenmoore's room to check on his welfare. His chamber was freezing, since no one could be bothered to light the grate. The chamber pot was full and smelled dreadful. I couldn't be certain when the last time was that someone had fed him." Charlotte shuddered at the memory.

"And you took care of him," he finished, feeling a flicker of pride to which he had no claim.

"I had to," she murmured, stroking his palm with her fingertips. "Animals are treated better."

Sliding further atop the bed, Hugh rested against the headboard and pulled her back between his legs, wanting to hold her and offer whatever solace he could. He stroked his hands down her arms and kissed her shoulder.

"You are so sweet, Hugh." She wrapped his arms around her waist.

He buried his face in her hair to hide his embarrassment. "Tell me more," he said gruffly, deflecting the conversation away from him.

"Glenmoore was ill but still lucid and sane. He didn't know who I was, of course, but once I explained, he took my presence in stride, and we spoke at length. I really liked His Grace. He had a sense of humor and a zest for life I admired. I couldn't leave him to suffer simply because Jared wished to be rid of him—"

"Why was his wife not caring for him?"

"Glenmoore wasn't married at the time. He wed not long after I arrived."

Hugh rubbed his lips against her shoulder, frowning. "What woman in her right mind would marry a man in that condition? He had an heir and was unable to produce further issue. She had nothing to gain."

"There are reasons for everything, Hugh." Charlotte rested her head back against his shoulder. "You must trust that hers were sound."

He snorted in disbelief, then said, "Carding must have been furious when you handed him his congé."

"Oh, he was," she agreed, snuggling deeper into his embrace. "He ranted and railed, and threatened to destroy me so that no other man would ever have me."

She took a deep breath. "But after the despicable way he treated his father, I wanted nothing further to do with him. I told him to do his worst."

"Bloody hell," he breathed, impressed. No one defied a duke, let alone a slip of a girl who relied on him to support her.

Charlotte laughed. "I'm no martyr, so don't think that. I was already planning to sever my arrangement with Carding, and I'd saved up enough to live comfortably. Offering to care for Glenmoore afforded me the time to discover what I wanted to do next and to help the old duke at the same time. It seemed a perfect arrangement."

"But something happened to your plans."

"I underestimated Carding. If I'd known how he would react, I would have handled things differently. I would have returned with him to London, collected my things, and then made arrangements to come back. Instead I sent my abigail—a stupid, stupid mistake. Carding wasted no time. He went through my house the night he returned and disposed of all of my clothes and jewelry, most of which I had acquired before I met him. He ceased paying the servants here, so they left. The ones we have now deserve better recompense for their efforts. All we can offer is food and a roof over their heads, hence the reason I don't overtax them with cleaning areas that aren't used."

"What of the money you'd saved?"

"It wasn't money I saved but jewelry."

"Which Carding stole," Hugh finished.

She ran her fingertips over the backs of his hands, a soft, absentminded caress he enjoyed far too much. "In deference to Glenmoore's feelings, I attempted to hide what his son was doing, but he knew. As his condition worsened, he gave me the map, books, and journal. He wanted to repay me for seeing him through his last days, and he hoped to ensure my future in some way."

"But once he was gone, why didn't you leave? As beautiful as you are, you must have known you could secure another protector."

She turned in his arms, a position that pressed her breasts to his chest. Hugh's breath hissed out at the contact, and he struggled to concentrate on her next words. "Everyone here relies on me. If I leave, what will happen to them? They are excellent servants, but very few employers can look beyond their handicaps. Besides it's not too dreadful. We eat well. We're clothed and warm."

"Then the map is just a hobby?" He stroked his hands down her back. "You appeared quite engrossed in it earlier."

"That is due to my pride." Charlotte arched into his caress. "I dislike living under the duke's thumb. It allows him to feel that he's won, that he's bested me. If I could acquire financial independence, I could control my own fate. That's worth studying the map with all the enthusiasm I can muster. Besides, there was nothing else to occupy me in this weather." She pressed a kiss to his nipple. "Until you came along."

Hugh tucked her hair behind her ear. "I've never considered keeping a mistress, but—"

"Why pay for what I give you for free?" she interrupted with a sly curve to her lips.

"You're avoiding the subject again." He slid lower and draped her body over his. "You are quite adept at evasiveness."

"I am adept at a great many things."

He laughed and kissed the tip of her nose, pleased that she'd confided so much in him. "Is Her Grace harmless?"

"Oh, yes," she assured him. "She's no danger to you."

"Then why did she venture into my room this morning?"

Charlotte's eyes lit with mischief. "Perhaps she wished to have her wicked way with you."

"That's not funny," he grumbled.

She giggled. "I think it is."

He began to tickle her.

"Stop it!" she gasped, laughing.

"Now this . . ." he said. "This is funny!"

Turning, Hugh pinned her beneath him and smiled.

"Oh, no, you don't!" she protested, pushing upward against his chest. "I must eat; I'm starved. I want to bathe and . . . other things."

Hugh rolled his eyes and then rolled to his back with an exaggerated sigh. "For a mistress, you're not very accommodating," he complained.

Charlotte tossed a leg over his hips and straddled him, still clutching the sheet like a toga. "I am your lover, not your mistress. And I've been accommodating you for hours, my lord. Now you must accommodate my hunger."

"Hugh," he corrected, needing the familiarity. He was beginning to believe his recent ennui was a result of his lack of close personal associates. Perhaps all he needed was a mistress, one woman he could concentrate his attentions on, rather than indulging in fleeting liaisons. But first he had to prove to Charlotte that she needed him in some way. "When we've finished breakfast and fucking, we'll go over the map and journals together."

She laughed and looked down her nose at him.

"You don't believe I can help you?" he asked, with a frown. Perhaps this would be more difficult than he'd thought. "I have some investment in Lambert Shipping and—"

Gentle fingertips drifted across his lips, searing him with their touch. "I believe you can do anything you set your mind to, but I don't believe you'll ever finish fucking."

Hugh growled, her belief in him causing his lust to surge. "Best you retire to your room now, before I prove you right."

Charlotte leapt from the bed and ran from the room in a fit of giggles.

"You should never have visited his room," Charlotte scolded. "Now he knows about the hidden passageways and the map."

"I'm sorry," came the contrite reply. "You said he was gorgeous. I just wanted to see for myself. Was he dreadfully angry?"

Charlotte took a seat at her vanity and relented with a sigh. "He might have been originally. But he's not any longer."

Soft hands settled on her shoulders. "I just wanted a good look at him."

Glancing in the mirror, Charlotte caught the reflection of the woman at her back. "Perhaps it's best if you don't see him. There is something fundamentally unfair about having a man that gorgeous around. It makes it nearly impossible to think clearly." Lowering her gaze, she was startled to discover that the woman who stared back was younger than she remembered, with flushed cheeks, bright eyes, and a kiss-swollen mouth.

Hugh La Coeur liked kissing. He took his time with it, tasting her, caressing the inside of her mouth with deep licks of his talented tongue. She'd had her share of selfish bed partners, men who couldn't be bothered with foreplay. Hugh, however, was a tactile man. He loved to caress her hair, her skin, her lips, and she preened like a cat under his touch, wanting to stretch and purr and soak up his affection.

Fierce and primitive in bed, he took her body as if it belonged to him, as if it existed only for his pleasure. The tiny glimpses of vulnerability she'd seen in him certainly didn't extend to the bedroom. His lovemaking was breathtaking, his stamina impressive. Twice she'd begged him to leave her alone, only to find that she craved him again within moments. He knew it, too, the arrogant man. It was rather like an addiction to chocolate, she supposed. She only hoped she would have her fill before the storm blew over and he went away.

Charlotte picked up her brush and ran it through her hair. "I told him about the map and Glenmoore."

"That sounds promising. What did he say?"

"He offered to help, actually." She thought of his reactions to everything he'd witnessed so far and had to admire his aplomb. Nothing seemed to catch him off guard. And the way he'd soothed Katie and offered to buy a dozen pitchers for her . . . Charlotte had been touched. She didn't trust people easily, but Hugh's flashes of kindness for her, for his footman, and for her servants made her believe he was someone who genuinely cared for her welfare.

"Do you think he can? Help, that is?"

She shrugged. "I'm not certain, but I don't see how it can hurt anything for him to try, and it will keep us occupied during the storm."

Laughter greeted that statement. "I didn't think you needed any outside influences to keep you two occupied."

Charlotte set the brush down with a firm click. "Now *that*, I'm certain, isn't proper at all!"

Chapter Five

Hugh stared into Artemis's single eye and refused to give ground. To cave in to a servant . . . Why, the thought was abominable!

"Listen, old chap," he said curtly. "'Tis a simple enough question."

Artemis set his hands on his hips. "And one ye need be askin' 'er Grace!"

"You answer the door, for Christ's sake! You know as well as anyone if Lord Glenmoore comes calling here."

"O' course I know! Doesn't mean I'll be tellin' you!" The bulbous eye protruded further as the butler narrowed his gaze. "You can ask from 'ere to perdition, gov'na, and I—"

"Hang it all!! The proper address for a peer is 'my lord.' Is that so bloody difficult?"

Artemis gasped. "'Ere now! Are ye complainin' 'bout the way I perform my duties?"

"Complaining?" Hugh snorted. "Good God, I'm astounded. Amazed. Stunned."

Artemis nodded in agreement. "And so you should be, gov'na."

"'Tis not every day one finds service of your caliber," Hugh muttered, running a hand through his hair.

"Are ye bein' sarcastic?" Artemis asked suspiciously.

"Who, me? Never."

"What are you two arguing about?" Charlotte asked as she descended the staircase. Dressed in soft floral muslin that was a few seasons out of style, she looked fresh and young, a vision of ripe innocence that belied her sensual past.

"You can ask *'er*!" The butler turned to leave without being dismissed. "A man shouldn't 'ave to deal with this sort of treatment in 'is place of employment," he grumbled as he shuffled away.

Hugh gaped after him.

Charlotte laughed, a raw, husky sound that made his cock hard.

Damnation! He scowled. He couldn't go around sporting a constant erection, which is precisely what he'd been doing since he arrived.

Coming to a stop before him, she brushed his frown away with the soft touch of her fingers. "Artemis is a good man, and whatever you asked, you shouldn't have asked him. You know as well as I that no respectable upper servants would ever divulge information about their employers."

Not accustomed to admitting he was wrong, Hugh stewed for a moment before nodding.

Charlotte's green eyes sparkled with amusement. "Now, what did you want to ask?"

Hugh released a deep breath. "I'd like to know if Glenmoore still comes to visit you."

A dark red brow rose. "In what capacity?"

He snorted. "In any capacity."

"He stops by occasionally," she said carefully. "But I no longer share my bed with him, if that is what you're inquiring."

The relief that flooded him was profound and, because of that, disturbing. "Why does he come, then?"

"I suspect he simply wishes to assure himself that the duchess remains here and poses no threat to his precious reputation." She laced her arm with his and steered him toward the drawing room, where tempting aromas made his stomach growl.

He was ravenously hungry, and once they were seated, he tucked into the delectable meal with gusto. Consisting of kidney and eggs, honey cakes and plum cakes, the food was delicious. Despite the rather frightening specter the cook presented, Hugh had no trouble admitting that her talent in the kitchen was impressive. She was much better than the resident chef at Montrose Hall.

When Katie came in a few moments later, bearing a pitcher of wildly sloshing water and favoring a bandaged hand, he simply smiled, unalarmed. Everything seemed different today. The candlelight that bolstered the dreary morning light seemed more golden, the food more appetizing, Charlotte more beautiful.

Suspecting it was contentment he was feeling, Hugh grinned, savoring the moment. He wanted to feel this way more often, and he knew Charlotte was the cause. Therefore a stratagem was required to convince his lover that having him around could benefit her in more ways than orgasms. Since she'd provided the solution already, he had only to take advantage of it.

"You're in a fine mood," Charlotte noted, smiling against the rim of her cup. Hugh La Coeur was also in fine form. Dressed in warm shades of brown, he made her mouth water, the handsomeness of his features intensified by a boyish smile.

"I am. More's the pity for you." He waggled his brows suggestively.

She laughed. "A girl could become accustomed to having you around."

"I hope you do." He pushed away his empty plate and stood, moving to her chair. "Shall we retire to my room and study your map?"

Charlotte rose, a sharp tingle of awareness coursing through her veins. She glanced at Hugh over her shoulder and batted her lashes. "I thought studying the map came later?" Her eyes dropped to his trousers, and she watched, fascinated, as his cock swelled before her eyes.

"Stop that." He grabbed her elbow and led her to the stairs.

"Stop what?" she asked innocently, biting back a smile.

"You know very well what," he said, his voice a slow drawl that made her toes curl in her slippers. "Drooling while staring at my cock."

"I did no such thing!" she protested, choking back a giggle as they ascended the stairs.

He shot her an arch glance. "You did, too, insatiable minx. A man can hardly get any rest around here."

She choked. "Horrid man! You wouldn't leave me alone. How many times did I roll over and attempt sleep?"

"Several," he said smoothly. "But it wasn't long before you reached for me again."

Charlotte paused on the middle stair. "Only because your erection was poking me in the spine!"

Hugh shrugged in exquisite nonchalance. "You were wiggling."

She stared at him, fighting back laughter, her entire body warming to the sensual amusement she found in his dark gaze. He was so devastatingly handsome, full of vigor and mischief. He was a man who lived life, while she'd spent the last few years in a daze. She was drawn to that energy, to that zest, wanting to absorb the thrill of it into the marrow of her bones.

Unable to help herself, she stepped forward and offered him her mouth. With a deep groan, he obliged, gifting her with one of his sensual kisses. Charlotte melted against him, her hands drifting to clutch the powerful muscles of his shoulders.

"See?" he murmured, licking her parted lips. "You are doing it again."

Achingly aroused, she laughed breathlessly. "You're a conceited rake."

"And you're a brazen wench." His hands cupped her breasts, teasing her hardened nipples.

She pulled back with a grin. "You like that I am."

Hugh leaned back against the railing and crossed his arms. "I quite like that you are," he agreed. "Now would you like to go over your map?"

Charlotte considered him for a moment, from head to toe. He was fully, impressively aroused, and she was obviously willing, but he wanted to study the blasted map? She chewed her lower lip.

"Think you can keep your hands to yourself?" he prodded.

She narrowed her eyes, enjoying the game. "Can you?"

He grinned. "Shall we see who can hold out the longest?"

"A wager?" She rubbed her hands together. "Certainly."

"What are the stakes?"

"The stakes?"

"There has to be something in it for the victor. 'Tis the possibility of winning something that drives a man to gamble."

"A tumble isn't enough?"

"I had intended that to be *my* prize," he said with a pout.

She laughed. "You can always choose the same."

A dark gold brow rose. "Ah, but my gain must be greater than yours, or your loss more than mine, to make it truly a wager."

"You appear to know a great deal about gambling," Charlotte noted.

"I've had some experience," he said smoothly. "So if you are able to keep your hands to yourself for longer than I, you shall win a hot, sweaty tumble. I, however, want a boon."

She frowned. "What sort of boon?"

"I haven't decided yet."

"You're cheating!"

"I am not. Of course, you can always forfeit now and save us both the trouble . . ." He dropped his arms and stepped closer, enveloping her with his scent and potent masculinity.

"Oh, no. I won't forfeit. I shall win."

He gripped her elbow and then gestured up the stairs with his other hand. "Excellent. Let's begin."

Her heart racing with excitement, Charlotte moved with Hugh up the staircase and to his room, her mind industriously considering all the avenues she could take to ensure her victory. The first thing she did upon entering his chamber was move to the fireplace and throw on more coal.

"What the devil are you doing?" he asked. "It's plenty warm in here."

"Truly? I feel a chill."

Hugh shrugged out of his coat. "If you want me naked, you have only to ask."

"I thought I had. You wanted to look at the map instead."

He shot her a mock glare, and Charlotte laughed. She hadn't had this much fun in ages.

No, that wasn't true. She hadn't had *any* fun in ages.

After removing his waistcoat and cravat, Hugh moved to the desk and bent over the map. "Can you bring me everything you have that pertains to this?"

"Of course." Charlotte left the room with a plan and returned a quarter of an hour later with her first salvo ready to fire.

Gliding back into Hugh's suite with a wide grin, she paused just inside the doorway, arrested by the sight of his bare back. He'd removed his shirt and shoes, the corded muscles of his shoulders bunching as he leaned his weight on his arms, his skin covered with a fine sheen of perspiration from the warmth of the fire. She sighed, thinking she could simply stare at him for days.

Without turning around, he said, "Drooling again?"

"You are the most conceited man," she muttered. She reached the desk and dropped the books with a loud thump. He lifted his gaze to look at her.

"Bloody hell," he breathed, taking in the black negligee she wore. Held up with ribbons at the shoulders and completely sheer, it was an erotic confection she'd had for years and never donned before. The gown flowed with her, changing opacity, teasing the eye with glimpses of her nipples and the curve of her waist.

Charlotte brushed her fingertips across his full lips. "Careful, darling. You'll drool."

His brows snapped together. "Cheaters never win," he growled.

"I'm not cheating."

His scowl clearly refuted her. "Why don't you show me what you've gathered so far, so I don't waste time pointing out things you may already know."

Shaking her head, she wondered why he was so determined to keep them out of bed and focused on the map. With any other man she might consider the possibility that the map interested him more than she did, but with Hugh she knew that wasn't true. He wouldn't be so frustrated if he weren't fighting the temptation she presented. Something was afoot, and if she wished to discover what it was, she'd have to play along.

Pulling the books closer, she grabbed the slender journal from the top and opened it. "According to Glenmoore, he won this map in a wager while traveling through the Caribbean. He dismissed it as nothing more than a souvenir, until he was approached by a local man who swore he was among the crew that originally hid the treasure."

Hugh stared at her with his intense dark eyes. "What exactly is this treasure?"

"Glenmoore was never able to discover the answer to that with certainty. There were two tales. The simple one was pirate's gold. The other featured a love story."

"A love story?" he asked skeptically.

Nodding, Charlotte turned the pages of Glenmoore's journal until she found a worn piece of paper tucked inside. Upon opening it, a lovely female visage appeared. "Her name was Anne," she explained. "According to the story Glenmoore heard, she fled an unhappy marriage to sail the high seas with a pirate named Calico Jack. They were together for a time, but Jack was eventually caught and hanged. It is said that Anne, who was pregnant when he was killed, fled the authorities and hid his ill-gotten gains."

Hugh rubbed the back of his neck. The pose emphasized his powerful arms and beautifully built chest. She licked her lips.

Good heavens, she *was* going to drool.

"Charlotte, don't you think—" He raised his eyes from the map and met hers. Then he groaned. "How in damnation is a man to concentrate on anything when you dress in that manner and look at him thusly?"

"Why are you so interested in the map all of a sudden?"

Reaching down, he stroked his erection through his broadcloth trousers. "I'd like to be useful to you for things other than sex."

Charlotte blinked, then moved to a nearby chair and sat down. All thoughts of seduction and winning their amorous bet left her head. "You'd like to be useful," she repeated softly, awed by the statement. "I don't believe I've ever had a man say that to me before."

"Yes, well, I, for one, have never said such a thing before," he grumbled. "Being wanted for simple fornication has its decided benefits. And giving in to such demands is certainly less painful to a man's genitals. I blame the water hereabouts for this madness."

He scrubbed a hand across his face before pulling the journal closer. "Do you truly believe in this treasure nonsense?"

She watched him studying the journal, obviously sexually frustrated and yet determined to find a way to be valuable to her, and her heart softened. What an odd man he was. She couldn't puzzle him out, but then, what did it matter? She felt alive and appreciated, and this man was the cause.

"Charlotte?" He glanced at her and muttered an oath under his breath. "Do you intend to assist me with this or not?"

"I forfeit." She'd never done such a thing in her life. Cursed (or blessed, depending on how one looked at it) with a competitive nature she took every challenge seriously.

"Beg your pardon?"

"You win. I forfeit. Can we have sex now?"

"Hell and damnation!" Hugh pushed away from the desk and began to pace. "You are not allowed to forfeit."

She stood. "Why not?"

"Because I need to help you with this."

"You can help me later."

He paused and faced her, holding his arms out, displaying

his perfection even as he displayed his frustration. "Why are you being so bloody difficult?"

"What do you want, Hugh?" she asked softly. "What do you gain by assisting me?"

Growling, he turned away. "The storm will pass soon, leaving me no reason to tarry here."

"Yes, I know."

"My carriage was new, damn it, and cost me a bloody fortune! I should be enraged, *furious,* that the wretched thing broke. Yet I'm grateful, because it gave me the opportunity to meet you. And I suspect once I leave, I shall miss you, and I never miss anyone."

Her heart racing, Charlotte crossed the small space that separated them. Her hands caressed his back, feeling the muscles tense beneath her fingertips. His words, his passion . . . she'd never witnessed anything like them. "Hush," she soothed.

"You left this morning to bathe, and you were gone forever. It's madness, I tell you. A horrid, insidious madness, to crave the company of a stranger the way I do yours. Yesterday at this time, I didn't even know who you were. And last night, when I was inside you, I wanted no more than that. But this morning, I thought perhaps more would be nice—"

"Shhh . . ."

"—and now—"

Too short to reach his lips, she pressed an ardent kiss to his nipple, and his hands fisted in her unbound hair.

Hugh pushed her roughly away, revealing fierce, dark eyes that might have frightened her if she hadn't been so aroused. "And now I want you to come with me. Become my mistress. You'll want for nothing, I promise you that."

"Oh Hugh . . ."

He crushed his mouth down on hers, and Charlotte was flooded with sensation, a sharp, almost painful racing of heat across her skin. All morning she'd craved him. She'd needed his touch, his smile, the warmth of his gaze. It was madness, she agreed, to want the attentions of a stranger, but that was how it was, and she couldn't be sorry, not when it felt this wonderful.

Sinking to his knees, he pulled her down with him, his hands leaving her hair and moving to her breasts, every touch rife with an underlying tenderness that cut her to the quick. "I'll replace all your jewels, all your gowns. I'll give you a home, and it will be yours, in your name—"

"Cease talking, damn you." She didn't want promises or dreams. She just wanted right now, just this moment, and nothing more. She was afraid to want more.

Spinning away, she dropped to all fours and spread her legs, waiting for the sweet, oblivious pleasure that filled her when they joined.

But when he moved, it wasn't as she expected. It wasn't with the fevered urgency he'd displayed only hours ago. Instead it was a hot brush of breath through her gown, the heated press of his cheek against her spine, the soft slide of his hands along her sides.

She dropped her forehead to the rug, her body quivering, her skin dampening with sweat from her proximity to the fire.

"I would like the luxury of touching you like this," he murmured, his fingers running along the length of her spine. "I want to take my time, savor you, instead of feeling so rushed, so desperate."

"Desperate?" she gasped, arching into his touch.

"That is how I feel, as if I must have my fill before it's too late." Hugh lifted her hair to his face and breathed deeply. "This is such a beautiful color. It's the most glorious shade of red I've ever seen."

Charlotte attempted to roll over so she could savor him as he was savoring her, but he held her still with a firm grip.

He slid her gown up slowly, using the soft material to caress her skin. She shivered as his hand dipped between her legs, tangling in the damp curls. "And this red—darker, more passionate. From the moment I saw you on that massive horse, I wanted to know what color the hair here would be." His finger circled her engorged clit with a featherlight touch, while his other hand reached around and cupped her breast. "When you lie naked in the bed, your hair spilled across the pillows, your skin so pale, your nipples and lips so dark . . . I can hardly bear it."

He kissed the curve of her derriere. "But it is the things you say and the sound of your laughter that move me most."

She closed her eyes, awash in feeling and emotion. Charlotte looked at life pragmatically, and she felt no shame for her past. The need to survive had long ago overridden her pride. But in all of her experience, she'd never had a man take such time with her, stoking her arousal, making her liquid with desire, as Hugh had done from the very beginning. The sexual act shouldn't feel this intimate, not when the situation was so temporary. But then he slipped a finger inside her, and she lost her trepidation. He entered a little more, and she tensed, sore from his earlier amorous attentions.

Hugh hummed a coaxing sound, and then his mouth was there, his tongue moving in deep licks, just the way he kissed. He parted her with his fingers, his other hand kneading her breast, rolling her nipple.

"Please," she whispered, circling her hips into his thrusting tongue, wanting him . . . desperately.

He straightened, and a moment later she felt the hard heat of him, pressing slowly into her, filling the empty ache she hadn't known was there until he'd arrived. Patient and tender, he stroked her spine, soothing her, as his cock stretched swollen tissues unaccustomed to such constant use.

"Yes . . ." she sighed, when his thighs touched hers, her body stretched to the limit to accommodate him. She arched her hips upward in silent invitation, and he slipped deeper inside with a soft curse.

"This feeling," he grunted, hunching over her and cupping her silk-covered breasts with his hands. "I cannot imagine ever having enough of this."

He slid out slowly and then pressed forward again, starting a leisurely rhythm and maintaining it, the steady in and out inundating her with pleasure. She whimpered and began to writhe, begging him to end her torment.

"Do you truly want it to end?" he asked in a husky murmur. "I don't."

Her short nails left scratch marks in the rug as he slowed his pace. She *didn't* want it to end—this moment, his visit, none of it. But if she didn't orgasm soon she was afraid she would die. "Please . . ."

He thrust deep and groaned, burying his cock to the hilt and coming, burning her from the inside with hot, pulsing streams of his seed.

Charlotte came just like that, convulsing around him, his chest to her back, his hands on her breasts, his groans with her cries, until she couldn't tell where she ended and Hugh La Coeur began.

Hugh brushed fiery red curls from Charlotte's face before kissing the tip of her nose. "I want you to come with me when I leave." Lifting her from the floor, he carried her to the bed.

She buried her face in his throat. "I cannot leave here."

"Why not?" He set her atop the counterpane and then slid beside her.

She caught his hand and brought it to her heart, her eyes a soft and misty green. "Because we're safe here, the servants and I. We have a home where we're comfortable. It may not be ideal, but it's reliable."

Resting against the pillows, Hugh studied her face. "I can be reliable. I shall open an account for you, in your name. I've promised you a house, and I'll provide it. Everything I give you will be yours to keep. Plenty to provide for you and the others."

Charlotte looked away. "I like Derbyshire," she said softly.

He stared at her, feeling as if he'd taken a physical blow. *She would choose this place, this life, over him?* He'd told her how he felt, revealed emotions he didn't know how to manage, and she shunned him. In truth she didn't trust him.

It's reliable, she said. Unspoken was the notion that he was not.

"Jesus," he muttered, sliding off the bed. He walked to the window and pushed aside the drapes, gazing at the winter scene outside. A few days more and he would be free to move on, free to return to the careless life he'd once enjoyed but now found sadly unfulfilling. If he expired today, what memory would he leave behind? That of a man who was unreliable and irresponsible? He didn't want to be that man anymore.

"There are things you don't know," Charlotte said behind him, her voice soft and tentative.

He kept his back to her but was acutely aware of every move she made. "Are you going to tell me what they are?"

"I . . ." She paused, then sighed. "No."

"Well, then." Hugh released a deep breath, his disappointment painful. "I suppose that answers my question."

"I wish I could explain."

"Please," he said, raising a hand. "Don't say anything further. I asked, you replied. There's nothing more to be said." But part of him wished she would tell him, would confide in him, would trust him. Then again, the more he knew, the worse his ridiculous attachment could become.

No, it was best to keep her as an amusement and nothing more, regardless of how he felt at the moment.

Hugh turned from the window and retrieved his trousers. Then he collected his shirt.

"Where are you going?" she asked.

He didn't look at her. "For a walk."

"Where?" The sheets rustled. "I can show you around the manse."

"I'd rather you didn't, if you don't mind." He could sense her hurt from across the room, but he forced himself to ignore it, moving into the adjoining sitting room to create much-needed distance between them.

Having spent most of his stay in the bedroom, Hugh wasn't familiar with any other wings of the house, but he didn't imagine it would be too difficult to find the study he'd stumbled into before. Most of his focus had been on Charlotte last night, but if he remembered correctly, there was a liquor-stocked sideboard in there.

And a drink, or several, was just what he needed, to find the frame of mind that kept his emotions far removed from his bedsport.

Chapter Six

It took only a few moments after leaving Charlotte for Hugh to find the study, which was just down the hall. He also found something else. Seated at the desk, with books scattered all around, was a young girl of no more than sixteen or seventeen years of age. Pausing on the threshold, he wasn't certain if he should enter or not. Propriety dictated the girl be chaperoned in his presence, but then he doubted anyone in this household would take offense.

Who the devil was she? She looked . . . normal. And the casual way in which she made use of the study made him think she must be a member of the household and not a servant.

The girl looked up at just that moment, and her face broke out in a delighted grin. With hair as dark as night and bright blue eyes, she was quite lovely. "Hallo, Lord Montrose," she greeted as she rose from behind the desk and came toward him. "'Tis a pleasure to make your acquaintance." She held out her hand.

Completely dumbfounded, Hugh moved out of sheer habit, reaching for her fingers and bowing. "A pleasure . . . ?"

She giggled. "Guinevere. My mother was a bit of a romantic. But you should call me Gwen as all my close associates do."

Arching a brow, Hugh studied the chit further. Tall and

slender, she held herself with the hallmarks of good breeding but deported herself with an informality that betrayed her lack of proper social training.

"Are you studying?" he asked, looking over her shoulder at the items on the desk.

"I was attempting to, yes." Gwen smiled. "But history is simply not holding my attention today. Where is Charlotte?"

"I'm not certain." Surely she wouldn't still be in his room. Most likely she'd never grace it again, leastwise not while he was occupying it.

"Ahhh . . . a lover's tiff," Gwen murmured sagely. "Surprisingly early, but inevitable, I've been told. And the deeper the attachment, the more hurtful the row."

"How the devil would you know of such things?"

Shrugging, Gwen turned back to the desk. "There's not much of interest out here, my lord, and few people with whom to talk. Around these parts the only true form of entertainment appears to be courtship, and I'm a curious sort. It's rather like an opera, you see, or a play. Quite fascinating the way the sexes associate with each other, wouldn't you agree?"

Hugh shook his head. He'd never encountered a stranger group of individuals in his life. "I require liquor," he muttered, moving with long strides to the sideboard, where several crystal decanters sat lined up with tumblers. Tossing back one drink, he savored the burning heat in his stomach, before pouring another and turning to face the young Guinevere again. "Are you related to Her Grace?"

Her brows arched. "I'm her ward."

"Right." He finished his second drink. To these people it would make perfect sense to leave a young girl in the care of a duchess not quite right in the head.

"'Ere now!"

Hugh glanced at the doorway, where Artemis stood with hands on his hips. "You shouldn't be talking to 'im," the servant scolded Gwen.

"Beg your pardon?" Hugh stiffened.

Artemis turned his bulging eye toward him. "I tole 'er

Grace you'd be nothin' but trouble. But she wouldn't listen to me. And look what you've done!"

"What the devil are you talking about?"

"She's cryin' and yer in 'ere imbibin' spirits and swearin' in front o' Miss Guinevere. And 'alf dressed, too! Disgraceful."

"Oh, dear." Gwen gave a regretful shake of her head and moved to make her egress. "That must have been some row you had."

"I've done nothing," Hugh cried, affronted at the unfair accusation, and a tad embarrassed. Artemis was correct. He wasn't acting the gentleman. "I've yet to be introduced to Lady Glenmoore. I'm certainly not the cause of her distress. Most likely it's *you*. Lord knows I'd be in tears if you worked in my household."

Artemis gasped, his hands coming to his hips. "See?" he blustered to Gwen. "I tole ye how they are!" He lifted a finger to the side of his head and spun it in a circle. "All the Quality are a bit—"

"Damnation!" Hugh slammed his empty tumbler onto the sideboard. "Of all the insolent—"

"Good heavens," Gwen interrupted, wrinkling her nose. "Artemis, stand down."

Hugh crossed his arms. "He's mad as you please."

"Eh?" Artemis snapped. "Ye can't even recall the name o' the lady you've been entertainin' all mornin'."

"Oh, my." Gwen blushed, her hands lifting to her cheeks.

Hugh froze. His horrified gaze shifted to Gwen. When she winced, all the pieces fell into place. Stunned, he shot a glance at Artemis, who for once had the grace to look chastened. "Good God." He leaned heavily against the sideboard. "Where is she?"

"Perhaps you should wait until you're less surly," Gwen advised.

"I am not surly!"

"You're yelling," she pointed out.

"I am not—" He took a deep breath and closed his eyes. He *was* yelling. Despite the foul mood brought on by Charlotte's lack of faith, he needed to control himself and deal with the situation rationally. "I need to speak with her." Opening his eyes, he said, "She'll be safe with me."

"I don't doubt that," Gwen said with a smile. "'Tis obvious you are both a bit soft on one another. Artemis, do you know where Her Grace is?"

The butler gestured toward the hallway. "'Er room. Third door down on the right."

"Thank you."

Artemis blocked the doorway for a moment. He opened his mouth and then snapped it shut, moving out of the way.

Halfway down the gallery, Hugh paused and took another deep breath. There was so much to comprehend at once, it was nearly impossible, and in the end, the only one who could clarify anything was Charlotte. And feeling a cad that he'd made her cry, Hugh was suitably contrite when he knocked on the closed door. He heard her bid him entry and walked inside.

She sat at the escritoire, studying the map. With her bright red hair piled atop her head and dark green dressing gown, she was a vision. When she looked up, her eyes were as clear as a field of grass in spring, her nose pert and not red. She hadn't been crying at all. It was easy to deduce that he'd been duped. Obviously the butler felt Hugh should know the truth.

Her chin lifted. "Good morning, my lord." Her voice was cool and impartial, far removed from the temptress who'd been on her hands and knees for him just a short time ago.

Goaded into it by her chilly demeanor, he replied, "Good morning, Your Grace."

Charlotte flinched, a slight movement of her brows that he would have missed if he hadn't been determinedly searching for it.

"Artemis," she muttered under her breath. "Drat him."

Hugh closed the door and waited.

She sighed. "Very well, then." Coming to her feet, she moved around the small desk and approached him head-on, just as she approached all her difficulties. "Is there anything else you discovered?"

"You refer to Guinevere?" He realized then that their meeting could not have been unplanned. Had the young girl studied in her room, he would never have learned of her existence. For whatever reason, the members of Charlotte's odd menagerie wanted him to know their secrets.

Pursing her lips, she gestured to the nearby settee, waiting until he sat to continue. "Everything I told you was the truth."

"Truth by omission," he argued.

"But the truth nevertheless."

"Was that you in black and shrouded in lace?"

"Yes, that was I."

He released a sigh of relief. He'd thought he was insane for feeling aroused by the darkly clad duchess. Knowing it was Charlotte in disguise put the whole encounter in perspective.

She pinched the bridge of her nose. "Gwen is Carding's daughter. Since he's not married, I'm certain you can deduce the nature of her association to him."

Hugh leaned back, noting the sudden weariness that weighted Charlotte's slender frame. "He left her with you?"

"Good heavens, no," she said, with a bitter laugh. "That man cared nothing for his own father. Think he would care for a bastard? It was Glenmoore who asked me to look after Gwen. He discovered her existence when she was a child, and started a small stipend for her mother. But the mother passed on, and there was no one to care for Gwen. Carding refused to do anything for her, so Glenmoore brought her here. He wanted a grandchild desperately, and Gwen is such a dear. One cannot help but adore her."

"And the marriage?"

"It was the only way Glenmoore could ensure Gwen's future. He could leave me a trust for Gwen, and grant me the rights to claim it, should Carding prove to be a problem."

"A pitiable trust fund," Hugh muttered. "This place is a disgrace."

Charlotte reached over and claimed his hand, jolting him with a spark of sensual awareness. "Glenmoore was afraid to bequeath too large a trust. Since the marriage was never consummated, as Carding well knows, the duke wanted to give as little provocation as possible for a contest."

She stood and began to pace. "No one can discover who the duchess is, Hugh. We cannot have outsiders questioning who Gwen is. Those were Carding's only requirements in allowing us the use of this house."

"What future does this place hold for her?" he asked, standing to face her. "What kind of life is this?"

"None. Which is why Glenmoore left me the map."

"Bloody hell, Charlotte!" Hugh scrubbed a hand over his face. "'Tis ridiculous to pin all your hopes on that blasted map. Pirate's treasure and other such nonsense . . . You shall rot out here. And Gwen, as well."

"And you would take us in?" she challenged, her cheeks flushed and eyes sparked with anger. "A mistress with a minor ward and entourage of disabled servants? Gwen would be thoroughly ruined. Or do you intend to hide us away? Perhaps the accommodations would be superior, but we would still be trapped, our futures dependent on the whim of a rake's temporary infatuation."

His hands clenched into fists. Would no one ever trust him to be responsible? "Tell me, Charlotte, what am I to you?"

She snorted. "A charming stranger. A man too devilishly handsome for his own good. An amorous libertine who shows flashes of kindness that startle me."

Hugh turned away and moved toward the door. He'd heard enough.

"What am I to you?" she called after him.

Pausing on the threshold, he turned back. "A beautiful woman whose sensuality calls to me. A nurse, a guardian, a champion for those in your care. A pragmatist who will do anything to survive, a trait I appreciate, since I lack it myself. An honest individual who said she admired me, who believed, if only for a moment, that I am capable of doing whatever needs to be done."

"You are."

"Only when it relates to you."

Charlotte's lower lip quivered, her fingers picking restlessly at her skirts.

He took a deep breath and said, "I've acted out of character ever since I stepped foot in this monstrosity of a house, and since I didn't much care for my character before, I don't mind at all. In fact, I rather like myself better when I'm with you. I like that I admire things about you other than your physical attributes, though I admit to spending a great deal of the last twenty-four hours admiring those." He sketched a bow, then turned again and left the room.

"Hugh, wait!" Charlotte hurried after him.

"Why?" he asked over his shoulder. "I understand."

"But you don't."

Hugh stopped but didn't turn around. She circled him, her lush floral scent enveloping his senses.

She tilted her head back to look at him. "If it were just you and I, and no one else, I would go with you. I would leave everything behind to be with you, for however long you would have me."

"But it isn't that way."

"No." Her hand reached for his, just as she'd often done since he met her. "And I am dreadfully sorry it isn't. You must realize, too many people depend on me to simply hand over everything and hope for the best."

His mind shifting industriously, Hugh reasoned out a way to prove he was someone on whom she could rely. "You want to find that treasure, and I can assist you. But you will have to trust me."

Her eyes widened, her wariness a palpable thing.

"I can take you to Lord Merrick," he continued, hoping to allay her refusal. "His father-in-law is Jack Lambert. If anyone could decipher that map, Merrick could, or at the very least he would know someone who could."

Charlotte swallowed hard.

Rushing ahead, he said, "Both my sister and Lord Merrick have holdings in Derbyshire. That was my destination before fate led me here." He brushed his fingertips across her lips.

"You shall have to travel by ship eventually. It would relieve me greatly to know you traveled on a Lambert vessel, with proper escort and protection. I can make arrangements for you."

"You would do that?"

He smiled at the softening he saw in her gaze. "Only one person in my life has ever relied on me for anything—my sister, Julienne—and I'm ashamed to admit I failed her. Miserably. You would be doing me a great honor if you would rely on me and give me the chance to redeem myself. You've carried your burdens for a long time. Why not pass the weight to me for a while?"

"From the moment you arrived, my burdens have felt lighter, even if in truth nothing has changed."

He kissed the tip of her nose. "I would appreciate your intimate companionship for the duration of our association, but only if you wish it. If you don't, I still promise to assist you in whatever way I can. This is not about sex, Charlotte. 'Tis important to me that you understand my motives."

Resting her head against his chest, she laughed. "I understand, Hugh. And continuing our association would please me as well. It's shameful, really. I've been nothing but a wanton since you arrived."

"Only when you're not rescuing the entire population of Derbyshire misfits," he said dryly.

"'Ere now!" Artemis complained, stepping out of the study. "We don't take kindly to that nonsense 'round 'ere!"

Hugh attempted to step away from Charlotte, but she held fast, and after a second he relaxed. Another second more, and he discovered he rather liked holding a female in a nonamorous position. It was soothing.

Looking over the pile of red curls, he locked his eyes with Artemis's one, which had the gall to wink.

Hugh chuckled, realizing he just might like the butler a little after all.

Chapter Seven

"It hasn't snowed in the last two days," Charlotte said sadly, as she looked out the window. She'd come to love the sight of snow, since the fall of it meant Hugh would stay another day.

Glancing up from the journal, the object of her affection gifted her with a boyish smile. The effect of that smile was so powerful, her breath caught and her hand lifted to shelter her rapidly beating heart.

Hugh ran a careless hand through his golden hair. "I noticed that this morning."

He was so achingly beautiful, she could hardly bear it. Thankfully he remained unaware of how he affected her. "If your carriage is repaired in time, perhaps it will be possible to set off tomorrow."

"My thoughts were similar." He closed the book and gestured for her to come closer.

The earl had been in residence for a fortnight, and so far his interest in her showed no signs of waning. He slept in her bed every night and spent every waking moment with her, maintaining his easy charm without any sign of boredom. If she moved to leave the room, he followed. If she wanted to take a nap, he went with her. For the first time in her life, the loneliness that was her constant companion was gone, replaced by the steadfast presence of the dashing Earl of Montrose.

"You seem nervous," he noted.

"And this surprises you? I haven't left the area in a very long time. My clothes are sadly out of date, and my social deportment is rusty."

Hugh chuckled, and when she came close enough, he tugged her into his lap. "No one will pay any mind to those things. Your beauty is so blinding, it outshines everything else."

"Perhaps *you* think so," she muttered.

"I *definitely* think so," he corrected, kissing the tip of her nose. "You have nothing to fear. The company we'll keep are infamous for their eccentricities. My sister and Remington aren't conventional by any means, and Merrick disappeared for years. To this day no one knows where he was. *That* sort of behavior is odd. My arriving with a gorgeous woman on my arm is positively commonplace, regardless of her attire."

Charlotte looked away, stung by the knowledge that she was simply one of many. She'd known he would be a temporary pleasure when she met him. Why she'd allowed herself to care for him, she couldn't say. But then, it was most likely inevitable. How could any woman deny him anything, including her heart?

"I have never taken a woman to meet my sister before," he said softly, and when she turned to look at him, it was clear he knew her thoughts. His dark eyes studied her face, a frown gathering between his brows.

To divert him from his intense perusal, she threw her arms around his neck and hugged him close. "Thank you for helping me, Hugh. I cannot begin to tell you what it means to me."

"No more, I imagine, than what it means to me that you trust me to do so." He tucked her against his chest and sighed. "Are you even a little excited to leave this place and mingle with the rest of the world?"

"Oh, I'm very excited. This will be Gwen's first time away from the district, and I eagerly anticipate meeting Lucien Remington. I've heard some—"

She squealed as she was tackled to the settee.

Hugh loomed over her with narrowed gaze. "You've been

trapped out here for three years, and the most excitement you can muster is for Lucien Remington?"

Charlotte made no attempt to squelch the thrill she felt at his possessiveness. She blinked innocently. "Well, he's rather legendary among the demimonde. I met his mother once. A delightful woman. She—"

Lowering his head, Hugh bit her bottom lip.

"Ow!" she complained, pouting.

"He's married. To my sister. Very happily, I should point out. It's almost sickening the way they fawn over one another."

She shrugged. "I can look."

"No," he said gruffly. "You cannot."

"You're jealous!" Giggling, she tugged his head down and kissed him. Against her thigh, she felt his cock swell. "You should know that women like to ogle handsome men. Usually with as much enthusiasm as men like to ogle attractive women."

"My sister might not approve," he said, against her lips.

"Oh, you see, women actually like it when the men they escort draw such avid attention. It makes us quite proud to possess something so desired."

"Hmmm . . ." Hugh's mouth twitched as he held back a smile. "I suppose I should round up some admirers. Perhaps then you'll pay more attention to me than to Remington."

Charlotte's smile wavered. She almost didn't want to leave the estate, preferring instead to remain trapped with Hugh, safe from the forces that would separate them.

"Ah, *some* women like it," he noted perceptively, his hands brushing the hair away from her face. "But you are not one of them."

The conversation was rapidly moving to areas best left unexplored. "You're heavy," she said, trying to create distance between them, even if it was only physical. It was a lie, of course. She relished the feel of his hard, powerful body stretched over hers. She loved how it made her feel cherished and cared for, instead of dominated.

"You bear my weight often. This is the first I've heard you

complain." His gaze burned her with its intensity. "Am I beginning to bore you, Charlotte?"

"No!" Her hands reached for his face. In the last fortnight, she'd learned many things about her lover, the most important being how deeply he feared being expendable. "Oh, Hugh, not that. Never that."

"Never?" He brushed his mouth across hers.

Arching up into his weight, she pulled him close. "Take me to bed now."

"Why?"

She offered a seductive smile. "You know why."

"Yes." He lifted away from her. "I know why."

Charlotte watched him, confused, as he rose from the settee and moved to the window where she'd stood a moment ago.

"What do you think about when we're making love?" he asked suddenly.

"What do I . . . ?" She shook her head and sat up. "I don't think about anything."

"Precisely."

"What are you saying?"

"You use sex as a way to avoid your feelings."

She was speechless for a moment, surprised by the accusation. "And you don't?" she scoffed, rising to her feet.

"No rows," came Gwen's chastising voice from the doorway. She swept into the room with her customary enthusiasm. Dressed in sprigged muslin, with her long, dark hair tied at the nape, she appeared younger than her seventeen years. "We've been trapped together for days. 'Tis inevitable that we would become a tad testy with one another."

"I've been here for years," Charlotte retorted. "Montrose is the testy one. Perhaps his lordship is the one who is bored?"

Hugh turned from the window, and the smoldering light in his eyes stole her breath. "With the games you play to keep me at bay? Yes, I weary of them."

"Keep you at bay? How can you say that after these last two weeks?"

He snorted, and her hands clenched into fists. He wanted everything, damn him.

Gwen coughed discreetly. "Cook outdid herself for tea. Katie will be bringing it up shortly."

Bowing, and looking damned dashing while doing it, Hugh said, "You must excuse me today, Miss Guinevere. I feel a headache coming on. I believe I'll retire for a nap." His glare blamed Charlotte as he walked past her and left the room without another word.

"Oh." Gwen's wide-eyed gaze moved to Charlotte. "He's not testy. He's angry."

"Apparently."

"Will he still take us with him when he departs?"

The plaintive note in Gwen's voice drew Charlotte from her thoughts. "Of course," she soothed. "He won't be angry in an hour or so."

Gwen's head tilted to the side. "Why not?"

"Men don't usually stay angry at women for long." Charlotte moved back to the settee as Katie entered with a cacophony of rattling china. "Even if the fault is ours."

Sighing, Gwen joined her, spreading out her skirts to avoid wrinkles, as Charlotte had taught her. "I don't believe I will ever understand men. The more I learn about them, the less they make sense."

Charlotte laughed. "Truer words were never spoken."

"If Lord Montrose is bored, perhaps I could play whist with him, or cassino, though it's not as much fun with only two."

"He'd probably enjoy that."

Hugh had taken a liking to Gwen, and his gentle, courtly dealings with the young girl warmed Charlotte's heart.

"But perhaps you meant to say, it is the company that bores him," Gwen said, wrinkling her nose.

"Oh, no, Gwen." Charlotte covered her hand and gave it a reassuring squeeze. "If he's bored with anything, it's me."

"I doubt it's that." Reaching for the tea, Gwen began to

serve, demonstrating a grace and social adeptness Charlotte had worked hard to teach her.

But Charlotte had no formal training. Everything she knew about proper social deportment was learned from studying others. She wanted Gwen to have a better start in life, and already time was running out. Gwen would come of age in less than a year.

"Montrose is smitten with you, Charlotte. It must be thrilling to have so handsome a man take such a keen interest in you."

"It is," she agreed. "I'm afraid, however, that I'm terribly smitten myself."

"Why be afraid?"

"Because we'd never suit."

"You suit beautifully," Gwen scoffed.

"In some ways, but in others we're worlds apart. You haven't experienced the class system yet, but you will."

"You are a duchess."

"I am a counterfeit duchess. The title doesn't change who I've always been. And this discussion is moot in any case. Lord Montrose is a man who holds only temporary interest in women."

Passing over a cup and saucer, Gwen smiled. "I propose a toast."

"Over tea?" Charlotte arched a brow.

"Don't tell me it's not proper. It's all we have at the moment, so it will have to do."

Charlotte laughed. Gwen's enthusiasm for life had never diminished, despite having spent so much of her childhood hidden away as a mistake. "Very well. What are we toasting?"

"New adventures."

Charlotte raised her cup. "To new adventures."

"Are we almost there?" Gwen asked. She craned her neck out the carriage window, her hand holding her bonnet to her head so it wouldn't blow away.

Hugh watched her antics with a wide grin, understanding how excited she must be to venture out after all these years. "How many times do you intend to ask that question, Miss Guinevere?"

"As many times as necessary for you to give me a straight answer." She shot him an arched look. "'When we arrive' is not a proper response."

"When have we ever done anything properly?" Charlotte teased, laughing as Gwen scowled in response.

"Oh, we're turning! We must be here!" Gwen nearly shook with excitement. "What a beautiful property. I wasn't aware they could make homes that big. And look at all the carriages!"

"Damnation," Hugh muttered, looking over Gwen's head to see the front of the Remington manse. Neoclassical in design, with fluted columns and overlooking a wide circular drive, it was stunning in its elegance. But the beautiful façade didn't hold his attention. Instead his narrowed gaze was riveted to the line of carriages that clogged the drive. Shunned by the highest tiers of Society, the Remingtons nevertheless had no lack of friends or acquaintances.

"Good heavens." Charlotte's hands went to her throat. "What will we do now?"

Hugh blew out a frustrated breath. He'd intended to tell Julienne about Charlotte, Gwen, and the whole mess with Glenmoore's map, but now he would have to alter course. Charlotte had taken great pains to hide her marriage to Glenmoore—encouraging Artemis to scare away visitors and hiding Gwen. Looking at her now, he could see the tension tightening her lips.

"Not to worry," Hugh soothed, thinking quickly. "Gwen will simply be your companion."

"And I will be Mrs. Riddleton," Charlotte finished, reaching for his hands and squeezing them tightly. "Your widowed paramour. You're brilliant, Hugh!"

"Riddleton?" he asked, even as warmth spread from her compliment up to his heart.

"My maiden name." Her eyes sparkled, and Hugh felt great satisfaction in having lightened her worries. It was a feeling to which a man could grow accustomed.

Gwen giggled. "It will be fun! Like a charade." She resumed her seat and rubbed her gloved hands together. "You are an angel sent from above, Lord Montrose. I cannot tell you how happy I am that your carriage was disabled near our home. If you hadn't come along, I would be studying right now and lamenting my boredom. Instead I am about to enjoy my first social gathering. I do hope there are more handsome men to ogle."

"Good God," Hugh muttered, arching a brow at Charlotte, who had the temerity to grin.

It took a few moments for the other carriages to dispatch their passengers and luggage, but it seemed all too soon that they were alighting by the front steps. Hugh was holding his hand out to Charlotte when a familiar deep voice sounded behind him.

"Montrose, we weren't expecting you."

Looking over his shoulder, Hugh smiled at his brother-in-law. "I couldn't allow you to have a gathering without me. Can you imagine how dreadfully boring that would be?"

Lucien Remington laughed aloud. "We're delighted to have you. And your lovely companions."

Charlotte stood on the bottom step with wide eyes. Gwen was worse, with her mouth agape. Both women stared at Lucien with obvious appreciation. Scowling, Hugh pulled Charlotte closer.

"Remington, allow me to present my very good friend, Mrs. Riddleton, and her companion, Miss . . ." Hugh cleared his throat to get Gwen's attention.

"Sherling," she blurted out, sticking out her hand. "Guinevere Sherling."

Lucien accepted the offering with a low bow, dazzling the young girl with a charming grin. Hugh began to tap his foot, not at all pleased with the reactions the ladies were having to the attractive former libertine.

And then Charlotte took his arm. Looking down at her, he caught her slight smile. "I prefer blonds," she whispered.

Suddenly Hugh's day was much brighter.

Remington gestured for the servants to collect the trunks and then led them inside. Gwen stumbled to a halt as they entered the foyer. A floating dual staircase directly ahead capped an expansive marble floor flanked by several doorways on either side. Overhead a massive crystal chandelier hung from a domed ceiling, featuring a painting of lush fern fronds on a pale blue background.

"This is so beautiful," Gwen breathed, clearly awestruck.

Lucien tilted his head in acknowledgment. "Thank you, Miss Sherling."

"Hugh La Coeur." All heads turned to the right, where Lady Julienne Remington stood in the doorway to the parlor. Dressed in pale blue silk with darker blue trim, his sister was a vision of beauty and poise. Heedless of the guests that milled around, she glided toward them with a brilliant smile and surrounded him in a fierce hug. "You should have told me you were coming, but regardless, I am very happy to see you."

Hugh lifted his sister's feet from the floor. "The sentiment is mutual," he whispered gruffly. Growing up without parents had made them closer than most siblings. After all the scrapes and mischief from which she'd rescued him, there wasn't anything in the world he wouldn't do for her.

Setting Julienne down, he drew Charlotte closer. She held out her hand and introduced herself.

"It's a pleasure to meet you, Mrs. Riddleton," Julienne said with a genuine smile. "This weather became so tedious, we decided to liven things up with a little winter house party. I'd warn you about some of my guests, but since you came with Hugh, I doubt anything you encounter will offend overmuch."

Charlotte laughed. "I thank you for your hospitality, my lady."

Julienne linked her arm with Charlotte's and smiled at Gwen. "Come along. I'll show you to your rooms and relate the scheduled activities."

With a quick wink over her shoulder, Charlotte moved to

the grand staircase with Julienne and Gwen, leaving Hugh staring after her.

"She's lovely," Remington murmured.

Hugh nodded his agreement, though he rather thought "lovely" was too tame a description.

"I admire your taste."

"That's quite a compliment coming from you, Remington."

Lucien laughed. "Shall we head to the billiards room? Most of the gentlemen are there."

As they left the foyer, Hugh asked, "Is Lord Merrick here?"

"Merrick is expected to arrive later this afternoon."

"Smashing." Hugh very nearly rubbed his hands together with glee. "I'd like to speak with him privately, if he'll consent."

"Certainly. You may use my study whenever you like."

Now that the matter for which he'd come was settled, Hugh looked forward to enjoying the afternoon. The last week with Charlotte and Gwen had been pleasant and the most relaxing time he could remember, but he missed the bawdy humor and salacious discourse he found exclusively in the presence of other gentlemen.

He entered the smoke-filled room behind Remington and raked his glance over the occupants. Lord Middleton, who stood with a group in the far corner, raised his hand in greeting and gestured him over. Hugh moved to meet him, but he paused midstep, his smile frozen, as a man standing near Middleton turned to see who approached.

"Montrose," the Duke of Glenmoore called out, with a wide smile. "It's been some time since we last met."

Hugh's jaw tensed. "Not long enough," he said under his breath.

After seeing Gwen comfortably ensconced with the other companions, Charlotte followed Hugh's sister down the hall. She couldn't help smiling. Julienne Remington was very easy to like. Blessed with the same honey blonde hair as Hugh and the same dark eyes, she was lovely. Bearing the poise and grace of a woman born to privilege, she nevertheless seemed open and accessible.

"Here we are," Julienne said, throwing open a door on the right. "I hope you'll be comfortable."

Stepping into the bedchamber, Charlotte gazed around in wonder. Decorated in shades of plum and taupe, it was spacious and luxurious. "This is beautiful," she breathed.

"I'm pleased you like it. Tonight we've scheduled a ball." Julienne lifted her arms in the air and spun about. "I've felt like dancing for months. It took great effort on Mr. Remington's part to acquire an orchestra, but he managed it, and I'm terribly excited."

"I lack suitable attire for such an event," Charlotte confessed. She had one evening gown with her that was simple enough in style to go without notice, but she would never attend a ball without Gwen. It would break the girl's heart, although she would never admit it.

Julienne studied her figure carefully. "You and I are not much different in build. I believe I have a number of dresses that would fit you. You can look through them and see which one most suits your taste."

"Oh, really, you mustn't trouble yourself."

"'Tis no trouble at all, Mrs. Riddleton."

"Charlotte," she corrected.

"Charlotte." Julienne grinned. "I like you, Charlotte. I have always enjoyed the company of straightforward and strong women. Hugh needs that sort of support in his life."

"He's quite capable of supporting himself."

Arching a brow, Julienne looked clearly dubious. "In any case, my brother is quite handsome."

"Yes, quite," Charlotte agreed with a laugh.

"And in evening finery, he's unsurpassed, as you must know."

Not willing to admit how little she and Hugh knew of one another, she said nothing, but she could picture him clearly. Showcased in stark black and white, his golden beauty would be devastating to the female senses.

"We mustn't have him wandering about unescorted," Julienne continued. "Wouldn't you agree?"

Charlotte clenched her fists. She might never be able to keep him, but for the next week Hugh La Coeur was hers, and she would do whatever was necessary to make certain every other woman present knew that. "Yes." She offered a grateful smile. "Thank you so much, my lady."

"Julienne."

"Thank you, Julienne."

"Did you bring an abigail with you?"

Charlotte shook her head, knowing the outmoded style of her garments most likely betrayed her limited means.

"Wonderful. You and I shall prepare for the evening together. My maid will take one look at your glorious hair and beg to style it. I hope you don't mind."

"No. That sounds lovely. Thank you. You've been so kind to me."

"Nonsense. It will be fun. Bring your companion, too, if you like." Julienne moved to the door. "Now, as much as I'd rather stay with you, I must see to the new arrivals. Your trunks will be up shortly. If you're at all interested, the other ladies are in the sitting room, a few doors down on the right. You'll hear the gossip as you draw closer."

Pausing with her hand on the knob, she offered a warm smile. "I'm very pleased you came, Charlotte. I shall track you down in an hour or two, and we'll have the opportunity to become better acquainted."

"I'd like that."

The door had barely shut behind Julienne Remington when a knock came. Gwen rushed in without waiting for permission. "Oh, Charlotte!" she cried. "There's a ball tonight. Isn't that exciting? My first ball. I cannot wait to see the clothes. And the men."

Laughing at the young girl's exuberance, Charlotte shrugged out of her travel pelisse. "You will wear my ice blue satin."

Gwen's eyes widened as she shook her head. "Oh, I couldn't possibly. That's your best gown."

"Lady Julienne has graciously offered me the use of one of her gowns."

Squealing with delight, Gwen spun around with her arms wide. "I really like her. She's as nice as Lord Montrose."

"Yes, she is." Another knock came to the door. When Charlotte opened it, she found two footmen waiting with her trunks, and a maid to unpack them.

Gwen came to her side. "Shall we retreat to the rear garden? Lady Canlow's companion said it was designed to look even prettier in the snow than it does in the spring."

Charlotte retrieved her pelisse and cloak, feeling a freedom and lightness of spirit that she doubted she'd ever felt before. And it was all Hugh La Coeur's doing, she knew. She linked her arm with Gwen's. "Well, we definitely must have a look, then."

Chapter Eight

"That has to be one of the more fantastic stories I've ever heard," Lucien said, with a shake of his head.

Hugh threw his head back and released a deep breath. "I know. Believe me. I thought I was going mad. You've never met such a ragtag collection of lovable misfits in your life." He started to pace. "Where in hell is your butler?" he snapped.

He'd sent the servant to locate Charlotte and bring her to him almost a half hour past. The Remington manse was vast, but not *that* vast.

"You are wearing a hole in my rug, Montrose," Lucien said dryly.

Cursing, Hugh stilled, staring down at the elegant Aubusson rug beneath his feet. He spun about as the door to the study opened. The butler entered, a prime example of an upper servant with his impassive face and unflappable demeanor. Snorting, Hugh realized he liked Artemis better. Artemis would have told him why Charlotte was absent immediately, unlike Remington's butler, who waited to be asked before he would speak.

"Out with it, man!" Hugh barked. "Where is Mrs. Riddleton?"

The butler turned his head to Hugh with a disdainful sniff. "Apparently there was a collision between two footmen as they carried Lord Merrick's trunks up the stairs. Mrs. Riddleton took the injured party to the kitchen. I informed her of your summons, my lord, but she said you would understand why she was unable to respond immediately."

Throwing up his hands, Hugh turned in exasperation to Lucien, who sat calmly behind his desk. "I swear, Remington, that woman is a magnet for the injured."

Laughing, Lucien rose and moved toward the door. "We'll go see how they're faring. Then we'll retire somewhere private, and you can inform Mrs. Riddleton about Glenmoore's presence."

When they reached the kitchen, they discovered a well-tended footman eating hot buttered scones, and no Charlotte. The servant leapt to his feet, flushing guiltily, but Remington waved him back down.

"Where the devil did she go?" Hugh asked a scullery maid, who stammered so terribly with fright in the face of his ill humor, he could hardly comprehend her.

"There was an ac-cc acci-ci-"

"Bloody hell. An *accident*?"

The maid nodded, and Hugh shot a glance at Remington, who was beginning to scowl.

"What happened now?" Lucien barked.

"Lady Denby broke her cup, Mr. Remington, and cut her finger."

"Where?"

"The upper sitting room."

Hugh and Remington took the servant's stairs to the upper floor, where they found Lady Denby with a bandaged finger, and no Charlotte.

Lucien sketched a quick bow before asking, "Do you have any idea where we can locate Mrs. Riddleton, Lady Denby?"

The buxom brunette batted her eyelashes and offered a coy smile. "Why, Lucien Remington, whatever do you need Mrs. Riddleton for?"

"*I* need her," Hugh growled. He was starting to feel a mild panic under his frustration. If Charlotte was traipsing all over the premises, she was very likely to run into Glenmoore.

Lady Denby arched a brow. "I see. Well, I would try the

stables, then, Lord Montrose. I believe she mumbled something about checking on a horse."

He released a deep breath and moved toward the door.

"The stables?" Lucien asked, following on his heels.

"Yes, yes, she's mad for horses." Hugh moved down the hallway with impatient strides. "One of my new carriage bays was injured when my wheel broke. She fussed over him the entire way here."

Lucien's soft chuckle earned him a scathing glance over Hugh's shoulder. "A magnet, you said."

When they reached the stables, Hugh found his horse sporting a liniment-covered foreleg, and no Charlotte.

"Damn and blast and bloody, everlasting hell!" Hugh cried, kicking a stall door and sending a fine spray of hay into the air. If he didn't find her immediately, he would go mad. Well-and-truly mad.

His heart raced in a desperate rhythm as he pictured Glenmoore finding Charlotte before he did. She'd promised to keep Gwen hidden in return for the use of the manse. Who knew how Glenmoore would react if he discovered the two had not only left, but were attending a large social function. The duke had discarded her clothes and jewelry, and spent the last three years ensuring that she had no life whatsoever. Hugh could only imagine the malicious temper that would goad a man to retaliate so viciously against a woman as kind and nurturing as Charlotte.

"I've never seen you like this," Lucien said softly.

"Like what?" Huge snapped, his hands clenching into fists.

"Like this. So concerned for another individual. Even when I wished to court Julienne, you weren't this upset."

Hugh growled. "'Tis the damned Derbyshire water. I've never been the same since. I'm completely mad."

"Yes, dear brother, I believe you are quite mad for her." Remington's hand came to rest on his shoulder. "It was bound to happen sometime."

"What was bound to happen? What the devil are you rambling about?"

"You're in love with her."

Lucien offered a commiserating smile as Hugh gaped and then sagged into the abused stall door. "I know just how you feel. Someone had to tell me, too. I think men who are accustomed to lives of carnal indulgence find it harder to acknowledge how dependent their happiness can become on one woman."

Shaking his head, Hugh considered himself carefully. He'd known Charlotte for such a short time. How could it be possible that he loved her already?

"How do you know?" he asked. "How can you be certain?"

"When you are in love, you cannot stand to be away from your lover. Her touch, her smile, her attentions, are necessary things. You admire her above all other women; her faults are what you find charming. You want to care for her, protect her, be all things to her. Your desire for her stuns you, humbles you, and makes every other female pale in comparison."

"Good God." Hugh scrubbed a hand over his face. "That sounds dreadful. And terrifying." He dropped his hand and sighed. "And very much like the way I feel about Charlotte."

Patting him on the back, Lucien gestured toward the stable door. "Let's go find her, shall we? Before you expire."

"Oh, it's lovely," Gwen breathed, running her hands reverently over the tiny pearls that encrusted the sleeves of Charlotte's gown. "I've never seen a garment so fine."

Charlotte eyed her reflection with both longing and trepidation. The satin gown was a beautiful green that complimented her eyes and brought out the striking hue of her hair. "I couldn't possibly—"

"Nonsense," Julienne cut in, resplendent in mauve-colored silk. "That dress looks much better on you than it ever has on me. You must wear it."

Turning, Charlotte gave Hugh's sister an impulsive hug. "Thank you so much." Having been occupied all afternoon with entertaining Gwen and helping wherever she was needed, she hadn't had the opportunity to see Hugh at all, and she missed him dreadfully. She was pleased to think that when he finally saw her, she would look as she did now, dressed in a green very much like the robe she wore the first night they made love.

She was also quite willing to admit that her infatuation with the handsome earl was rapidly progressing to deeper waters. A few hours without him, and she felt bereft. She wondered where he'd been all day, how he'd occupied himself, if he'd thought of her at all and missed her, if only just a little.

"I cannot wait until the moment Hugh first lays eyes on you," Julienne said, with a smile. "I've waited so long for him to find his footing and a steady companion."

"Find his footing?" Charlotte asked.

"Yes." Julienne waved her arm carelessly. "His entire life he's fallen into one scrape after another. Don't misunderstand, he's very intelligent and inherently kind. He simply has a tendency to leap before looking. He says and does things before considering all the consequences, and then regrets his actions later. Hugh has made an effort to change over the last few years, but it may be a while yet before he becomes a man that one would call responsible. There were a few times when I wondered . . ." She shook her head. "But you are a sensible sort, confident and poised, and Hugh is obviously quite taken with you. You'll be a good influence on him, I can tell."

Charlotte frowned, attempting to reconcile the picture painted by Julienne with the image she bore of Hugh—a man who was strong and resourceful.

"Shall we go down to dinner now, ladies?" Julienne asked, effectively squelching the questions Charlotte had been about to ask.

"Oh, yes, let's!" Gwen cried.

Shaking off her sudden unease, Charlotte turned to look at Guinevere. Dressed in the ice blue gown, Gwen's creamy skin was displayed to perfection. But there was something missing from the ensemble, and despite how hard she considered it, Charlotte could not remember what it was.

Collecting the elbow-length gloves the abigail held out to them, they left Julienne's dressing room and headed toward the main staircase. Several other guests also left their rooms, and Charlotte studied the latest fashions carefully, eager to see what was new and popular. A bright bauble on a passing baroness caught the light, and suddenly she remembered what it was Gwen's dress was missing.

"Please go on ahead," she said, stopping in the middle of the gallery. "I forgot something."

Gwen frowned. "What is it?"

"The diamond brooch that goes so beautifully with that gown."

"You would allow me to wear that?" Gwen's eyes widened.

It was one of the few pieces of jewelry Charlotte had remaining, and it was one of her favorites.

"Of course. I think the dress looks almost naked without it." And the fact was, after this week the chances of Gwen mingling with Polite Society were very slim indeed. Charlotte wanted to ensure the young girl enjoyed every moment to the fullest.

"Well, we should retrieve the brooch, then," Julienne said with a smile.

"Please proceed without me," Charlotte urged. "You have guests to attend to, and Gwen is so excited. I hate to delay either of you."

As the two women moved away, Charlotte lifted her skirts and ran to her room. Hugh was certainly waiting downstairs by now, and she couldn't wait to see him. There was so much yet to learn about each other, so many questions to ask. Clutching the diamond-encrusted piece in her gloved palm, she backed out of her chamber and shut the door.

"I thought that was you."

She stiffened at the familiar voice behind her.

"Only a woman of your breeding would run down the hallway like a hoyden."

Taking a deep breath, she turned around. "Good evening, Your Grace."

The Duke of Glenmoore smiled and sketched a mocking bow. "Good evening, Your Grace."

"I detest it when you call me that," she said tightly, her gaze raking his stocky form. He remained unchanged from the last time she'd seen him, a year ago. He was still handsome, with his dark brown hair and even darker, almost black eyes—eyes that radiated none of the warmth she found in Hugh's. Once she'd found Jared appealing; now she wondered why.

"I detest that you married my father. Some things cannot be changed. Such as our agreement." He stepped closer. "What are you doing here?"

She lifted her chin. "Whatever I please."

Jared laughed, a harsh sound lacking any humor. "Decided to make a laughingstock of the old man after all?" His gaze narrowed. "I will not allow you to besmirch the Kent name."

Charlotte forcibly restrained herself from taking a step back. Any sign of weakness would only fuel Jared's ire. "No one knows who I am."

"Charlotte," came the soft, hesitant voice down the hall. "Are you well?"

She turned her head toward Gwen and managed a reassuring smile. "I'm fine. Please go wait downstairs."

Jared glanced down the hall, and his face darkened with fury. His hand lashed out, gripping her upper arm in a brutal vice. "You brought my bastard to a social gathering? Are you mad?"

Gwen gave a pained gasp, then turned on her heel and ran back down the hall.

Furious, Charlotte slapped his face, inwardly cursing the material that prevented a satisfying sting. "Unhand me. You make me physically ill."

"As does the sight of that mistake, dressed in finery and mingling with Society," he bit out.

"She is not a mistake! In fact, Guinevere is the only decent thing you've ever accomplished in your lamentable life. In return for your scorn, she has remained hidden, at the cost of her childhood and the chance to make friends. What more could you ask of her?"

"To know her place, something you never appeared to have learned."

"I have remained hidden as well," she argued. "No one knows who I am, nor do they know who Gwen is. Ignore us, and no one will be the wiser."

He yanked her closer, hovering over her like an avenging specter. "I want to know why you're here and what you intend, and I want to know *now*! If your aim is to extort money from me, I'll tell you now I refuse to give you a shilling more than what was bequeathed to you."

"Release her, Your Grace." The voice down the hall, though soft, was laced with menace.

Charlotte turned her head to find Hugh coming toward them with obvious predatory intent. His shoulders squared, his jaw tense, he looked ready to do damage, and she was awed. She simply couldn't think for a moment, arrested by the sight of him, beautiful in black and shrouded in fury. A force to be reckoned with.

The duke, unaware of the danger, didn't even spare him a glance. "This is none of your affair, Montrose."

"I would listen to him, Jared," she murmured, having no doubt, by the look of him, that Hugh was willing to ignore the Glenmoore title to protect her.

As she relaxed under his touch, Jared stiffened and glared at Hugh. "What do you want?"

"At the moment I want you to release my fiancée. Then I want you to step away and go about your business."

Charlotte gaped. Then her heart began racing so fast, she swayed on her feet.

Jared looked at her with raised brows. "Marrying down, Charlotte? At least this peer isn't on his deathbed."

"Go to hell," she snapped, tugging at her arm. Rescuing her was one thing. Lying to a duke of Glenmoore's power would only lead to trouble.

Releasing her, Jared stepped back. "She's after money, Montrose. She's a mercenary female, if I ever saw one. Do you know anything about her? Her past? Anything?"

Hugh stopped mere inches way. "I know everything about Charlotte and Gwen and the whole morass. I shall be taking them all off your hands. The only thing you need concern yourself with is the dispersing of Charlotte's trust, which I'll set aside for Gwen, as your father intended."

Jared's face broke out in a grin. "Ah, I see. What a perfect match you two are."

"What are you talking about?" Charlotte asked crossly.

"This is about the widow's trust, Charlotte dear." His gaze returned to Hugh. "You should know, Montrose, that the stipend is negligible. Not enough to keep you in the style to which you've become accustomed. Certainly not enough to wager."

Hugh stiffened. "This is not about money."

"It is for Charlotte," the duke said. "It's always about money for Charlotte." He looked at her. "Do you know anything about your intended, dear? Did he tell you how he wagered away almost every shilling of the La Coeur funds? He was forced to sell his sister to Remington to bail them out of debt. Why do you think an earl's daughter married a bastard?"

Suddenly Charlotte's nausea became a very real hazard, and she clutched her stomach in a vain attempt to still its roiling.

"Lady Julienne chose Remington of her own accord," Hugh growled.

"She was set to marry a marquess," Glenmoore continued, digging in deeper, as he relished Charlotte's obvious distress. "But then Lord Fontaine cast her aside when he realized how far in his pockets Montrose was."

"Lies!" Hugh glanced her way, his face flushed, his fists clenched.

Glenmoore arched a brow. "Are you claiming you weren't nearly destitute from irresponsible gambling?"

Hugh's expression could have been set in stone. "That was long ago."

"Only a few years, I believe." The duke's smile was filled

with malice. "Regardless, I was on my way to join the rest of the party, and I don't wish to hold up the proceedings. Congratulations, Montrose. Charlotte. I'll await your missive detailing where I should direct Charlotte's pension. Also, since you won't require the manse anymore, I'll make arrangements to sell it." Glenmoore walked away, leaving destruction in his wake.

Hugh was so furious for a moment, he could hardly think. When Gwen collided with him on the stairs and blurted that her father had cornered Charlotte, the rage he'd felt had almost overwhelmed him. If he had any doubts earlier about his feelings for his paramour, he didn't any longer.

"You should never have told Glenmoore we were affianced!" Charlotte groaned. "He will mention our engagement to someone just to embarrass you. This is a disaster."

Hugh stepped closer to offer comfort. She was frighteningly pale, her mouth and eyes rimmed with lines of tension.

Trying for levity, he placed a hand over his heart and gave an exaggerated sigh. "You know, a man could be irreparably damaged by such a response to his proposal."

She flinched. "We must go down and correct this mistake. Whatever will your family say when they hear of this?"

Hugh tapped a finger to his chin. "Congratulations?" he suggested.

"You are impossible. Lady Julienne warned me that you were known for being irresponsible and jumping into situations headfirst. I had no notion what she was talking about until now." She attempted to pass him, and he sidestepped into her path. "Hugh, the guests will gossip if we hold up the meal."

"Perhaps, but it won't be too untoward in this company." At her raised brow, he explained. "Julienne and Remington have been relegated to the fringes of Society for years. Only the most daring and licentious of guests will deign to associate with them. Glenmoore attended only because he wishes to enter into a partnership with Remington, who has the devil's own luck when it comes to making money."

She tilted her head back to look at him, her entire body tense and expectant, like a bird prepared to take flight. Hugh's heart sank to his stomach. She didn't look even remotely like a woman pleased with an offer of marriage.

A sick feeling of dread pooled and then hardened in his gut. "Don't you think we should discuss my proposal?"

Charlotte stumbled backward, her eyes wide and stricken. "Good heavens, you weren't serious!"

Hugh moved toward her, his heart racing in near-panic. "You were afraid my affections would be temporary. You worried I would cast you aside and leave you and your menagerie destitute. I've resolved that. As my wife, your comfort will be assured."

She shook her head. "We hardly know one another."

"I think we know each other very well." He stepped closer and reached for her hand, which she didn't raise to meet his. "Don't you care for me, Charlotte?" he asked softly. "Even a little?"

Her fingers tightened on his. "Of course I care for you, Hugh, very much. But . . ."

"I searched for you all afternoon."

"You did?" She began to tremble.

"I did." Lifting her hand, he held it to his cheek, despising the glove that separated his skin from her touch. "I needed to find you, to warn you about Glenmoore, but you kept moving, and I could never catch you. I was quite desperate for you, actually."

"Hugh . . ."

He nuzzled into her palm. "I waited in your room for nearly an hour. Where did you go after you left the stables?"

"I-I was in Julienne's room."

"Ahh . . . I was sick with worry. I couldn't bear to think of you facing Glenmoore alone."

"Oh, Hugh . . ." Her fingers curled, cupping his cheek. "I am accustomed to caring for myself."

He leaned into her touch, the warmth of which burned through her glove and heated his blood. No other woman had ever affected him as Charlotte did. "There is no weakness in relying on someone to assist you and care for you. The only weakness is in allowing yourself to suffer when support is at hand."

Beloved green eyes swam with tears. "But I cannot rely on you, Hugh. I do not know you well enough. Just in the last half hour, I've learned things about you that have shocked and disturbed me, not just from Glenmoore, but from your sister as well."

Raw pain, piercing and wounding, cut him to the quick. His eyes slid closed. "Please don't say that," he murmured hoarsely, pulling her against him, needing the physical closeness, because he felt her withdrawing. "Don't judge me by my past."

"There is more at stake here than just you and me, Hugh. You'll regret this rash proposal later. I am not a suitable wife for you. The burden of those I bring with me will begin to weigh on you. You will come to resent me and then hate me. I lack the breeding to be a proper countess. You would—"

Hugh covered her mouth with a kiss, cutting off her words. Her lips melted into his, and he groaned, pressing his advantage, his hands stroking her back until she opened with a whimper. She returned his ardor in equal measure, kissing him as if it were the last time, as if they never would again. Her arms lifted, her small hands cupping the nape of his neck, holding him close. The lush, ripe mouth that he loved so much moved feverishly under his, forcing his desire to rise up to match his anger and fear, then far surpassing both.

Pulling away, he rested his damp forehead against hers. "What are you afraid of?" he asked softly. "Being abandoned or discarded? I'm not Glenmoore. I won't take all that you are or all that you have, and leave you with nothing."

"I-I'm not afraid."

"You are. Afraid to trust. Afraid to hope. Afraid to love."

"Hugh—"

"Have I disappointed you, Charlotte? Have I promised you something and then not delivered?"

"Not yet, but—"

"Not ever. You either trust me to support you, trust me to be a good husband, to love you and care for you . . . You either trust me, or you don't."

She melted against him, her slight weight necessary and welcome. He hugged her close, squeezing her, until there was no space between them. He held his breath, waiting.

"Please understand," she begged. "I am responsible for the care of Gwen and the others. My decisions must be made with my head, not my heart."

He recoiled as the import of her words struck home. "You refuse me." His voice was a pained whisper, his heart aching as he stepped away. Her touch, which he had been longing for, was suddenly painful.

Hugh struggled to control his breathing, unsure of what he could do or say to erase the tormented look he saw in Charlotte's eyes. There was sadness there, a deep well of it. Her gaze said good-bye as surely as her kiss had.

It was then he realized there was nothing he could say. Her fear was too powerful. Even with an offer of marriage, she still couldn't trust him. Shaking his head, he turned away, his throat clenched tight. He strode down the hall, suddenly anxious to be away from her and the cloying agony that twisted inside him.

"Wait!" she cried after him. "Please don't go. Not like this."

He knew she would chase him down as she had before, so he lengthened his stride. Hugh left her and the wondrous dream of happiness far behind him. He didn't look back. He couldn't.

He loved her too much.

Chapter Nine

"I miss Lord Montrose." Gwen dropped her cards on the table.

"Pick those up," Charlotte scolded. "I can see your hand."

"I'm no longer in the mood to play. Where is he? I haven't seen him in two days. I inquired after him with Lady Julienne, and she said only that he was 'about.' What does that mean?"

Releasing a deep sigh, Charlotte set down her cards and leaned back in her chair. Tired and abjectly miserable, she hadn't been interested in playing anyway. She'd suggested the game in an attempt to cheer Gwen, who was taking Hugh's absence almost as hard as she was. "It means he doesn't wish to be found, Gwen."

Blue eyes narrowed. "What did you do, Charlotte?"

"What did *I* do? Why is his behavior my fault?"

"I may be young and naïve, but I'm not stupid. The duke is strolling about, puffed up like a rooster, and you glance away whenever Lord Montrose is mentioned."

Charlotte swallowed hard. Part of her hoped every moment that Hugh would walk into the room just so she could see him with her own eyes and assure herself that he was well. The other part of her dreaded such an event, knowing how badly she had wounded him. Her heart ached every moment.

"Mrs. Riddleton."

Glancing up, Charlotte's eyes widened at the sight of Lord Merrick. Tall and radiating savagery barely restrained, he was intimidating, with his long, black hair and intense blue gaze. Standing in the parlor full of women, his presence was overwhelming.

"Lord Merrick." Her heart leapt into a faster rhythm, knowing the only reason the earl would seek her out would be related to Hugh.

Gesturing to one of the two empty chairs, he asked, "May I? I won't take up too much of your time."

"Certainly, my lord."

He settled his powerful frame into the seat and clasped his hands in his lap. "Lord Montrose has shared your map and other items with me, Mrs. Riddleton."

Charlotte's hand went to her throat. "He did?"

"Yes, he did. Lady Merrick and I travel to the West Indies at the end of every Season to visit with her father. Lord Montrose has asked that I take you with us on the journey next year, and he has provided enough funds to retain a large expedition for the search. He's also spoken with Lord Glenmoore and made arrangements for you to continue to have use of the residence here in Derbyshire."

Swallowing hard, she glanced at Gwen, whose pursed lips and narrowed eyes condemned her. She was condemning herself, knowing how difficult it must have been for Hugh to speak with Jared and reveal her negative reply to his proposal.

Lord Merrick cleared his throat, and she returned her gaze to his. His handsome face was impassive, betraying none of his thoughts. "I will relate to you what I told Montrose. A great many adventurers have searched for that treasure over the years, Mrs. Riddleton. I doubt your chances of locating it are any better than theirs, even with Montrose's substantial largesse. However, he insisted this be done, and because I consider him a friend, I have agreed to assist you." He stood. "I have your direction, and I will contact you to make arrangements as the date of departure nears."

She grabbed his arm and blurted, "How is he?"

Merrick arched a brow and studied her carefully. "As well as any man can be when he's disheartened."

"Oh." Her hand fell away. The tone of Merrick's voice told her much. "You don't like me, do you, Lord Merrick?"

"I don't like that you have wounded my friend, but I very much appreciate your rejection of his suit. I was fortunate to find true happiness in my marriage. I wish nothing less for him. He's heartbroken now, but he'll recover. I hope one day he will love again, as unfashionable as that is, and next time I hope the lucky woman loves him as well."

Charlotte looked away quickly, biting back a sob. The picture evoked by Merrick's words cut her deeply, clenching a fist around her heart. "*I* love him," she said, her voice wavering but clear.

"Mrs. Riddleton," he said, sighing, "I am not privy to the state of your affairs, but I can assure you, for you to remain seated here while a man who loves you suffers is not love by any means."

She looked at him. "My decision was made for his benefit as well as mine. I have reasons. I—"

"I'm certain you do. But love requires a leap of faith, and often it has no reason. It simply exists." He bowed. "Montrose has made arrangements for you to depart tomorrow. Is that acceptable to you?"

She gave a jerky nod, and Merrick walked away, his departure drawing the appreciative gaze of every woman in the room.

Gwen stood. "You coward," she accused, in a sharp whisper. "You want to run back to the manse and allow the best thing that ever happened to us go without argument!"

Charlotte blinked, never having witnessed Gwen saying an unkind word to anyone. "That's not true. I'm doing what is best for all of us. We hardly know him and his history—"

"'Tis not his history that is the problem, but yours. You are afraid to rely on anyone. You have fended for yourself and all of us for so long, you don't know how to allow someone else to lighten your load."

"You are too young to understand, Gwen."

"How could living with Montrose possibly be any worse than the way we are living now? Even if he were to become destitute, which I doubt, from what I've managed to overhear, we would live no less in poverty than we do at this moment, and we would have *him*!"

Standing, Charlotte lifted her chin, fighting off the tears that threatened. She had managed hardly a wink of sleep in the last two nights, and the conversation with Lord Merrick had her thoughts in chaos. Looking around, she saw the curious glances. "I refuse to discuss this any further while we have an audience." She swept out of the room with Guinevere fast on her heels.

"Think on it, Charlotte. Think how happy we have all been. Tom and Henry carry themselves with a pride they never had before, because Lord Montrose has never condescended to them or made them feel inferior for their handicaps. Katie adores him. Even Artemis has a grudging like of him." Gwen's voice became breathless as she chased Charlotte up the stairs. "It wasn't an accident that I went to his room that night. I wanted him to find the secret door. I wanted him to know to look deeper."

Charlotte halted on the upper landing, her breath coming in heaving gasps. She spun around. "Beg your pardon?"

Gwen held out a hand and leaned against the railing, catching her breath. "When Tom and Henry told me about the earl, I thought he might be the one. When Katie told me the story about the pitchers, I began to think of how I could be certain. And when I saw your face with its rosy glow and bright eyes, I *knew* he was the one, and Artemis did, too. Why you cannot see it is beyond me!"

Shocked, Charlotte could say nothing.

"I have admired you for as long as I've known you, Charlotte. Please don't take that away from me." Gwen moved past her and disappeared around the corner, leaving Charlotte with a tear-ravaged face and far too much to consider.

* * *

Charlotte pushed aside the sheer curtain that covered the window and looked out upon the winter scene below. Her heart thrummed a restless rhythm as she watched Hugh and Lucien Remington walk their mounts back to the stables, the horses' hooves leaving clear tracks in the snow.

As Hugh disappeared from her view, she turned and gazed at the room around her, a room in which she'd spent most of the last twenty-four hours deciding what it was she wished to do with her life. Her trunks were packed and waited by the door. She was leaving today, and once she departed she knew there would be no turning back. However, before that happened, she was willing to make one last, desperate bid.

She'd discovered something about herself over the last sleepless night, something she should have acknowledged long ago—she *was* a coward, just as Guinevere had said. A coward who was afraid to believe that someone would care for her, worry about her, and wish the best for her. To give control of *anything* into the keeping of another was difficult for her, a woman who had cared for herself with no assistance almost since birth. But she was a coward who was more afraid of losing Hugh La Coeur forever than she was of placing her fate and the fate of her dependents in his hands.

The hands of the clock on the mantle moved with torturous leisure. It seemed forever before a half hour passed. Once it had, she left her room and traversed the winding hallways until she came to the wing where Hugh's suite was located. She paused at the door to his room, her hands shaking, her breath coming in unsteady pants. Before she lost her courage, Charlotte reached for the handle and walked right in.

"Go away," Hugh said curtly. "I didn't send for anything."

Her eyes filled with tears at the sound of his voice. She'd missed it, missed the way it spoke to her in the darkness, embracing her as surely as he did. Soft and encouraging, or husky and raw, it had offered her a lifetime of joy, and she'd thrown it away like a fool.

He stood by the window, looking out at the rear lawn. He'd

removed his coat and waistcoat, his broad shoulders covered in a white linen shirt, his powerful legs encased in breeches and boots. For a moment she simply absorbed the sight of him—the firm curve of his ass, his wind-tousled hair, the graceful arc of his arm as it held the curtains back. She'd missed him so much, she thought she would die of it. Even now her throat was so tight, she doubted she could speak.

He glanced over his shoulder and froze. For an instant, she glimpsed raw pain in his dark eyes, but it was quickly masked with the studious impassivity of a seasoned gambler. "What do you want?" He looked away.

Charlotte stepped into the room and shut the door behind her. "Lord Merrick has informed me that you've arranged for me to travel with him to the West Indies."

Hugh said nothing.

"He says you've paid for my journey and financed an expedition."

"I told you I would help you without any obligation on your part." He snorted. "But I suppose with your lack of faith in me, your surprise is to be expected."

She bit her lower lip and took a moment before she could reply. "I deserved that."

"Aren't you departing today?" he asked gruffly.

"Yes. Gwen and I shall be leaving in just a few hours."

"Godspeed." He waved his hand over his shoulder in a gesture of dismissal.

Charlotte's chin lifted. His anger was her due, and she would bear it. She would pay whatever penance he required if he would find it in his heart to love her again.

Taking a deep breath, she stepped closer. "Don't you wish to say good-bye to me, Hugh?"

"We've already done that."

"'Tis apparent you've said farewell, but I haven't. Not properly."

That spun him about. He'd removed his cravat, leaving his throat bare and revealing a light dusting of golden hair in the slender opening of his shirt. His gaze raked from the top of her head to her slippered feet. She made no attempt to hide her longing or desire.

He gave a bitter laugh. "Ah, I'm untrustworthy and have no self-restraint, but I can fuck well. What a relief to know I'm good for something."

Charlotte winced. "You are good for a great many things, Hugh La Coeur. And I am a thousand kinds of fool for making you doubt that."

His jaw tensed. "I'm not in the mood for your games."

She stepped close enough to smell him, a rich combination of the scent of his skin, horses, and the wild outdoors. His nostrils flared as she neared; his gaze narrowed.

"I've missed you," she whispered. She reached for his hand, but he backed away quickly, an action she took as a positive sign. He couldn't be as indifferent as he appeared, or he wouldn't fear her touch. "I didn't believe Glenmoore. Not even for a moment. He simply provided the excuse to be a craven I was looking for."

"Get out," he snarled.

"I can't." She smiled sadly. "I need you, Hugh."

Shaking his head, he moved away. "No, you don't. You can care for yourself; you don't need anyone to rescue you. I, however, have discovered I require being needed. And for more than just my cock."

She stepped up to him and placed her hand against his back, flexing her fingers to absorb the feel of muscle and sinew beneath the billowing linen of his shirt. He tensed, and she rested her head against him, trusting him silently not to move away, for if he did she would stumble. "I do need you and want you. You've no notion of the torment I've suffered these last three nights without you. It's not merely your body I missed. I've missed your voice, your laughter, your smile. I cannot go another day without those things in my life."

"Charlotte." His voice was a harsh rasp. "Don't say any more. Just go."

She wrapped her arms around his lean waist, loving the feel of him. Splaying her hands across his abdomen, she felt the ridges of muscles shift as he groaned. Burying her face in his back, she breathed him in. "I want to link my future with yours, Hugh. I trust you to be the type of man I can depend upon."

His fingers laced with hers, and then he pulled her hands away, stepping out of her embrace. He turned to face her, his expression cold. "Why are you doing this?"

There was no room left for pride or fear, not any longer. "Because I love you."

"Your feelings will pass."

"I don't want them to pass."

"I'm sorry, I don't know what more I can say to you."

Charlotte held out her hands to him. "Tell me you have no tender feelings for me and I'll leave. I won't trouble you again."

There was no hesitation. "I wish you well in your future endeavors, but that is the extent of my interest."

She winced as his words cut deep. "You're lying."

Resolved, Hugh moved around Charlotte, then through the open doorway to the sitting room. His entire being ached for her and cried out for her touch, but he forced himself to leave her and kept his face impassive. There was too much at stake. She'd abandoned him so easily due to just a few cutting words from a man she despised. Before he risked himself further, he had to know she was sincere. He had to know it wasn't simply gratitude for his largesse that brought her here, but her love.

He poured himself a drink. And then another. A moment later he felt Charlotte's tiny hands caressing his back. He closed his eyes as he savored her touch. When her hands cupped his buttocks and squeezed, he reached down and tore open the placket of his breeches, freeing his swollen cock. He took himself in hand and began to stroke, needing to ease his lust before he reached for her.

Three nights he'd spent alone in this suite, knowing she was close, wanting her with a biting, penetrating need. To have her here, just as he'd imagined, was excruciating. His hunger was too powerful, his desire too great. Goaded any further, he couldn't say if he was capable of even a modicum of control.

"Allow me," she murmured, her hands reaching around his waist, her pert breasts with their erect nipples pressing into his back. When she circled his cock with both hands and began to pump, his breath hissed out between his teeth, the pleasure searing in its intensity. She rested her cheek against his back. "I've missed touching you, holding you."

"I am the same man I was three days ago," he growled, his head falling back, his eyes drifting closed.

"Yes," she whispered. "The man I love."

His hips began to thrust rhythmically into her talented hands. Charlotte knew just how to hold him, how tightly to grip him, how fast to take him to the ecstasy only she could bestow. He began to pant, the heat of his lust washing over him, bringing him to the edge of reason. His cock swelled, his balls drew up, a tortured groan escaped as he prepared to come . . .

Her movements stilled, and she stepped away just as he was on the verge of release.

"Damn you." He slammed his glass on the sideboard. Clenching his fists, he couldn't stop the tremors that shook his frame. "Is your goal in life merely to torment me?"

Charlotte stepped around to face him, her eyes shining like emeralds and burning with desire. "My aim is to comfort you, Hugh, to please and satisfy you, so that I may prove my love and win you back."

Her hands cupped the edge of the sideboard, and she jumped to sit upon it. Above the scoop of her bodice, the ripe swell of her breasts was flushed and covered with a spattering of reddish freckles he knew intimately, because he'd licked and worshipped every one.

Gripping fistfuls of her skirt, she yanked the hem of her gown upward, the fevered haste of her movements betraying how desperately she desired him. The length of her lithe, stocking-clad legs was revealed to him first, and then she spread her thighs, displaying the deep red curls that sheltered the plump lips of her sex.

Drawn to her, Hugh closed the distance between them, until her soft floral fragrance swirled through his senses with potent familiarity. Charlotte leaned back carefully until her shoulders rested against the wall, angling her hips to give him greater access. Watching his own movements with ravenous hunger and deep adoration, Hugh parted her lips with one hand while rubbing the tiny nub of her clit with the blunt fingertip of the other.

She gasped, and arched her back, thrusting her breasts toward him. Unable to resist, he bent and licked along her slender neck. "Yes . . ." she breathed. "I've hungered for the feel of your hands, the warmth of your mouth . . ."

His skin was burning hot and covered with sweat. Hugh could barely think, could hardly breathe. Shifting his hips, he was there, the broad head of his cock covered in her cream. She was so ready, he slipped the first inch inside her without any effort. The tight clasp of her body welcomed him and was nearly the end of him. His breathing harsh and ragged, his fingers digging into her thighs with bruising force, he paused and locked his eyes with hers.

And waited. Even though it was killing him.

Charlotte's hands moved to his shoulders and then around his neck, her calloused fingers entwining in the hair at his nape. "I belong to you, Hugh. In whatever way you'll have me."

His heart stilled before resuming its near-frantic beat, his thighs quivering with the need to fuck her, to claim her, his arms aching to hold her. "Any way?"

"Wife or mistress—I care not. Just don't send me away. I love you, Hugh." She pressed her lips to his, and he groaned. "I love you," she whispered against his mouth, her tears wetting his face and salting her kiss. "I'm so sorry I hurt you. This is so hard for me, to trust someone . . . but I do. I do trust you . . . and I love you so much."

Covering her mouth with his, he cradled her spine and slid her hips to the edge of the sideboard, dragging the creamy heat of her body over his cock until he was buried inside her. "Damn it," he breathed, crushing her to him. "I almost thought you wouldn't come to me. I feared you would go, and I would lose you."

"Never. Oh, Hugh . . ." Her cunt tightened around him. "Please . . ."

He lifted her and stumbled to the settee, every step nudging him deeper into the wet, clenching heart of her. By the time he sank into the cushions, he was certain he would expire. "Ride me," he ordered, his hands at her thighs urging her to move.

"Remove your shirt," she said.

He tore the garment in his haste to be rid of it, and his reward was sweet. Charlotte lifted until he was barely within her and then lowered, encasing him in her silk, her soft whimper of need spurring his ardor. He felt maddened, wild. He wanted to grip her hips and lead the way, plunging into her, until the desperate hunger he felt was thoroughly sated. Instead, he spread his arms and held onto the settee, knowing he was mere moments away from a magnificent orgasm. An orgasm made all the richer by the love of the woman who held him so intimately.

Gripping his shoulders for leverage, Charlotte set a hard, fast rhythm, pounding her lush body onto his cock as if she couldn't get enough of him. His eyelids grew heavy, the drugging ecstasy tightening every muscle in his body, his fingers holding the wooden rim of the sofa so tightly, he feared it would snap.

"I love you," he said, his voice hoarse with emotion.

Charlotte faltered.

He didn't.

Moving quickly, he had her on the rug, her thighs over his, his cock driving deep. His strokes were strong and steady, his gaze locked with rapt attention on her face. Her skin was flushed, her full lips parted, her emerald eyes bright with love. She came on a gasp, her back arching upward, her shivers tightening around his shaft until it became difficult to withdraw, difficult to return, the soft sucking sounds of their lovemaking filling the room along with her cries.

Hugh followed directly, pouring into her, flooding her with his joy and his love in a release so devastating, he knew he would never be the same again.

"You shall marry me, Charlotte."

"Are you certain? I'm not suitable."

He snorted. "You are entirely suitable. And marriage has decided benefits you're failing to consider."

Charlotte curled into him where they lay on the floor and stroked her hand across his chest. "Such as?"

"The marital bed, for one."

"Ah, yes, a bed. That would be lovely. Perhaps with marriage, we will make it there more often . . ."

Epilogue

London, August 1815

Sebastian Blake, Earl of Merrick, took the steps of Montrose Hall two at a time. He rapped with the knocker and waited. A moment later the door swung open, and he was faced with a stooped butler sporting the largest eye he'd ever seen in his life. He blinked, quickly comprehending the reason his footman had returned to the carriage in a fright.

"Aye?" the old man queried, in a gravelly voice.

He held out his card. "I've come to collect Lord and Lady Montrose. They are expecting me."

The butler lifted the card to his oddly protruding eye, squinted at the lettering, and then dropped his hand with a grunt. The servant stepped aside. "Come in, gov'na, and I'll inform 'is lordship yer 'ere." He shuffled off, leaving Sebastian to carry his own hat and shut the door himself.

Pausing by an open doorway, the servant gestured wildly and said, "Wait in 'ere."

Moving into a well-appointed parlor, Sebastian frowned. The Earl and Countess of Montrose never held social functions in their home, which he'd not thought untoward, considering their newly wedded status. The rest of the *ton,* however, found them mysterious, and their aloofness only fueled the rumors that they ran a bizarre household. The butler was an oddity, to be sure, but . . .

An odd noise caught his ear, and Sebastian cocked a brow as it drew closer and increased in volume.

The next moment a young serving girl appeared in the doorway, her slim arms weighted with a beautiful china tea service that wobbled horrendously. He'd never seen such a spectacle in his life. Every item was jumping and rattling—spoons clinking against each other, cups dancing in their saucers.

Sebastian gaped for a moment and then moved to assist her, shaking his head in wonder. He would remember to speak to Montrose about this later.

He definitely wanted an invitation to dinner.

"The Merrick carriage has arrived," Charlotte noted, looking down at the front drive from the upper-floor window. A moment later warm arms encircled her waist, and then her husband's deep voice was purring in her ear.

"Are you still excited?"

"Are you jesting?" She spun in Hugh's embrace and stared up into his handsome face. "Of course I'm excited."

"You seem pensive."

"I miss Gwen," she said with a sigh. "I know she's having a wonderful time at the finishing academy, but still . . ."

Hugh kissed the tip of her nose. "I miss her, too."

Wrapping her arms around his lean waist, Charlotte squeezed tight. "Thank you so much."

"For what, love?"

"For arranging this treasure hunt. I know you believe it to be nonsense."

His mouth curved in a smile that stole her breath. "And you don't?"

"I'd like to think it exists."

"You'd like to believe in the romantic version of the tale as well." Hugh's large hands smoothed the length of her spine and cupped her derriere. "What happened to my pragmatist?"

Charlotte laughed, her heart light and filled with love. "I've never been a pragmatist where you are concerned." Hopelessly addicted, she wondered how she ever considered living without him.

He squeezed her close before turning away, moving to the trunks that had yet to be taken downstairs. He was preparing to close one, then paused. Picking up a brown-paper parcel, he shot her an inquiring glance before untying the twine. A moment later his laughter, warm and rich, filled the air and warmed her heart.

"What do we have here?" He held up an eye patch.

"The journey is long I've been told."

Hugh's mouth twitched. "So it is."

"It could become tedious."

"You and I alone in a cabin? Never."

"I have a fantasy," she confessed, moving toward him with salacious intent.

"Umm . . . I like the sound of that." Hugh tossed the pirate costume in the trunk and caught her about the waist.

She winked. "You'll like the doing of it much better."

"Fetch your pelisse," he growled. "I want to get to that ship."

Author's Note

The characters of Calico Jack and Anne Bonny, mentioned in "Her Mad Grace," did indeed exist. However, their "treasure" is entirely fictional.

Don't miss Kathy Love's latest novel,
FANGS BUT NO FANGS,
available now from BRAVA!

She reached her bedroom, a tiny square room at the very end of the trailer, just like Christian's. An image of him lying on his bed flashed in her mind. All smooth skin and hard muscles. She glanced at her bed covered with a Strawberry Shortcake comforter that she had gotten for five dollars at a yard sale when she moved here. She told herself it was such a good deal she couldn't pass it up. But secretly, she also wanted it. Strawberry Shortcake had been popular when she was younger and she'd never had any of the toys. She pictured Christian lying among the pink bows and red strawberries. Even pink bows wouldn't detract from the sheer masculinity of him.

She stopped looking at her bed and twisted the silver knob on her radio. A pop song from the sixties filled the silence. Not as good as real company, but the tune was cheerful and made her feel less alone. She opened the top drawer of her dresser and pulled out a pair of pajamas, light blue boxer-style shorts and matching camisole top. A picture of a sassy-looking fairy decorated the front of the top with the word "Naughty" scrawled underneath in glittery script. Another bargain purchase.

Christian would seriously wonder about her taste, and her age, if he saw the bedspread and the pajamas together. She chuckled. Well, that wasn't likely anyway. Christian certainly hadn't shown any signs of being interested in her tonight. In fact, he'd kept plenty of distance between them. She had to forget his kiss, or she was going to make herself insane.

She changed into her pj's, assuring herself she just wouldn't think about him anymore tonight. Naked on pink bows and red strawberries. Kissing her with gentle worship brushes of her lips. Groaning, she tugged on her top. This wasn't working. She marched to the bathroom to wash her face. With very cold water.

She'd just finished drying her now tingling cheeks, when a loud, almost impatient knock banged on her front door. Startled, she threw the towel over the rack by the sink and hurried to see who was there. Relief swept over her as she saw Christian's handsome face in the window.

"Hi," she said, both surprised and curious about why he'd changed his mind.

"Can I come in?"

"Of course." She stepped back, holding the door.

He entered, his hands in the pockets of the black pants he'd worn to work. He also had on the same black silk shirt from earlier. A night of bartending and he still looked like he walked out of a designer clothing ad.

He even had the sexily pensive expression down as he strolled into her almost empty living room and glanced around. Finally his gaze found its way back to her.

She crossed her arms over her chest, feeling self-conscious in her cotton pajamas with her freshly scrubbed face. The fact that he was just staring at her with those contemplative eyes didn't help.

"Are you all right?" she finally asked.

"I don't think so." He shook his head slightly as if to clear some vision or thought from his mind. His eyes focused on her, his gaze wandering over her.

Her body reacted, even though she didn't get the feeling that his look was one of desire. He appeared almost pained.

"What is it? Do you need to eat?" she asked, stepping closer to him.

He blinked, his attention now focused back to her face. "If only that would help."

She took another step closer. What did he mean? Did he need to go to the hospital? His color looked fine. His eyes, while troubled, were clear. He didn't look crazed like he had the other times, only distressed.

"Is there something I can do? Do you need to go to the doctor? I'm not great with stick shifts, and your car is a little—intimidating, but I can drive you if you want."

"A doctor wouldn't help."

The dullness of his voice alarmed her. "Christian, what is wrong?"

He shook his head, the strangest look of incredulity on his face. "I want you. Sexually."

Take a peek at Amy Garvey's
I LOVE YOU TO DEATH,
available now from Brava!

The place was packed, and the atmosphere was pure Friday night, loose and hot and crackling with energy. A Shins song pounded from the speakers and the postage stamp of a dance floor was crowded with bodies.

Shouldering her way through the people at the bar running the length of the room, Alex waved at the bartender. The girl turned bright blue eyes on her and flicked one of her black braids over her shoulder.

"What can I get you?"

"Nothing . . . yet," Alex shouted over the noise of two guys arguing about the Mets. "I'm actually looking for someone I'm supposed to meet here. I know it's crowded, but . . ."

The girl grinned as she swiped the bar with a damp rag, shouting back, "A guy? Tall, dark hair, leather coat? Kind of slick?"

Oh, good. She swallowed. "That should be the one."

The bartender jerked her head toward the tables in the back corner, on the other side of the room. "Make him pay for the first round," she said with another grin. Her tongue was pierced with a tiny silver barbell.

Alex nodded as she walked away, nudging past a girl doing a Jell-O shot of something the color of Windex. It was hard to see very far beyond the shifting crowd of bodies, but as she got closer to the back of the room, she spotted her date, sitting alone at one of the corner tables, just like the bartender said.

Wow. Sydney wasn't wrong.

He was gorgeous. Well, maybe not gorgeous in the traditional sense, but definitely her type. The secret type she hadn't even known she had until she laid eyes on him, in fact, and found his close-cropped dark hair and strong jaw shadowed with stubble the sexiest thing she'd ever seen. He was leaning back in his chair, the fingers of one hand carelessly circling the lip of his empty glass, his dark eyes shifting back and forth over the crowd, watching, waiting.

He didn't look like a real estate broker. Unless he only sold homes to the mob, or in the kind of neighborhoods other agents were afraid to drive through. And his leather jacket wasn't exactly what she'd pictured, either. She'd been thinking tailored, metrosexual, buffed to a buttery sheen, and his looked as if it had been tied to the bumper of a speeding car and dragged across uneven pavement. Scuffed, worn, lived-in—but, she had to admit, as natural on him as a second skin.

He looked . . . dangerous. Which was certainly different, for her, at least. She'd never known *dangerous* could look so tempting.

With a deep breath for a courage, she edged past a couple who were taking turns sipping from the same drink, and walked up to his table. *Now or never. Nothing to lose.*

"Hi," she said. "Alex Ramsay. I'm sorry I'm late, but . . . well, there's never a good excuse for that, is there? I hope you haven't been waiting long."

His mouth curved into a smile and he shook his head slowly. "Not long at all. Just long enough, I guess."

She pulled out a chair opposite his and sat down, nestling her bag on her lap. Now what? He was looking at her so strangely, as if he wasn't exactly sure what she was doing there, but definitely not unhappy that she'd shown up. Except for the way he kept glancing past her toward the short hallway that led to the bathrooms, if the stick figures of a man and a woman posted above the archway meant what she thought they did.

She wanted him to look at her again, she realized suddenly. Maybe it was the heated, sexually charged atmosphere, or the simple fact that she'd taken the plunge and come on this date, but she wanted to make the most of it. Getting out of a rut seemed a whole lot more appealing if she was going to be doing it with someone who looked like him.

"Have you been here before?" she asked him, wishing she had a drink in front of her. It would have given her something to do with her hands, at least.

"A couple of times," he said, that same slightly confused smile playing around his mouth. "Usually on business."

What kind of business could he do here? She couldn't imagine discussing escrow and variable-rate mortgages in a place like this.

"You?" he asked, leaning forward, his elbows on the table. Beneath the sweaty, faintly electrical haze of too many bodies, the sharply spicy scent of perfume, and too many speakers blaring at once, she could suddenly smell him—warm and dark, like a crisp night in front of a fire.

Delicious, she caught herself thinking as she looked up and into his eyes. Oh yeah, they weren't bad either. A rich dark brown, intent and curious and intelligent, the kind of eyes that saw everything.

"No," she answered finally. "I work a lot of nights."

His gaze sharpened, and she found herself explaining before he asked. "Teaching. Adults usually need evening classes, and after a few hours of the tango and the fox-trot I'm usually too beat to do anything but collapse in front of the TV."

"The tango, huh?" His head tilted sideways as his mouth quirked into another grin. "I didn't know anyone did that anymore."

"Oh, lots of people still want to learn." She crossed her legs under the table and her foot brushed against the solid weight of his calf. "Sorry. I'm usually more graceful than that."

His grin changed into a sultry smile. "I believe it."

She fought a blush. What were they talking about? Was this flirting? Because it felt pretty good—a little vague, certainly, and a little dangerous, but exciting. As if the conversation could twist into something new at any moment.

Maybe she should slow things down a little. She cleared her throat. "So how long have you been in real estate?"

Now his grin was a frown. "What makes you think I'm in real estate?"

"Uh . . . " *What?* She was trying to think of how to respond to that when someone tapped her on the shoulder. She turned her head to find the bartender she'd talked to earlier leaning down to speak to her, blue eyes wide.

"The guy who told me he was waiting for someone?" she whispered fiercely. "That's not him."

"So, what does a girl have to do to get an ale around here?"

So caught up in his reverie, Brodie hadn't realized Daisy was standing across the bar, an expectant smile on her pretty face. He'd also been so caught up that he hadn't noticed the hush that had fallen in stages across the breadth of the pub. Those seated at the tables first, followed by those in the back, shooting pool or tossing darts.

"What?" challenged an irritable and entirely familiar voice. "Did I grow another head when I wasn't looking? Rhys, you better snap your mouth shut before you catch a fly. And Conner, I believe you owe me a quid from that thrashing I gave your dart game last week, so the first round is on you."

Brodie stood there, damp rag clutched loosely in one hand, a look of pure shock likely etched on his face. "Kat?"

The object of his attention, and everyone else's judging from the complete silence, turned and scowled at her apparent partner in crime. "See? I told you this was a ridiculous idea. Everyone knows I can't pull this off."

"I'd like to see you pull it off," Fife shouted, his words slurred more from the toothless grin that accompanied the offer than the amount of ale in his belly. He raised his empty mug in her direction, finally breaking the extended silence as a riff of laughter skated through the crowd.

Daisy leaned closer to her compatriot and whispered none too quietly, "Well, it would help if you weren't quite so surly about the whole thing."

"Surly?" She turned to Brodie. "Am I surly? Never mind," she added quickly, seeing his grin reappear. "And not a word from you about this." She motioned to the brightly colored sundress she was wearing. And quite fabulously, if he did say so himself.

He nodded easily in response, knowing once he got over the absolute shock of seeing Kat Henderson in anything other than dungarees or coveralls, he would have a lot to say about it. All good, he was thinking.

"Besides," she went on, "you'd be surly too if you had to dress up like this."

"Oh, I imagine I'd be more than surly," Brodie agreed, folding his arms. "I'm not big on dresses. I have the devil of a time finding ones that fit across my chest. I'll stick with the occasional kilt." He shot Daisy a wink. "My legs I don't mind showing off." He leaned over the bar and glanced down. "I'm just wondering why you've waited so long to show off yours," he told Kat, much to the agreement of the rest of the pub patrons, if the sudden lusty cheer was anything to judge by. Instead of being flattered, however, Kat turned six shades of red and clutched Daisy's arm.

"That's it, I'm out of here. I appreciate the idea and the effort, really I do. But the last thing I need is a drink. My judgment is obviously already impaired beyond recognition."

"Would you hush?" Daisy leaned closer then and whispered something in Kat's ear. Brodie could barely make out what she was saying, but it was something along the lines of, "It's working, you idiot. Isn't this what you wanted?"

Was what, what Kat wanted? And since when were Kat and Daisy bosom pals? Last he saw Kat was staring daggers at the Yank. But before he had time to puzzle any of that out, Kat replied, "I don't know what I want, but I do know I can't go about it like this." She gestured to the flowery shift she had on, then flipped at her hair. "Or this."

That was when Brodie realized that, for once, Kat was wearing her hair down. He'd been so caught up with the dress . . . and those legs . . . Of course he'd seen it down over the years, but usually that was only when she was in the process of braiding it back up again. It was all shiny and wavy, tumbling over her shoulders and partway down her back.

"I like it," he said to nobody in particular. Both women looked at him and he shrugged a bit sheepishly. "The hair I mean. And the dress." When Kat's eyes narrowed, he quickly added, "Of course I liked your hair before, too." Women. Damn but he never knew what was going on in their minds. Here she went to all this trouble, but she was mad now that anyone was noticing? Like they wouldn't have? Somebody explain that to him.

"See?" she told Daisy as if his comment explained everything. "Honestly, Daisy, I really can't do this. He's all yours."

"But I don't want—"

Daisy's protest was cut off when Kat made a beeline to the door.